Pippa Roscoe lives in Norfolk, near her family, and makes daily promises to herself that this is the day she'll leave the computer to take a long walk in the countryside. She can't remember a time when she wasn't dreaming about handsome heroes and innocent heroines. Totally her mother's fault, of course—she gave Pippa her first romance to read at the age of seven! She is inconceivably happy that she gets to share those daydreams with you. Follow her on Twitter @PippaRoscoe.

Jackie Ashenden writes dark, emotional stories, with alpha heroes who've just got the world to their liking only to have it blown wide apart by their kick-ass heroines. She lives in Auckland, New Zealand, with her husband, the inimitable Dr Jax, two kids and two rats. When she's not torturing alpha males and their gutsy heroines she can be found drinking chocolate martinis, reading anything she can lay her hands on, wasting time on social media or being forced to go mountain biking with her husband. To keep up to date with Jackie's new releases and other news sign up to her newsletter at jackieashenden.com.

Also by Pippa Roscoe

The Diamond Inheritance miniseries

Terms of Their Costa Rican Temptation
From One Night to Desert Queen
The Greek Secret She Carries

The Royals of Svardia miniseries

Snowbound with His Forbidden Princess
Stolen from Her Royal Wedding

Also by Jackie Ashenden

The Wedding Night They Never Had
The Innocent's One-Night Proposal

Pregnant Princesses collection

Pregnant by the Wrong Prince

Rival Billionaire Tycoons miniseries

A Diamond for My Forbidden Bride

Discover more at millsandboon.co.uk.

CLAIMED TO SAVE HIS CROWN

PIPPA ROSCOE

STOLEN FOR MY SPANISH SCANDAL

JACKIE ASHENDEN

MILLS & BOON

First published in Great Britain 2022
by Mills & Boon, an imprint of HarperCollins*Publishers* Ltd,
1 London Bridge Street, London, SE1 9GF

www.harpercollins.co.uk

HarperCollins*Publishers*
1st Floor, Watermarque Building,
Ringsend Road, Dublin 4, Ireland

Claimed to Save His Crown © 2022 Pippa Roscoe

Stolen for My Spanish Scandal © 2022 Jackie Ashenden

ISBN: 978-0-263-30094-9

08/22

MIX
Paper from
responsible sources
FSC **FSC C007454**
www.fsc.org

This book is produced from independently certified FSC™ paper
to ensure responsible forest management.
For more information visit www.harpercollins.co.uk/green.

Printed and Bound in Spain using 100% Renewable Electricity
at CPI Black Print, Barcelona

CLAIMED TO SAVE HIS CROWN

PIPPA ROSCOE

MILLS & BOON

To my writing friends who were with me from the beginning of this series to the happy-ever-after:

Rachael Thomas, Carrie Nichols, Lucy Monroe and Rachael Stewart.

Thank you for your fabulous company and your incredible support!

xx

PROLOGUE

SHE WAS LOST. Completely lost.

Henna dashed at her tears and bit her lip to stop the trembling turning into a sob. All she could see were thousands and thousands of tiny little green leaves everywhere she looked. This was useless. She turned back down the narrow path and around the corner, hope creeping into her heart until she came to another dead end. She was completely lost.

She wished her stepmother had never brought her to this stupid party. She felt as if she'd been stuck in the garden maze of Svardia's royal palace for hours and was half convinced she'd still be here when night fell. What if no one came looking for her? What if no one found her? Heart pounding, she told herself she'd been stupid to believe that Viveca would wait for her. Her stepsister was only two years older than Henna and, though she didn't want to admit it out loud, Viveca was mean.

Henna's hair fell out of the band she'd tried to tie it back with and she angrily pulled at the short strands that had been cut by her stepmother's hairdresser. Another tear threatened to spill onto her cheek. She'd loved her long hair. It reminded her of the way, every morning, her father had woven it into plaits and every night he had brushed it out for bedtime. At the top of a sob, the sharp sting of pain cut deep in her chest. She missed him so, so much. And no matter how many times Marcella told her that twelve years was too old to cry, and three years was too long to mourn, it didn't stop the ache filling Henna's entire body until she was exhausted and heavy and hurt. All the time.

She turned and went back the way she had come. Or at least the way she thought she'd come. She heard a laugh and her stomach twisted, imagining Viveca's delight at her misery. The tears began to fall faster, the hurt began to throb harder and when she tripped over an overgrown root in the maze floor Henna wanted to stay on the floor and never get up.

Gravel bit painfully into the skin on her knees and palms and even as the muffled voice—deeper than her sister's—grew closer, she still couldn't move. A tear fell into the dry dirt and she heard the voice tell someone to head back to the party and soon the sound of footsteps forced her to look up.

Immediately she regretted it. Of all the people who could have found her, it had to be *him*. For a second she wished it *had* been Viveca. Not only was he the coolest boy at school, popular, top of his class in sports and smart too, he was also the Prince of Svardia. He must have been speaking to Kristine, his girlfriend. Even though some of the kids at school whispered about what a strange couple they were, she was kind and pretty too.

Prince Aleksander crouched down and Henna scuttled backwards in the dust, as if he were a dangerous creature. He raised his hands up and leaned back. 'I just wanted to see if you were okay.' He looked at her, his deep brown eyes unwavering. 'My sister once got lost in here and it took us ages to find her.'

His words made her feel a little less foolish for getting lost, but not for trusting Viveca. The thought brought a fresh wave of heat to her cheeks and she stood up and dusted off her hands on the pale silk party dress. Marcella would kill her for ruining it.

Henna threw a glance at him, hoping it didn't look like she was staring. Older than her by three years, the Prince had thick dark hair, eyes that were warm and a smile that was easy and offered to everyone. They'd nicknamed him Prince Charming at school because he was so nice.

'Are you?' he asked.

She looked blankly at him.

'Okay?' he repeated. There was laughter in his voice, but he wasn't laughing *at* her. The thought made her even more sad because she would never be someone he would laugh *with*. She nodded, but her face must have given her away because he narrowed his eyes on her and she looked away.

'You're Viveca's half-sister?'

She nodded. He pulled a face that was so comically full of disgust Henna couldn't help but smile.

'Come on. We should get back to the party,' he said, interrupting her chain of thought. His hand reached out to hers and she stared at it for a second before tentatively placing her hand in his. 'Tell me,' he asked, the curve of his lip welcoming and warm, 'have you met my sister?'

And with that innocent question, little Henna had no idea how much her life was about to change.

CHAPTER ONE

FREYA STARED AT HER, startling amber eyes glistening and hands twisting in her lap. She mouthed the word 'please', the desperation in her eyes tearing at Henna in a way that made her helpless to do anything but whatever it was that the Princess of Svardia needed.

'You know, it would serve you right if I refused,' she groused, rolling her eyes as Freya sprang out of her chair, arms wrapping around Henna's torso and pulling her into a series of jumps that threatened to topple the pile of carefully ordered paperwork on Henna's desk.

'Thank you, thank you, thank you. You are the best lady-in-waiting *ever!*' Freya cried.

'I'm your *only* lady-in-waiting,' Henna said, unable to hide her smile at seeing her oldest friend so easily happy.

'And you're sure it's okay? It's not too much trouble?' the Princess asked.

It would be a mountain of trouble and at least three hours' extra work that evening, but Henna wouldn't tell.

'Of course. Now, go! You've got a handsome fiancé waiting to whisk you away for a secret escape to some exotic location in a private jet.'

Freya pressed her hands to her chest. 'I do, don't I?' she said as if she couldn't believe it herself.

'Say hello to Kjell for me,' she called as Freya disappeared through the door.

Henna sighed, staring at the literal mountain of paperwork on her desk, before making herself a coffee and settling back in front of her computer.

Kjell's romantic gesture was sweet but it was going to be a little tricky to explain to the French Ambassador, who had expected to be meeting with Her Royal Highness at the end of this week. It would be the last getaway Kjell planned for a while, because once they were engaged he would be added to the roster for royal duties and would no longer be able to be so beautifully impromptu. In fact, Henna was half-convinced that was *why* the newly titled Duke had chosen to whisk Freya away two weeks before their engagement party.

For a moment she wondered what that would be like— to be whisked away to some luxurious isolated escape, wined, dined and pleasured by a handsome man—and then laughed at herself. She had far too much to do here. Henna picked up the phone and dialled the French Embassy and while she was waiting to be put through to Ambassador Toussaint her gaze snagged on an email appearing at the top of her inbox. Frowning, she clicked on it and stared.

'Hello? Ms Olin?'

Shaking her head clear of the mental fog that had paused her brain function for a second, she spun the chair away from the distracting computer screen and focused on the task at hand.

'Ambassador Toussaint, I'm so sorry to have to ask but I'm afraid I'm going to need your help.'

It took fifteen minutes to carefully pick through the minefield of cancelling a diplomatic event with a foreign embassy without ruffling feathers, bruising egos or over-compensating with undeliverable promises and Henna did it perfectly, all the while resolutely ignoring the email that pulsed in the back of her mind.

By the time the call ended she had swept her hand across an overly warm forehead so much that her fringe had an upward-bending kink. Finally, after steeling herself, she returned to the email that had rocketed her heart rate.

Dear Miss Olin…

…trusted member of the Svardian royal staff…highly recommended…believe you would be a perfect fit… very competitive salary…

Headhunted. She was being headhunted.

She squinted her eyes at the screen to see if just a little peek at the invading email would make it less… *tempting.* But no, what they were offering was a once-in-a-lifetime position. And as a lady-in-waiting, that was saying something. The details didn't include the name of the would-be boss, but there were enough clues in there for her to piece it together. The female CEO was internationally renowned, energetic, enthusiastic and determined to work exclusively on projects that had big global impacts. Henna shook her head, confused by the enticement of the email.

She would *never* leave Freya, or her younger sister Marit. But, even as she thought it, she couldn't deny that things were changing. With Marit secretly engaged to Lykos Livas, the Greek billionaire, and Freya and Kjell's very public engagement ball in just two weeks, the Princesses were growing up and moving on with their lives. They had found their partners, their *confidants*. They wouldn't need her as much. Henna looked to the pile of paperwork on her desk. There would always be enough work between the royal siblings to keep her busy…but what if she wanted more than that?

She shook her head again and whispered 'no' into the empty room. She loved Svardia. She'd lived here all her life and while she'd travelled all over the world in her duties with Freya, coming home had always been the best part. She loved watching the seasons change in the leaves of the large trees in the palace gardens. Loved the way that the salt-touched breeze swept in from the sea, the dramatic craggy coastline that looked prehistoric, and the explosion of Svardian technology that harnessed the very best of nature without destroying it in the process. It just wasn't something she wanted to walk away from.

Henna's mobile phone rang, shocking her from her thoughts, and she saw Freya's name as she accepted the call.

'Are you meeting your sister?' she heard Freya ask over the sounds of the gravel drive crunching beneath the tyres of the car taking her to the private airstrip at the back of the palace grounds.

'Stepsister,' she corrected as numbness spread quickly through her. 'No. Why?'

'I saw her pulling up in her car. I thought I'd give you a heads-up. I wonder what she's doing here.'

Only Henna didn't need to wonder.

Aleksander.

Aleksander was beginning to believe that his 'great idea' was, in fact, deeply flawed.

On paper, she was perfect. She would inherit her mother's Marchioness title, she was rich, beautiful, educated and sophisticated. His family had known hers since they were children. She moved in similar circles as he did. But clearly there was something he had forgotten. Just at that exact moment, she opened her crimson-coloured mouth and once again he resisted the impulse to cringe.

'So, I said to him that he couldn't possibly have got me confused with Lady Annabelle because the woman spends her entire life looking as if she were dragged through a hedge, backwards! I mean, look at me.' The vicious comment cut through the air as successfully as the dramatic sweep of her hand down the length of her body.

Viveca Lassgård was perched on the edge of the settee in a position that could hardly have secured a single pert cheek and could not have been anything other than deeply uncomfortable. Her legs were dramatically crossed high at the thigh, revealing more of her than Aleksander had any intention of ever seeing again. The patent red leather of her shoes matched the crude colour of her lipstick, separated by a bright honeybee-yellow dress that clung to angles rather than curves on her body.

No. Aleksander, King of Svardia, was man enough to admit—to *himself*—that he had made a monumental mistake. How Henna could have grown up in the near vicinity of this woman and not committed murder would be one of his life's greatest unanswered questions.

Aleksander conceded that he had been somewhat *hasty*, enticed by the ease with which a possible fiancée might be found. Because that was what he needed it to be—easy. Four months ago, as tradition decreed, his father had abdicated on his sixty-fifth birthday and

Aleksander had ascended to the throne of the Scandinavian kingdom. The day after his coronation his mother and father had left for the twelve-month sabbatical that allowed each new monarch to find their feet as ruler.

Aleksander might have laughed, if he'd been in the habit of such things. He could have ruled Svardia at any point since his twentieth birthday if needed. The fact that he'd had to wait nine years was merely incidental. He had been six years old when his uncle, the King, had died, forcing his father to take a throne he'd never wanted, but he had ruled with absolute focus and determination. Nothing had come between his father and his duty and he'd ensured that his children felt exactly the same way. Whether they wanted to or not. It was a cause of quite considerable distaste to Aleksander that he was now in a position to inflict a similar fate on an heir of his own.

That teeth-grinding thought pulled him back into the present, and the living area of his palace suite where Viveca was currently removing a cup of tea from a tray held by a server she had yet to, and he doubted ever would, acknowledge. Instead, she was eyeing up the Italian baroque furnishings and design elements that ran through the entire palace because some long-forgotten ancestor had taken a liking to the style. Aleksander hated it. Imagine having to have a conversation with world leaders about nuclear disarmament in a powder-blue room with gold filagree.

'It is beautiful,' she said lasciviously.

He grunted in response and she didn't even raise her carefully pencilled eyebrow. He had seen women like her on the arms of rich old men. Aleksander didn't judge. He *never* judged. If she wanted to throw her body away for financial security and gain that was her choice. But he wasn't ever going to be that rich old man. With years of practice, he made barely polite small talk while he reassessed his position. Viveca clearly wouldn't do—at *all*—but it didn't change the fact that he was still in need of a Queen.

Time was running out. That the devastating news that Freya was unable to carry a child to term was still a secret was nothing short of miraculous, but it wouldn't stay that way for long. The situation had to be negotiated carefully. Aleksander hated that it was the case, but he knew what the press were like. If it wasn't handled perfectly, they would tear Freya to shreds and then start on Marit, questioning her fertility next, which was unacceptable. Faith in the royal family would be at its weakest in years, so if Aleksander needed to be married to help his sisters and his country navigate such a serious crisis so early in his rule, then he would marry.

He would do whatever it took because he wanted Svardia to be one of the greatest countries in the world. His father had protected their country when it was reeling in shock from the sudden death of their King. It was Aleksander's job to make it *thrive*. And to do that, the nation needed to trust its King. And if they needed a Queen beside him to do so, then he would give them a Queen. Even if it was the last thing he wanted.

Glancing at Viveca, he was about to bring the whole farce to a close when his body started to react to some yet unseen presence. Instinctively he turned to the open doorway in time to see Henna at the threshold, tucking a look of sheer fury behind that delicate mask of hers.

Curious.

Henna was surprised that she heard Viveca's patently *unwelcome* greeting above the high-pitched ringing in her ears.

'Sister. You look…well.'

The pause indicated that her stepsister thought she looked anything but. Punctuated by an imperious eyebrow, it was her tone that hurt the most, as if Viveca was surprised Henna had the audacity to breathe the same air. Viveca looked *svelte*—there was no other word to describe her—and Henna suddenly felt invisible in the clothes that she had taken such pride in that morning.

'Th-thank you,' Henna replied, stuttering over the words and feeling embarrassed. Not because Viveca would notice. She was always stilted around her. But in front of Aleksander? 'I just came to…' In the infinitesimal moment it took for Henna to realise that she genuinely had no idea what she had come here to do, her sister rose to the occasion.

'Oh, wonderful. I'll have another tea. I'm sure you remember how I like it. Aleksander?' Viveca turned, as if she had every right to offer the King a drink in his own home, a wide perfect smile on her face.

For a second Henna was caught—helpless, stuck in a childhood prism of anger, hurt and dismissal that made her body immobile but her heart rage with injustice. And Aleksander got to witness the whole thing.

Viveca had treated her like a servant from the moment her mother married Henna's father six months before his death. But she hadn't had to bow to her stepsister's demands since she'd moved into the palace staff quarters. And Viveca *knew* that she did more than make tea and coffee. It was a dig, just like so many others, as if Viveca wanted to see how far she could be pushed before she broke.

That was what brought Henna back to earth. The memory that no matter what—*no matter what*—she never gave Viveca what she wanted. It might have taken Henna years, and one particularly brutal betrayal, but she'd learned and she knew how to play this game.

She steeled her spine. 'Your Majesty,' she said, turning her attention to Aleksander, 'if the staff have been remiss in providing refreshments to your guests, please allow me to take the matter to the Principal Private Secretary to the Royal Household.'

Not a single member of staff positioned discreetly around the room moved—knowing her threat was empty—but a collective breath was held while Viveca squirmed and a battle of wills commenced between Henna and Aleksander.

Would he side with his guest and sacrifice his staff, or would he reveal Viveca's spoiled behaviour?

'Did you resolve things with the French Ambassador?'

Anger, hot and heady, bubbled up from a well so deep she hadn't known it was there. It stained her cheeks and stole her breath, slicked her palms with sweat and *burned.* Henna told herself that it was because he had side-stepped her challenge and not because he was considering Viveca as a fiancée…not at all.

'Of course, Your Majesty.'

He narrowed his gaze on hers and, just a second too late, Henna realised that she had revealed her emotions in her tone. Unfolding from the chair, he stood to his full height. 'Miss Olin?' he asked before making his way across the room and gesturing for her to precede him through the door which he held open.

The hairs on the back of her neck lifted and a shiver stole through her as she passed the King of Svardia and left the drawing room. An apology was on her lips but he held up his finger to silence her, as if trying to sort through his thoughts. She'd never been sharp with a member of the royal family before and had never been warned over her behaviour. In fact, the only people to have ever found fault with her were her stepmother and stepsister.

Lazy. Selfish. Rude, they'd called her. And it had hurt because she genuinely hadn't thought she had been. Bewildered, she'd spent hours thinking over her actions and tone. She'd doubted herself terribly. So she had worked harder, been nicer, become more selfless but it had only seemed to make things worse. But this time she had not only been rude, but she'd been rude in front of staff and his guest.

She opened her mouth once more to try to apologise, but he raised his eyebrow as if reminding her that she wasn't to speak until she was told to. She bit her lip and wished, so much, in that moment that his arrogance didn't look so good on him. The arch of his eyebrow added even more power to an already imperious visage and a flex of muscle drew her attention to a jawline that had its own Pinterest page.

Thick and carelessly sexy, his tawny-coloured hair was the perfect blend of his sisters', and served to draw attention to eyes the colour of molasses. Only there was nothing sweet about this man, despite his rich, complex colouring, which had garnered an impressive amount of attention from the international press.

Henna was convinced Aleksander purposely cultivated the enigmatic persona that was world-renowned, but she'd discovered that she could decipher him when she needed to. Yes, his control over his temper, features and body language was legendary, but his eyes were the one thing that betrayed him.

Perhaps if she hadn't known him since his mid-teens, if she hadn't known him before he'd changed, it might have been harder. But she still remembered the charming, laughing, teasing boy who she had met fourteen years ago and who had brought her to his sister, given her a friend, and eventually a job and a home. But now the King's eyes sparked warnings like fireworks, snapping her back to the present.

'You can't marry her,' she blurted out, ignoring the threat of danger. 'You just can't.'

That he'd been thinking exactly the same thing was neither here nor there. No one dared to tell him what to do. Not usually anyway. But Henna was different. She always had been, he thought, before veering away from the thought.

'Why would you think I might be considering—?'

'I'm not stupid, Your Majesty,' she interrupted, not helping herself one bit. Red slashed across pale cheekbones as if she realised the same thing.

If he'd had less control he might have reacted to her tone, but he didn't. Despite that, Henna stepped back and bowed her head as if she had sensed his shock.

'Explain,' he commanded. Because if Henna knew then…

'Even though in the last few weeks you've taken every measure to ensure that Freya is the most loved of the Svardian Royals, it will only go so far when the press discover her diagnosis. Marit's engagement will also help somewhat, but only your marriage would provide the stability needed to ease the release of information regarding Freya's fertility.'

He raised an eyebrow, daring her to go on.

'It would be only logical for you to have your future Queen on your arm at both engagement announcements, thus taking credit for being deferential to your younger siblings before announcing your own, whilst also testing the people's opinions of your soon-to-be bride.'

He clenched his jaw. If he were that transparent…

'Your Majesty, as the only person who has been made aware of both of the Princesses' engagements, and Freya's diagnosis, it is easier for me to…' She shrugged, clearly not wanting to drive home the point that she had seen through his plans. He cocked his head to one side, opened his mouth to admonish such impertinence when—shockingly—she interrupted him again.

'And then, of course, you asked me about Viveca three weeks ago.'

She had been wasted on Freya, he thought for only a second before realising that he would never have chosen anyone else to have been by his sister's side all this time. Henna had always been there, for Freya and even Marit when she was feeling forgotten by their parents. Henna had been there when he couldn't be and he didn't like how reliant he had become on her.

'So why shouldn't I marry your sister?' He knew why *he* didn't want to marry her.

The purposely blank look that shuttered her features niggled. There was something she was not telling him and that was absolutely unacceptable to him.

'Henna,' he warned.

'You just…' It was unusual for Henna to struggle over her words like this and it slithered through his gut unpleasantly. 'You can't trust her,' she finally got out.

Her words were like a knife, cutting through his plans for her stepsister.

'Why?'

'Personal reasons.'

Aleksander got the distinct impression that the Spanish Inquisition wouldn't get more out of his sister's lady-in-waiting, and he barely resisted the urge to say so. 'Okay, but that doesn't help me resolve my situation, though, Henna,' he warned.

He watched her wisely bite back what must have been another inappropriate response. She was right about Viveca, obviously, and her grasp on that was surprisingly astute. Henna was efficient and discreet, he reasoned. He had already taken her into his confidence with his plans for Freya and Marit. In theory, this shouldn't be any different. A low hum began to sound in his mind, faintly reminiscent of a fire alarm. The instinct to keep his plans to himself was years old and hard-learned—forged from a betrayal so shocking that it still had the ability to steal a breath and a heartbeat. His trust had been broken once and he'd vowed to never let it happen again. But if Viveca wasn't evidence enough that he needed some help in the matter...

Henna was frowning up at him, so he saw the exact moment jade daggers of awareness flashed in her hazel-coloured eyes, as if she had followed his chain of thought.

'Oh, no. No, Your Majesty.'

'No, what, Henna?'

'That is *way* beyond my job description.'

'Freya is away for two weeks.'

'You say that as if you think that my work stops when she's not here.'

'I am your King.'

'And she is my boss.'

He glared at her, but her raised eyebrow challenged him to overrule a bond she clearly believed superior to that of her King's. He could have laughed at her audacity. But he played his trump card. 'And that makes me your boss's boss, so clear your schedule, Henna. I need you to help find me a fiancée.'

Without waiting for an answer, he pushed open the door to the drawing room and several curious eyes swerved back to a hazy middle distance.

'Viveca? You may go.' And with that he turned on his heel and marched down the corridor as if he didn't know that he'd left both sisters with their mouths hanging open.

CHAPTER TWO

HENNA HAD WOKEN with a headache at five-thirty that morning and despite the quick twenty minutes of yoga, the two painkillers, the three cups of coffee and the green smoothie the staff chef knew she liked best, it hadn't gone away. But then she hadn't really expected it to, she realised, looking out across the perfectly manicured spring green lawn as Aleksander, in a white shirt, tan trousers and dark leather shoes, waved and gave his best toothpaste smile to the international press. Objectively, he looked *good*. This was the perfectly polished, sanitised version for mothers and little children to warm their hearts.

But in her mind's eye she saw him as he had been at the Vårboll, the annual Spring Ball held at the Palace. He'd towered above her, dressed in his cream thigh-length military coat with gold piping at the shoulders and neck. He'd been draped with military decorations and more finery than half the women in the room, but he had made it look *fierce*.

Despite Aleksander's plan to force Freya back into Kjell's arms, Freya had returned from Sweden devastated but determined to do her royal duty and at the Vårboll Henna had stood beside Aleksander, her heart breaking as Freya had said goodbye to the man she loved and thought she could never have. The raw umber of Aleksander's eyes had turned nearly black but his fury had been nothing compared to her own. She'd been angry with him for manipulating her best friend, even if he felt he had the right as her older brother and King, and furious with him for inflicting more hurt on Freya.

And for the first time since he'd come across her in the maze all those years ago, she'd had the audacity to order him to fix it. To fix Freya's broken heart and the mess he'd created. And a connection had formed between them, despite his status and her role, a shared moment of understanding. She had commanded a king. And he'd *obeyed*. And *that* was when things had changed between them. From that moment on, his gaze no longer passed over her. Each time she felt it, it caught, snagged on her and tugged. Not to get free, but to pull her to him, to draw her in as if she had no choice.

And now, as if he'd heard her very thoughts, across the lawn and in front of at least thirty of the world's press and photographers, he looked straight at her and she had no time to brace herself for the impact. The fake smile didn't matter, the way he was crouched down, shaking the hand of a little girl… No, it was the look in his eyes and even though it lasted barely a full second it was enough time for her breath to stutter, the hairs on her skin to lift and her heart to bruise. Turning away, she called herself all kinds of fool. Because it was now her job to find the King of Svardia a Queen.

Twenty minutes later Aleksander joined her as they walked away from one of her favourite charities. Founded by Aleksander, The Children's Garden Party recognised children for overcoming life-changing events to their families and loved ones. It celebrated resilience and showed the children how much support they had within their communities beyond the finite boundaries of family and it never failed to remind her of the assistance the royal family had given her. Instinctively, their steps fell into a rhythm as Henna looked over the schedule she'd been sent by the press office.

'You're running a little behind,' she observed as they made their way to the staff entrance at the back of the Palace.

His hand lifted almost to his temple before fisting and returning to his side as if he were unwilling to display any sign of frustration or weakness. Instead, he nodded. 'The Prime Minister can wait. He won't like it, but he will at least understand. The CEO from Nordact, however… Could you look into organising a palace tour for him? That would buy me, what, thirty minutes?' he asked without looking at her.

'It would buy you forty-eight minutes, Your Majesty, and if you had a secretary, they would be able to—'

'It is not my fault that Anders retired when my father relinquished the throne,' he snapped, uncharacteristically terse.

'But it is your responsibility to find a replacement,' she replied, aiming for delicacy and failing, given the look in his eyes. 'It has been four months,' she pressed. 'It is—'

'Enough.'

She pressed her lips together to prevent another ill-advised response from escaping, aware that Aleksander had no need to justify himself. So she was surprised when he said, 'I was expecting Lars to continue on with me.' She remembered the quiet, self-contained assistant who had been with Aleksander for almost as long as she had been with Freya.

'Where is he now?' she dared to ask.

'I believe he is teaching personal assistant courses at an exorbitant fee.'

She couldn't imagine it—just up and leaving like that. The relationship between a royal and their assistant—it was a bond unlike anything else. She thought back to the email she had received offering her a role away from the royal family. The job invitation she hadn't yet replied to. An email she should just delete, but for some reason hadn't yet. Shaking the thought clear from her mind, she focused on the task at hand.

'We need to talk about your...' Henna struggled for a word that wasn't offensive or rude '...requirements.' She thought she heard him grunt in response. Really, she was beginning to get more than a little frustrated. This was supposed to be something he wanted after all. 'Your Highness, we need to discuss timelines and—'

'Two weeks.'

Henna missed a step.

'Are you unwell?' he demanded.

'I have a headache.'

'I know the feeling,' he muttered, and she resisted the urge to roll her eyes.

'Two weeks is all we have, as she will need to be on my arm for Freya's engagement party,' he said, tucking his hands into his trouser pockets. He squinted off into the distance. 'She must be educated. Degree level at least,' Aleksander plucked from an invisible list.

Henna noted it down on her tablet.

'Scandal-free, preferably,' he continued, and she ignored the way it sounded horrifyingly like ticking boxes on a medical health form.

'Able to handle the press and public events,' Henna added, adding it to the list only once Aleksander had nodded in approval. 'Titled,' she continued, starting to type before he could respond.

'No.'

'What?' Henna asked, stopping to stare at him.

'No, my future Queen doesn't have to have a title.' He was peering at her as if she had started to sprout leaves.

'But what about Freya? And Marit when she thought she would have to replace Freya as second in line to the throne? The second in line has to marry someone with a title. It's the legislation.'

'I know that you might find this hard to believe, but I do know my country's constitution. Can we?' he asked, gesturing impatiently to the pathway that would bring them to the back of the palace.

'But why not you?'

He stared at her impatiently. 'Do you not consider my title enough for both of us?'

Us. She knew he hadn't meant it like that, but her unhelpful mind inserted herself into that impossible equation and suddenly she *did* feel unwell.

'I have a one o'clock meeting,' he said over his shoulder as he marched towards the palace.

'And I have one at twelve-thirty,' she threw back.

His gaze snapped to hers and embarrassment stained her cheeks and burned her skin.

Aleksander turned away, wondering how the woman currently blushing with such discomfort had managed to extract an apology from the French Ambassador *and* three hundred words of glowing praise currently taking up space in his email when they had all known that Freya had been in the wrong.

The stark contrast reminded him of years ago in the palace maze, where he'd first seen Henna looking devastated in a way he'd not yet experienced. It had hurt him to see her pain so clearly and instinctively he'd reached out to her.

But she'd pulled back, flinching from him, as if he already wore a crown, as if the thing created a shield between him and everyone around him. His girlfriend, who'd hated the spotlight of being associated with a prince. His father, whose lessons and teachings had been unrelenting. His mother, who'd been so picture-perfect she'd remained that way even when the press had gone home. But when Henna had placed her hand in his it had cut through the numbness surrounding him. She had given him her trust and, as it turned out, her loyalty.

'What about Sonja Hund?'

Henna's question yanked him from the memory and dropped him mid-stride towards the Palace. He thought of the blonde banking CFO who had done a lot of good charity work throughout the Scandinavian Peninsula.

'No. She's about to launch a coup against the CEO of Lungrandst and that would be...'

'Distasteful?'

'... To the world's press. My fiancée can't be seen as more—'

'Powerful?'

'*Aggressive* than me.' That aside, he hadn't minded her suggestion. 'What about Marian Fastvold?' he asked her, curious about what Henna would think.

'Gambling addiction.'

'Really?' he asked, genuinely shocked. He was very good at reading people and he'd never seen a hint of it.

'Really,' she confirmed. 'Would you consider English-speaking?'

He winced. 'Might be harder, unless they were fluent in at least one of the Scandinavian languages.'

Henna cocked her head to one side. 'Natassia Malthe?'

Hmm… He hadn't considered the Norwegian businesswoman, though she did meet the requirements of his future fiancée. 'How old is she?'

'Twenty-eight.'

They were finally approaching the Palace building. 'And you think she would be amenable?'

Henna considered his question. 'Yes.'

'This would have to be done quietly.'

'Of course, Your Majesty.'

He clenched his jaw. 'I am serious, Henna.'

'As am I. It can be done very discreetly.'

'How? Is there some secret cabal of assistants I should know about?'

'Absolutely. And the first rule of the secret cabal is not to *talk* about the secret cabal.'

And, with that, she left him standing at the back entrance to the Palace wondering what perfume she was wearing, because it reminded him of both roses and cucumber and it was driving him a little crazy.

Eleven hours later, Aleksander could still smell it, the scent lingering as if it had transferred onto his clothes, but she'd not touched him once.

'I'll table the conversation for our meeting in Öström.'

'You can table it,' Aleksander growled into the phone, 'but it won't be a conversation. It is done. Ilian Kozlov threatened my sister—he crossed a line and there is no turning back from that.' A fury exclusively born from the need to protect his family filled him with white-hot rage. Aleksander had hated every interaction he'd had with the Russian oligarch but as a fellow member of the extremely secret organisation Aleksander belonged to there'd been no escaping him.

Aleksander had been in his early twenties when his business mentor and old friend had initiated him into the organisation just before his death. Comprised of some of the world's richest and most influential leading figures, its purpose was to support—in secret—0those that would advance the world for the better. Kozlov had inherited his membership only a few years ago but was the antithesis of everything they stood for.

'Removing a member from the organisation hasn't been done for a very, very long time, and with good reason.'

'He has been engaging in illegal business practices for too long and he has got away with it because he was part of the organisation. No more.'

'Kozlov knows too much. Outside the organisation he will be an untenable liability. So you need to be very clear about what you expect from the organisation, should you make this happen.'

'I am very clear,' Aleksander said darkly.

'Does the Greek know about us?'

'No. Lykos Livas had a pre-existing relationship with Kozlov and only approached me because he discovered my shares in the Russian's company.'

A respectful grunt came through the telephone line. 'Impressive.'

'Yes. It is.' Aleksander had hopes to initiate his

brother-in-law into the highly secret organisation, but that was a conversation for another time. Now, Aleksander's sole focus was Kozlov. 'When Lykos got too close to toppling Ilian, the Russian threatened Marit because of their association. But Kozlov knows she is my sister and he knows the rules. Family is sacrosanct. I will see you in Öström,' he said before ending the call.

He left the desk in the corner of his suite and, whisky in hand, made his way towards the living area where two large butter-soft leather sofas bracketed the open fireplace. Although the cold bite of spring was giving way to warmer winds, Aleksander enjoyed the fire. The flames twisted and turned, hissing and licking over the hunks of wood, but all Aleksander could see was Henna's hazel eyes. His sister's closest friend had proven herself to be nothing other than excellent in her work and he had no doubt that she would bring the same quality to her search for a suitable fiancée.

But he couldn't deny privately that the thought left a bitter taste in his mouth. It was, in fact, the last thing he could conceive of wanting, and the pun was intentional. The only thing he needed from his Queen was a child. It would take the focus and the pressure from Freya who— unable to carry a child to term—would come under some of the world's most intense scrutiny for what would be perceived to be a failure on her part.

He fisted his hand. The world could be cruel, he knew that. Royals were expected to behave as if they never made a mistake, as if they never had a selfish moment, as if they never wanted something just for themselves. And if they dared take it, then more often than not the punishment was bordering on cruel.

I'm sorry.

Kristine's long ago whispered words brushed against his consciousness and he washed his anger down with whisky.

Me too, Aleksander mentally replied before his grief could take hold.

'I think you'd be perfect together,' Henna said as she sorted through the files on her desk. With Freya away with her fiancé, Henna's duties should have lessened. But staff kept coming to her with queries about His Royal Highness.

'And I think you've lost your mind,' came the laughing response from Natassia Malthe.

Henna had used her contacts, which weren't quite a cabal, to reach out to the Norwegian businesswoman, who had apparently returned her call only because she was curious.

'You don't think you're fit for a king?' Henna asked, genuinely intrigued. Natassia's confidence and self-composure were the envy of many a person.

'I absolutely think I'm fit for a king. Just not *that* king.'

Henna frowned. 'I know he can be—'

'Difficult? Moody? Manipulative?'

She couldn't refute the adjectives being fired down the telephone line. But she wanted to. Because he hadn't always been like that. The boy who had found her in the maze, brought her back and introduced her to Freya... was not, she could admit, the same as the man who ruled Svardia as if it were an art form.

'I can't deny that,' she said to Natassia, 'but he is also kind. He might not have the time to be nice about it, he does have a country to run. But—'

'Are you trying to tell me there's a cinnamon roll under all that bluster?'

'That is not…no,' Henna concluded, her tone revealing how unlikely just the thought of it was. Natassia laughed. 'But he will respect you and your career. And he will treat you well and allow you the freedom to pursue what it is you want to do with your life. And you will be able to use a position by his side to achieve anything you want. That is more than most.'

'But is it enough?'

That wasn't a question she could answer, but Henna had heard the curiosity in the woman's voice and knew she had her. 'You'll have to meet with him tomorrow to find out.'

'He *is* handsome.'

Henna kept her tongue firmly in her mouth while her mind flashed back to the look he'd given her earlier on the lawn.

'Okay,' Natassia sighed. 'What are the details?'

Henna rattled them off, disconnected the call and started the hour-long process of clearing Natassia and the dinner with the royal security team and the restaurant. Through it all, the email from the head-hunter kept sparkling at her like a diamond in her inbox. She'd replied when she'd got back from her meeting with Aleksander, thanking them and buying herself some time with a request to consider her options. And it hadn't been a lie.

Henna knew that Freya was going to need her less as a friend, as a source of emotional support, and more as an assistant and the thought made Henna feel…lost. The thing that had made them work so well *was* their relationship. It might be unusual for secretarial and assistant roles, but that was what made being a lady-in-waiting so different. But if their relationship changed, then wouldn't her role also change? And she wasn't sure where that left her. Marit was blossoming in her relationship with the Greek billionaire Lykos Livas and had started looking into ways she could share more royal responsibilities. And now that Aleksander was looking for a fiancée everything was changing.

Fear bloomed in her blood like ink in water just from the thought of it, having been scarred irrevocably by the monumental shift in her world when she'd lost the father who had never let a single day go by without telling her how much she was loved.

Her father had been a tech entrepreneur with a vast financial empire behind him, but the day Gustav Olin lost his wife only weeks after the birth of their child he'd handed over the reins of his company and spent every minute of the day raising his daughter. Henna's love for her father was a wondrous, huge, bright, beautiful thing. And then one Christmas he'd developed a cough that wouldn't go away. Over the next year or so, doctors' visits and hospital stays had stolen weight, energy and years from them, but never love. She'd seen the worry about her future etched in his eyes and the only thing that had taken that concern away was when he'd met with the friend of an old business associate. Marcella, a Marchioness, had agreed to marry him and take care of Henna in return for the financial security he would provide.

Knowing that securing her future had brought her father peace in his last days, Henna hadn't been able to protest, even though just meeting the woman had made Henna miserable. Focused on what was in front of her, Henna had spent every minute she could with her father, playing his favourite card games and chatting happily, ensuring he was entertained by silly futures that she made up. She was able to keep up a happy façade because she had felt loss before, she knew her mother's absence, so she'd thought she would be able to handle it when the time came.

Only when her father passed it had been nothing like what she had expected. Henna had been hit with such an avalanche of grief she'd felt buried, suffocated by the weight of it. She'd been furious with her father and the world for not telling her how painful it would be—an acute betrayal, as if they had all kept this devastating secret to themselves. Because the distant throb that her mother's absence had left her with was nothing like the searing, shocking horror of losing her father. Each day she'd felt as if a hand pressed down on her chest, trying to squeeze out more tears from a well that was exhausted and dry. She'd been so blinded by her loss that she'd not seen the changes that Marcella had started to make to the only home she'd ever known. The estate had been carved up, modernised, painted and wallpapered. Everything she'd ever known swept away by a decorator and she'd been numb to it all.

She'd seen the changes with her eyes, but she hadn't been able to feel it until it was too late. And Henna just couldn't shake the feeling that it was happening all over again. She was seeing the changes with her eyes, but she refused to sit around waiting for the blow to land, as she had done as a child. No. Now, she had a choice. Allow the tide to wash her towards something new or stand and buckle, as she had before, under the tsunami that was on the horizon.

Maybe the job offer was a sign that she should be moving on—it had certainly come at a fortuitous moment where she could take pause and consider her future. And if she did want to move on, then maybe helping Aleksander find a fiancée would be the full stop on this part of her life.

The fact that it took fifteen members of the palace security team, three close protection officers, a press embargo and an hour and a half to get to the restaurant might have had something to do with why Aleksander didn't date. Outside of that, he worked very hard to make sure the press didn't find out about the affairs he did have—ones that were short-term, mutually beneficial and extremely pleasurable for everyone involved. Consenting adults who knew—and were happy with—the boundaries in place was easy, uncomplicated and all that he needed.

Anything more? No. It was off the table for him and had been ever since Kristine. A part of him hated that she was still a shadow hanging over him, but the other part welcomed the reminder. Always. Because it was a lesson he needed to remember, especially now—that he couldn't trust anyone not to betray him, even those closest to him. The past swirled, thick and heavy, pulling him into a hurt he refused to revisit, but when his limousine pulled up to the back entrance of a Michelin-starred restaurant on the edge of Svardia's capital city he turned his thoughts from the past, determined to make the most of an evening with an intelligent, beautiful woman.

He walked through the kitchen, nodding at the bowed heads of staff in chef's whites, to where the head waiter greeted him at the kitchen pass as if he'd just stepped off the red carpet. Beyond the smartly dressed man was a restaurant entirely empty of customers. While it would certainly impact on the atmosphere, it would at least allow for privacy. Privacy that would be needed if they were to reach an agreement that suited them both. Just as he was taking his seat, the doors in front of him swept open and he stood, ready to greet the woman he hoped might turn out to be his future Queen.

His gaze started at her feet. He'd only ever really seen Natassia a few pages into the same newspapers he was regularly headlining so he was surprised by the impact the sight of an impressive height of heel beneath slim ankles and shapely calves had on him. His fist instinctively curled as if he'd taken her calf into his palm and smoothed his hand upwards. The black velvet dress clung to legs that made his mouth water, the tauntingly respectable hemline at odds with the direction of his thoughts. Soon his eyes were racing upwards, over hips, waist and, refusing to linger obtusely anywhere between there and her face, he finally looked up.

And was shocked.

'I'm sorry. Natassia has—'

'Stood me up,' he concluded before Henna could finish. He mentally cursed and then, without a hope in hell of calling it back, laughed.

CHAPTER THREE

THE BARK OF laughter caught Henna by surprise. Not for a second did she think it was aimed at her. No, he was many things but cruel was not one of them. There was something cynical, self-deprecating even, about it. Aleksander was laughing at himself, though she couldn't think for the life of her why.

Frowning, she made her way towards the table that occupied the middle of the room, sure he was muttering about being careful what you wished for. She'd known that coming here to let him know that Natassia had been called away was going to be awkward, but now that Aleksander had his temples bracketed with thumb and middle finger, she was wishing she'd simply called him.

Only she could never have left him here, alone in a mostly empty restaurant that, she thought with a repressed shudder, looked horribly bare. *Was this how a king was supposed to woo his future queen?* She stopped a foot from the table and dropped her head to a bow—the subtler form of the curtsy staff used when there were no civilians present.

'Your Majesty, I—' As she raised her head, she faltered slightly as she caught his penetrating gaze.

'If you've come to stand me up, Henna, there's little point standing on ceremony,' he interrupted.

'Aleksander,' she corrected, really not enjoying the feeling of his name on her tongue.

He nodded and she looked away, not that she could forget the way his dark wool jacket clung to his broad shoulders, or that the sheer arrogant laziness of the un-buttoned shirt collar made her want to clench her teeth together and the shock of his slow perusal of her body from foot to face had made her hot and damp and...

'I should go. Natassia sends her sincere apologies but,' she said, looking back to him, but still refusing to make further eye contact, 'an unavoidable personal mat-ter came up at the very last minute.'

There was silence until she raised her eyes to his and, even bracing herself this time, she was hit with that bank of heat, as if she'd just emerged from an air-conditioned airport into the height of summer. And then, as if she'd reversed the trip, it was gone. With a blink of his eyes he'd turned it off and she was coward enough to admit she felt relieved.

'You might as well sit,' he said, gesturing to the chair on the opposite side of the small square table laid for two.

Henna's discomfort increased and she was self-conscious in the dress that she'd worn because...well, she couldn't come to a Michelin-starred restaurant to dump a king in her office clothes. But, unfortunately, she was tired, incredibly hungry and didn't like being ordered around by Aleksander, who—when he was in *this* mood—was incredibly unpredictable and liable to manipulate small countries. She wanted to tell him that she wasn't a dog, but instead a polite, 'No, thank you. I should be getting back,' slipped from her lips.

'Henna, sit down.' It wasn't a request and even the discreet security team stood up that little bit taller.

'Yes, sir,' she said quietly as she sat down in the chair.

'Don't, sir me,' he said under his breath as much as she had.

'Then don't behave like an—' She could have bitten off her own tongue. Had she really been about to call the King of Svardia an *arse*?

Once again, Aleksander laughed, which seemed to surprise him as much as her and completely changed the mood in the room. Apparently having decided it was safe, the head waiter came over and offered them a menu each. Even though Aleksander studied it intently, she couldn't shake the feeling that *she* was the object of his considerable attention.

Henna accepted the menu with a smile and waited while the waiter poured them each a glass of water and explained that they were welcome to order from the menu or, if they would like, the chef had prepared a special meal with wine pairings that was, in his humble opinion, excellent.

'That would be wonderful, Jakob, thank you,' Aleksander replied, gently snatching the menu from her fingers and handing it back to the waiter.

Reluctantly, she let a smile pull at the corner of her mouth. There was a cheek to his actions and a spark in his eyes she'd not seen for a very long time. This was who she remembered. Not the manipulator, not the brooding power of the throne—*him*.

'So, I'm behaving like an—'

'Only, apparently, on special occasions such as these,' she fired back, belatedly shocked by her audacity.

'Special occasions?' he asked.

'When you're left to your own devices you have a tendency to become…'

'A monster?'

'Hardly. A beast, perhaps.'

He inclined his head to the side, as if saying *touché*.

'Great, big, hairy—'

'That's quite enough of that, thank you,' he said as the waiter appeared with a bottle of wine and Henna felt a warmth in her chest, radiating outwards. Really, she should have known better, because Aleksander was like one of the very best predators, lulling his prey into a false sense of security before striking. Because that was precisely what he did the moment the waiter left.

'Tell me what happened between you and Viveca.'

Aleksander half wished he could take the question back. Beneath the soft lighting in the restaurant, Henna had visibly paled. But something had happened between Henna and her sister and it was something bad. A protective instinct had risen in him watching their interaction and he neither liked it or wanted it in his life and had therefore decided that only by knowing what had happened would he be able to remove it.

'It is none of your business,' she said tightly, and he could see how much it cost her to refuse his demand.

She reached for her wine, her fingers plucking the thin stem from the table and bringing the rim of the glass to her lips. It was wrong of him to be so aware of a woman so clearly angry with him. But it was more than anger. He could tell—just as he had done the first time they had met—that she was holding back an avalanche of hurt and he didn't like it. He'd never liked it.

'Tell me and I will find a secretary,' he offered, utterly aware of how much work she had shouldered on his behalf in recent months.

This time it was Henna who laughed. It was half disbelief, half humour, and it was all honest. That was a hard thing to find when you were King and a long-forgotten part of him was delighted.

'A secretary *and* a fiancée. Just make sure you don't get them confused.'

'That really would give the press something to talk about,' he mused.

'And the palace HR department, I'm sure.'

The gentle humour lay between them, heated in the flame of the table's candle and evaporated. He could see her thoughts turn back to his question, could read the internal struggle she was having at the thought of telling him. He held his breath until a sigh signalled her defeat.

'You're aware I stayed in Svardia when Freya went to Switzerland for her degree?'

Aleksander nodded, remembering. His sister had desperately wanted to stand on her own two feet, be truly independent for the three years of her studies without protection officers or assistants and staff. And although their father had agreed, he'd lied and had secretly sent an undercover bodyguard, Kjell, to keep an eye on her. It had been devastating for his sister when she'd discovered the truth.

'I went to college here in Torfarn. It's such a beautiful campus and the lecturers were wonderful. And… I didn't want to be anywhere else,' she said, shrugging as if she should apologise for her love for Svardia. The candlelight flickered in her middle-distance gaze. 'That's where I met Nils.'

Beneath the table, Aleksander's hands fisted reflexively and it took an inordinate amount of energy to undo the unconscious action.

'He was studying biology, but his flatmate had a few lectures with me. Nils was,' she said, finally turning her gaze back to him, 'nice.' She nodded as if agreeing with her own assessment. 'He was quiet, easy, uncomplicated. And I felt safe.'

He could hear the longing in her voice, as if she still felt the need for such things—safety—and a small part of his mind filed the important fact away.

'When he proposed, I thought that it was done. That *I* was done. That my future was a home with him and a family. He was so different from the hysteria of Viveca and her mother, there was no game playing, no drama. He was quiet and...'

'Safe,' Aleksander completed.

She nodded, and reached up to sweep a hand through her fringe. 'I didn't want him to meet them. I thought they would devour him and that he might run away. Might decide that it wasn't worth it.'

Aleksander read between her words. She'd feared that he might find that *she* wasn't worth it. He didn't quite know where this story was going, but he didn't like it and he most definitely didn't like the idea that Henna would think at any point that she was unworthy. From the corner of his eye, he saw the waiter hovering at the kitchen pass with the first course and subtly held him off with a hand.

'But I took him home and, surprisingly, it went well. My stepmother behaved herself. Viveca was on her best behaviour, which simply meant ignoring us both for the most part which, of course, I was more than fine with,' she said with a smile that trembled a little. Her inhale drew the candle flame ever so slightly towards her as if it too was waiting on what happened next. 'And then, about two weeks later, I came home and the bed wasn't made. It was a silly thing—Nils must have been in a rush that morning. Only when I shook out the duvet, Viveca's earring came flying from the sheets. It was gold and long and nothing about it being there was a mistake.' Henna looked at the napkin she was twisting in her hands, her cheeks as pale as the white cotton. 'She wanted me to know that she'd slept with my fiancé.'

He had imagined Viveca callous and cold, but the intent behind her actions was vicious. During his stunned silence, the waiter appeared and placed the first course on the table, having incorrectly identified a lull in the conversation. Ignoring both the man and the food, he asked, 'What did you do?'

'Nothing,' she replied, taking a small sip of her wine before carefully placing the glass back on the table.

'What do you mean?'

'I did the opposite of what Viveca wanted,' she said, finally looking up at him with eyes that exposed her hurt. 'I ended my relationship with Nils and never spoke to either of them about what had happened.'

'You didn't confront them? At all?' he asked, shocked.

'No,' she replied.

'But she got away with it.'

Henna shook her head. 'She's a bully. She wanted the drama. She wanted the responsibility for ending my relationship with Nils. I refused to give her that.'

He understood the logic, had now seen enough of Viveca to know that Henna was right. But that kind of hurt, that kind of devastation…to keep it all locked in and not let it out…he knew the toll it took.

'I'm sorry,' he said, for asking, for forcing her to admit such a thing, and for such an awful thing to have happened to her. He could see the hurt and betrayal simmering beneath the cloudy honey colour of her eyes and recognised that particular brand of poison.

She nodded, accepting his apology even through the clawing sense of shame and hurt unspooling in her chest. She'd never told anyone what had happened with Nils, the betrayal one so shocking that it had spread a numbness through her. A shock so close to grief that for just a moment, in that bedroom, she'd been tempted to ignore the earring.

Yes, she'd felt the hot sting of humiliation because Nils had slept with Viveca, but the deeper cut, the real source of shame was that for one moment she'd considered disregarding it. Her longing for safety and security, for a home where she was loved once more was so strong she would have lied to herself and deny that she'd ever seen the earring.

Even Freya didn't know about Nils, the entire situation over and done with before her return from university in Switzerland. And when Freya had come back she'd been so broken-hearted by the lie that had severed her burgeoning relationship with Kjell that Henna had had no time to wallow in her own heartache, moving into her role and lodgings at the Palace immediately.

How could she explain the devastating loss of a future she had believed in because she'd been so utterly convinced it was *safe*? The way that it had crumbled everything around her and beneath her and left her shaking for months after. How everything had suddenly felt less real than the fantasy of a future she had created where she would be happy.

Nils had been her future, her safe harbour and her security. Viveca had destroyed that, and she still didn't know what she'd done to make her stepsister do such a thing. Logically, Henna had told herself, it had been better to find out the nature of her fiancé before she'd married him. And she had been so utterly thankful to throw herself into royal service, which gave her a home and a purpose. But in her most secret heart she wondered if she had forged a bond with Nils because of the future she'd thought he could offer her. Maybe if she hadn't lost her father at such a young age, if Marcella and Viveca hadn't been so cruel, it wouldn't have impacted her so severely. But it had made her determined never to build her safety, her *home*, around one man ever again.

'Did Natassia really have a family emergency?'

Henna felt Aleksander's eyes watching her reaction to his question and decided to go with the truth. 'I'd say the chances are fifty-fifty at this point.'

'Interesting,' he said, spearing the delicate flesh of the salmon with more enthusiasm than he'd seemed to give his date.

'Well, it might have something to do with the rumours about you and Reina—'

'Michaels!' Aleksander said, snapping his fingers in recollection.

'And something to do with a maid's uniform?'

'Yes. Well, that would make sense.'

'Do I want to know?'

'Absolutely not,' he assured with one hundred percent arrogant conviction.

Henna failed to suppress the smile that pulled at her

mouth. 'Well, I did actually try to find a replacement, but apparently it's a little harder than I'd thought.'

He narrowed his eyes and Henna couldn't account for why that made their exchange feel more intimate, other than being the sole focus of his fierce intellect and sometimes wicked humour.

'Who did you ask?'

'Agnes Ullman.'

He winced. 'Ouch. No, she's—'

'And Ingrid Harr.'

Henna thought she might have heard him groan. How he'd managed to keep all of this from the international press was inconceivable to her.

'I could be persuaded to admit that I'm a little difficult,' he offered graciously.

Henna snorted. 'I hadn't noticed.'

He was chewing and, honestly, there really shouldn't be anything remotely sexy about a man chewing a mouthful of food, but it was his eyes. He looked for just a second as if what he found most delicious in that moment wasn't the mouthful of exquisite food but her teasing him.

And then she realised it was highly unlikely that anyone had teased him in a while. Certainly not since he'd become King and probably even long before then, maybe not since his late teens, after the breakup with Kristine. Because after they had split Aleksander had become a completely different person. Henna was tempted to ask him about it. After all, he'd certainly delved into her personal history, but she was reluctant to lose this moment.

'Where did you go?' he asked of her train of thought.

'Nowhere important. So, you won't tell me about the maid's uniform, but will you explain about the significance of the honey, because—'

Aleksander cut her off with a shocking display of Svardian curse words and the look on his face was one of horror combined with a little bit of fear.

'How on earth do you know about that?' he demanded.

'Secretarial cabal,' she whispered before taking a sip of her wine.

'Bloody hell,' he said, leaning back in his chair and now looking at her with something a little like awe.

The waiter appeared and discreetly whisked away their plates, while another server replaced their white wine with a red in a fresh glass, filled up their water, changed their knives and disappeared with as much speed and efficiency as a racing car pit stop.

And throughout it all Aleksander held her gaze.

And throughout it all she wished he didn't. Because this wasn't a date. This very much wasn't *her* date, that was for sure. A tingling began at her fingertips and her heart felt full and thick as it thudded in her chest, each beat sending fissures of need around her body.

Looking away, she caught the eye of one of the security detail standing at the far end of the room, and the small smile and nod of acknowledgement reminded her that she was one of *them*. Not the person who was taken for dinner by the King. Not purposely so, anyway.

It wasn't her role to tease the King. It was—as they had agreed—her role to help him find a fiancée. And whether or not she found him attractive was neither here nor there.

'Did you…?' she started and had to clear her throat gently. 'Did you have any other women in mind?'

There was only one woman he had in mind at that moment and he would never be able to touch her. Because what he needed was complete indifference. And what

Henna Olin meant to him... He could categorically confirm that it was most definitely *other* than indifference.

The waiter returned with their main course, buying Aleksander some time. 'Aged sirloin steak with a stout jus, celeriac purée, baby vegetables poached in cumin butter and...' Aleksander stopped listening and watched as Henna bestowed a beatific smile on the waiter. There was nothing fake about the warmth that she shone on the people around her. No matter the hurts and losses she had experienced, it hadn't made her brittle, harsh or manipulative and for just a second he was jealous that she hadn't *had* to become those things. Remembering why and how he'd melded himself into the King he'd become hardened something that had melted a little under the warmth of her attention.

She flicked a gaze to him, concern firing in her eyes like a spark, which was banked before it could be seen by the waiter, who finally left them alone.

'It doesn't matter,' he said, forcing himself to answer the question Henna had asked.

'Of course it does,' Henna replied lightly, still holding on to the ease of conversation they'd had just moments ago. An ease that couldn't be allowed to continue.

'No, it really doesn't. Anyone will do,' he stressed. Henna's eyes were focused on where his hands were firmly braced against the edge of the table. He needed her to understand this, not because she was going to help him find his future bride, but because they had blurred the boundaries he had worked hard to put between them.

He should never have asked her to stay for the meal. If he hadn't seen her dressed like that, if he hadn't seen the way she had looked at him...desire, curiosity, need. *No.* He couldn't, *wouldn't,* place the blame for this on her at all. He knew his limits. They had been hardwired into him the moment Kristine had told him what she'd done. The moment that he'd realised the devastating loss of what could have been and never would be.

'Henna, let me be clear. Whoever I marry will have to know that love is not on the table. It is not a possibility. I will provide them with whatever they need or want, and they will provide me with an heir. But beyond that? The only requirement is that under no circumstances whatso-ever will they engage me emotionally.' Aleksander had given up, lost, too much to allow for any other possibil-ity. 'All I have, everything I do, it is for Svardia. *Noth-ing* else matters.'

He watched the lovely flush that had coloured her cheeks drain away, the spark from her eyes dimming as if the night sky was readying for the palest dawn, her fingers released her knife and fork onto the plate qui-etly and none of it touched him. It couldn't. He'd told her the truth. He'd loved once and would never again be so foolish because he honestly didn't think he'd survive the loss and betrayal that love always led to.

She nodded, her gaze on her plate.

'Tell me you understand, Henna. I need to hear you say it.'

The look in her eyes when she raised her gaze to his was a slap to the face. Sharp fury burned him from across the table.

'It is clear that you feel the need to pursue this path for your own needs. But that is a harsh punishment to inflict on your future fiancée,' she accused, her words striking hard and fast.

'If they know what they're getting into, then it is their decision to make,' he responded harshly, lashing out because of the damage he'd caused himself. He had lowered himself in her estimation and he'd done it on purpose.

'I understand, Your Majesty. But I am afraid that I will not be any part of this.'

Aleksander pressed his teeth together to stop himself from taking it all back. Instead, he nodded once and she placed her napkin on the table beside her unfinished meal. Sliding the chair back, she stood and with a quiet, 'Your Majesty,' she turned and he watched her leave the restaurant.

It was only when the waiter arrived some time later that he realised he'd stared after her for so long that the food had gone cold. And still he told himself that he'd done the right thing. He'd done what he needed to. And he might even believe it if the scent of her perfume hadn't lingered to tease him that he was lying to himself.

CHAPTER FOUR

HENNA STARED AT her computer screen, trying to read the words in the email in a way that would make some kind of sense. It had been two days since 'the meal' with Aleksander, which had suited her just fine. She'd hoped that a bit of distance between them would put things back to the way they had been before. But then she would remember the way his eyes had drawn up her body, heating her skin and making her heart race, how his eyes had sparked with a desire that inflamed a need she'd thought long gone, but instead revealed itself to be simply dormant. Back then, her feelings had been nothing more than a teenage crush. This? This was a different beast altogether. This lived and breathed fire, and had wings to make it soar and was absolutely impossible, she warned herself every time she felt it stir. So she'd pushed Aleksander and his terrible plan for a loveless marriage to the back of her mind. Until she'd started receiving the calls.

'Henna, rearrange my meeting with the Russian consulate.'

'Henna, arrange a video conference with the British Prime Minister for Thursday afternoon.'

She had fielded ten such directives the first day and

it had doubled yesterday. So she'd started screening her calls. And then the emails had started. And the last had her screaming at the screen, causing a member of staff in the corridor to duck suddenly and run away.

From: Restad, HRH Aleksander
To: Olin, Henna
Subject: Urgent
12th April 11:45 a.m.
My current meeting is overrunning by twenty mins and the CEO of Nordstad Enterprises is already waiting. Distract him?

From: Olin, Henna
To: Restad, HRH Aleksander
Subject: Urgent—not really
12th April 11:47 a.m.
Your secretary is more than capable of doing this.

From: Restad, HRH Aleksander
To: Olin, Henna
Subject: Urgent—really
12th April 11:49 a.m.
I don't have a secretary.

From: Olin, Henna
To: Restad, HRH Aleksander
Subject: Urgent—not really
12th April 11:51 a.m.
Exactly!

From: Restad, HRH Aleksander
To: Olin, Henna

Subject: Please answer the phone
12th April 11:55 a.m.
Are you there?

From: Restad, HRH Aleksander
To: Olin, Henna
Subject:
12th April 11:59 a.m.
Henna?

Henna had left her office before she did something even more stupid than she had already done by responding to *the King of Svardia* with emails like that. She had come to the Palace gardens to try to regain a sense of calm, inhaling the crisp bite in the air and letting the sunshine warm her skin.

Pulling her shawl tighter around her shoulders, her heart turned as she admitted that she didn't recognise herself at the moment. Her behaviour was not that of the person who genuinely enjoyed helping people find solutions to problems, who drew a great deal of satisfaction from coordinating people and events in a way that created smooth and seamless transitions through the day. She'd always found it orchestral and harmonious, and it had given her great pleasure to be the conductor. But ever since the Vårboll, things had been discordant.

No. Discordant wasn't the right word. It was more like frantic, nervous, *wanting*.

Every time his name appeared in her inbox, her pulse leapt, her mind tuned into a frequency of pure static and she felt that same electric current zipping through her veins. Every time she remembered the heat in his eyes as he'd looked at her in the restaurant it wrecked her pulse and put thoughts in her mind she couldn't take back. Images. Hot, heavy, intimate images. And when he pushed at her she wanted to push back. She wanted to chip at the arrogance on his shoulders, put *him* on the back foot. Press and push until they were up against a wall and...

She groaned out loud, startling a bird in the hedgerow. She couldn't work like this. She couldn't *live* like this. Aleksander was her best friend's brother. He was the King. A king who would one day in the very near future choose a queen for whom he felt absolutely nothing.

Love is not on the table. It is not a possibility.

The crunch of gravel behind her broke into her thoughts painfully and she turned round, her heart racing from shock.

'Henna—'

'You scared me,' she accused.

'And you interrupted me,' Aleksander shot back angrily. 'The CEO of Nordstad has left without the meeting and I could really do without the bad press at the moment. I have three meetings this afternoon and I don't even know what they are.' His hand raised as if to bracket his temples, but it dropped again as if he wouldn't even allow that moment of self-comfort.

The heat in his words enraged the embers of her frustration and she couldn't help but match his exasperation. 'You have a meeting with the Principal Private Secretary. The co-ordinator for Freya's engagement party wants to finalise the order of events, and Sven needs the information for the delegation arriving from Japan in two days' time.'

'Why am I meeting Anita Bergqvist?' he asked, as if it was perfectly natural for her to know his every move.

'Because you need a secretary!' she screeched, reaching the last thread of the very frayed edge of the thinnest tether in the world. 'Your Ma—' She cut herself off with a sharp exhale. She *knew* that he had an inordinate amount of work at the moment. He was only four months on the throne and the world was watching for his first mistake. To know that, to feel that every second of his actions and every single one of his decisions were being watched at all times—she couldn't imagine such a thing. 'Aleksander, you *really* need a secretary,' she said gently.

'I know that,' he said through gritted teeth as frustration seeped into his bones. He *did* need a secretary. 'I just don't have time to train someone up,' he concluded, evading his reluctance to place his trust in yet another person who might let him down. And Henna was here. 'Can't you just—' He stopped with the realisation that he was about to beg. And he didn't beg. *What on earth was this woman doing to him?*

'Find the time, Aleksander. And find a secretary,' she said and turned away from him.

'But you could do it much more quickly,' he called after her, only to have her spear him with a raised eyebrow he would never have accepted from anyone else under any circumstances. 'You could use your secret secretarial cabal to find me someone.'

'We prefer "personal assistant" these days.'

'Henna, you could be called God's gift for all I care. I just need—' He cut himself off before finishing the sentence.

'You can say it, you know. It's not a sign of weakness.'

'I will do no such thing,' he said, offended. He'd not asked for help in more than ten years. He'd not had to since he'd started to engineer situations that achieved his preferred outcome. But for some reason it was, in this *sole* instance, not working. What it boiled down to was that he simply couldn't trust anyone to handle his affairs in the way in which he needed them handled. And as for Henna—he already relied on her far too much for his liking.

'What are you doing here anyway?' he asked, irritated that he had to resort to such a blunt about-turn in the conversation to move away from the subject altogether.

'I was *trying* to clear my head,' she said as her short strides closed the distance to the Palace maze.

'I meant why *now*?' he said, falling into step with her, belatedly realising that his words revealed he knew that every night after she finished work she would take this walk. He'd first seen her from his office window three years before and somehow it had become part of his daily routine too. He'd told himself that it was her regular evening walk that coincided with his after-hours whisky because it simply couldn't be the other way round.

'I needed to clear my head *more* than usual.' She hitched her shawl up around her shoulders an inch but it only drew his attention to the curve of her neck and a little mole he'd never noticed just in the hollow beneath her earlobe. 'What about your three meetings?' she asked as he kept pace with her.

He threw his hand to the side, still distracted by the contraction in his body that was, irrefutably, arousal. 'I need to clear my head,' he said, disliking that he had such little control over his body around her.

The corner of her lips lifted and he'd let Anita Bergqvist wait for another hour just for the sight of that alone. The strange silence between them settled into something expectant; the crunch of their shoes on the gravel felt like a slowly turning screw, tightening everything in him. So what Henna said next came like a bucket of water in the face.

'When my father got ill…when he realised *how* ill he was, we started this. Taking a walk every day while he still could.' There was a tone to Henna's voice that was soft and warm. Yes, grief was there, but it was tempered by love. 'He'd ask me so many questions, but always the first was, "What was one thing today that made you smile?" He was fascinated by what made me happy.'

A quick trio of fists punched deep into his heart. The first was for Henna and what she had lost. The second was a reminder that his own wouldn't care at all if he were happy—only that he was doing the best for Svardia. And the third…was a phantom, a could-have-been, and just the thought of it stole the air from his lungs even now. 'That is the sign of a wonderful father,' he said the ache in his chest.

'He was,' she said, love shining ever so brightly in her eyes. 'He didn't have to give up his job and his company to raise me, but he did. And I had nine precious years knowing that I was loved utterly and completely and nothing, not even grief, would have me take that back.'

The ferocity and brightness of her love was something Aleksander couldn't understand. It was there, swirling around her in bright warm colours, and he envied her that. But at the same time he took her words as a line in the sand between them. A clear indication of what Henna wanted from her life—as if he hadn't known already. She was soft and good and kind and deserved nothing less than a future with exactly that kind of love.

'He would have been proud of you,' he told her, offering her nothing but the truth.

She huffed a small laugh. 'Really?'

'Yes. You've travelled the world—'

'With Freya,' she interjected.

'And you've bent French Ambassadors to your will.'

Her smile exploded into full bloom and it was marvellous for him to see.

'That I have,' she said with pride, arriving at the entrance to the maze. She looked to the ground and when she gazed back up at him her eyes were unreadable. 'Have you found a suitable…candidate?'

Aleksander knew she wasn't talking about the personal assistant role now and his mind flew to Tuva Paulin. They'd found themselves in the same social circle on occasion and he'd detected a reasonable amount of interest on both their parts. She was savvy, intelligent and poised. As the daughter of two prominent actors, she was media aware, well-liked and respected. She was also, in person, as cold as he needed her to be and therefore completely safe.

'Yes. We are having dinner tomorrow night.'

Henna nodded and once again he was frustrated that he couldn't tell what she thought or how she felt about it. And then he became thoroughly irritated with himself because he shouldn't give a damn what she thought or how she felt.

He took his leave then with a swift nod, heading to the first meeting of the afternoon, which he would give only half of his considerable attention to, while the other was spent leashing his body's reaction to his sister's best friend.

Henna hadn't stopped thinking about what Aleksander had said the day before, that her father would have been proud of her. Would he have been? Had she achieved all that he'd imagined for his daughter? Whether it was the shifting nature of her feelings for Aleksander or the second email from Veronique about the job offer making her question things, she wasn't sure. But the HR director had replied to Henna's request for more time with a bit more information about the role. And it sounded too good to be true.

She would be the chief of staff to the client, mediating between the client and their direct reports as well as being in charge of three personal assistants, all of whom worked together to ensure that the client had three-hundred-and-sixty-degree support whenever needed. There was an insane amount of holiday, scope for travel, working from home options and a more than generous housing allowance provided for the upheaval. Because that was the other thing. The role was located in London.

Looking at a map, she'd realised that the client was based a ten-minute walk from where her father's offices in Knightsbridge had been. He'd worked there for two years and had met her mother there. He'd promised to take her there one day, but his diagnosis had come before they could ever make the trip. And Henna couldn't shake the feeling that there was something fortuitous about the job offer. It fitted so many missing pieces she hadn't known she'd lost in the last few years, as if the universe was sending her a message, or a gentle nudge to take her life into her own hands and step out into the world. She opened the email again and reread the answer to the question she had asked them: why had they chosen to approach her?

Because we have heard that you are the best.

Who would have told them such a thing? Had Freya

been the one to tell them? Had she realised that Henna would be better off spreading her wings, or did she also feel that impending change on the horizon, as inescapable as a tsunami and just as terrifying?

She had just switched her computer off when the phone rang. Frowning, she answered, checking her watch. Whatever it was couldn't be a good thing at nearly seven-thirty at night.

'Henna, I'm so glad I caught you. Did His Majesty give you the information for tomorrow?'

'No, he was supposed to give that to you.'

'He said he would. It's just that we have the delegation arriving at nine a.m. tomorrow and the kitchen has no idea what to do.'

'Just call him,' Henna said, already knowing he wouldn't.

'Henna, please.' The word was a theatrical whine. 'He's been in such a foul mood for the last two days and we've already had one of the staff in tears. You're the only one who knows how to handle him.'

'That is patently untrue.'

Another dramatic whimper came down the phone line and Henna rolled her eyes. 'Okay, okay, I'll go.'

But as she made her way towards Aleksander's office she knew already that she didn't want to see him. She didn't trust herself around him. Rather than going away, each time she saw him her feelings got worse, making her say and do and want things that she really shouldn't.

Henna stopped outside Aleksander's office door, her gaze snagging on the patch of new plaster and paint covering the damage done by Lykos Livas a few weeks ago and proof that Aleksander drove people to their limits. Even now she felt her heartbeat gather in speed at the mere thought of asking him for the information Sven needed.

No. She wouldn't lie to herself. It wasn't the thought of a confrontation with the King that made her pulse rate pick up. Thrusting the wayward direction of her thoughts back, she knocked on the door.

'Come.' The sound of his frustration penetrated the closed door and she closed her eyes, gathering herself, before pushing the door open and entering his domain.

The office was bathed in the evening's shadows, the low lighting making it something altogether different than what she was used to. Logs burnt gently in the fireplace despite the easing of the cooler months into the warmth of summer. A half-drunk whisky was on the mantelpiece and she turned to the lamplit desk that mirrored her own in terms of sheer volume of paperwork. The door to Aleksander's private living area opened and he came through, buttoning up his shirt, forcing Henna to look away as if she had caught him in a state of undress.

Heat spread to her cheeks that had nothing to do with the fireplace and she cleared her throat. By the time she looked back, Aleksander had looped a tie around his neck and still she felt as if she were seeing more than she should. It was personal. It was...too much.

'What is it?' he asked abruptly, looking around the room for something.

'Sven needs the dietary information for tomorrow's delegation,' she forced out around the pulse beating heavily in her throat.

Aleksander threw a curse into the room and leaned over the desk to retrieve a file. Her eyes were drawn to the way his torso turned, his thin hips bracketed by a leather belt, and a low thrum started in her body. It started as something quiet, but as he turned and stepped towards her, closing the distance between them, it grew louder and louder until she could hear it above the pounding of her heart.

Kiss me, kiss me, kiss me.

He handed her the manila folder but hadn't let it go by the time her fingers had wrapped around the top of the file. They were barely an inch apart. Surprise crossed his gaze before desire drowned it out like an inkblot exploding his iris. At the sight of it, her skin flooded with pinpricks, thousands of them, raising the hair on her arms and peppering her heart with little electric shocks, tripling her pulse and taking away the ground beneath her feet.

'I'm quitting.'

The words burst from her lips, surprising them both, and Aleksander stepped back, accidentally taking her with him from where she still held the paperwork.

He shouldn't have been able to hear her words above the roaring in his ears, but he did. They cut through his thoughts like a hot knife through butter, zeroing his focus while simultaneously going to work on the threads of his restraint.

'Okay.'

The moment he'd said it, he knew it was wrong. There was nothing okay about it at all, even though it really shouldn't have come as a surprise. But, beyond that, it was clear that Henna didn't like his response either.

It was in the blank shock in her eyes.

'Henna—'

She pulled the paperwork from his hands and stepped

back, shaking her head slightly as if trying to shrug off a physical blow. The sight of it was too much so he reached for her and tugged her back to him, *into* him, and for a shocked moment they stood like that—breaths held, hearts mid-beat.

And then he made the mistake of looking down into her eyes. Lush lashes framed hazel eyes, rich with a complexity of colours, arrowing straight to his own arousal. They moved simultaneously, coming together, lips finding each other's. Aleksander didn't know what he wanted more—the taste of her, the feel of her or the scent of her; he knew only that he wanted it all.

Her kiss soothed the feral beast that had lived within him for the last two days. The paperwork dropped from her hands as she reached for the fabric of his shirt, curling her fingers and the cotton into her fists, pulling him to her, his heart pounding at the contact. His fingers splayed through the hair above her ear, cradling her head, angling her so that he could deepen the kiss, so that his tongue could thrust. Open-mouthed, she welcomed him, her fingers curling tightly in his own hair, her nails scraping deliciously over skin that was overheated and sensitive.

He laid his hand above her breast, the pounding of her heart beneath his palm powerful and impossibly fast, an aphrodisiac all of its own. It was as if their desire feasted upon each other, exponentially increasing with no end in sight. He felt as if he were being driven out of his own skin and the loss of such control was both heady and impossibly frustrating. In an attempt to leash it, he dominated the kiss, crowding her with his shoulders and body, only to feel her push back just as strongly. Deep within him an animalistic part of him roared in satisfaction at finding his equal.

The taste of her drove him wild, and he forgot everything. Where he was, who he was, who she was. The moment she hooked her calf around his leg, bringing their bodies closer, the heat of her fitting perfectly against the hard length of his need, he groaned, low and deep. Unthinking, he picked her up, spun them around and, holding her to him, he swept an arm out, clearing the desk, before placing her on it. She looked up at him, eyes wild and glazed with desire and need, making room for him between her legs as a pen pot rolled beneath the desk and sheets of paper fluttered to the floor.

One hand slipped behind her, bringing her forward against the evidence of his desire for her, the gasp that fell from her lips music to his ears. Flexing his hips, her pupils exploded, shards of jade and ochre drowned in black, and she arched her back, pressing the delicate juncture of her thighs against him even harder.

'Again,' he commanded, the exquisiteness of her pleasure igniting his own irrevocably. For a second she looked unsure, so he pulled her harder against the ridge of his arousal and her head fell back, her eyes unfocused beyond need and pleasure. The cry that came from her lips was an appetiser of the feast to come and he wanted more. Keeping her pressed to him, his fingers bunched the material of her skirt at her thighs. Hot, needy and incessant, his pulse pounded *more, more, more* through every beat around his body. His fingers slipped beneath the hemline, inching up smooth skin to the crease of her hip, as his thumb dropped dangerously close to where he so desperately wanted to put his mouth.

Henna's breath was coming in short sharp pants, full

of need and want, each one a delicious scratch against his chest. He'd never felt this before. As if he couldn't get enough, as if he needed it more than air. He inhaled more and more of her into him, chasing a high that had no end in sight. His chest burned with a need beyond the point of pain and the only thing that cut through the haze of the fiercest arousal he'd ever had was the chiming of the mantel clock above the fireplace. With each toll, he was pulled back closer and closer to the present, until he realised exactly where he was, who he was—and who was waiting for him in a restaurant three miles away.

He cursed out loud. Exhaling heavily, he pressed his heated forehead to hers. 'I have to cancel Tuva.'

'What?' she asked, the hazy desire clearing from her gaze.

'The…date,' he finished, distaste like ash on his tongue.

'No! You can't.'

'What?'

The look in his eyes turned from molten lava to glacial.

Her heart pounding in her chest, Henna couldn't get her thoughts straight. 'I… This…' Her lips were swollen by the passion of their kiss. A passion that had marked her skin and dampened her thighs and…

Aleksander had a woman waiting for him in a restaurant who might be his wife one day.

She felt sick.

'It shouldn't have happened. I…have to…' She slipped off the desk.

'Henna—'

She ran from the room just as the first tear started to fall.

CHAPTER FIVE

FOR WHAT FELT like the hundredth time that day Aleksander slammed the desk phone back into its cradle. Nothing was going as planned. Marit had returned two days ago and, while she was taking on more royal duties, she simply wasn't as up to speed as he needed her to be.

Following his meeting with Anita Bergqvist, his Principal Private Secretary, she had provided him with several CVs of supposedly suitable candidates for the role of his personal assistant, but he'd found each one wanting. One was too young, the other too old and yes, he knew he sounded like Goldilocks. He told himself that he was managing to make do with the interim assistant Anita had loaned him until he found someone he could trust.

But he knew that he was spinning too many plates. He was running between obligations, patching them up with interim solutions and barely hanging on. And the world was watching Svardia's new King, praying—he imagined—for him to make a mistake for their entertainment alone. He wasn't stupid, he knew he needed to find an assistant that he could trust, but whether he liked to admit it or not, losing Lars had cost him. Time, effort, efficiency. Aleksander didn't like making the same mistake twice and putting his trust in someone else was too damn much to ask. Because the last time someone had betrayed his trust, made a decision that he could never have imagined making himself, it had left him utterly destroyed. He had survived only by numbing himself to all emotion and he would never open himself up to that kind of pain again.

Surprisingly, the only time he hadn't felt that internal warring was when he'd finally arrived for dinner with Tuva. He'd been intent on making his apologies and excusing himself, but she had surprised him with her frank response. Tuva had been exactly as he remembered her, direct and efficient. She had laid her cards on the table and he had followed suit. She too was in need of a marriage that wouldn't challenge her emotionally and they had decided to take some time to consider their options and reconvene in the days preceding Freya's engagement ball.

She was, he thought, looking out of his window, perfect. Until he realised that he was searching the palace grounds for Henna, who he hadn't seen in the three days since…since the encounter he was refusing to think about. That he was working predominantly out of his assistant's office next door proved only that he had enough sense of self-preservation *not* to work on the same desk he would have thoroughly satiated both himself and Henna given half the chance.

Which only turned his thoughts back to that evening and infuriated him even more. He simply hadn't expected it, that was at least half of his problem. And for someone always two steps ahead it was warning enough. Yes, he'd known that he was attracted to her—Aleksander didn't make a habit of lying to himself. He liked and respected her, and beyond that she was utterly beautiful. But the kiss had gone from sensual to searing in less than a second and he felt as if something fundamental had changed deep within him. It was the single most erotic experience he'd ever encountered, enough to make him mindless in a way that went far beyond something as simple as lust. Even now he wanted to take a cold shower just thinking about it. That alone proved how dangerous she really was.

But he couldn't fault her. Henna had been right. The kiss shouldn't have happened. Not only because Tuva had been waiting for him, but because he would never be able to offer Henna what she needed. And she would never be what he needed. She threatened his emotional equilibrium too much.

As the phone rang he realised that he was running late again, serving to prove his point. Snatching it up, he listened to a stream of apologies from the assistant Anita Bergqvist had provided for him. He'd managed to arrange for two meetings with two very different world leaders at exactly the same time and had then painted himself even more into a corner by cancelling on them both at the last minute in a panic.

Aleksander slammed the phone down *again*, cursing loudly and not caring this time who heard him. He bracketed his temples with his thumb and forefinger and stared at the travel plans he'd intended to ask the assistant to make to get him to Öström, a pit opening in his gut.

The organisation's meeting in Öström was one of the most important events on his schedule. It would never be found on public record, it would never be spotted in a newspaper, it would never even be known outside the smallest of circles that he'd even been there. But it was still absolutely vital that he attended. He had given his word to his future brother-in-law that he would handle Kozlov, even though Lykos Livas did not truly know the extent of his relationship with the Russian oligarch. Aleksander had absolutely no intention of letting the Russian's threat to his sister slide and it was of the utmost importance that he was dealt with once and for all. And he refused to entrust his travel plans to someone as monumentally inept as the kid who had just cancelled not one but two world leaders.

It wasn't up for debate any more. Whether she challenged him or not, he needed Henna's help if he had any chance of getting to his sister's engagement ball with his throne and his sanity still intact.

Henna folded the last of her pullovers and placed it into the bag she would keep beneath the bed until winter came back around, until she realised that she wouldn't be here for winter. She sank onto the bed, the cashmere soft in her hand, knowing that, especially now, there was no going back. She had irrevocably and completely burned the bridge that had connected her to Freya, to Marit and to… Aleksander.

She had called Freya earlier that morning, not wanting to interrupt her and Kjell's precious time away but knowing that each minute that ticked by was another spent fearing that Aleksander would tell Freya first. Not out of meanness but just because he didn't always think. She'd been avoiding it because telling Freya would make it real. But Henna knew now that she *needed* it to be real.

'*You can't!*'

It had eased a scared part of her to hear Freya's response. Henna hadn't realised just how afraid she'd been that Freya wouldn't care, that she didn't think of them as sisters, as Henna did. And she would have absolutely buckled under Freya's plea to stay, had it not been for the kiss.

Pressing her fingertips to her lips, she could have sworn they were still bruised by the force of their passion. And while she could never tell Freya what had happened with Aleksander, she had instead slowly unravelled her feelings about working in a new role and being offered this new position. Forming the words and sharing them with her friend had made her realise that this *was* the right time for her to leave. She was good as Freya's lady-in-waiting—excellent even. But she was also unchallenged and it had left her too much time to think.

She supposed, had she been another type of person, she could have done anything. Gone travelling, moved to some far-flung destination and taken up a thousand hobbies. She was lucky enough to have financial security outside her job, thanks to her father, but Henna had always seen it as a financial security that had cost her too much and had never touched the inheritance her father had left her. She really did enjoy working and she knew she would never be happy unless she was doing something that helped others.

There had been a lot of tears between her and Freya and her eyes would probably still be puffy in the morning, but some of that restless slithering she'd felt in her stomach had eased a little. Not completely, and it returned the instant she thought about Aleksander, but she felt much better. Freya had asked Henna to clear their schedules for the day she returned so that they could spend it together and it had warmed her so much to know that Freya would miss her. She was the closest thing Henna had to a real sister, to family, but it was time to find her own way in the world.

Henna thought back to Freya's first reaction.

'Did my mean brother scare you off? That's it, isn't it?'

And Henna's reply was the first lie she'd ever told Freya. 'No. Not at all.'

Henna's attention had snagged on the word 'mean' and inside she had protested. Yes, Aleksander was moody and demanding and difficult. But Henna had seen mean. She had experienced mean. And Aleksander was *not* it. And when they'd been out at dinner she'd even caught glimpses of the charming, easy, fun teen he'd once been, before whatever it was that had happened to take all that away.

Casting her mind back, they'd been at school. It had been the start of a new school year, around the time she was fifteen and Aleksander seventeen. The news had filtered through the school that he'd broken up with Kristine, his girlfriend of three years, because she'd moved away. Had he been so broken-hearted that it had changed him so much? If so, why not track her down later as an adult? Henna wondered how she would have felt in the same situation. She had never thought of tracking down Nils because of what he'd done. But if he hadn't…if he'd simply had to move…would she have gone with him? Frowning, she realised that she wouldn't, and she wasn't sure what that said about her feelings for him at the time. Had she been detached? Had he noticed? Was that why he'd slept with Viveca?

A knock on the door of her suite pulled her from thoughts so all-consuming that when she opened it to find Aleksander standing there she simply blinked at him, waiting for him to morph into Sven or another member of the staff who lived on this corridor.

His hair was ruffled and yet still somehow sexy and, although his hands were in his pockets, tension thrummed through the corded muscles of his forearms, visible thanks to the rolled-back shirtsleeves. His jaw pulsed as they stared at each other, and she wished for all the world that she knew what he was thinking.

Wrestling the spike of adrenaline that had lurched through her at the mere sight of him, she pressed her lips between her teeth, stepping back and gesturing for him to come in. She supposed it was silly to be self-conscious of her living space, given it was just the same as any other live-in staff member's. But feeling silly and Aleksander seemed to go hand in hand these days.

He stalked to the centre of the room, gaze on the floor until she closed the door and turned to face him.

'I need you to come work for me,' he said, his dark brown eyes revealing absolutely nothing.

The statement drenched her body in a volatile combination of heat and fury. Heat that he dared look that good, and fury that he dared ask her that.

'No.'

Internally, Aleksander reeled. People just did not say no to him—usually because he made sure of the answer before he asked the question, if not by knowledge then by orchestration. And although he allowed for the fact that the manner in which they had last parted made his question extremely difficult, if not downright inexcusable, he was still King of Svardia.

'Just for three days,' he bartered.

'No.'

He snapped his jaw shut, before he could say something he couldn't take back. Taking a breath to calm the pulse that was unusually quick for such a simple confrontation, he couldn't help but register that the perfume that was uniquely Henna was so much stronger here than he'd been prepared for.

'What will it take?' he asked.

'For you to get a secretary, I would imagine,' she said, reaching for a jumper on the bed that was part of the open-plan living arrangement and he immediately looked away. That wouldn't help either of them.

He didn't want to be here. He disliked intensely that she was the only person in the entire palace that he needed while he was in Öström, but what really pushed him to the edge was the lack of control he had over his body around her.

'You could ask for anything,' he threw at her.

'Really? What *should* I ask for?' she enquired.

'A good reference?' he bit out in frustration.

Her eyebrows skyrocketed. 'You would give me a *bad* reference?' She held his gaze until he felt the air in his lungs press against his ribs.

'No. No, I wouldn't,' he said.

A large window dominated the space, a small table right in front of it. He could so easily picture her there in the mornings, hair twirled up in a messy bun, flicking her fringe from her eyes like she did when it irritated her. A fist formed in his stomach when he realised Henna wouldn't be at that table for many more mornings.

'When do you start?'

He watched her unfold and fold the jumper in her hands. 'A month,' she replied.

'So soon?' he couldn't help but ask. He was worried for Freya, of course.

It was strange to be in her living quarters, the space enclosed and intimate in ways that were unexpected and undesirable. He looked around, realising that it was the first time he'd seen any staff member's suite. The entire surface area was perhaps half the size of his private living room and it didn't make him feel much better.

'What is it that you need?' she asked, and he wondered if it were too much to hope for that she would relent.

'I have to attend an event that needs to be completely off the radar. No press, no schedule, no travel plans, no trace whatsoever.'

'An event?' she demanded, bright red slashes marking her cheeks. 'If you think,' she said, impassioned and outraged, 'even for *one minute* that I am going to arrange for you to have some… some… *assignation—*'

'Oh, God, no!' he said, horrified that she would think him capable of asking her to do such a thing after… And then he remembered that he had left the palace with the taste of her still on his tongue and met with Tuva. He bit back the impulse to groan. He was making such a mess of this.

He gestured to the table. 'Can we sit and I'll explain?'

Reluctantly, she sat at the table and he took the chair opposite, but she still looked as if she might bolt at any minute. The only way he could get her on side was to tell her the truth. And everything in him warned him against it. Nothing good ever came of trusting someone. But he had no other choice.

'I have an important meeting with several people who must not be seen with me for various reasons, none of which are illegal,' he said when he read the question in her eyes. 'And I need you to run interference for me during what will most likely be, at least, two full days of intense discussions.'

'What kind of interference?'

'I'll need you to create a cover story and to answer and field emails and messages during that time.'

Her eyes widened. He knew he was asking a lot of her, and he knew it was ridiculously last-minute. 'We'd fly out this evening.'

'Aleksander!'

He held up his hand to ward off any more admonishment. 'I know, I know.'

'I need more information than that.'

'You don't. And I won't give you more than what I've told you.'

That he'd told her this much was more than he'd ever told anyone, even Lars, and it was costing him. The meeting in Öström was the only thing outside of the kingdom of Svardia that meant something to him. It gave him the chance to do good in a way that would not be manipulated or misinterpreted by the world's press and he valued that chance and the responsibility that came with it. He would never betray the organisation's secrets.

'It is definitely not illegal?'

'Definitely not.'

She levelled him with a gaze that could only mean trouble. 'I'll do it on one condition.'

'Anything,' he said, truly that desperate.

She bit her lip, and it curled his stomach, but not in a good way; it was a warning and he braced for impact.

'I need to know what happened. What made you so incapable of trust that you cannot find a secretary, and so resistant to love that you would cut it from your marriage?'

'You don't,' he said, his heart turning hard.

'Then find someone else to run interference, Aleksander.' She got up and, absolutely incensed, he slammed his palm down on the table, making her jump, but she did not give him the satisfaction of turning to face him.

'You do not know what you're asking, Henna. If you did, you wouldn't—' He bit his tongue before he could say another word.

Staring at the table, he heard her say, 'I know that, whatever it is, it's eating you up inside and making you reckless. And you can't *afford* to be reckless, Aleksander. You're playing Russian roulette with your meetings and your schedule and you're manipulating people into outcomes that you think you can control, but you can't.'

It was a warning that he didn't want to hear but couldn't deny. He got up from the table and paced across the room, feeling as if he were in a cage. Henna was right, he knew that. But so was he. She really didn't know what she was asking of him. His fingertips tingled and he released the fists he'd formed, restoring circulation.

He hadn't told anyone what had happened to him at seventeen. He wasn't sure he even had the words. It was twelve years ago, and he could swear it hurt as badly as if it had been yesterday. He felt it like the fresh hell that it always was, a knife twisting in a gut full of grief and loss and guilt.

He could walk out of here now and not look back. He'd find a way to go to Öström; he wasn't a complete imbecile. But her accusation had hit home, cutting closer to the truth than she'd probably realised. He needed to face it.

'My world used to be a happy one,' he started slowly, his words stilted. 'Charmed, even. I was the Prince of a beautiful and wealthy, thriving kingdom, school was easy for me, the lessons nothing in comparison to the studies my father would have me learn in preparation to becoming King. Despite my status, I had friends—good, funny, naughty, silly—every single thing I could ask for. And Kristine. She was...'

'Lovely,' Henna filled in. Kristine had been quiet but always nice. She certainly hadn't been like Viveca and her friends, whose vicious tongue-lashings had sometimes bordered on bullying. There had been something about Kristine that remained apart from it all but anchored to Aleksander. They had always been hand in hand, despite the school rule about remaining eleven inches apart.

'You remember her?' he asked and for a moment she thought he sounded surprised.

She nodded rather than answering because of course she remembered the girl who'd put an end to Henna's childhood crush on the boy who had found her in the maze and given her a best friend. She had seen their relationship and known that it was special.

'We'd been together for three years. I think, outside of the time she spent with me, she hated every minute of being with a prince. She was naturally shy,' he said, pausing his back-and-forth march across the small breadth of her living area. 'And I didn't take that seriously enough.' The halting nature of his words made it seem as if he were talking about this for the first time in a very long time. Thinking about it in a way that, perhaps, he hadn't done before. 'I should have,' he sighed. 'I should have taken it so much more seriously.'

He sat on the edge of her bed, leaning his elbows on his thighs and staring at his hands. He had never looked less like a king to her. And suddenly she wanted to take the question back. A pit opened in her stomach, warning her that she didn't want to know, that she should never have asked.

'It didn't matter that we were careful…' Henna's hand flew to her lips. 'Kristine fell pregnant just at the end of the summer term.'

Henna's thoughts scattered, going through every single possibility in a broken heartbeat, knowing there was no possible good ending to this story.

'I told her that I wanted to marry her. I had thought about it and wanted to tell my parents, I wanted to have our baby. I…had never wanted anything more in my life,' he said, looking up at Henna so that she could read the truth in his gaze. The truth and the devastation…

Breath shaking his words, he pressed on. 'I asked her to wait for me and she said she would. She promised. I needed to figure out how to tell my parents but, before I could, I heard that her family had literally packed up overnight and moved halfway across Svardia. I…' he shook his head, as if he still couldn't understand it '… I managed to convince one of the security guards to take me to them and when I got there…it was done.'

A knife slashed through her heart for him. She didn't need to ask what had been done.

'She cried so damn much. Tears falling the whole time, she tried to explain why she couldn't have married me, why she couldn't have borne to be in the public spotlight, how young we both were, that neither of us were ready. This way, she said, no one needed to know, as if it hadn't even happened.

'Do you know how hard it is to look into the eyes of someone you love and for them to say that your child never happened? To not have a choice about it? And worse…to know that you failed to protect either of them from what happened…because of who you were?'

Henna watched as Aleksander blinked back tears.

'No one needed to know,' he repeated. 'So for a long while I didn't tell anyone. I kept it all deep, deep down.'

Her heart ached. That this terrible tragedy had happened to him and he had no support, no love or compassion to comfort him. At seventeen, to be dealing with so, so much. Grief, love, loss, guilt. She couldn't even imagine.

'Eventually my father called me into his office and told me…to stop *moping*.'

The gasp that fell from Henna's lips sounded an awful lot like horror to Aleksander, but it didn't quite penetrate the thick icy fog of the past winding itself around him until it froze his fingers and stung his chest.

'He knew,' she stated, and Aleksander could only nod as he heard his father all those years ago.

'It is my job to know everything that happens in my country. And it is my job to ensure that mistakes do not derail this country. A job that will be yours one day.'

'He didn't…' Henna couldn't finish the question, but she didn't have to. He understood what she wanted to know.

'My father said that when he visited Kristine's family

they were already decided on…a course of action.' The words hurt his heart as he said them, as he described the end of a life that would never be. For so long, anger and grief had lashed his soul, and beneath all that…responsibility. *His* responsibility.

A hand pressed against his forearm, the skin-to-skin contact a shock. Henna was kneeling before him, the sympathy in her gaze, the compassion…it was wasted on him.

'So,' he said, clearing his throat and gently shaking her off as he rose to stand. 'Now you know. And now you will come to Öström.' It wasn't a question. He had paid the price she had exacted and she would do as he demanded. 'And we will never speak of this again.'

She nodded.

'The helicopter will be ready to leave at four.'

He turned and, just before he could open the door, 'What happened to Kristine?' Henna asked gently.

He clenched his jaw and, forcing a small smile to numb lips, he turned to Henna. 'She's married to a tax accountant with whom she has three children.'

Aleksander left the room before he could see the flare of sympathy in Henna's compassionate gaze. As he'd thought before, it was wasted on him.

CHAPTER SIX

THE HELICOPTER LIFTED into the sky, leaving Henna's stomach back on the Palace grounds. Swallowing a swell of nausea, she looked down at the paper in her lap. It was a hand-written schedule that she would destroy at the end of this event. This journey had all the makings of a spy film, which should seem ridiculous if it wasn't for the fact that every single aspect of Aleksander's life was fodder for journalists and newspaper oligarchs, waiting to make money from his mistakes more than his successes.

The stark realisation that they would have torn the young Prince of Svardia and his girlfriend to pieces over a teenage pregnancy was devastating. Her heart ached for the decision Kristine had been forced to make and it broke for Aleksander, who'd had no choice at all. She could imagine just how much he'd tried to keep bottled in—his grief, his anger, his loss, not being able to speak to anyone about it. And then to discover that his father had known. Had known and not provided him with comfort, or compassion, or support... To a woman whose father had been the sun and moon in her life, constant, nourishing and loving, it felt unnatural to her. And her heart swelled with the need to give Aleksander some of those things, even if it was twelve years too late.

Not that he would accept anything from her. Aleksander was a man whose sense of trust had been crucified and he saw emotional bonds as a threat to his control—a control that was sorely tested by the responsibility he'd felt for Kristine, for the pain they'd shared and for the loss of what they could have had. Henna feared that his plan for a loveless marriage was a form of self-punishment for the mistakes of a young man's passion.

The helicopter banked suddenly, forcing her to thrust out an arm to the side of the cabin to steady herself. The close protection officers were still grim-faced and silent in their disapproval of their King's command. They had reluctantly agreed to remain close by, but outside the area of the tiny peninsula of Öström.

The cover story she and Aleksander had concocted was a three-day tour of a military base, where it would be expected for details to be scarce. The helicopter would land, before they took a two-hour drive, in secret, to Öström—an area that had a population of six, comprised entirely of the live-in staff members of a hotel that was so exclusive it didn't have a website. There had been no photographs for Henna to look at and she was unfamiliar with the area. She knew nothing about how many people would be in attendance, or who they were, only that during the hours Aleksander spent in meetings she would be fielding any incoming correspondence and—if necessary—pretend to be him on email.

They hadn't had much time to talk about what specifically would happen when they got to Öström and, with so many people around, Henna knew that now wasn't the appropriate time to ask. Outside of managing the details of the trip, Aleksander had been neither the commanding King she had come to recognise nor the charming teenager she'd once thought she'd known. There was a seriousness to him that she'd sensed as a middle level between the two. As if, perhaps, now she knew, Aleksander didn't have to pretend any more.

Gunnar, who had until recently been the head of Freya's security detail, motioned to the headset and Henna flicked the button that would allow her to hear the conversation.

'Ms Olin, we will be landing at the base in fifteen minutes. From there Aleksander will drive you onward.'

Henna frowned.

'Don't worry, you're in safe hands,' Aleksander said absently as he looked out of the window, completely unaware of how the thought of being in his hands undid her.

Her pulse jerked, as if he'd flipped a switch in her body. A throb, hard, fast and just a little damp, pulsed between her legs and she forced her gaze away from the cabin and out of the window, hoping that she had hidden the sudden blush on her cheeks.

'Gunnar—' she heard Aleksander sigh as if tired of having to explain himself to the head of security '—the security threat level is practically zero, you have been allowed to vet the area before anyone's arrival, so you know the layout and you will be within a five-minute reach of us at all times. There is nothing to worry about,' the King of Svardia insisted.

Only Henna was beginning to realise that being secluded with Aleksander for three days meant that there was a *lot* to worry about.

Aleksander was worried, and it had nothing to do with the fact that he was due to meet a startling array of the world's most powerful players in the morning. No, it had everything to do with the woman sitting beside him in the sleek matt black two-seater that he usually loved driving. Large sweeping slow corners of grey tarmac cut through the craggy coastline and a gunmetal-grey sea as he changed up a gear and hit the accelerator.

Whether it was because they were alone, or that her perfume was once again wreaking havoc on his senses, but from the moment they'd left Svardia his body had been on high alert—as if sensing he was under threat. And he supposed he was. Aleksander had imagined that revealing what had happened in his past would change things between them and he'd been right. He'd thought that it would have made him vulnerable to her somehow, but instead it had made the connection between them stronger—at the exact time he needed it to be weaker.

Henna shifted behind him, crossing her legs and accidentally revealing an expanse of thigh that he was intimately and deliciously familiar with. His gaze flickered down the length of her legs and his fingers wrapped around the steering wheel instead of her skin just as Henna pulled two sections of the blue skirt together. Never before had he paid such attention to the design of women's clothing, but the wrap-over skirt Henna wore seemed nothing short of devious. The silky lining he'd seen far too much of slid over her skin and constantly revealed too much leg. Or not enough.

Fighting a ferocious wave of arousal, Aleksander forced his body back under his control, just in time to take the last turning onto a peninsula that looked as if it had been carved from volcanic rock. He watched in the rear-view mirror as the security detail peeled off in the opposite direction, heading to the smaller camp they'd reluctantly agreed to stay in. Returning his gaze to the road, he was struck by the desolate and primeval landscape, ancient in a way that felt about as base as his urges towards Henna. So no, even the setting wasn't helping.

The dark, jagged, blackened jutting rocks, however, hid a hotel so exclusive that it couldn't be found online in any form. There was a central building, around which eight cabins were situated in such a feat of architectural design it had become one of Aleksander's favourite places to be. He had come to Öström to meet with the others twice a year over the last eight, but this would be the first time he had come as King. It had been easier before, when the press could be distracted by either an easy-to-sell minor scandal or a dramatic world event, but as King it was different.

Not that the change in his status would mean much to the people he was meeting. More than half of them had more wealth than thirty percent of the world's smaller countries, and each and every one of them would be willing to disagree with him or they wouldn't be there. The organisation had been the secret of the world's most powerful players for the last one hundred years and would probably be so for another hundred. And tomorrow Aleksander had to convince the five highest members that he was demanding Kozlov be removed from the organisation.

He pulled into the small circular drive in front of the main building and asked Henna to wait in the car. She nodded, her gaze locked on to the incredible horizon visible from her window. It took him less than five minutes to confirm his arrival with the hotel, the arrival of the other guests and to request that dinner be sent to the cabin in an hour's time.

He returned to the car and drove it around to the cabin

at the furthest edge of the rocky outcrop. He was out of the car and halfway to her door when she thrust it open to stand and stare at the end of the peninsula, where grey and white waves crashed against black rock. Her mouth was open, shock, surprise and delight all clear in her gaze.

The wind had blown her fringe back, away from her forehead and wisps of hair whipped around her. She reminded him of a Vettriano painting, as if she stood strong and alone in the eye of a storm, preyed upon by his voyeurism. Then she looked at him and everything he'd been trying to deny rushed to the surface—want, desire, hit him hard and he knew that he'd made a monumental mistake in bringing her here.

Standing by the floor-to-ceiling window at the edge of the seemingly simple cabin that she was set to share with Aleksander for the next three nights, Henna shivered, and it had nothing to do with the gentle heat inside and everything to do with the way that the last third of the cabin hung away from the rocky outcrop of the peninsula and directly above the swelling sea beneath. The waves were relentless, hurling themselves dramatically against the rocky harbour curving around to her left.

She'd noticed that there were other cabins, but the distance between them all was surprisingly vast. The sense of isolation here was like nothing she'd ever experienced and that she was sharing it with a man who had driven her almost to an orgasm when his thumb barely touched her thigh sent blood and sparks rushing around her body in equal measure.

The single-storey cabin was surprisingly compact. All on one floor, the larger part of the cabin on the land end housed the two bedrooms, each with windows that displayed more of the dark and twisted coastline, along with the most exquisite bathroom Henna had ever seen. At the end of a room covered in bronzed golden tiles was the largest bath she'd ever seen, pressed right up against the window—the only thing separating the bather from the sea.

She'd been staring at it when Aleksander had called her to the table where their evening meal had been served. Dinner had been silent, the delectable food lost on Henna as her stomach roiled as much as the waves. Cured fish, celeriac remoulade, gently pickled beets, caviar—it was as if the chef had known her favourite things and brought them together in a dish that should have torn her attention from the man opposite her, but didn't. The silence was building between them into something that had become impossibly loud and she really didn't know what would break it.

She saw his reflection in the glass behind her, saw the whisky he offered her.

'Drink with me?'

His request was strange to hear when, before, he would simply have demanded. She reached for the glass, avoiding his fingers as she retrieved it from his grasp. The cut crystal was still warm from the palm of his hand, her skin, her body, instinctively seeking it out.

She refused to meet his gaze, instead turning back to look out at the sea as she took a sip of the whisky and all she could think of was that she would never see this incredible coastline again. She would never come to this unimaginable hotel again. She would never be alone with a man as powerful and devastating as Aleksander again. It had become an urgent refrain in her mind and she couldn't make it stop. It hurt, and it was loud, and she was tired of fighting the desperate need she had to feel his hands on her skin, to let him finish what he'd started in his office on his desk.

Maybe then it would stop, she lied to herself. Maybe then she wouldn't react to just the thought of him, she wouldn't pant his name in the midnight hours from dreams that had fuelled night sweats. Maybe then she would finally be able to say goodbye and take up the promise of the next phase of her life in a new job and a new city.

She bent her head over her glass of whisky, defeated by her desires, and just when she was about to give up, to run away and hide in her room, she felt the faintest trace of his breath against the back of her neck. Heat exploded between her legs and her heart raced as if she were running, long and hard towards a finish line that felt impossible to even consider. First it was his breath, then it was the pad of his thumb, pressing lightly at the bottom of her hairline, down her spine to the collar of her silk shirt. She felt the skin flush at her cheeks and between her breasts, and thought she heard him curse, but the pounding of her pulse was so loud in her head she wasn't sure.

Her nipples pebbled beneath the oyster silk of her shirt, cold and aching for his touch, while the heat of his body drenched her from behind, a tantalising promise of what could be. She turned beneath his touch, his palm cupping her neck, and they were finally face to face with barely an inch between them.

The moment their eyes locked, she wished she could look away. The heat in his gaze burned so hot she felt it soul deep and knew she would never be the same again.

She began to tremble and even the gentle warmth of his palm on her neck couldn't steady her.

He cursed and drew her towards the wood burner in the centre of the living area. He took plush pillows and soft throws from the sofa and chairs and gently led her to the floor. She wanted to tell him that she wasn't cold. Wanted to tell him that only one thing would make the trembling stop, but she couldn't form the words and once again Aleksander pressed a glass of whisky into her hands and she drank from it as she couldn't from him.

Aleksander shifted back on the floor so that he rested against the sofa opposite to where he had led Henna closest to the heat of the fire—even though he was half convinced that she hadn't been trembling from the cold.

Elbows on bent knees, he watched her drink from the glass of whisky, her eyes shielded from his gaze by the turn of her face towards the fire. Slowly the shakes racking her body began to lessen and with it a little of the concern in his chest, but not enough.

'Are you okay?' he asked.

She nodded, but he needed more. 'I need to hear it, Henna.'

She looked away from the fire and pierced him with her gaze. 'I'm okay.'

Her words were steady, but her breathing was too controlled to be natural. He ran his hand across his forehead and threaded his fingers into his hair and gripped. He needed to hold something because Henna would see that she wasn't the only one trembling. He'd felt it in his fingers as she'd turned in his hand; her skin against his had been almost too much for him to bear. And while she was brave enough to wear her desire, to own it, he

knew instinctively that should he betray just how much
need he felt for her they would both burn that night.

She cleared her throat. 'You've been here before?'

'Yes,' he said, ignoring the train of his thoughts.

'So, this is a regular thing, these meetings?' she asked,
reaching for her glass, her fingers shaking less.

In that moment he doubted he would ever come back
here again. His request to move the meetings elsewhere
would be granted without question. But he'd never be
able to look out of that window again without seeing
Henna's head bowed, without feeling her skin beneath
his touch, hearing the hitch in her breathing hardening
his arousal to the point of near pain.

'Twice a year in person,' he replied, forcing the words
out through the haze of desire he was taunting himself
with.

'Huh,' she said, swallowing a delicate mouthful of the
rich amber alcohol he'd poured for her, his tongue curling
in his mouth as he imagined that she'd taste of the orange
peel, smoke and sea salt the whisky was renowned for.

'What?' he asked, trying to distract himself from
needing to taste her.

'You have a secret cabal of billionaires.'

His gaze left her lips, jerked up to her eyes, twinkling
bright with tease, and he barked out a laugh. His reaction
made her smile and for a moment they shared a lightness
that banked the tension from before.

'I will neither confirm nor deny,' he said, the smile
on his lips forming the tone of his words.

'Because the first rule of the cabal is—'

'Not to talk about the cabal.'

He reached for his own glass, not because he wanted
to drink but because he needed to taste her, and this was

as close as he could let himself get. He could lie and tell himself that the reason he couldn't touch her was because of her friendship with Freya, or because they worked together…but he hadn't lied to himself for a very long time. The truth was that Henna already challenged his emotions. He had made decisions based on what she would think or do, he had created a charity for children that had been inspired by the loss she had overcome as a young girl because she had been there, entwined with his emotions, for years. He threw the whisky back, relishing the burn of alcohol as a punishment. Because, no matter how much he knew she was a risk to him, he still wanted her. And when he looked back to Henna, he saw the same need in her eyes.

She had to know. She had to understand.

'I can't give you what you want, Henna.'

'Who are you to tell me what I want?'

'Your King,' he growled.

'You're the boy who found me in the maze. To me, you will always be that first.' Rather than tearing a strip off him for his arrogance, her tone was simple, sincere and it cut him off at the knees.

'You're trying to avoid the issue,' he warned, even though it was he who was hiding.

'I don't think I am,' she said, sitting up straighter against the sofa. 'We started something in your office and…' despite the blush of discomfort painting her cheeks a rosy pink, she pressed on '…and I want you to finish it.'

Aleksander cursed. He almost shook from the need to cross the distance between them, lay her on her back and feast on her as she wished, indulge her every delight and lavish her in pleasure. He fisted his hand to stop himself from reaching for her. She deserved more than that.

'You would be happy with that? One night?' He watched as her pupils bled out into the thinnest of amber rings. 'You would let me into your body,' he asked, his stomach tightening around the words, the images it conjured, the *feelings*, 'knowing that I would then go on to marry another?'

At that her skin blanched. He had been right. She might want him, she might even have the same wild need that cried and lashed in her chest as it did in his, but she wasn't ready for what she wanted. She wasn't prepared for the consequences of what she wanted. Yet neither could he leave her like that—poised on the same precipice, hurting and wanting and needing.

'But,' he said, damning himself to hell, 'if you want, I can finish what I started.'

Her head jerked up, her eyes burning with the reflection of flames from the wood burner, heat from the whisky and need from the deepest part of her—he recognised that it matched his own. And in that second he realised that he needed this as much as she did. He needed it more than his next breath.

He put down the glass in his hand, knowing it wasn't the alcohol that would satiate his thirst. 'Let me taste you,' he asked, watching the colour flood her cheeks. 'Let me drink from you,' he all but begged. 'Let me bring you pleasure.'

His words turned a key to a locked box she'd not known was in her mind. It unleashed images that cascaded like an erotic kaleidoscope across her mind's eye, all the while unable to tear her gaze away from the promise in Aleksander's eyes.

'Yes.' The word poured from her lips like the whisky they were drinking, heady, intoxicating, powerful. But she wasn't mindless with it. She knew what he was offering—and, more importantly, what he wasn't. She knew that things would change between them, but hadn't they already? She was leaving her job with his family. She would be leaving the country too. They were already past the point of no return, but what that meant beyond what he was offering her tonight she would consider later. For now, she wanted to indulge in everything he had asked.

Aleksander heaved in a breath as if he were surprised that she'd agreed to his request. With one leg stretched out before him and the other bent, supporting the arm crooked on his knee, he looked more like a rake than a king. His eyes had become ferocious with intent and he looked as if he were battling an internal war.

'Are you sure?' he asked, his eyes blazing.

'Absolutely,' she replied with soul deep conviction.

Her heart pounded in her chest as he unfurled from where he leaned against the chair opposite and prowled to where she sat, hands fisting in the thick sheepskin rug, holding herself back and utterly destroyed by the intent in his gaze.

He leaned over her, dominating her not with aggression but the force of his passion.

'You can never wear this skirt in front of me again.'

'Wh-wh-what?' she asked, the word stuttering through the shakes that had returned to her body.

His hand swept up her thigh and slipped between the gap in the wrap-over skirt, his skin against hers a delicious friction, her body instinctively unwinding and pressing closer to his, bringing her chest closer to his. Aleksander's eyes had never left her face, as if he were fascinated with her every expression, every reaction to his touch. Her head drifted backwards as her lips opened on a gasp beneath his, he inhaled as if trying to capture her exhale.

One hand had bunched the skirt at her thigh, while his other slipped to the damp heat between her legs. He closed his eyes and cursed, before conquering her mouth with his, the shocking thrust of his tongue the most that he would give her, filling her in the way he had refused to, but still sending her higher than Henna had ever been before.

All too soon the kiss ended, as Aleksander tore his mouth from hers. For a moment she felt such an acute loss she couldn't breathe, until he leaned back, gently spreading her legs, her skirt falling either side of her thighs. Instinctively she tried to press them closed.

'There is no need to hide from me,' he said gently. 'Unless you would like me to stop?'

'No. No, don't stop…don't…' She didn't need to finish her sentence. All of his considerable focus was on removing her panties, all the while staring at her as if he had never seen anything more beautiful. He made her feel that.

He bent down, his palm snaking around her ankle, sweeping up over her calf, sending goosebumps across her skin—her legs, her stomach, her breasts—and she felt them like little electric shocks across her heart, making her breathless as she forced oxygen around the starbursts.

Her eyes drifted closed as he placed kisses on the inside of her thighs, painting fireworks on the backs of her eyes. The first delicious sweep of his tongue curved her body, her hips raising beneath his palms and his mouth, her back arching as she felt the gentle growl of his own delight through his tongue to her body.

Oh, God.

He kissed, teased and sucked her clitoris, sending shivers through her body, hurtling her towards a climax she half feared. His thumb gently hooked on her entrance, pulling ever so slightly before he filled her with his fingers. Her breath became urgent, her legs shifting restlessly, her hands fisting his hair, holding her to him when he growled his delight, pushing him from her when he stopped. She wasn't sure any more.

Let me taste you.

Let me drink you.

Let me bring you...

Her orgasm took her by surprise, exploding through her body like a meteorite, decimating any thought or sense she had. When she opened her eyes she was looking at the velvety sky above Öström, the stars myriad and beautiful, and she felt herself bright and burning as strong as any one of them. She felt both boundless but tethered, safe and protected. It was only then that she realised Aleksander was still holding her to him.

CHAPTER SEVEN

WATER SLUICED OVER Aleksander's heated skin. Eight hours after he'd brought Henna to orgasm and then put her to bed, *alone*, his body was still burning for her, his breath was still catching in his lungs and he could absolutely *not* go into his meeting like this.

Damn it.

He'd kept the curse in, but it was a loud shout in his mind. Soaping up his hands, he swept them across his body efficiently, until he came to the jut of his erection and groaned. The slippery lubricant of the soap was too much. He had denied himself pleasure yesterday in favour of hers, and he would make the same decision over and over again. But as he firmed his grip on his arousal his hips surged against his will, one hand braced against the golden tiles of the bathroom, the other gliding to the tip of his penis, circling the head and sliding back down, and this time the groan fell in with the rush of water pounding down against his skin.

Henna's eyes flashed in his mind, the way her thighs had parted for him, the damp heat between her legs, the taste of her, woman and sensuality, dripping on his tongue… He cursed again and he pressed his forehead against the tiles, the cool ceramic leaching the heat from his fevered brow, his breath coming in pants, harsh in comparison to the melodic litany of Henna's from the night before. The way her cheeks had flushed as her climax grew nearer and nearer had Aleksander fisting the base of his shaft, a small pearlescent bead joining the drops of water against the bruised head of his need. But it was the memory of how she had fallen apart on his tongue, how she had let him hold her as her orgasm racked her body, that finally drew his own from him, his muscles corded, thighs locked and gut tight as he came.

By the time he opened his eyes the water had washed away the evidence of his need, making him a little more clear-headed, thankfully. Until he'd dressed and made his way towards the kitchen and he saw Henna at the table, head bent over the laptop she had brought with her. She had swept her hair into a messy bun and in doing so exposed the length of her neck, and instantly he was transported back to last night, to the feel of her skin beneath his fingers as he traced—

'Coffee?'

'Yes,' he replied without missing a beat, even as his heart tripped over itself to catch up. She stood from the table, approached a coffee machine that hissed and spat, and magicked an espresso without looking him in the eye. Clenching his jaw, he fought the instinct to reach for her chin and turn her face to his so that he could see what he needed to. That she was all he could think about when he should be planning Kozlov's downfall was dangerous and that she affected him so after what little they had shared was unacceptable. She threatened his focus and that was dangerous. To be the man he needed to be, the King his people needed, it was absolutely vital that he remained unaffected at *every* level. He had given her what he could last night and there would be no more, and with that thought he left the cabin.

Klaus Brandt stood by the open window, blowing the smoke from his cigar out into the world, much to the disapproval of Olena Kelinski. The tension between the two was simmering, as it usually did whenever they were in the same room, but considerably less than when Ilian Kozlov was present. The Russian oligarch had the uncanny ability to ratchet up the tension with even the most mild-mannered of people, Sakura Maki being the perfect example. Aleksander rubbed at the dull tension at his temples, trying to focus on the most important matter for their consideration.

'It won't be easy,' Sakura warned.

'When did we ever shy away from hard work?' he growled, drawing an assessing look from Javier Casas, the Spaniard with an incalculable net worth.

'Something you want to share with the group?' Javier teased.

'Not particularly,' Aleksander groused.

'She's very pretty,' Olena's rich Ukrainian accented voice purred.

Aleksander's head whipped up. 'She is none of your concern.'

Olena inclined her head, accepting his possessiveness over Henna.

The lower-level members of the organisation came from the UN, the IMF, Presidents, Prime Ministers, royalty and billionaires. But the group in this room comprised of the highest members. Every person had more money than a third of the world's lowest income population, *each*. But all of them were united in one purpose:

to use this organisation to redistribute the better part of that wealth where needed, to support initiatives that were denied backing because they didn't know the right people, or weren't prepared to offer the right investment incentive. Each and every person in the higher echelons of the organisation had a driving desire to see the world improve, economically, ecologically, technologically. Apart from Kozlov.

'Revoking a membership hasn't been done in over eighty years,' Klaus said on a plume of blue smoke.

'The man is a menace,' Javier observed, distaste clear in his tone.

'I'll allow that he's not a person I would have chosen, but the rules are the rules. Membership is passed down before the death of a previous member and their choice is inviolable,' the German replied.

It was a way to keep the numbers steady and the organisation circumspect. There were certain criteria that must be met before the membership could be ratified, but Kozlov's predecessor had been an ornery bastard and Aleksander couldn't help but think he had chosen the Russian on purpose.

'He skates too close to the edge,' Sakura insisted.

Olena huffed. 'Now is not the time for niceties. His dealings are illegal, his manner offensive and I'm appalled that it's taken us this long to consider ousting him.'

'In the past, members have done much worse,' Javier reminded them.

'And for an organisation determined to positively affect the future of the world, we might be putting too much stock *in the past.* Kozlov threatened,' Aleksander said, his tone forbidding, 'my *sister.*'

Slowly, one by one, each member nodded their consent to his removal.

'But how?' asked Klaus.

'There are ways,' Olena said, not so cryptically.

'The Greek, Livas,' Javier asked. 'He gave you his shares in Kozlov's company?'

'Yes, and combined with mine, we could have used them to bribe him to leave,' confirmed Aleksander. 'But the moment Ilian realised he'd lost the controlling shares of his company, he sold out.'

'What's he playing at?' Klaus demanded. 'He's been parading that company around like it was his firstborn.'

'Well, it's orphaned now.'

The group digested that as they realised they'd lost their only decent bargaining chip.

'We could—'

'No,' the others said unanimously when Klaus began to offer what they all knew would be highly illegal and downright violent.

Aleksander glanced at his watch. 'Let's take a break and meet back here in an hour.'

Henna had left the cabin when the staff had arrived to set up lunch. She told herself that the necessary secrecy surrounding this visit meant she hadn't wanted to be seen, but that wasn't the reason she had come out to the furthest edge of the peninsula and the view that had bewitched her on first sight. Salt burned her tongue as she breathed in each wave that crashed against the rocks at her feet.

Last night had felt like that. Waves, crashing over her, drenching her in a pleasure she'd never experienced before. It had never been like that with Nils. No, Alek-

sander was raw and powerful like the force of nature she
was witnessing now. He had drawn a line between what
would and wouldn't happen between them, but he had
not held back. It had been a passionate onslaught that
still sent tremors of pleasure through her body even now.

But, no matter how much he had given her last night,
it wasn't enough. Everything in her roared with need and
she wanted to fight him, make him change his mind,
make him see that there was so much more than he was
limiting himself to. Not with her, no. Henna wasn't naïve
enough to think that they could ever be more than these
stolen moments. He was a king and she—simply the girl
he'd picked up from the floor of the maze in his garden
one day many years ago.

The crunch of footsteps behind her startled her and
she spun round to face Aleksander, who seemed surprised by the emotion she knew was in her eyes. He
stepped towards her. For a moment they stared at each
other, joined in the knowledge that they both saw what
the other was trying to hide. The want, the longing.
Henna realised that for her it had always been there,
and in that moment she believed that it always would be.

She opened her mouth, wanting to say something,
wanting him to know, but he interrupted her, as if he'd
known and was refusing to hear it.

'Lunch is ready.'

Ten minutes later she was sitting at a table filled with
coal-roasted fish, sea vegetable salad, perfectly toasted
rye bread sliced so thinly and a brooding king. His arms
were crossed, head turned out towards the sea and body
so tense the only two things that moved were the finger
tapping out a catastrophic rhythm at his elbow and the

muscle flexing in his jaw. He'd been like that ever since he'd piled his plate with food he hadn't yet touched.

She sighed and put down her knife and fork. 'Can I help?' she asked, hunger completely forgotten.

'Help?' he queried, pinning her with that mahogany gaze.

'I have very little experience with the kind of world domination you're planning,' she only half joked, 'but perhaps I could...offer a different perspective?'

He seemed to consider her question seriously, which surprised her.

'I...believe that we're at a stalemate,' he hedged.

'Okay.' She nodded, wondering if he'd continue.

'We have...a problem that we need to solve.'

'Aleks,' she said softly, 'you could continue to be cryptic and all cabalesque, or you could simply trust me enough to tell me what's going on so that I might genuinely be able to help.'

His eyes flared as if fighting a years-old instinct to secrecy, but when he pushed his plate out of the way she knew he'd given up the fight. He explained about the organisation, how he'd been approached by a business mentor he'd encountered at university in London. How they had become fast friends and, until his death, Aleksander hadn't known a single thing about the secret organisation. The fondness with which he spoke of his mentor made Henna glad that Aleksander had met someone who had perhaps helped him to heal a bit. His mentor had been in the upper echelon of this organisation, and in taking his place Aleksander was given access to some of the world's greatest financial, political and scientific minds. For the most part, members had the same goal—to do everything they could to ensure the future stability of the world as a whole, rather than focusing on any country. But then came Kozlov. A man whose business dealings were barely legal, whose personal dealings were vicious, and when they weren't they were lecherous. The only satisfaction Aleksander had *ever* had when dealing with him had been obtaining controlling shares in his precious company.

'He is not a reflection of our values and each and every month he seems to get worse. He threatened Marit when Lykos came too close to taking over his company,' Aleksander concluded.

Henna's fury that Marit could have been in danger from this man was fierce, he could see it blazing in her eyes. Her desire to protect his family floored him. He forced his mind back to the conversation. 'We thought the easiest way to bring him to heel would be via his company.'

'How did you end up with the controlling part of his shares?'

'I won a large section of them from Kozlov playing at cards.'

'You play cards?'

'I am very good at hiding my vices,' he said, the double entendre out of his mouth before he could stop it, the words landing between them both true and poignant.

Henna blinked, whatever she had been about to say stalled by his careless response.

'And Lykos gave me his. Together they would have been enough to force Kozlov's hand.'

'But because he sold it, the company is no longer a way to punish him.'

'Yes.'

She frowned and sat back in her chair. 'You can't punish bullies,' she stated.

He frowned. 'What do you mean?'

'Kozlov is a bully, like Viveca. He is looking for a fight, always. And you will never win while you give him what he expects.'

Aleksander considered her words, unable to forget what she'd told him about her stepsister. 'Go on,' he encouraged.

'So…' She sighed, looking over his shoulder in concentration. There was a little furrow between her brows that he wanted to smooth with his thumb. He could have watched her think all day. And when he caught himself thinking that he mentally slapped himself. 'You want him to go, but you can't terminate his membership because of the rules.' He nodded. 'So…you make leaving his idea.'

'That's what we were trying to do with his company,' Aleksander said, throwing his hands in the air.

'No, you were trying to force him to go, using his company. You need to make him offer you his membership.'

'But how?'

She laughed at him then, a sound that hit him in the solar plexus. 'I can't do it *all* for you. *I'm* not a member of your secret cabal.'

'You have your own, remember?' he fired back, before realising that she was completely right. 'I have to go,' he said, getting up from the table and slipping into his suit jacket. He looked back in time to see the tease leaving her eyes, to be replaced by something else. It wasn't quite sadness, but it wasn't soft either.

'What is it?' he asked, his stomach clenching instinctively, preparing for a blow. She swallowed, the little flex of muscle at her jaw showing how much she was fighting whatever it was. 'You can tell me anything, Henna,' he replied truthfully.

She lifted her head and the look she gave him pierced something deep within him. 'I want more.'

Aleksander wasn't petty enough to pretend he didn't know what she was asking for. 'I can't give you that.'

'There's a difference between can't and won't.'

'Do you know what you're asking?' he demanded, angry that she was pushing him, making him want more than he could have.

'I'm asking for nothing more than the remaining days. But I'm asking for everything in them.'

'Everything?' he asked tonelessly. 'You are asking for the impossible. There is nothing more in me, Henna,' he said, turning from the table.

'I'm sorry,' she said, and he paused, half wanting to know why and half not. Unable to resist, he turned back to face her. 'I'm sorry that no one was there for you while you grieved. The way,' she said, her eyes glistening with unshed tears, 'that you were there for me.'

'I gave you nothing, Henna.'

'You gave me your hand, you gave me a friend, you gave me a family and a home. You gave me what I needed.'

It was a gut punch—that she knew what he'd wanted following Kristine's shocking decision devastated him. But she didn't understand that it was precisely not having that support that had made him who he was today. The king he was: accomplished, driven, single-minded…and broken. But, instead of admitting that to the smart, sexy woman sitting at his table, he turned and left the cabin.

Javier Casas was talking on his phone outside the hotel but terminated the call when he caught sight of Aleksander.

'You have an idea,' he correctly guessed when Aleksander came close enough.

'I do, but it's a risk.'

The Spaniard grinned, a light in his eyes, his arm thudding around Aleksander's shoulders. 'Since when did we play it safe?'

'We don't have much time.'

'Tell me.'

'Kozlov is all ego and would love nothing better than to best me, since I am why he lost his company. What if I gave him that chance?'

Javier's eyes narrowed in concentration. 'Go on.'

'He's in Macau right now,' Aleksander said, thankful for Gunnar's efficient intelligence-gathering. 'He's there for two days and then he's off. If we were to be in the same casino, what are the chances that he'd be so damn desperate to beat me at cards that he'd bet anything?'

'You think you can force him to put his membership as the ante?'

'Only if I offer him mine.'

Javier whistled. 'That *is* a risk. I'm not sure the others will like it.'

'They won't, and I don't have the time to talk them round.'

Javier grinned. 'You want me to do it.' After a brief

consideration, he nodded in agreement. 'But,' he warned, 'you will owe me.'

'Fair enough,' Aleksander said, turning back to their cabin, his attention already on the fact that he and Henna would now be heading to Macau. Henna, who had been the key to solving the Kozlov problem. Henna, who had asked him for everything…and he had refused. Because in less than a week his future bride would be presented to the world…and it wasn't Henna.

CHAPTER EIGHT

HENNA HAD TRAVELLED to many places with Freya over the last five years, but never in the King's plane. The aircraft had a shower, a bedroom that was as big as her suite and chair and table combinations that were cream leather and mahogany that screamed luxury.

She had taken the news about their new destination in resigned silence. She had stripped herself raw asking for more than he was prepared to give. But it had been her only chance to have the man she'd wanted from the first time she'd seen him. She could admit that to herself now. That all these years she had been hiding from the truth. Aleksander was far more than the older brother of her best friend, more than her employer, more than her King even.

Aleksander's awareness of her was as powerful as a touch. He might be staring intently at the emails she'd handled for him during his meetings in Öström, but she couldn't shake the feeling of it, the *weight*. She gratefully reached for the cup the air steward had brought her, the smell tingling her senses as she inhaled deeply and tiredly. Taking a sip, she sighed as the familiar flavours of bergamot and citrus hit her tongue. She let it soothe some of the tired hurt she felt pressing at the edges of her heart.

'It's good.' He nodded again, clearing his throat. 'Very good.'

She nodded, accepting his praise awkwardly. That was the problem. Since they'd left Öström—since he'd refused her request—they were out of step with each other again, even more so than since the Vårboll. It scratched at her skin and scrabbled back and forth across her stomach. It made her feel... She sighed and pressed her head back against the seat.

Things had shifted between them, of course they had. But she'd not been able to get her feet back on steady ground. She'd only made things worse.

'What are you drinking?' Aleksander asked, as if confused by the scent of her tea, an unusual type for Svardians.

She smiled, genuine warmth spreading through her as the memory rose in her mind. 'Earl Grey. It was my mother's favourite. My father told me that she was very specific about how the cup was made. Tea first, then milk.'

'No lemon?' he asked, familiar with the English tea.

'Though I'm sure there are those that would say she had it wrong, but she wouldn't have it any other way.'

'Is it okay for me to ask what your mother was like?'

Henna met his gaze, the look in his eyes one of some-one who knew loss only as a deep wrenching pain. Her own was so different because of the way her father had shared her loss and grief, and his memories of her moth-er's joy and vibrant personality.

'Colourful. Every picture of her is full of intense bright colours,' she said, seeing the framed photographs she had taken from around the house and hidden in her bedroom before Viveca's mother arrived. 'My father met her in England, when he worked in his London office, and they fell in love. She didn't think twice about following him to Svardia. She passed away shortly after I was born from an aneurism, but my father would tell me something new about her every single day, even after he got sick. He made my feelings of loss for her something else. He turned it into curiosity and familiarity and warmth,' she said with a shrug. And when the echo of pain thudded in her chest for her father, she wrapped her arms around it and held onto the ache of her love tightly.

Aleksander was watching her intently in that way of his that made her feel seen. 'Who was there for you when you lost your father?'

You.

Henna shook the word from her mind, fighting her way back through her feelings to answer his question. 'My father had married Viveca's mother six months before he passed.' Henna knew her grief, accepted and cherished it even, but still the words were sometimes hard. 'He wanted someone to look after me when he was gone, and he and my mother had no other family. Marcella was a friend of his colleague and…she seemed nice,' Henna concluded.

'But she wasn't?'

'No.' She had stopped sugar-coating her experience with Viveca and her mother a long time ago. 'For the first year it didn't matter, because I was so shocked by my grief. I hadn't expected it. I thought… I thought that because I knew what it had felt like to not have my mother there, I…' She shrugged, even now chasing a breath because grief had filled her lungs. She desperately wished to comfort the utterly devastated child she'd been. 'But it shook me. And by the time I began to come back to the world around me everything had changed and they made it very clear that they didn't want me there,' she said simply.

Her home had become a place where every meal was painful and endured in silence from fear of making her stepmother even more frustrated with her or incurring the wrath of her stepsister. Where around every corner was absence and loss and reminders that her father was no longer there. Where every second felt as if she was a stranger and unwelcome in her own home. Was it any wonder that she had held on to the friendship Freya had offered with both hands and never let go? Any wonder that the Palace had been the truest home she'd had in years? A home that she was now about to leave.

'You will always have a place here,' he said, and he was looking at her the way he'd first looked at her, when they'd met in the maze, and she wanted so much to believe him. To believe that what they'd shared the other night hadn't ruined everything.

Aleksander watched as Henna made her way to the bathroom, leaving a sense of sadness behind that seemed to fill the cabin. He couldn't imagine what it would be like to not feel safe in your place in the world. For him, he had been told over and over and over again until it was as sure as breathing, *You will be King.* His place in the world had always been, and would always be, a solid, certain thing. And he wasn't naïve about the fact that in taking this new job Henna was about to leave her sense of security behind…but he hated to think that she might have taken the role because she felt unwanted.

Unwanted.

The word teased and taunted. He didn't think that he'd ever wanted someone more. Ever. Mentally he was desperate to hold her to him, to pull her in and never let go, and emotionally he wanted her as far away as humanly possible. Because if he let her in...what would he let out?

The way Henna had described her grief, the shock, the numbness—he *knew* that feeling. He *knew* that pain. He'd never spoken about the loss of his unborn child, not even with his father, who had known of the pregnancy all along. Kristine had moved before he'd even had a chance to talk to her. To ask her if...if...

He clenched his jaw, fighting the questions that built in his mind, the anger, the hurt, the fear. The fear that it had been his fault from the very beginning, that it was his fault that he'd brought that pain down upon them and that Kristine had been forced into the most horrendous decision anyone could ever make. Emotion welled to the surface of his heart, drawing pinpricks of sweat across his spine and neck as he battled with the intensity of it.

His hands fisted on the armrests of the chair, knuckles white, fingers bruised red, until Henna's palm swept across the back of his hand and gently prised his fist open, because how could he hold on to such tension beneath such gentleness? He looked down to where she crouched beside his seat, her eyes not on his, but where she swept circles across his hands, her head bowed, and this time, rather than arousal, pure and simple, something complex wrapped around them, as warm as it was hot, as calming as it was urgent, as lasting as it was fleeting. In that moment Aleksander knew that, whatever it was, it was unique to her. Only to her. Only ever to her.

Apparently satisfied that he was no longer under the

same ferocious hold of anger, she smoothed his now relaxed palm one last time and returned to her seat, turning her head into the crook of the cushion and closing her eyes.

'There's a bed,' he said, choosing to ignore what had passed between them.

'It's *your* bed, Your Majesty,' she replied, the title drawing a line between them that he was both angered by and thankful for.

He turned back to the laptop and stared at emails he couldn't see while he wrangled with the feelings that Henna brought to the surface and then swept away beneath her touch.

Twenty minutes later, Aleksander heard the slide of Henna's hair against the leather of the seat and tried to ignore it, but she had been restless in her sleep and every time she moved it drew his attention. The stubborn woman had refused to be comfortable and that it was fracturing his concentration was unacceptable.

The air steward had noticed and was about to approach to wake Henna, but Aleksander threw up a hand to ward him off. Henna had gone above and beyond in the last few days. As the staff member withdrew, Aleksander rubbed the tiredness from his eyes and stood, deciding that what he was about to do made practical sense and nothing more.

He rolled his shoulders before crossing the cabin and allowed himself one stolen minute just to look. Henna was about as watchful as he, so rarely had he got the chance to take her in. She really was exquisite. Beneath her fringe, long lashes swept downwards from her eyelids, curling and dark. Her skin was slightly flushed, but the thick dark brown ropes of her hair, shot through with gold, framed cheekbones that were gentle but defined, as if everything in her was balanced between soft and strength, and he marvelled at it.

Her head turned again and her legs shifted. She clearly wasn't comfortable in that seat. He bent, slipping his hands to her back and beneath her legs, and gently pulled her into his arms. Instinctively she curled into his chest, her head resting against his shoulder as he turned towards the bedroom at the back of the plane. Of all the emotions he'd fought in the last few days, this was the most at peace he'd felt.

Right. It feels right.

Ignoring his inner thoughts, he carefully manoeuvred them into the bedroom and gently placed her down on the covers. Her body relaxed into the soft mattress, pinning his arms beneath her and bringing her chest to chest with him, the warm scent of her rising to tease his senses and beckon him over the line he'd placed between them. Shifting in his arms, her head turned towards his, their lips but a breath apart, and his heart leapt in his chest, pulse pounding like a drumbeat, impossible to ignore, urgent, needful and strong. Henna's eyes drifted open and he watched as the flare of surprise and desire obliterated the hazel ring to black. The sight of her reaction to him had need thickening his throat, a weight in his blood, hardening his arousal, and tension straining his muscles and just when he would have taken her lips in his she turned her head to the side, away from him.

A fist grabbed his gut and squeezed. He didn't have that right. He had refused her and now expected a kiss? He was a bastard and forced himself to see, to *know*, the hurt that she tried to hide. He closed his eyes and turned to go, but a hand sneaked out to grasp his wrist.

'You're tired and need to sleep too.'

'Henna, I—'

'Just sleep,' came her reply as she turned her head back to the pillow and closed her eyes.

Unable to deny her command, unable to fight the connection between them that had revealed itself, he toed off his shoes and, without breaking the hold she had on his wrist, lay down beside her, his body mirroring the curve of her back. There were mere inches between them, but Aleksander's last thought before being pulled into a deep sleep was that it might as well have been miles.

Henna stood by the window—another floor-to-ceiling reveal, but the view couldn't have been more different. Bright neon colours flashed and danced across skyscrapers which were mirrored in the sea below, bisected by the three bridges that connected Macau peninsula to Taipa and Coloane. From the seemingly impossible height of the hotel, Macau lay beyond her like a scattering of sequins on silk, the slightest ripple drawing her gaze to new and startlingly bright colours exploding across the cityscape. Her gaze feasted upon the sight, working so very hard to ignore the dress that Aleksander had procured for her.

She'd awoken on the plane's bed alone, but the warmth of the sheets beside her told her he'd only just risen. And she wondered if that was how it would always be between them now, her just a step behind, following in his footsteps. The thought had stung the backs of her eyes, before she'd pulled herself together and returned to the cabin, where the air steward had placed another Earl Grey tea beside her seat.

Typing away, Aleksander had barely spared her a

glance as he'd informed her of the suite he'd booked for her and the clothing he'd arranged to be provided for her. Of all the things that had happened between them, it had been that which had angered Henna the most. She was well versed in last-minute change of plans, arranging clothing for Freya or Marit, suitable for any occasion, no matter where they were in the world. She was more than capable of providing for herself. So when she'd first seen the covered dress hanging on the back of the bedroom door, she had refused to look at it for at least twenty minutes. Until curiosity got the better of her and when she did…

Her heart had pounded. *Was this how he saw her?* Showered, and silky from the frangipani-scented body mousse that had left her skin feeling supple and smooth and worthy of the midnight-coloured creation, she stared at the dress, a boldness creeping over her skin and into her heart.

She held the spaghetti straps wide and slipped into the dress, sliding it up over her sensitive skin. The audaciously deep vee cut into the silk covering her chest took her breath away, the skirts parting high on her thigh as she walked closer to the mirror to inspect her reflection, and she drew her hand to her lips in shock. She turned, her entire back exposed but for the thin X of silk straps that held the dress in place, the blue silk gathering at the base of her spine scandalously.

Seeing herself like this, knowing that Aleksander had imagined her like this, she felt changed by it. The dress exposed as much as it concealed and the duality of it made her feel both sensual and beautiful, confident and powerful in a way she hadn't experienced before.

A message appeared on her phone, asking her to meet

him at the bar of the hotel's casino. Her fingers flexed around the thin case.

You are asking for the impossible. There is nothing more in me, Henna.

She believed that he was wrong. But she'd asked. She'd asked and he'd refused her and she wasn't going to ask again.

Aleksander exited the private lift from his suite to the ground floor, frustrated that he'd been delayed by a call from Javier, confirming the organisation's agreement with his plan. That it gave him what he wanted was nothing compared to the fact that he'd made Henna wait.

The thought pulled him up midstride and he paused, his hand reaching towards his temples and lowering again before betraying such an obvious sign of frustration. The realisation of just how important she had become to him had him almost turning on his heel. Until he caught sight of a flash of blue silk. Fists flexing and heart pounding, he took one step and then another, enthralled by the siren's call of her exposed skin and the need to feel it, anywhere against him and any *way*. He watched as the barman placed a martini glass on the marble top in front of Henna and in the reflection of the mirrored glass behind the bar she caught his gaze.

A hundred little explosions shattered his equilibrium to the point where he was genuinely surprised the entire bank of bottles containing some of the world's most expensive alcohol hadn't collapsed and smashed to the floor. Shards of jade scattered across Henna's irises before she blinked them away and lifted the glass to her lips without breaking their connection.

He felt his own pupils widen in response to the power

of her gaze. There was neither challenge nor submission in it—simply a recognition of self-worth and it made her devastating. The acute awareness of the impact she had on him was to the point of near pain as the physical and emotional threatened to coalesce. Her lips opened just slightly—as if perhaps she was about to say something—when Aleksander became aware of a figure approaching from his left.

Marshalling himself with a ruthlessness honed from years of practice, he turned to greet the short, stocky suited man and his extremely tall companion. Aware of the attention they were drawing, Aleksander was conscious that it was unusual for two members of the organisation to greet each other so openly, but then again Kozlov had just sold his shares in the company he'd built from the ground up because Aleksander and Lykos had been able to obtain controlling shares. It would be best to remember that Kozlov was a man who would cut off his nose to spite his face. It made him dangerous. It also made the Russian very angry.

'Your Majesty,' Kozlov greeted him with a considerable amount of venom.

In response, Aleksander inclined his head, his features masking his own fury. Looking closely, he could see the suspicion beneath the anger simmering in the Russian's gaze.

'What are you doing here?' the oligarch demanded and Aleksander couldn't work out if it was the man's stupidity or intolerable arrogance that made him feel he could address royalty in such a way.

'I heard that the Sultan of Bur'hran was here and I plan to relieve him of his favourite thoroughbreds, so if you'll excuse me,' Aleksander said, making to walk away.

'What, you do not wish to try your hand against me again?' The jeer in Kozlov's tone was music to Aleksander's ears, slowing his steps and turning him back. 'Worried you might lose this time?'

'You have nothing left that interests me, Kozlov,' Aleksander dismissed.

For a moment the mask slipped on the face of the statuesque blonde on the Russian's arm, her eyes widening in shock, before Kozlov yanked her back into place on his arm. The move nearly pulled the woman off her feet and Aleksander's hackles rose with the need to wipe the sneer off the billionaire's face. He should never have been permitted as a member of the organisation. The organisation should be there to protect others from people like this.

'But you have something *I* want,' Kozlov snapped. His tone grated against Aleksander's nerves, but the way he ignored the evident discomfort of the woman beside him was unconscionable.

'Spit it out or hold it in, Kozlov. You're wasting my time,' Aleksander said, not bothering to hide his disdain.

Ilian glared at him, the man's cheeks going an unhealthy shade of red.

'I want a seat at the table. The *top* table.'

Aleksander's smile was lethal. 'No.' He walked off, his pulse racing in his chest, counting the footsteps that took him further and further away from the Russian. *One, two, three—*

'I'll play you for it. If you win, I will give up my membership. If I win, I will take yours.'

The thrill that went through Aleksander was like lightning. He turned back, making his response seem behind disbelief. 'Without complaint? I don't trust you, Kozlov.'

'We can draw up an agreement in advance. The house will witness and hold the ante.' Such agreements were ill advised and irregular, but not unheard of and exactly what Aleksander had hoped for. All the sweeter that Kozlov believed it was his idea. Desperation practically dripped from the man. A desperation that was all too familiar to Aleksander.

Consenting to the wager Kozlov thought was his, they went through the requirements with the casino's concierge and Aleksander realised that there had been a time in his life when things could have been very different for him. Publicly, he had never put a foot wrong, he'd never come off the rails, missed an exam, received anything less than a merit in school and college. But privately, he had skated very close to a very thin edge. Alcohol and gambling had been within easy reach of a very rich royal who was happy to roll the dice between the temptation of oblivion and the pressure of a role that had cost him the girl he'd loved and a child he'd desperately wanted. Because he *had* always wanted children. Whether because it was required of him and the role he was born to play, or whether it was innate within him, it hadn't mattered.

But when that possibility had been taken away from him it had shattered that softer, happy, carefree part of him. Until he'd played a single hand of cards with the man who would become his mentor. Aleksander honestly couldn't have said what the older man had seen in him, but he'd be eternally thankful that he'd been pulled back from the brink of disaster before he could ruin his life irrevocably. Aleksander had lost that innocent part of him, but he had been stopped from embracing the darkness completely.

But even now, sitting at the private poker table away from the murmur of conversation and voices placing bets and bemoaning losses, Aleksander felt that same sweep of recklessness pulling at him. Half of his attention was back at the bar where he'd left Henna twenty minutes ago. He would give her any number of apologies she needed, but Kozlov had to be handled now.

He lifted the tips of his two cards and looked at the four in the centre of the table. He'd played Kozlov enough times that they didn't need to feel each other out. Although he often seemed erratic, there was a blunt driving force behind the way the oligarch played his hands. He quickly assessed the Russian's chips—he was down against Aleksander, but that could change in a hand or two. Even then, he decided to let go of this hand and folded.

Kozlov swept up the chips on the table and ordered a vodka. Aleksander checked his watch before the waiter turned to him, distracting Aleksander from the approach of the concierge.

'Gentlemen, we have another player. This is amenable to you?'

Another player was the last thing Aleksander wanted, but when he caught the look in Kozlov's gaze he wondered whether it might present a distraction for the Russian.

'Our deal would not change?' he asked.

'The winner retains the loser's membership,' Kozlov confirmed, his gaze flicking between Aleksander, the concierge and the third player.

'And the new player?' he demanded, unwilling to break eye contact with the Russian.

'Plays only what's on the table,' Kozlov replied, meaning they wouldn't have to offer an equal stake to the agreement regarding the membership. After a quick calculation Aleksander agreed. It wasn't as if this new player would pose any kind of threat, he was confident in his skills.

The thought burned to dust when he saw the player take their seat. He snapped his jaw shut before an expletive could escape and betray him. With a buy-in of five hundred thousand he couldn't fathom how Henna had made it to the private table.

CHAPTER NINE

SHE WAS BLAMING her audacity on the dress. *And* that she only had a short time left in Aleksander's employ. *And* the fact that she hated the idea of him confronting Kozlov alone. He'd explained enough about the man for her to not want Aleksander anywhere near him and she hadn't liked the look of the bodyguards the Russian had placed either side of the entrance to the private tables. It was unexplainable and, probably for Aleksander, inexcusable, but Henna simply knew that she had to be in here.

'Kozlov,' the Russian said by way of introduction.

'Olin,' she replied in kind. The oligarch narrowed his eyes and she could have sworn she felt Aleksander still dangerously, as if he were watching every single move.

'As in Technologies?' Kozlov asked.

Henna inclined her head in acknowledgement, even though Olin Tech was no longer owned by her family.

'I met your father once. He was…ferociously intelligent.'

'He was,' she said, refusing to let her dislike for the Russian colour her reply. Even had Aleksander not told her about the man, he made her skin crawl, though she couldn't have said why. While Kozlov's attention was on her, Aleksander's fury was clear in his eyes, but the moment the Russian returned his gaze to the table it was masked.

'Your Highness,' she addressed him.

'You two know each other?' the heavily accented question split the table.

'Everyone knows the King of Svardia,' she dismissed easily. She was aware that Aleksander thought her in need of protection, but she'd meant what she said back in Öström: *she* knew bullies. She also knew cards. At first when she'd been very young, her father had taught her how to count quickly, with a simple game. He would turn over a series of cards and she would have to add them up. Then he taught her games like whist, and rummy, and vingt-et-un, and when he'd been stuck in the hospital they would play poker. It had been her father's favourite and had quickly become hers.

'The ante is ten thousand,' Aleksander warned, and she inclined her head, realising that he had no idea of her financial situation. It might have seemed strange to some that Henna would continue to work whilst she had a not so small fortune in her bank account. Her father had been a billionaire in his own right and while he'd married Marcella and given her the estate and a monthly income upon his death, Henna had received the larger part of his considerable wealth.

Henna placed her chips on the table, realising that she enjoyed surprising Aleksander. He, who seemed to know all and see all. It made her proud—as if she'd accomplished something that very few people did.

The dealer looked to each of them and started to deal. The first few hands were played in silence, each of the players getting used to the new dynamic. Henna surfed the rise and fall in her adrenaline levels and the mental agility required to mask her responses from two intelligent and very different opponents, while looking for tells that would betray their cards. Occasionally the statuesque blonde would appear at Kozlov's side, pout and require some money before she disappeared, but for the most part the focus was on the hands.

She'd just folded a mediocre hand when Kozlov said, 'I don't think you have played here before, Miss Olin. I'm sure that I would have recognised you.'

She locked her gaze with the Russian's, rather than meet Aleksander's piercing glare.

'It has been some time since I played,' she admitted, while feigning interest in a possible pair.

'Well, I have had the pleasure of playing the King of Svardia quite recently, and I must admit he won a considerable stake from me. I have not forgiven him.'

'If you lost your hand, Mr Kozlov, the fault lies not with him.'

'My intent is simply to warn you that he often has another agenda,' replied the Russian, his gaze boring into hers. 'He's always thinking two steps ahead.'

Henna willed everything in her not to tense, the way her stomach had. She couldn't give the game away. But there was something in his warning, something that she felt she should not so easily disregard.

'Stop pontificating, Kozlov, and play your hand,' Aleksander growled, glaring at Kozlov.

Kozlov threw another ten thousand into the pot without taking his eyes from Henna. 'He has no patience,' he mocked.

That Kozlov was taunting Aleksander was unsurprising to Henna. That he was using her was either spite or he somehow knew that Henna worked for the royal family. The bet was to her and she chose to raise, drawing a glimmer of attention from both men, before the dealer revealed the turn.

'I find honesty is the best way to play,' she said, this time looking straight into Aleksander's stormy glare and refusing to bow to the power of that tempest. She felt the words like a spell casting them both to hell—hot, fiery and delicious until they burned whatever this madness was between them.

The fourth card in the centre of the table got her close to the hand she wanted, but she would have to wait to see how the men chose to bet. Her heart was thumping, adrenaline coursing through her veins, and she wrestled her body under control, determined not to betray her feelings.

'Honesty. How novel,' remarked the Russian, as if amused by such an idea. 'Aleksander? What are your thoughts on honesty?'

'Final bets,' the dealer announced into the brief moment of silence.

Aleksander pushed three hundred thousand onto the table. 'My thoughts are simple, Kozlov. You threatened my sister. My intention is to make you pay for that for a *very* long time.'

Henna's gaze flashed between the two men, surprised that Aleksander would reveal such a thing. Kozlov met the three hundred thousand on the table.

'Well, I suppose that depends on who wins, doesn't it? he sneered, dripping arrogance and venom in equal measure. If either man noticed that she added her bet to the pot she couldn't say, prompting the unflappable dealer to reveal the fifth and final card.

Everything in Henna stopped—her heart, her breath,

her blood. The men were still staring each other down but all she could see was the one card she'd needed.

The King of Hearts.

'Well, Your Majesty? Can you beat this?' the Russian growled as he threw down a straight.

White noise filled Aleksander's ears, his eyes almost seeing stars from the adrenaline coursing through his veins. He wasn't looking at Kozlov's hand, though, but Henna—her eyes bright, round and impossible to read. Her skin glowed against the indigo silk of the dress, the deep vee he wanted to slip his fingers beneath, the flicker of her pulse at her throat that he wanted to taste. In an instant, his thirst for vengeance was quashed and all he wanted was her. To give her what she'd asked for—*everything*.

Aleksander tossed his cards across the table, revealing the flush that beat Kozlov's hand. 'Your membership is mine,' Aleksander said, pushing back from the table, impatient to get Henna away from the oligarch and alone in his suite.

'And your money is *mine*,' said Henna, looking at the Russian as she stood, her eyes blazing with victory.

'Four of a kind,' the dealer observed, yanking both Aleksander and Kozlov's gazes to Henna's hand. 'Miss Olin wins,' he said, pushing the chips towards Henna. Aleksander's heart pumped fiercely in his chest, pride, power, awe, delight filling his body until he felt fit to burst. Henna slid a chip to the dealer and her considerable winnings were taken care of by the concierge, who slipped away discreetly.

'You were both in on it? You cheated!' Kozlov yelled.

The dealer signalled to Security.

'One should not question the integrity of the King, nor the casino in their ability to spot a cheat, Kozlov,' Aleksander warned as suited men appeared, already flanking Kozlov's bodyguards.

'Nor should one underestimate the women of Svardia,' Henna added. 'You will stay away from Marit, from our country *and* from the organisation,' she commanded.

Kozlov's mouth opened and closed wordlessly, until a fierce purple bruised his cheeks. Aleksander skirted the table to meet Henna, his palm pressing gently against the bare skin at the base of her spine, sending an electrical firestorm through his body and, without a single glance back at the Russian, together they left the private tables.

In silence, Aleksander ushered her through the public tables of the casino, passed the bar where he'd first seen her and across the black and white marble floored foyer to the private elevator, beyond the main bank of elevators. The heat of her skin taunted him, burned him as they waited for the gold doors to the penthouse suite's elevator to open. He shifted so that he stood behind her, his chest to her back, giving him access to her neck and the sensitive place he knew would drive her wild, just beneath her ear. It certainly drove him wild.

His heart pounded as it worked to force blood around his body, sluggish with desire and want.

'Before, you asked me for everything. Is that still what you want?' he demanded, his voice dark with a lust he could leash only if she commanded it.

'Yes,' she said, meeting his gaze in the mirrored reflection of the elevator doors.

'Even though it will never be more?' he warned.

'If you give me everything tonight, it will be enough,' she assured him.

And even though he knew it was a lie—because it would never be enough for him—he allowed it because his need for her was now too great to be stopped unless she commanded it.

The elevator doors opened and he ushered her forward, keeping her back to his chest. The rise and fall of her chest drew his gaze, his fingers instinctively grasping her at the hip and pulling her back against his body, against the clear evidence of how much he wanted her. As the doors closed behind them, desire pulled and pushed at him, ebbing between his possessive need for her and his instinct to reprimand her. He had hated that she had been near Kozlov but he rejoiced in her triumph and besting them both at cards.

'When did you learn to play poker?' he whispered as the thumb of his free hand came up to caress her shoulder blade. Her skin pebbled as his breath rolled over it, his lips barely an inch from the curve of her neck. Consciously or not, she had bent her head to give him better access. Her nipples pressed points against the midnight silk of her dress.

Her silence drew his gaze to her reflection in the mirrored walls. 'Before you, I'd imagine,' she teased. This bold Henna, this powerful, sensual creature, was his for the night and there would be no holding back. She deserved what she'd asked for. Not because she had beaten both him and Kozlov, but because of who she was. Because she was more regal and more worthy than anyone he'd ever met. He raised an eyebrow and she bit her tongue, little tremors beginning to filter through her body, but her gaze was steady, the look a challenge, a dare.

'Everything,' she replied to the question he'd been about to voice, as her arm swept up so that her hand could reach his neck, her fingers tangling in the hair above his nape. The gesture pressed her breasts forward and his hands itched to cup them, to feel the delicate weight of them in his palm. He read the truth in her eyes, the fire and heat of her need for him, and could no longer deny her a single thing.

He smoothed the silk straps from her shoulders and the dress dropped from her body like a magician's reveal. Her gasp was drowned out by the ferocious pounding of his heart. He covered her breasts with his arm, pulling her against him, and she shifted against his arousal, her back arching her breasts against his forearm. He was wearing too many clothes, while Henna was in nothing but a midnight-coloured thong and high heels.

Her body was on fire, branded by Aleksander's touch, by the scorching heat of his gaze, and it was glorious. Every single touch, every single lick, kiss, bite, she felt it all over her body. It was shameless and she didn't care. Her head fell back against his shoulder and he devoured her neck with open-mouthed kisses and growls of need that arrowed to her pulsing core.

The door to the elevator opened behind them, the swooshing sound audible until she let out a delicate cry as he swept her off her feet and into his arms. Her arms instinctively looped around his neck as her shoes fell to the floor, her hands interlocking and her gaze fastened to his. The thread of humour that had begun from embarrassment at the sound of her surprise evaporated beneath the heat of his scrutiny.

He stalked through the penthouse suite and came into a room bathed in an array of colours: fuchsia, ice-blue, rich gold, lush green and effervescent purple. He laid her on the bed beneath a kaleidoscope of city lights through the window and he was still the most glorious sight she'd ever seen.

He shucked the tux jacket from his shoulders and tossed it aside. He yanked the bow tie from his throat, snapping one end free and sliding it from round his neck. She backed up on the bed as his eyes stalked over her, devouring her without laying a finger on her.

'You are my weakness—do you know that?' he asked as his hands pulled the shirt from his trousers, and all she could do was watch. His words were fire through the ice in her veins, heating her from deep within. His movements were efficient, impatient even, and there shouldn't have been anything erotic about the sharp, tension-filled actions that undid buttons, but there was.

'You could ask for anything right now and I would give it. Do you understand?' he demanded furiously, as he tore the shirt from his shoulders and threw it across the room. His anger only fuelled her desire. Because she was angry too. Angry that he could never be hers. Angry because she suddenly understood why. 'I have spent years ensuring that no one would ever get close enough to betray me again. But you? You wouldn't have to. You could take everything from me and I'd still want to give you more.'

She saw it then—how vulnerable he thought she made him, how weak. She saw his thinking as if it were being written in the air between them. He had been made to pay the ultimate price in order to rule, and to make it worth it, to make *Kristine's decision* worth it, he had to be the best ruler—no weakness, no vulnerability, no emotion. She wished she could show him that there was another way to be, another way of living that didn't involve him cutting himself off from everyone around him. But he was clinging so desperately to the belief that had enabled him to survive his grief, the belief that cutting off all emotion was the only way forward, that she didn't dare take it from him. Tears gathered in her eyes as she nodded. 'I understand.'

'Henna, I—'

He shook his head, cutting off whatever it was he would have said, kneeled on the bed and pulled her into a kiss that stole as much as it gave, that thrilled as much as it drugged, that soothed even as it broke her into a thousand pieces.

His lips opened hers, worshipping her, breathing life into the far reaches of her desires, of her sense of self, and she couldn't explain how much she wanted him, how much she needed him. She reached for the button of his trousers, pulling back to see his eyes glazed with a heady need. She palmed the length of his erection, the solid heat of his arousal just for her. He caught her wrist, stopping her when she pulled at the zip.

'You said I could have everything tonight,' she whispered, her desire to taste him as he had tasted her so strong it had become a mantra. Admitting it painted her cheeks with a blush that stung, and she feared he might refuse her, until he cursed and let go of her wrist.

She slid the zip down and ran the pad of her thumb delicately over the soft dull pink head of his penis where it crested the band of his briefs. His body shivered beneath her touch and she marvelled at such clear evidence of how she affected him. She swept the briefs down over his erection and hips, freeing him, and he shifted so that she could slip them from his legs.

Turning and lying back against the silk bedding, Aleksander watched her, his gaze revealing the sheer intensity of his anticipation. Sliding between his thighs and lowering, she licked slowly up the length of his hardened erection as it jerked against her tongue, the power, the heat and the dusky taste of him all for her. As she took him into her mouth, his hips bucked lightly and she clasped the base of his shaft, pushing down gently, delighted when his hips bucked again and a curse fell from his lips.

Slick and salty on her tongue, his thighs tense and corded beneath her touch, she felt the power of having Aleksander trembling beneath her, mindless with pleasure *she* had brought him, and surprised by the pleasure she brought herself. Her tongue swept a caress across the head of him and this time Aleksander reached for her with both hands. 'If I have only one night with you, Henna, do not make me wait,' he said, staring down at her, his eyes ablaze.

He pulled her up the length of his body and kissed her with an intensity that seared her soul, that teased already taut nipples and pulsed an over-sensitised core, before he rolled her beneath him.

Braced on one arm, his hand swept down her body, his fingers hooking beneath the thin band at her hip and sliding the thong down her legs and from her feet. He clasped her calf, his fingers travelling up over her knee and thigh to luxuriate in the soft crosshatch of curls. Restless, her legs shifted against his thighs, wanting more and more from his touch, and when he finally parted her to his scrutiny, rather than feel exposed, the raw ferocity in his gaze made her feel powerful, wanted, *needed*. He cupped her, pressing the heel of his palm against her clitoris and teasing her with two thrusting fingers.

He was brutal in his determination to drown her in as much pleasure as he could and, unlike last time, her orgasm built with a decadent inevitability, first sweeping at her feet like the tide, then rising inch by delicious inch through her body, warming her skin with tingles and dusting it with a pink flush. Her thighs quivered as it passed, it tripped over her ribs and flooded her lungs, making her gasp for air, it filled her throat and rolled her eyes and, when it finally hit, her body arched the wave and her soul soared into the midnight sky.

'Aleksander.'

His name was a sob on her lips and he'd seen every single second of her pleasure and it had humbled him. He couldn't stop touching her. His palms stroked her thighs, her hip, waist, anything he could touch, because for this night only she was his. He marvelled at her skin, pebbling beneath his palm, flushing beneath his gaze, dotted with golden freckles and dark moles that were a constellation he wanted to trace each night until he had mapped her, until she was *known*.

The thought was enough to scare him. Her eyes found his, as if she had sensed the change in him. He smiled away her concern as he pressed the feeling down deep within him and bent to kiss her shoulder, her neck, and beneath his lips she arched against him.

'Henna—'

'Please, Aleksander.'

Her whispered words tore at his heart.

'Even with a condom—' he began, hating that the thought of duty and the whisper of grief had entered their bed and become stuck in his throat.

'I am also on the contraceptive pill,' she explained, holding his gaze with compassion, understanding and so much more than he deserved. It was as safe as it could ever be, and it was still the most dangerous thing he could ever do. 'But I would never ask you to do something you didn't want to do,' she said solemnly.

He huffed out a grim laugh. He wanted her more than he had ever wanted anyone. For so many years he had kept so much to himself, bottled up, fizzing beneath the lid, and finally he felt understood by her and it was the absolute worst thing that she could do. Because she would know that it was his carelessness that had cost him and Kristine so much, even if they had only been teenagers.

But he wasn't a teenager now, and neither was Henna. They were as protected as they could be. The slide of her thigh against the outside of his calf started a silky friction that quickly incited a firestorm of need. He couldn't change the way he was, the way he'd made himself twelve years ago, but he could give Henna what she wanted tonight.

He reached for the bedside table drawer and withdrew a condom, her heavy-lidded gaze steadfastly on his as he tore the foil wrapper and drew the latex over the length of his erection. Turning back, he braced himself on forearms that bracketed a face he would hold in his heart until he could no longer remember anything else.

She parted her legs for him and just before he entered

her, just before he pushed into the softest heat he'd ever known, his last thought before need became a crashing urgent thing was that he felt safe. But the smooth, slow slide robbed him of all thought, leaving him capable only of the growl that left his lips, met and matched by Henna's gentle moan, as if they both finally crossed an invisible threshold that they'd fought against for too long.

A part of Aleksander wanted to lie there, luxuriating in the silken muscles that gripped him more intimately than he'd ever felt before, but the raw animal part of him wanted more. He withdrew, pulling a whimpered protest from Henna, urging him back into her deeper and faster, and the sigh of satisfaction that met his every thrust was all he needed. Again and again, he drove them to the brink of her orgasm, and again and again, he pulled her back with gentle hands, telling himself that it was for Henna, that he wanted to bring her what she deserved.

It wasn't a lie, but it also hid a truth. That, buried deep within her, was the closest thing to complete he'd ever felt and he wasn't ready to let it go.

He luxuriated in the feeling, drawing it out until he thought that he might be able to take it with him for the rest of his life. And finally, when their bodies were sweat-soaked and fevered, when the pleas from her lips met the desperation in his chest, when his body trembled with the effort of holding back and could no longer fight, he thrust them into an abyss of such infinite pleasure he wasn't sure he even wanted to find his way back.

CHAPTER TEN

ALEKSANDER WAS STILL sleeping when Henna quietly padded back into the room after her shower. She pulled the soft robe tighter around her shoulders as if to protect herself from the impact of the sight of the King of Svardia sprawled across the bed, the sheet draped across his abdomen *just about* protecting his modesty.

The thought drew a smile to her lips, then a warmth to her cheeks as she remembered that he had absolutely nothing to be modest about. Before they had fallen into an exhausted sleep, Aleksander had stayed true to his word and given her everything she could possibly have desired from a night with him. He had lavished her with pleasure and she had come apart beneath the ruthlessness of his focus. Even now a pulse between her legs flared to life and just for a moment she thought she could feel him again. There had been times when he had moved so deeply within her that the lines had blurred between them, as if they had become one and…and… Her heart stuttered. She had felt as if she had found a part of herself she'd never known she missed. As if she might never be lonely ever again.

The ground suddenly felt unsteady beneath her feet and her heart began to shake in her chest. She loved him.

She *loved* him. Complex and infuriating, but always with a core of unshakable integrity, he was a king who loved his country and a billionaire determined to make the world better in secret, a man who had compassion for her grief and no patience for his own. He was resolute in his convictions, ambitious and determined, but when the reins slipped he could be funny and charming, surprising and desperately sexy. Aleksander wasn't easy, but his care for those he considered his was fierce. And she *knew* he cared for her. But he saw her as a threat to his country and to him—that was unacceptable and nothing she could say or do would change his mind.

Silencing the sob on her lips, she turned to the window but for the first time couldn't see beyond the glass. Instead, she saw their return to Svardia, her office, welcoming Freya back, completing the final arrangements for her engagement party, travelling to London and all the little things that would be her future without Aleksander. From the moment they left this room she would never feel the heat of his body against hers, his lips against her skin, she would never feel warmed by the connection between them that had felt so pure and so private.

Her heart began to pound in her chest, her breath coming a little quicker, a cold sheen gathering at her nape, making her shiver, tremble in some awful contrast to how she had shaken in his arms. She was grieving for a loss she had refused to consider before, but now it demanded recognition, demanded to be heard. She loved him but she could never have him because he had closed himself off from anything that would remotely engage him emotionally. He had imprisoned himself within a maze so convoluted and complex, designed in grief and duty, that her heart just broke for him. Tears pressed at the corners of her eyes and her arms, wrapped tight around her ribs, were the only things holding her from falling apart.

A movement in the reflection of the window caught her eye. Aleksander was behind her, the white sheet wrapped around his waist, his body full of the kind of push-pull tension she'd begun to recognise in him when he wanted something but wouldn't let himself have it— and it broke her heart that it was her.

'Do you regret it?' Aleksander winced as the words raked his throat raw. Everything he wanted to say but couldn't was trying to get out, fighting tooth and nail. It was a question that he'd never had the chance to ask Kristine, but he wouldn't shy away from the truth this time. Henna deserved more than his cowardice. Everything in him braced for the words that would send him to a hell of his own making. His hands were fisted, jaw clenched, thighs rock hard, holding him in place. He didn't think he'd be able to bear it if—

'No, Aleksander,' she said, turning. The sincerity written across her face wasn't even enough to break the hold that fear had on him. Her hand came up to the side of his face and he turned into her palm, seeking a solace he didn't deserve. Warmth spread from her skin to his body, pushing back the cold darkness that had threatened to overwhelm him.

'No,' she said again, as if knowing he needed to hear it. Then she pressed her lips to his, once, twice, and a third time. Gentle brushes, slowly teasing his mouth open beneath her caress, and when he gave in it felt like his victory, not hers. Drawn into the sensual dance as if hypnotised by her touch, he pulled at the thin tie holding the robe together and slipped his hands beneath the silk to find the glory of her skin.

His hand swept around her waist and pulled her fiercely against his body and not once did she break the kiss or protest, even though they both knew she should. He lifted her up, bracing her with one arm as her legs wrapped around his hips, and he drew the silk away from her body and threw the sheet from his waist, bringing them skin to skin in a way that had them both trembling in seconds.

She fitted against him as if she'd been made to be there and everything in him roared against the restraint that pulled him back from simply plunging deep within her, seduced by the need to slide skin to skin with no barrier between them. Need was a war cry in his mind, but one he would never give in to.

He took them to the bed, aware of just how little it had taken for them to go from caress to carnal and the look in her lust-filled gaze appeared dazed by the same thought. 'I can—'

'Finish what you started, Your Majesty,' she interrupted, the challenge, the tease, the desire so clear beneath the command she had uttered, he delighted in it and determined to do just as she had asked.

'Henna?'

She turned to see Lisbeth coming down the corridor towards her. She smiled at the young woman she had worked with for three years, who would—happily—be taking over as Freya's lady-in-waiting after Henna left. And then her smile turned into a frown when she saw the first look of concern mar Lisbeth's features since accepting her promotion.

'Is everything okay?' Immediately her thoughts flew to Freya, then Marit, and finally her heart stopped altogether when she thought of something happening to—

'Yes, yes.' She nodded, a little frantically. Henna had never seen her so unsettled, and it wouldn't bode well for her future if she didn't get that under control. 'I just... Are you going to your office?'

'Yes, I left some paperwork there.'

'Right, only...'

Henna heard her office door open behind her and turned to find Freya, leaning half out of it. 'Ah, there you are. Can you...?' She beckoned Henna forward.

Had Freya been looking for her? As promised, when she and Kjell had returned from their break, the two friends had spent an entire day together, no work, just catching up. It had been wonderful and Freya's newfound happiness was glorious to see.

But what about you? You deserve your happiness.

Her father's voice had whispered into her mind as she'd laughed and smiled with her closest friend. Twice Freya had asked if she were okay. Both times, she'd been thinking of Aleksander and both times she'd lied and said she was fine.

She had thought it would stop when they returned to Svardia—the strange sense that she knew where he was. It was a kind of foresight that warned her when he was near, raising the hair on her arms and neck, her pulse suddenly beginning to spin out of rhythm. Unable to marshal the reaction she had to him, it was as if he owned her, body and soul. The battle between fire and ice raging across her body made a part of her long for the end of her notice period but the other cling on desperately, hoping against all odds that he might change his mind.

And then she realised how foolish that was. As if he, King of Svardia, would pick *her*. That voice sounded horribly like Viveca's, but she couldn't shake it off. Henna had told him the truth in Macau. She didn't regret spending that one night with him. If that was all she would ever have, she would keep it with her for the rest of her life. But she wished she'd known beforehand just how much it would *hurt*.

'Come on.' Freya hurried just as Henna's feet grew heavier. Despite Freya's and Lisbeth's now palpable excitement, Henna was certain that Aleksander was in her office. Determining to relax, Henna let the two pull her into her office, where—

'Surprise!' a chorus of voices shouted out.

Her little office was packed full of people—so many that they were overflowing into the adjacent office through the open connected door. A banner had been hung across her desk and paper streamers thrown about, little plates of food were being shared and when a glass was thrust into her hand by Freya and she found herself pushed back into a chair in the centre of the room she couldn't help but allow a wobbly smile to pull at her lips.

'You thought we'd just let you go without throwing you a goodbye party?' Freya teased.

'Well, I thought that most of you would be preparing for *someone else's* party,' she teased. Most of the staff members groaned and then laughed when Freya said, 'Hey, I haven't been that bad!'

This was what Henna loved about working at the Palace. It wasn't the prestige. It wasn't the access to some of the world's most influential people. It was the family that they had created. The work was long hours, intense and incredibly locked down due to the sensitive information they had access to. But the core staff, they were more than friends, and Henna realised for the first time that it wasn't just Freya and Marit and their brother she would be leaving. It was Anita Bergqvist, who had been one of the first people to congratulate her, it was Jean and Ella from Admin, it was Mikael, Anders and Birgit from Security, it was all the people who had come together today, happy for her, and sad to see her go.

'No, *you* haven't been that bad,' someone groused, clearly thinking of how difficult Aleksander had been recently.

'I heard that,' said a voice from the back of the room.

While good-humoured apologies were given, the soft centre of Henna's core began to shake a little and goosebumps raised on her skin. Not that anyone would have noticed—she had become expert at hiding her reaction to Aleksander.

'Speech! Speech!'

She let out a purposely audible groan. 'No, no,' she said, shaking her head, but the cries were insistent. She looked around at the sea of faces, all bright-eyed and so thrilled for her. She felt the heat of Aleksander's focus on her back, torn between being pleased that he'd come and sad at the distance between them.

'Not many people know what we do,' she began, 'which is, admittedly, the *point* of what we do,' she stressed to their laughter, 'but it *is* important. Important that the people of Svardia have faith in our…our family.' She looked to Freya, her heart warm with love for a woman more sister than friend. 'Faith in our Princesses and our King,' she said, angling her head to the side, acknowledging him but unable to meet the gaze she felt burning into her skin. 'Often this requires sacrifice, and almost always that sacrifice is unseen, and unknown. But *we* know. *We* see. We understand and we…thank you for it,' she said, her words shivering with emotion.

Although tears glistened in Freya's eyes and many of her colleagues', she knew that Aleksander had heard her words, her message to him. She wanted him, *needed* him, to know that, no matter how much it hurt, she understood. Understood the sacrifice that had been made for him in the past and the one he was making now, so that Svardia would have the incredible King that he would be.

'We're supposed to be thanking you!' cried Freya, pulling her into a fierce hug that Henna honestly needed in that moment. Especially when she felt the King slip from the room in the middle of the fuss. And even though she shouldn't, even though she knew it was wrong, she excused herself for a moment and hurried into the corridor.

The sound of the door opening stopped Aleksander mid-stride. He pulled up short, his pulse pounding in his chest. He was too close to a line he wanted to burn. He didn't want to let her go.

Even though he shouldn't, he couldn't not turn. He *had* to see her. Because he knew that once she left, that would be it. There would be no more teasing, no more understanding. There would be no more gentle smiles easing into pleasure-filled sighs. There would be no more shivers to soothe beneath the palm of his hand. He would return to a world where he kept secrets and trust behind locked doors. So right now, here, he would take in as much as he could of her. Slowly, his body moving from his heart not his head, he turned, and immediately wished he hadn't.

She was so utterly beautiful and she had no earthly idea of it. Her eyes gleamed with a knowing sorrow, but she wasn't cowed by it. It had made her strong, stronger than he ever would be, he thought as, step by step, they closed the distance between them until he felt the heat of her through their clothes and there was but an inch between them.

There were so many things he wanted to say, but nothing came to his lips. Instead, his eyes ravished her features, committing them to a memory he was already pushing deep within him. He teetered on the brink, fighting himself and the roaring in his ears that demanded he kiss her, pull her to him and never let go. But he couldn't. He just couldn't risk it. He would burn it all down for her if she asked him to, and what would that make of him as a man? As a king? What would that make of the sacrifice Kristine had made so that he could be the King Svardia needed? It would make it worthless and he could *never* allow that.

He felt her gaze across his face, as if she too was taking this moment, memorising it, locking it away for some unimaginable future apart. His heart ached even as it was soothed by her presence and in that silent shared moment he passed through every possible feeling. He shared it with her in the silence as it couldn't be shared out loud, he shared and took until there was nothing left. Because he was her King and she was the only woman he could never marry, for the simple reason that she was too much of a threat to him.

Something shattered in him then. He felt it, an actual loss deep within him. Henna took the smallest step

back, as if she'd realised it too. He'd been about to follow, to reach out for her like the drowning man he was,
when the door to her office opened and Freya emerged
into the corridor.

Aleksander pulled back but it was too late. He knew
his sister had seen too much, even without taking his
eyes from the woman in front of him.

'Henna, is everything okay?'

It said something that his sister's first thought was
for Henna.

This was it, he knew. The last time that he would see
her as she was. The last time he would let himself near
her without the barriers his heart was already looking
to hide behind. He drank in one last sight of her, Henna
doing the same. The curve of her cheek and the little
dark mole in the hollow beneath her earlobe, the gold
and green shards in her eyes, the fringe he wanted to
push back from her forehead, the lips he had not nearly
kissed enough... His hand fisted at his side and, without
another word, he turned on his heel and left.

Henna watched him go, her heart breaking into a
thousand pieces as Freya came to stand beside her, looking between her brother's retreating form and Henna, a
worried look in her eyes.

'Henna—'

Whatever Freya had been about to say was stopped
by the bright smile Henna pasted on her lips. She took
her friend's hands in her own, pulling them to her chest,
and willed Freya not to ask. Because she would want to
seek solace with her friend, to tell her everything, all
the things that she could never take back, but she would
never betray Aleksander like that. So if Freya asked she
would have to lie, and Henna really didn't want to lie.

As if understanding, Freya freed her hand and rubbed a gentle circle against her back, the soothing gesture one she remembered from years before her father passed, and it made her want to cry all over again.

'Are you ready for the engagement party tomorrow night?' Freya asked.

Henna let out a teary laugh. 'It's *your* party, Freya.'

'Yes,' she replied, unable to hide the love and joy that shone from her like a lamp in the darkness. It hurt Henna to want to shy from it, aching that she couldn't feel that same sense of light, but she wouldn't turn from her friend's happiness. She deserved it so, so much.

'Freya, do you think you'd mind if I left a little earlier than planned?'

'From the party?'

Henna shook her head. If nothing else, what she'd just shared with Aleksander was a goodbye and she couldn't bear to work out the next two weeks of her notice.

'You go whenever you need to, Henna, but...' Freya looked at her as if wanting to say something but deciding against it.

'Freya?'

Losing the fight against whatever held her back, Freya said, 'Are you sure you want to do this? *Really* sure? There are so many things you could do.'

Surprised by what Freya had *not* said, it took her a moment to orientate back to her question. 'It's such an amazing opportunity. And I like helping people.' The words had come automatically, from a place of ease rather than of thought. And the look Freya gave her said as much.

'But you don't need to hide behind someone else to help people the way you could. You are a woman of considerable means,' Freya reminded her gently. 'Means that you could make work the way you want them to. Just think about it?'

Freya smiled, pulling her back across the threshold of her office and into the party, while Henna worked to ignore the afterimage her words had left in her mind.

The following evening Henna unzipped the white covering over the dress she'd chosen for Freya's engagement ball, the strange sense of déjà vu unsettling her. Usually she would have worn a dress that was unobtrusive, that would have disappeared into the background, leaving her faceless and unremarkable to the other guests. But, as of one hour ago, she was no longer employed by the Svardian royal family and was now welcome as a guest to her best friend's engagement party. The knowledge of that had been the impetus behind her unusual purchase.

For many years Henna had ignored the account that she had accessed when she'd withdrawn the money needed to gain entry to the private tables at the casino in Macau. At first, she had seen it as her father's money and she hadn't wanted it or anything to do with it. It had been a poor replacement for the man who had loved her with such strength that she still felt it now. And as the years had gone by it had been pushed to the back of her mind, mainly because she simply hadn't needed it. Freya had offered her the role as lady-in-waiting as soon as she had finished university, her housing was included with the position, her expenditure was minimal.

But Freya was right. Henna *was* a woman of considerable means. And while she hadn't quite worked out what that meant to her yet, she had known that this evening she had wanted, *needed*, to look stunning. It was a vanity, but it was also an armour. Aleksander would be presenting Tuva Paulin at the ball and while Henna knew she would be forgiven for not going, she also knew that she needed to see it. Needed to face this so that she could finally draw a line in the sand between herself and Aleksander, the present and the future. It would hurt, yes, but hopefully it would also cauterise her wounded heart so that she might go on.

She slipped the white garment bag from the hanger to reveal the midnight-blue dress she'd been unable to resist buying. Somewhere in there was the dress she had worn to Macau, the same midnight-blue silk at the very core of the dress, but embellished with a million sequins and sparkles. A thousand layers of embroidered tulle cascaded from the waist into a skirt fit for a princess, falling into a slight train that would fan out on the floor behind her.

Henna reached up to feel the exquisite beading and stitching that reminded her of the sky from the cabin's window in Öström. The texture beneath her palm, sharp and smooth, grounded her. She felt as if this dress told her story, her journey to here, where even though it would hurt and quite possibly damage her heart irrevocably, she would still have the power to stand and bear it. This dress made her feel strong and feminine and courageous—all things that had been in her but hidden…until now.

On the other side of the palace, Aleksander looked out of the window, unseeing of the grounds wrapped in the night's darkness. There was a strange sense of numbness to the evening. Freya's joy had been inescapable since her return from her time away with Kjell, and she had extracted promises from him to visit the cabin in Sweden that she had fallen so in love with. And Aleksandar was glad. Glad that she had Kjell, glad that Marit had Lykos—the latter couple arriving soon.

Aleksander had orchestrated situations that had thrust both of his sisters into the arms of men who loved and valued them beyond compare, which *some* might call manipulation, but that Freya and Marit knew love, thrived in that love, was the one bright light in his life so he was at peace with his actions. Time and time again it had been proved to Aleksander that people could not be trusted to make the right decisions, for themselves or others. He engineered situations where he could be sure of an outcome that would benefit everyone. But as he thought of the last situation he had engineered, he wondered if perhaps he had been wrong to do it. His conscience twisted in warning, but it was too late to change it.

The mantel clock, a present from an old British prime minister, chimed its way through seven tolls and the red-haired woman on the sofa behind him shifted.

'Are you sure this is what you want?' Tuva asked.

It didn't matter what he wanted. It was what was needed.

'Absolutely.'

CHAPTER ELEVEN

IF THE VÅRBOLL had been exquisite, Freya and Kjell's engagement party was nothing short of magnificent. Having done much of the preparation for it before Freya had left with Kjell, Henna got goosebumps looking at the Rilderdal Palace ballroom. Huge wide strips of white tulle were draped from the ceiling below strings of fairy lights, creating an illuminated vee between each of the chandeliers. Freya had requested boughs of Norwegian spruce and trails of ivy throughout, bringing the outside in and achieving a magical quality to the decorations. Even the staff passing round canapés and drinks had been caught staring at the beauty of it.

Henna smiled. Freya and Kjell deserved nothing less. Breaking a little with tradition, they had been the first in the room, there to welcome every single guest personally. It was what made Freya such a well-loved princess, the personal touch she afforded to everyone equally. Marit and Lykos appeared at the back of the ballroom, clearly not wanting to interrupt the line waiting to wish the happy couple their best. Something in Henna's chest eased at the realisation that this was the first time all the siblings would be together since Aleksander's coronation. Whether his sisters knew or not, he needed it, needed them by his side. Because while he might feel threatened by emotion, he was completely fuelled by it, or it never would have mattered to him who his sisters had married.

Marit approached with Lykos, her eyes staring holes into the back of her sister's head until Freya turned and gave her an affectionate wave before returning to her duty. Only a year ago, Henna knew Marit would have seen it as a dismissal, not being secure enough in herself or the love of her family, but Lykos had come along and stolen her on her wedding day—*twice*—and changed that for her.

Marit pulled Henna into a fierce hug and whispered, 'You can't go. I won't let you.'

Tears threatened to spill at the strong bond of love she felt between them. 'Oh, Marit.'

'What are we going to do without you?' she demanded, pulling back.

'You don't need me any more,' Henna replied, with a smile at the Greek billionaire beside Marit.

'It is nice to finally meet the famous Henna I've heard so much about,' he said, inclining his head over her hand as if to kiss it.

Charmed instantly by the old-fashioned gesture, she replied, 'Likewise.'

As Marit regaled her with stories of Paris and Milan and Athens, Henna realised that the fear she'd had of being only a tool, someone to rely on, to achieve things for Freya and Henna was gone. The easy conversation and the shared humour erased that fear and healed something deep within her, not completely but enough to see things a little more clearly than she had done in the past. She was just about to check on the catering when—

'Who is that?' Marit demanded, looking up to the first-floor balcony.

There was only one possible answer.

'Your brother's guest is Tuva Paulin,' she replied, bracing herself as she turned to face Aleksander and his future fiancée.

Aleksander stood at the top of the stairs, able to see that his sister only had two more couples to greet before he could make his entrance. Tuva's hand was tucked into the crook of his arm, on the side opposite his sword. Everything about this evening had to be perfect. It would set the tone for Freya and Kjell's future—ensuring that, no matter what, she would have the support of the royal family, and hopefully the country, behind her when facing the announcement that she was unable to have children naturally.

Tuva cleared her throat quietly beside him and he realised that the music had transitioned to announce his arrival. He just stopped himself from clenching the fist by his side, gave Tuva a smile and then led them down the grand staircase. Freya and Kjell stood at the bottom on one side and Marit and Lykos on the other and for a second he allowed himself to feel the simple joy of having both of his sisters here with him.

Family. He wanted them near, not because it would look good for the country, or bolster his image, as his parents would have suggested. But because he loved them. For the first time he wondered what it would have been like if he'd been able to talk to them about what happened in the past. Whether he would have been this emotionally closed off. Whether he might have healed enough to...

He looked up just at that moment and the sight of Henna stopped his thoughts and his heart. In the second it took to take her in, a kaleidoscope of images from their time away pressed against the back of his eyes. The midnight-blue silk of her dress in Macau, the stars in the sky over Öström, the way her blue skirt parted either side of her legs before he tasted her, how the straps of blue silk had slipped from her shoulders in the elevator, how she had stood there, bearing the weight of his fevered gaze, strong and powerful, daring him to be even remotely worthy of her—the way she was looking at him now.

Gentle pressure pulled at his arm and everything came back in a rush, the musical accompaniment, the sounds of the guests, the trace of concern in Freya's knowing gaze, the painfully perfect smile of the woman beside him. The woman who would be beside him in everything to come. He wasn't fool enough to compare her to Henna. Tuva would lose every time, in every way but one.

Tuva's gaze was heavy on him as he introduced her to his sisters and their partners. Both Kjell and Lykos were still a little wary of him—as they should be—but if Freya and Marit noticed, they didn't let on. Lykos whispered something to Marit and with a long, surprisingly serious glance from his sister, Marit enticed Tuva and Freya away, leaving the three men alone.

A server appeared with a tray of drinks and all three men chose whisky over champagne.

'Something on your mind, Livas?' Aleksander said before a tipped salute of his glass to his future brothers and taking a mouthful of peat, vanilla and burn.

Kjell, ever the military strategist, seemed content to have one eye on them and the other on his fiancée.

'Kozlov.' The word dropped like a bullet from the Greek billionaire's mouth.

Aleksander glared at him but, even without looking at the Viscount of Fjalir beside him, it was eminently clear he had no wish to discuss the matter in public.

The silver-eyed Greek shrugged. 'Kjell is now family. Marit is…teaching me the importance of it and I am embracing it.'

Aleksander looked at Kjell, who held his gaze. 'Russian oligarch, billionaire several times over, questionable dealings in the Ukraine, morally abominable and violent towards women. Nasty piece of work,' Kjell concluded his accurate précis on the man.

Lykos leaned his head towards the man as if to say, *see?*

'He will soon experience the loss of several major contracts that have, until now, afforded him a level of financial security,' said Aleksander, giving in to the bonds that would tie him to even more people.

'And with blood in the water, the sharks will start to circle. Good,' Lykos said with a finality that appeased both men's need for vengeance.

'What you choose to do and who you choose to do it with in your free time is all on you,' Kjell stated, leaning a little close to Aleksander's secrets for his liking. But the man had been a Lieutenant Colonel in the Svardian army, so Aleksander trusted him more than most.

'So, you chose Tuva then?' Lykos observed.

'Not who I was expecting,' Kjell commented. 'You?' he asked the Greek.

It was on the tip of his tongue to demand to know what they were talking about, when he found both of their gazes locked onto where Henna was talking to a clearly besotted French Ambassador.

'No. Shame.'

'Agreed.'

With the distinct impression that they were ganging up on him, Aleksander stalked off, ignoring the sound of gentle laughter behind him, and went to find Tuva.

Henna extracted herself from the French Ambassador, whose crush on her was nothing but sweet harmlessness. She was just about to find Freya when the music quietened in preparation for the first dance. This was it. This was the line in the sand that Henna needed. This was the inescapable truth that he would never be hers.

The three siblings took up positions around the dance area of the ballroom. It looked like an image from a period drama, the stunning perfection of the clothes—Kjell in military dress uniform, while Lykos Livas shone just as gloriously in his tux. And the women—Henna bit her lip until she tasted a faint metallic thread, releasing it as the sharp sting struck. Tuva was beautiful and poised, perfection in a cream gown that matched Aleksander's ceremonial uniform. They stood in a tableau, waiting for the music to begin, and for a moment she wondered if perhaps this was a dream. That this was where she would wake, but no. The music started and the couples spun around the floor in perfect synchronicity.

And even though she knew that she was strong, knew that she would survive this, she was once again on the outside looking in and it hurt like a thousand cuts to her soul. Aleksander never once made eye contact, but she felt his focus like a touch, slipping down the nape of her neck, her spine, spanning her shoulder blades and holding her in place. Holding her to the press of a body that would never be there. Would never hold her again. Would never pleasure her or protect her.

Her phone vibrated in her clutch and, as if ready for any possible excuse to break the hold he had on her, she reached in to check her screen. It was a reply to her request to begin her new role as soon as possible. Quickly putting in her code, she read the email, knowing that even if her request had been denied she'd be leaving first thing in the morning. Because, no matter what, she wasn't a masochist. She'd needed to see this, to feel it as real and know it as truth, but...

Her thoughts trailed off as she reread the email.

No.

She read it again, fury painting her cheeks with a flush.

Your email couldn't have been more fortuitous—if you can start at the beginning of next week it would be greatly welcome. We're so pleased that HRH recommended you and he was right, you really are a godsend!

Her knuckles turned white around the phone. She had, until now, believed that she had been headhunted because of her reputation, because of her skill. She'd thought it had been fortuitous. A sign that she should reach for more while connecting to her mother, even. But all this time it had been Aleksander. He'd kept that from her. Lied to her. Manipulated her into thinking that leaving was her choice, when he'd arranged the entire charade.

She looked up, the full horror of it dawning on her. He'd taken the first opportunity he could to remove her from the Palace. Once his sisters were settled and they no longer needed her, she was nothing to him but a distraction. Expendable and removable. In the way. Just like she had always been.

For the first time that night, his eyes found hers, the bitter chocolate a harsh taste to swallow. Turning from the room, blind to the guests, she picked up her skirts and ran, tears clouding her vision and pain tearing her heart apart.

Aleksander felt a knife pierce his chest when he saw the expression on Henna's face. He knew it wasn't because he was dancing with Tuva, he knew it was something else, something more. She'd been holding her phone and… He didn't even realise he'd left Tuva and was halfway across the ballroom floor, following hot on Henna's heels before it was too late. He heard the gasps and whispers around him as he pursued her out of the door and down a corridor.

His pulse pounded wildly in his veins, fear and hurt coagulating, making his blood thick and hard to push around his body. Everything in him told him it was fruitless. Everything in him told him to let her go, but he couldn't. For all his determination to keep her at arm's length, to push her away even, now, when it came down to it, he couldn't let her go.

Leaving the sounds of the ballroom behind him, he entered the staff wing of the Palace, following the clip of Henna's heels ahead of him. He spun blindly round another corner in the maze of corridors, following the way she led until they were deep in the heart of the Palace. He quickened his pace, no longer able to hold himself back, but she had too. Was she running from him?

The thought spurred him on, until he rounded a corner and came to a sudden stop, seeing her standing there, braced to confront him, fury and accusation shining in her eyes. He wavered, needing to close the distance between them.

'Henna—'

'How could you? How could you do that to me?'

He shook his head. 'Henna, you knew that—'

'I'm not talking about Tuva!' she yelled.

Force of habit had him quickly scanning the corridor for staff or guests, not even half as relieved as he should be to find it empty. They couldn't stay out here. He shoved at a door to the side, opening into an empty office. Satisfied, he grasped her hand and guided her away from ruination for them both. He kicked the door closed behind them and stared at Henna, her chest heaving with her ragged breaths, fury riding hard in her eyes.

'What happened?' he demanded.

'Do you not know already, Your Highness?'

He clenched his jaw, the lashing bitterness in her tone painful because he was sure he had put it there.

'After all, you pride yourself on ensuring that you know every move a person will make before they make it, do you not?'

Realisation crept into his thoughts. She knew. She knew he had engineered the job offer.

As if she saw the train of his thoughts, she nodded. 'How could you do that? Of all the things that you have planned and manipulated, this was particularly cruel.'

He flinched, unable to deny her accusation.

'You move people around a chessboard so that they cannot hurt you, but do you ever think how much hurt you cause?' Henna demanded.

'All the time,' he growled, the confession wrenched from the deepest part of him. 'It is all I *ever* think about.'

She shook her head, clearly disbelieving his words, her eyes full of a pain that swarmed around her like a tornado. 'Was it *all* a lie?'

'I have *never* lied to you.'

'You told me that I would always have a home here!' she cried, her hurt stabbing daggers into his soul. 'That was a lie!'

'Henna—'

'You let me believe that I would be safe here and the entire time, the *entire* time, you were planning for me to take a job in another country!'

'Henna, you earned that role, you *deserve* that role.' He was desperate for her to know that.

'But the price of it is here! The cost of it is to know that you didn't want me here!' she threw at him.

Rage tore through him. Anger, frustration and helplessness. 'You're right, Henna, I didn't want you here. I *don't* want you here.' She reared back as if he had physically struck her. 'How on earth am I supposed to find a fiancée when you are less than five corridors away from me? How am I supposed to be the king that I need to be when you are making me feel everything that I have spent years trying to forget? Tell me, Henna, because if you can make it happen then stay, by all means.'

He had shocked her into silence and he took full advantage. 'Even before Öström, even before we kissed, even before Freya was engaged, I knew that you were more of a threat to me than anyone I had ever known. Even then I knew that you—alone in an entire palace of people—would see the truth. That my need to control everything is beyond trust, beyond betrayal—' His breath shuddered in his lungs. 'Because if I let myself feel for you, then how will I not be destroyed by the feelings I have for…for…my child?' he demanded. 'The decision that was made for me, *without my choice*, was done so that I could rule this country. That can and will only ever be my one purpose now.'

She stared at him, as if sifting through his words, seeing to his soul, and finding him wanting. 'So you refuse to acknowledge your grief and loss and guilt and love and all the things that make us human, because you think it makes you a better king?' she asked incredulously.

'If that is what I need to do, then I shall do it.'

'That is a poor way of honouring the loss of your child.' Her words slapped him so viciously he took a step back, an irrevocable wound cutting into his heart. 'You were a lost teenager then, isolated from the very people who should have helped you and vulnerable to your grief. So you hid it deep down, untouched and unacknowledged. I understand that. You weren't strong enough then, but you are now. And you know better now.'

'Get out,' he whispered, with no less power in his words than the force of a tsunami.

And still she stood against him, immovable, her power that strong.

'I am your *King*!' he yelled.

'And if you say that enough times, will you finally believe that it is an excuse for your manipulations? For taking the same choice away from others that you were denied yourself?' she demanded, seeing straight to the heart of him.

'Don't,' he warned.

'Don't what? Challenge you? Question you? Are you such an autocrat that you would rule by your will alone?'

He took a step back as she took one forward.

'It is time for you to honour your pain and hurt and guilt. Use the support you have around you now, overcome it and be better for it. You deserve it, and so do they.'

He shook his head as if trying to ward off her words.

'Can't you see? If you did, then you would know that you are loved, that…that *I* love you,' she said, her words penetrating the walls he was hastily building around his heart.

Aleksander shook his head and Henna tried to hold her heart together even as it slipped through her fingers like sand. The pain was incalculable, tearing and ripping at her even as she stood before him.

'You don't,' he replied.

She let out a helpless laugh. 'It's not something you have the power to control this time, Aleksander.'

A look of determined sincerity passed over his features. 'I know,' he said, as if finally admitting a limit to his authority. 'But I was telling the truth. You don't love me. You love the boy who found you in the maze, who introduced you to his sister. That boy, he was funny and charming and easygoing, but I am not that boy any more. What happened to me changed me on a fundamental level.'

If he had been angry, if he had hurled accusations or manipulated her words, she would have something to fight against. But this? This was a surrender she didn't know what to do with, and no matter how much she tried she couldn't stop the pain pouring from her heart like life blood.

'You have built a dream around me and it's time for

you to wake up,' he said, his words and tone gentle but so unbelievably destructive.

Tears filled her vision and he reached out for her, but she pulled away before he could make contact. She wanted to deny it, she wanted to refuse what he was saying was true, but could she? Yes, she had looked and looked for the boy who had given her so much, but had she been so desperate that she had made it all up? Imagined the man she had fallen in love with? Had she done it again and built herself a future around a man she thought would never hurt her?

Her chest ached and her head hurt and she looked deep into her heart and knew the truth. 'I told you that I loved you because you deserved to know. But I deserve *more*,' she said, and turned from the room and the man she loved, but not before she saw the look of devastation in his eyes.

Henna slipped through the quiet Palace, most of her belongings already packed and sent ahead to her hotel. She retrieved her bag and coat from her now empty suite and a taxi was waiting for her at the staff entrance. She didn't turn, didn't pause, didn't slow as she made her way towards the car waiting on the gravel driveway. And as the clock chimed midnight from within the Palace, Henna didn't even look back. The past was gone and only the future lay before her, even if it broke her heart.

CHAPTER TWELVE

ALEKSANDER STARED AT the door Henna had left through for what felt like hours, his mind spending every second of that time replaying what she had said, what he had said…why it had happened and how. Two steps ahead—he had always been two steps ahead, but this time he was very much behind.

Even though he knew that there could never have been another outcome, his mind processed an infinite number of scenarios that might have ended differently. If he hadn't said… If she'd just… Each one made his head and heart hurt more and more.

On numb legs he forced himself from the room and found his way back to his quarters. He slammed the door shut behind him and was halfway across the living room when he realised that Freya was standing beside the fireplace and Marit sat at the end of the sofa, both staring at him with accusation in their eyes.

He sighed and bit out a curse. 'What do you want?' he demanded.

'We want—'

'To know if you are okay,' Marit said, her worried words cutting off Freya's angry outburst. He was sure that Freya had plenty to say, and not just because he'd ruined her engagement party.

'Oh, God,' he said, hands bracketing his temples, just realising what a monumental mess he'd made of things. 'How bad is it?' he asked, perching on the arm of a sixteenth century chaise longue.

'Tuva told everyone it was food poisoning, so there's that,' Freya revealed.

'Food poisoning?' He barked out a laugh—the last thing he thought he'd be doing that evening.

'There may have been a little glee on her part in sharing such a…frank explanation for your disappearance,' Freya replied, her own delight very close to the surface. 'And I suppose it's less embarrassing than being run out on by the King of Svardia.'

Guilt dug into his stomach and he groaned, bracketing his temples with his fingers. He felt his sister's hand on his shoulder.

'Tuva will be fine,' Freya said, trying to reassure him. 'When we left, she seemed to be having *quite* the conversation with the Austrian Ambassador.'

Nevertheless, Aleksander promised himself he'd find a way to make it up to her.

'Yes, but never mind all that,' Marit said. 'Are you okay?'

It was on the tip of his tongue to dismiss his sisters' concern, but Henna's words came back to haunt him.

'You know better now.'

'Use the support you have around you now…'

Henna was right, he realised with a shocking twist of the knife deep in his heart.

He shook his head slowly. 'No, I don't think I am,' he replied to Marit's question. And finally, after twelve years, he slowly told them the story of what had happened to him, to Kristine, about the pregnancy and how it had affected the years that followed. How he had shut everyone out because it was easier to close off all emotion than to open up to even the smallest amount of hurt. How he'd felt it was the only way for him to rule. How it had led to this—his search for someone to marry who didn't engage him emotionally—and how he'd arranged for Henna to be offered a position elsewhere.

'She is my friend, Sander.' Her words were an accusation but her use of his childhood nickname warmed a part of him he'd thought frozen solid a long time ago. 'You should not have done that.'

Everything in him wanted to refute her accusation. He rubbed his chest. He'd been so focused on not letting anyone close enough to inflict the kind of hurt that he had experienced, the hurt he had inflicted on Kristine, that he hadn't realised how Henna had already slipped into his palace and his heart and become irrevocably lodged there. It was she who had made him feel safe, she who had enticed his trust, she who had been more than his equal, who inspired him to be and do better. And he had betrayed her in the most painful and deepest way.

He cursed.

'I think he's getting it.'

'Shame it's a little late,' groused Freya.

'Oh, give him a moment,' Marit scolded. 'He's learning.'

Ignoring their chatter, Aleksander thought through his options. Henna had been right, of course, about everything—but, most importantly, about finally facing his feelings about the past.

'I need...' He looked up to find his sisters waiting expectantly.

'Whatever it is, we're here and we'll help,' Freya said, reaching for him and pulling him into a hug.

'Oh, you guys!' Marit cried, before trying to stretch her arms around them both, and they descended into teary-eyed giggles. Well, the girls did. Aleksander would never admit to such a thing.

Two days later, Aleksander watched from the back of his car as the man said goodbye to his children, got in his car and left for work. He waited another five minutes to make sure the man didn't return and if Aleksander needed that time to steel himself, then that was what he needed. He was done denying the things he felt and although he knew that this might be one of the hardest things he'd ever do, he knew it was one of the most important. Not just in his hope to get Henna back, but for himself too.

He exited the car and approached the modest two-storey home. His close protection officers were present but discreet, knowing how important it was that this remained away from the public eye. Not for him but for the woman in the house and her family. His footsteps sounded loud on the paving stones that led up to the front door in the quiet of the early morning and, before he could think again, he knocked on the door.

Kristine opened it and for a moment there was shock in her gaze and then an understanding so acute and so empathetic he nearly buckled under the weight of it and when she smiled he felt tears stinging the backs of his eyes.

'Can you come in?' she asked, her gaze looking for the protection officers she knew would be there.

'If that is okay?'

'Aleks, come in,' she said, as if telling him off and welcoming him at the same time. She stood back from the door and he entered her home. She ushered him into a sitting room filled with toys and sofas and pictures and DVDs and books and all the things that seemed so normal he ached.

A little blond boy came running into the room, took one wide-eyed look at him and made to run back out again, before being scooped up by his mother.

'Dani, this is an old friend of Mummy's. Say hello,' she said.

'Hello,' came the shy response, and it took a second try for Aleksander to greet Kristine's son, but he did.

She sent him off to play with his older siblings, before seeming awkward for the first time. 'Can I get you tea, or coffee?'

'No, thank you,' he said, shaking his head. 'How are you?'

She smiled and gestured for him to take a seat on the sofa, which he did when she took the armchair. 'Good,' she said, nodding. 'I'm good. How are *you*?'

'Is it that obvious?' he asked ruefully.

'Only because you're here.'

He nodded. 'I have some things I want to say, if that's okay?'

'Of course it is, Aleks.'

He twisted his hands, forgetting to stop himself before the sign of his feelings could show. His throat was thick and rough, but his words came out clear. 'I'm so sorry.

I'm sorry you had to make that decision. I'm sorry that I didn't, couldn't, protect you from that.'

'Aleks. I don't blame you. I never did. I thought…' She trailed off, but he understood.

'You thought I blamed you?' he asked. She nodded. 'I couldn't,' he replied quickly. 'Ever. I understand why you made the decision you did. I just… You should never have been in a position to make that decision—alone. Or, worse, with pressure from my father.' He could barely bring himself to say the words.

'Your father made it clear that he would honour any choice I made, and that I would have his support. He is not a bad man, but I know that it must have been difficult growing up with him.'

Relief hit him, so strong that if Aleksander hadn't been sitting he might have fallen. But his smile was sad. 'It wasn't easy, but this helps a little.' She understood, he could see that. 'I loved you,' he said, feeling it even now, but as a faint echo, something similar but in no way close to the other love burning bright in his heart.

'I know. I felt it. I loved you too. But we were too young. And…' She paused, as if unsure whether to say her next words or not. 'And I would never have been your Queen,' she said sadly.

He shook his head. He understood that too. In some ways, not having a normal ending to their relationship had meant it was stuck in time, leaving him unable to heal and grieve and recover like he might have done otherwise.

'Who is she?'

His head jerked up to see her gentle affection for him.

'I imagine,' Kristine continued, 'that, whoever it is, she is the one who helped you find your way here.'

This time he smiled. 'Henna Olin.'

'I remember her,' Kristine replied fondly.

'You do?' he asked, surprised.

'Yes, of course. She could never take her eyes off you.'

They caught up for a short while after, talking on the past, on their families, both knowing that this would likely be the last time they would see each other. Aleksander made sure that he left nothing unsaid, and when he returned to the car that would take him back to the Palace he felt as if he was finally ready to face the hardest fight he would ever have.

Because he had no intention of letting Henna go.

She could have used her keys but had chosen to ring the bell, so waited for one of the staff her stepmother employed to answer the door. The maid looked at Henna curiously and asked if she could be of help, clearly not recognising her.

Henna couldn't work out if it was funny or desperately sad that the people who occupied her childhood home didn't know her. Viveca appeared behind the woman and said, 'Oh, it's you. Come in then,' and disappeared off towards the living area, or at least where it had once been.

As Henna crossed the threshold she was torn between how big her father's estate was, but how small everything looked. It felt as if she was viewing it through a different lens than the last time she'd been here, her focus narrowed by loss. Twin strands of grief wrapped themselves around her, giving her just enough space to move, but nothing near the freedom she needed.

'What are you doing here? Mother's out, if that's who you were after,' called the disembodied voice, the monied, aristocratic accent sharp enough to cut glass. It had struck Henna a little while after she had joined the Palace staff that, for all the superiority and class Viveca and her mother wore like mink, they had nothing of the class she had witnessed through the years. A class not born from wealth or status, but rooted in kindness, grace and generosity.

She was glad in that moment that her father had never discovered the truth about the person he had entrusted with the care of his child—he would have been devastated. She looked around the large entrance hall that he had chased her through playing tag, the memory of their joint laughter fading in her ears but strong in her heart. And now she realised that she had not come here to get the last of her things, she had come here to say goodbye.

As if drawn by her silence, Viveca appeared, drenched in pale silk and fur, wearing crimson lipstick and cruelty in her eyes. 'Well, has the stupidity in your brain finally taken over your tongue? What are you doing here?' she demanded, as if Henna didn't have a right to be in her family home—her *father's* home.

'What was it?' Henna asked, stopping Viveca midturn, having become bored waiting for an answer. When Henna finally had her attention she pressed on. 'What was it that I did to you that filled you with such hatred?'

'You mistake yourself. You are so insignificant to me that I can't even summon up enough energy to hate you.'

'So you are simply this mean to everyone?' Henna asked.

'How dare you?' Viveca screeched, charging towards Henna across the black and white checked flooring of the hallway. 'Is this because of Nils? Have you finally decided to grow a backbone?'

There was a temptation to be cruel. To meet her poisoned barbs with taunts just as cutting and hurtful—to belittle Viveca. But that wasn't who Henna was and it certainly wasn't who she wanted to be. She'd told Aleksander that she knew how to deal with bullies, but she had been lying. She had never dealt with Viveca. Ignoring her hadn't made her go away. It hadn't made her any less hurtful or mean.

'No, this is not because of Nils,' she replied truthfully as the scales fell from her eyes. She *had* been lying to herself, just as Aleksander had accused, only not about her feelings for him. Being here after her father's death, with Viveca and her stepmother, had been awful. Truly awful. But making herself useful to them, making herself invisible to them, had pacified the two to the point where it had made Henna's life easier. And somewhere along the line it had become habit. It had become her way of being.

She had told herself that she liked helping people and being efficient because that was how she'd survived Viveca and her mother, but was it true? Was it what she wanted? Or had she simply been on autopilot?

She was distracted from unravelling her thoughts by her stepsister, who pulled up just short of invading her personal space.

'Or maybe it is,' Henna said, Viveca's betrayal with Nils leading her back to her childhood. 'Because I want to know what it was that I had that you wanted so much that you needed to steal something else from me.'

Viveca looked as if she had been struck, the sting bringing a sheen of unshed tears to her vivid blue gaze. '*Everything,*' she answered after a heartbeat. 'Everything. He may have died when you were young, but your father—he loved you. You couldn't stop *telling us* just how much he loved you. Your perfect father. Mine?' She laughed, bitterness and pain audible in her tone. 'He left. Walked out when I was four and that was the last time I saw him.' Henna took a step forward, but Viveca held up a hand to ward her off. 'And *then*,' she said, the meanness returning to her voice, 'you took Aleksander. He was supposed to be mine. Mother said. She'd wanted *me* to befriend him at that party, not you!'

All the violence and rage she saw in Viveca in that moment teetered on the brink of turning on Henna or turning back on herself and for a moment Henna felt a crawling fear scratching at the back of her neck, before she shoved it aside. There was nothing to fear here now, and truly she only felt sorry for Viveca. All that anger and hurt… And her mother had been no kind, loving or generous presence in Viveca's life at all.

No, she wouldn't forgive her for sleeping with Nils, but that kind of hurt had rotted something deep within Viveca. Aleksander might have buried his, locked his away, but he'd never been mean with it. He had hurt her, yes, but it hadn't been an act of cruelty. She could see now that it had been an act of self-preservation. And in his own way he had tried—as he had with his sisters—to give her something else. To nudge her towards a position and role that she had genuinely been interested in.

'Viveca, if you ever want to change the way things are between us I would be open to that,' she said, thinking of how she felt about Freya and Marit and hoping that if Viveca did ever confront her demons they might at least become friends.

Viveca frowned, as if not understanding or believing her words and, before she could be stopped, Henna swept her up in a fierce hug, before leaving and not looking back. There was nothing more here for Henna. It hadn't been her home for a very long time. Now, she wanted to look to her future.

'Are you sure you want to do this?'

Freya's question sounded in her ears. She was still excited by the prospect of the role waiting for her in London. But Henna needed a little more time. Seeing Viveca, coming here…it had cleared the path to making a decision. Yes, Aleksander's betrayal had cut deep, even now she felt the sting and burn in her chest, as if she'd inhaled winter's bite. Her heart had broken, but her soul had kept her standing and she owed it to herself to fight for the very best for herself. In her heart, her father smiled and some of the pain from the loss of Aleksander eased just a little.

Can you meet me in the maze? I need to talk to you privately but I can't leave the Palace. Please, Henna, I wouldn't ask if it wasn't desperately important. F xx

It was the day before her flight and the last thing Henna wanted was to return to Rilderdal Palace, but Freya had sworn that Aleksander was away on business. She hadn't even wanted that much information because her mind had quickly filled with questions about the organisation, whether Kozlov had kept his word, whether Tuva was with him…

Henna had refused to read any newspapers, listen to any news reports. Her only social media had been through the palace communications team so even that was closed to her now. She felt oddly isolated and out of tune with Svardia and hoped it was for the best, even if it felt wrong deep in her heart. The car Freya had sent for her passed smoothly through Security and took the private road access to leave her just beside the maze.

Unable to resist, her hand reached out to swipe across the hundreds and thousands of tiny little vivid green leaves. They tickled her palm like the memories playing in her mind. As a child, the walls of the maze had towered over her. They were still taller than her, but only just, which made them feel so much less intimidating.

She peered into the entrance and called out for Freya, but heard no response. Was she supposed to meet her here or at the centre? Henna checked her watch and, hating the idea of keeping Freya waiting, she started on the path she had forced herself to learn after getting lost. She had discovered that it had been designed as a labyrinth rather than a maze, there being only one true path to the centre, with many dead ends and confusing junctions along the way.

As she followed the route she knew in her mind, she couldn't help but feel that she was taking the first steps on the right path of her own journey and she was excited to tell Freya what she'd decided about her future. Henna was lost in the thought of her best friend's reaction when she turned into the heart of the maze, so it took her a moment to register what she was seeing.

Aleksander had clearly been pacing back and forth, but he stopped the moment she emerged at the centre of the maze. She had never seen him like this. His hair was messy and his shirtsleeves rolled back. His fists clenched and unclenched at his sides, and even then he *still* looked devastatingly handsome. The sun glinted on the golden strands of his hair, and the flex of tension in his jaw only served to make him look glorious.

Henna shook her head, intensely disliking the fact that she hadn't built up an immunity to him.

'What am I doing here, Aleksander?' she demanded, hurt and angry that he would do this to her, manipulate her, *again*.

In that moment Aleksander saw the pain he had caused Henna. He was struck silent by it and all the things he had prepared to say, had written and tried to memorise disappeared. Refusing to wait any longer for his answer, she turned to leave, forcing him to cross the distance between them in quick strides, rounding her and cutting off her exit. She had to pull up short to stop from crashing into him.

His heart pounded at the sight of the dark circles beneath her eyes, knowing that he deserved to witness her hurt and far, far more. He had manipulated her and in doing so betrayed her. He had taken her choice away, just like his had been taken away, and worse—he had taken away her home. It had scarred him to his soul that he had done that to her.

'I'm sorry,' he said, the words pouring from his soul with the most sincerity he'd ever felt. 'I am so truly sorry.'

'Do you know what you're sorry for?' she asked, glaring up at him. 'Or are you just saying what you think I need to hear?'

'I *know*,' he said, reaching for her hand, but she pulled it away. 'I…there is so much I want to say, things I'd like to…' He winced. This was coming out all wrong. As if surprised by his ineloquence, she took a step back from him. 'I went to see Kristine.' The words burst from him, stopping her in her tracks. He could see the questions in her eyes—the concern for him so pure and powerful and clear in her gaze it gave him hope. It made him *stronger*, which he should have realised a long time ago.

'How is she?' Henna asked hesitantly.

'Happy,' he said, finally at peace with the past. 'She loves her quiet life, her husband is kind, her children healthy and delightful. Speaking to her was something I should have done a long time ago. Freya and Marit said the same.'

'You told your sisters about what happened?' Shock filled Henna's question.

'Yes. You were, *unsurprisingly*, right,' he acknowledged. 'I hadn't realised how much I had cut myself off from them until you opened my eyes to it.' He dared to take a step towards her and this time she didn't move away. This time, he opened his heart and bared it to her with his words. 'Henna, for years I thought my grief, my guilt, was a cage. But in truth it was a maze. I just couldn't find the way out, until you.' Henna's eyes grew round with surprise and he pressed on. 'You guided me, like Ariadne—leaving me a string, a thread, for me to follow that led me not just out of the maze, but to you. My strength. My *heart*.'

Her eyes flitted across his face, as if searching for the truth, and he felt every movement like a touch, like a caress.

'But…but what about Tuva?'

Aleksander shook his head. 'There is no Tuva. There is no one else. And Henna—' he reached for her chin, gently holding her gaze to his, for this was the important bit '—there never will be. If you choose to leave I will understand, but know that there will *never* be anyone else. No other woman will wear my ring, or my crown.'

'But—'

'I love you. You are the *only* person I want by my side,' he said, taking the sudden flare in her eyes as a sign for him to continue. 'For so long I was fighting my feelings for you, I was so busy counting the ways that wanting you, needing you, could hurt me, that I didn't realise the many, *many* ways that you made me better. I was so sure that my love for you made me vulnerable and weak, opening me to manipulation and giving me over to you for you to destroy, I didn't stop to think, to realise, that you would *never* do that to me. The entire time, you gave me the truth when I needed it, and you asked me to share my hurt when I would have buried it. You gave me so much and I...' he struggled, forcing himself to confront his greatest sin, guilt burning and branding him '... I betrayed you. I took away your home, your *safety*, and I will never forgive myself, nor will I dare ask for your forgiveness. But I owe you the greatest apology and I vow to you that, no matter what, you will always have a home here, in Svardia, in Rilderdal Palace, you will *always* be part of our family,' he promised, hoping that she could read the truth in his words.

Shivers broke out over Henna's skin, Aleksander's words touching her far more deeply than she could ever have imagined. Her heart was soaring, but her mind still urged caution. What Aleksander was offering was more than she had ever imagined but...

'You hurt me.'

'I know. And I am so, so truly sorry for it. You deserve the world, and if you are not by my side please know that I, Freya and Marit will all help you in whatever way you want or need. And if you still want to leave for London then I completely understand.'

'London?' Henna asked, momentarily confused. 'I'm not going to London,' she said.

'You're not taking the job?'

She shook her head. 'I turned it down.'

'Because of me? Henna—'

'No—' she couldn't help but laugh '—not because of you,' she said, her heart easing into the realisation that he loved her. It was an excited, fizzing, *filling* kind of feeling that she wasn't quite used to yet. Aleksander searched her gaze and she realised he was waiting for an explanation. And suddenly she knew that it was Aleksander she had been waiting to tell. Yes, she would love to tell Freya, but this moment was what she had wanted since making her decision about her future. Pride unfurled in her soul, knowing that she was about to share her plan with someone she respected, someone she wanted to impress but didn't need to. She was excited about the future now and where it would take her. It felt *right*. Just like being in Aleksander's arms.

'I realised that I could do more—*be* more. And…you helped me see that,' she said truthfully. She would have enjoyed the job in London and she most definitely would have excelled in it. But after visiting Viveca, realising that so much of what she thought she wanted had been shaped by habit and denial, she had forced herself to think about what she really wanted to do with her life. 'As you discovered in Macau, I am sitting on a considerably large amount of money. Money I had ignored because it felt wrong, a tainted compensation for the loss of my father.' He reached for her then and pulled her into a hug. She let him hold her as the wash of memories flowed over her, more easily with him by her side.

'But I know now that I can use that money to do some

good. That I *want* to do it and be recognised for that myself, not hide in the shadows behind someone else. So I am flying to Paris with meet with Célia d'Argent.'

'Chariton Enterprises?' Aleksander asked, surprised, aware of the excellent reputation of the company that matched wealthy clients with deserving causes.

'Yes. They have a selection of charities for me to consider so that I can help people directly.'

'Any one of them would be lucky to have you,' he said, his fingers smoothing her hair, a silence descending between them. She felt his breath lock in his lungs, an unspoken question pressing against his lips. Hope and desperation warred in his gaze and she knew what he wanted to ask, was asking—she felt his need as if he were part of her.

She cupped his jaw, connecting her heart to his, her soul to his. 'I love you. You found me when I was lost and you gave me so much. And it helped, it slowly eased my grief, and it was magical and wonderful—the handsome prince who gave me what I needed before I even knew it myself.' His heart pounded beneath the palm of her hand, fierce and strong and all hers.

'Henna Olin,' he asked, eyes bright and full of hope, 'will you do me the greatest honour and allow me to be your husband, your partner, your lover and your home?'

Tears filled her eyes and spilled, and she felt no shame in them because they were true and honest and full of love.

'Yes, Your Majesty. I will.'

And there, in the centre of the maze in the grounds of Svardia's Rilderdal Palace, where they had lost their hearts, only to find them again, Aleksander and Henna didn't have the slightest idea that their love and marriage would soon become a real-life fairy-tale that generations would grow up knowing and admiring around the world.

EPILOGUE

HENNA STOOD IN the bedroom doorway in the private wing of Svardia's Rilderdal Palace, watching her husband, the King of Svardia, soothe their son. She leaned her head against the doorframe, the smile familiar on her lips, knowing that she would never forget the sight of him holding their children, never forget the way it made her feel. Henna kept expecting her heart to burst, unable to take any more happiness and love. But, as it had done when Aleksander had proposed, then when they had married, when they'd had their first child, Henriette, and three months ago their son, Jonas, it simply stretched to accommodate as much love as she was capable of feeling.

The last five years had been a whirlwind and there had been times that had sorely tested them both. The news of Freya's fertility difficulties had been accepted mostly with positivity, understanding and compassion. And, despite some tensions and grumbling, Aleksander had passed the legislation changes he'd wanted, removing the title requirements for royal family consorts, but also incorporating the line of succession to include adopted children.

She had taken to the role of Queen Consort surprisingly well, even though Aleksander still joked to anyone who would listen that she was the real power behind the throne. She had decided with Aleksander not to have a coronation ceremony because the planning for the second of their two weddings—the public one—had utterly exhausted her. Especially as she had been in her first trimester at the time. Heads of state had flown in from around the world and Henna had even caught the familiar names of two members she knew belonged to the organisation. It had been watched by more than thirty-two million people worldwide but it still didn't mean as much to her as the small private wedding conducted in the chapel in the Palace grounds two weeks before, with just Aleksander's sisters and their partners in attendance.

Henna had hoped that she might one day be able to create some kind of relationship with her stepsister, but Viveca had remained almost intentionally mean and, while it hurt a little, Henna knew that Viveca's pain was greater. Aleksander had talked it through with her and she knew he thought she was crazy for hoping, but Henna refused to close that door.

For their honeymoon, Aleksander had taken her to London. They had stayed in an apartment in Knightsbridge, done all the touristy things, and then Aleksander had tracked down some information about her mother and where she and her family had lived. They'd visited the area but, understanding her family were no longer there, she hadn't wanted to impose on the new tenants. Henna had thought she might feel a connection to it, but realised that her home wasn't in the memories of the past but in the connections in her present. It was Aleksander, Freya and Marit…it was Svardia, the country and the people.

Aleksander had maintained his twice-yearly visits to Öström and she had gone with him every time, thoroughly enjoying the peace and quiet and relishing the powerful force of nature that was the sea and the tide along that craggy peninsula. Thankfully, no one had heard anything from Ilian Kozlov in the years since his abrupt departure, and every now and then Aleksander persuaded her to play him at cards. Sometimes she won, sometimes he did, but every time it ended up in bed, the cards forgotten and pleasure the last thing on their lips.

She heard the pitter-patter of little feet in the hallway and looked down at the irrepressible mop of blonde curls Henriette had inherited from some long-forgotten family gene.

'Mama,' her daughter whispered, reaching for her hand, 'is Jonas okay?'

Henna swept her daughter up into her arms. 'Of course, Ette. I think he just missed his papa,' she explained with a smile.

'But he's right there,' Ette pointed out as Aleksander turned to face them, Jonas tucked against his chest.

'Which is why he's stopped crying,' Henna whispered to Ette. 'Papa did the same thing for you when you were that small.'

'He did?' Ette asked, beautiful brown eyes big and round.

Aleksander looked up at them and in that moment she knew that her husband felt what she did. Awe that this was theirs—their family, their life. They never took it for granted, all that they had and all the good that they could do. Aleksander had promised to give her a home, one where she would always feel safe and loved in, and he had done just that.

'Are we still going to Narna tomorrow?'

Henna bit her lip, knowing that Ette meant Dalarna, in Sweden, where Kjell and Freya had their cabin. 'Yes, we are,' she said, struggling to keep hold of her when Ette started wriggling in joy.

'We're going to see Alarik and Mikael and Malin?'

Henna nodded. 'And guess what…' she asked her daughter. 'Marit is pregnant!'

'Again?' Ette demanded with excitement.

Henna heard Aleksander stifle a laugh.

'Yes, now, let's say goodnight to Jonas and leave so he can get some sleep.'

Following a very gentle kiss from Ette, Henna took in the sleepy-eyed smiling face of her son, his surprising head of hair all his father's, but his eyes were hazel just like hers. Although she wasn't quite sure how to feel about it, their son had a Pinterest page with more followers than the one of Aleksander's jawline.

She looked up then, caught the love blazing in his eyes for her, for their children, and knew that he was thankful. Thankful for the journey they'd been on together to be here, now, and happy.

'I love you,' he mouthed, not wanting to disturb Jonas.

'I love you too,' she returned. Since his proposal in the maze not a single day had gone by without him telling her that she was loved, and not a single day ever would.

* * * * *

STOLEN FOR
MY SPANISH
SCANDAL

JACKIE ASHENDEN

MILLS & BOON

Carry on my wayward son…

CHAPTER ONE

Jenny

I ONLY WANTED one last glimpse of him, the man I once loved.

The man I now hated with every breath in my body.

Constantine Silvera. My stepbrother.

It wasn't the best choice of occasions—his father's wake—but I didn't want to go near him or talk to him. I only wanted to see him and from a safe distance.

Domingo Silvera, once CEO of Silver Inc, one of Europe's most powerful conglomerates, was being farewelled at the Silvera family's ostentatious Madrid mansion, and I'd sent Constantine a short, impersonal email offering him my condolences and promising I'd be there.

But I wasn't there for Domingo. I didn't care about Domingo. My mother had married him when I was nine and then promptly sent me to boarding school in England, so I'd never had much contact with him. Which was a good thing since he was a very difficult man.

No, the man I wanted to see was his son. One last time before I cut him out of my life.

It was probably a bad idea, and my poor heart had

been through enough the past three months, but I needed to say goodbye. Even if it wasn't actually to him. Even if it was only for myself.

So here I was, hiding behind a column in the white marble-covered ballroom, hoping I'd be lost in the crowd of dignitaries trying to catch a glimpse of him.

Not that it was difficult to catch a glimpse of him when he towered above everyone else in the room and drew every eye.

They called him cold, merciless, ruthless, and maybe in business he was. But he'd never been that way with me. Initially he'd been reserved and distant, yet I'd come to know the man beneath the ice. A kind, caring man.

At least until I'd moved to London permanently four years ago, and then, for some reason, he'd cut off all contact with me.

All contact except once, three months ago, when I'd discovered something else about him: there was fire deep in his soul, a fire that only I knew about.

A fire I'd discovered the night I'd seduced him.

At his engagement party.

My gaze drifted to the woman at his side, tall and blonde and poised. Olivia Wintergreen, CEO of Wintergreen Diamonds, an old and very successful jewel company. She wore a fitted black dress and her pale lovely face was composed. She was everything I was not.

She was also his fiancée.

A business arrangement, I'd heard through the grapevine, since certainly Con himself hadn't told me. An old friend of the Silvera family, chosen as a potential wife and mother for his heirs. He didn't love her, so the gossip columns reported, but she had good genes and came from a good family and, as CEO of a large company, she was his match in every way.

And I was…not.

I was short and round and not at all beautiful. I was not a CEO. I worked with the homeless in a shelter in London, much to my mother's disgust, and I had no poise to speak of.

I was not his match, as he'd told me that night, after he'd had me on the grass near the rosebushes in the garden outside. And I never would be.

The memory made my throat close with pain, but I ignored it. Normally I tried to be optimistic, to look on the bright side of things, but after that night in the garden looking on the bright side had been more difficult. And I was tired of pain. Fury was so much better, so I reached for that instead. Not that I was angry with Olivia Wintergreen, or jealous. How could you be jealous when your own personal god wanted to marry another goddess?

No, there was only one person I was furious with, and he stood in the middle of the room, tall and arrogant and icier than any glacier.

He was in a perfectly tailored, horrifically expensive black suit that clung to his wide shoulders and hugged his broad, muscular chest, emphasising his narrow waist and long, powerful legs. He looked like an emperor from ancient Rome, as if he should be wearing a laurel wreath, a snowy white toga and a cloak of imperial purple.

His face was as familiar to me as my own, and it made the ache inside me deepen. There were his imperious cheekbones, his straight nose, his hard and yet somehow sensual mouth. His inky hair was cut very short, and his eyes were even blacker, and he projected the sharp, ruthless menace of an apex predator.

He was beautiful. So beautiful.

People were afraid of him. They thought he was just as merciless and as ruthless as he appeared, and twice as cold. Detached from all emotion. But they hadn't seen him tuck a blanket around me when I'd fallen asleep on the chair in his office, or frown in concern over a nest of sparrow chicks I'd rescued and demanded help with, or give one of his very rare laughs when I told him a funny story.

He was only like that with me, and he had been right from the day I'd first met him, when I'd first arrived at the mansion at nine years old. And he hadn't been detached that night in the garden, when he'd dragged me down onto the grass. Somehow I'd unlocked his passion and fire had burst out of him…

But I couldn't think about that night. That way only lay heartache, and it wasn't the lesson I wanted to learn from my relationship with him.

I was going to take some of the ice he gave to other people and place it in my own heart, so I'd never be so stupid again as to fall in love with a man I could never have.

Constantine's black gaze raked the ballroom as if he was looking for something, or someone, and I wanted to shrink back behind my column, to stay safe out of his sight. Except another part of me, a harder part, wanted to show him that he hadn't destroyed me with the harsh words he'd said to me that night. That I was stronger than he thought.

That I hated him with every part of me.

So I stood my ground, and lifted my chin, and waited for the Sword of Damocles to fall.

And it did.

His gaze found me in the crowd, as I knew it would, and all the breath left my body. But I didn't go cold—I never went cold when Constantine looked at me—I went hot, like a fire blazing high.

He was already statue-still and his expression betrayed nothing. I'd always been able to read him, and yet tonight I had no idea what he was thinking.

His attention raked over me and for a moment or two I trembled. With heat. With desire. With desperate hunger.

Then he looked away, dismissing me as if I was dirt he'd wiped off his shoe.

Tears of rage prickled behind my eyes. Rage at him and at myself for coming here, for thinking I could bear one last glimpse of him without my heart breaking all over again.

I was stupid. I was so stupid.

Blinking fiercely, I fought back my tears and turned away.

I'd had my last glimpse. I'd said goodbye. Now it was time to leave, and the sooner I got out of here the better.

I threaded my way through the crowd to the closest door and stepped out into the relative quiet of the white marble hall.

I was starting to feel a bit sick, since I'd skipped dinner, and the emotion clogging my throat didn't help. So I was distracted, too wound up in raging at Constantine, to notice a man in a black uniform suddenly appear at the end of the corridor.

'Miss Grey?' he asked politely as I approached.

I recognised him. He was one of Constantine's security staff. 'Yes?'

'If you would follow me, please? Mr Silvera has instructed that you are to wait for him in the small study.'

I blinked in surprise. Constantine wanted to talk to me? Why? What could he possibly want to say to me that he hadn't said that night in the garden? Not that I wanted to hear him say anything at all. In fact, the very last thing in the world I wanted to do was to talk to him.

'I'm sorry.' I tried to be polite, even though I felt anything but. 'I have a plane to catch. Please tell Mr Silvera that he—'

'I'm afraid Mr Silvera insists.' The man gave me an apologetic look. 'Just following orders, miss.'

Shock rippled through me. Constantine was *insisting*? But…why? Hadn't he said everything he needed to three months ago? Things such as, 'No, I don't love you. What a preposterous idea'. And, 'Did your mother put you up to this?'. And, 'If you think I'm going to marry you, you're sadly mistaken. You have no money and have no power. You have nothing I want. Your looks might be passable, and you might be good in bed, but sex is not a basis for marriage.' And, 'This was a mistake. And it will *never* happen again.'

Perhaps he'd forgotten to say a few things. Perhaps he hadn't finished tearing my heart to shreds and now he wanted to finish the job.

I didn't want to give him that opportunity, but the way his security man was standing made it obvious that no wasn't going to be an acceptable answer. Which left me with either an undignified struggle or going willingly.

Well, didn't you want him to know how much you hated him? This could be the perfect opportunity.

That was true. The night of his engagement party, after I'd fled the garden, weeping like the stupid child I was, and finally got back home, I'd lain awake, my heart in ruins, allowing fury to fill me. Thinking of all the things I wanted to say to him. Things that would destroy him the way he'd destroyed me.

I'd loved him for so long—since I'd been sixteen—and the way he'd cut me off after I'd moved to London had hurt. And after the passion in the grass, where he'd fallen on me like a starving man falls on a feast, I'd thought that finally, *finally*, he was mine, and the past four years of silence had been an aberration. I hadn't expected his complete and utter rejection. It had come completely out of the blue.

Naive of me. I hadn't even realised it was his engagement party. I'd gone because my mother had told me that Constantine was having a party. He'd wanted me to come and my invitation must have got lost in my inbox. I'd arrived late, not knowing what the occasion was, and gone straight to find him. He'd been out in the garden, alone, and…

Yes, I'd been stupid, and that night he'd shattered me. I'd been too broken to say a word. I'd turned around and run away from him instead.

But things had changed now. It was three months on and I'd found strength in fury, so why shouldn't I give him a taste of his own medicine? Say all the things I'd dreamt of saying to him that night? Perhaps even demand to know why he'd been so distant with me for so long.

None of that would matter at all to him, but it would certainly make me feel better.

Ignoring the clutch of anxiety, I nodded and let myself be led down another corridor and into a small room.

As a child, I'd gone to stay at the Silvera mansion every school holiday, and in that time I'd find myself some out-of-the-way place to sit and read peacefully. Away from my mother constantly picking at me.

Usually it was Con's office, but sometimes I'd come in here. It wasn't the most appealing room, though I appreciated the shelves lined with books. However, the couch that sat in front of the fireplace and the two armchairs that flanked it were hard and uncomfortable. The floor was tiled too, and there were no rugs on the floor, no soft surfaces anywhere.

This was a room you showed your enemies into when they came to visit, not your friends.

I'd only taken a couple of steps into the room when the security man shut the door behind me. And I heard the lock click.

Then all the lights went out.

For a second all I could do was stand there, frozen in shock. From outside I could hear shouts, and a few screams, and fear caught at me. I had no idea what was going on, and now I was…locked in.

My heartbeat thumped as I turned and tried the door handle, just as someone on the other side turned it.

And pushed the door open.

I stumbled back, gasping, then the lights flickered on again, illuminating the man standing in the doorway, filling it completely with his height and breadth.

Constantine.

His cold black eyes found mine instantly, the way they had downstairs, and some expression I didn't understand shifted in them. Then he stepped through the doorway and shut the door behind him, trapping me in the room with him.

My heart thumped harder, all my earlier bravado leaking away as if it had never been. My knees had gone weak and my stomach twisted. What a pathetic mess I was. Nothing like his cool, poised fiancée.

No wonder he didn't want you. You should have listened to your mother.

I shoved that thought away and tried to swallow, tried to find my voice, but my throat was so dry I couldn't speak. While Constantine stood in front of the closed door, staring at me, studying me like a scientist examining a flaw in an otherwise perfect experiment.

'Wh-what happened?' I managed to force out. 'Why did the lights go out?'

'Nothing you need concern yourself with.' His voice was icy and deep, the lilting Spanish accent I'd always loved colouring the words. He took a step towards me. 'I'm glad you're here.'

He was? He didn't look glad. He looked cold and forbidding, all trace of the man I'd come to know and love gone.

I desperately wanted to say all the words I'd been fantasising about saying for the past three months, to tear him to pieces with my anger. But all the words had vanished from my head and all I wanted to do was cry.

Because even now I missed him. Even though he'd broken my heart, I missed him so much.

Pull yourself together, idiot. And don't you dare cry.

I shouldn't, because to do so would give away my anguish, and I wasn't going to do that in front of him. That had been my mistake the last time and I wasn't going to lower my guard again.

But there was a reason why my emotions were all over the place, wasn't there? A very good reason.

'Why are you glad?' I forced out between numb lips.

His black winged brows drew down very slightly. 'So you haven't come here to tell me?'

Cold swept through me, twisting my gut and making me feel even more ill. I put a hand on the back of the uncomfortable couch, steadying myself. Because he couldn't know. He couldn't. I'd told no one. It was my perfect little secret and that was how I'd wanted it to stay.

'Tell you?' I tried to sound as innocent as possible, to let my expression show nothing but polite enquiry. 'Tell you what?'

His inky brows twitched as he looked down on me from his great height, his beautiful face as expressive as a mountainside. 'That you're pregnant, of course.'

Did you really think you could keep it a secret? From him?

I had. I really had. I'd even found a doctor well away from where I lived to confirm it. She wouldn't have told anyone, would she? Weren't doctors supposed to keep their patient's information private?

Fear cut like a knife inside me, combining with hurt and anger and the anxiety of the last three months, plus the lack of food, and making my gut twist again, more violently this time.

I clutched hard to the back of the couch, fighting the nausea, but it was relentless.

I didn't want to be sick in front of him. I'd already humiliated myself enough, hadn't I?

Yet my body didn't seem to think this was a compelling argument. And there was nothing I could do as I stumbled forward a couple of steps and threw up my breakfast all over his expensive handmade leather shoes.

CHAPTER TWO

Constantine

WHEN THE LIGHTS had suddenly gone out downstairs, I'd allowed myself one crystal-clear moment of intense rage. In the darkness no one would see me let out a soundless roar of fury and so I had.

But it was only one moment.

The instant the lights had come back on I was myself again, the way I had to be. Impervious. Detached. Frozen solid all the way through.

Nevertheless, the fury had remained, so when I stepped into that room and my little stepsister threw up all over my shoes I was very tempted to roar again. But that would have been one slip too far, and my control around her already had cracks in it miles deep. So all I did was clench my teeth around the rage until my jaw ached.

I'd known she was here—put me in a dark room anywhere and I'd know the second she stepped into it—and I'd seen her hiding behind a column downstairs in the ballroom. And the instant I had, the frustrating indecision that had dogged me for the past two days, ever since I'd learned of her pregnancy, had coalesced into hard certainty.

My twin brother's not entirely unexpected appearance not fifteen minutes earlier, returned from the dead, had only sealed the deal.

I already knew Valentin was alive. Three months ago I'd had word that he hadn't been killed in a car accident fifteen years earlier, the way we all thought, but was alive and well and CEO of a legitimate company he'd built off the back of various shady enterprises.

I'd known he was going to make a play for Silver Inc, the huge European conglomerate my father and his father before him had built from the ground up, because it was just the kind of thing he *would* do.

I'd even suspected he'd take Olivia, my fiancée. And sure enough, with his usual dramatics, he'd cut the power and spirited her away.

However, I'd been expecting him to make his move during the funeral, not the wake, and no small part of my fury was directed at myself as well as him.

Clearly I'd been complacent.

Now my fiancée had been taken, and while I knew he wouldn't hurt her—Olivia had a considerable history with Valentin—it was a tremendous…inconvenience.

I'd spent a lot of time choosing the right woman and she'd ticked all the boxes. Intelligence, strength, poise, beauty. She was the CEO of a diamond company and had power and influence in her own right.

She was exactly what I wanted, and the best thing about her was that she wasn't anything like Jenny Grey, my little stepsister. My lovely little stepsister. The one woman in the world I could never have.

Except all that had now changed.

Olivia had been taken, and the woman I'd been protecting ever since she was a child—the woman I was still protecting even now, though she'd never know it—was pregnant with my child.

Which made everything very, *very* clear.

For the past four years I'd been holding Jenny at arm's length to keep her safe, both from my father and from me, but one night had ended that. One night and my own lack of control. For two days after I'd found out she was pregnant I'd thought of and discarded various plans that would involve me only peripherally, while at the same time making sure she and the child were safe, yet I hadn't been able to settle on one that would satisfy me.

However, Valentin's little escapade had made the decision for me.

I'd never believed in the inevitability of fate, and yet there was something inevitable this. About Jenny being here, and pregnant, at the same time as Olivia was taken.

So instead of fighting the inevitable, I embraced it.

I'd already given the order to make sure Jenny was shown to this room, since I'd wanted to talk to her about the pregnancy anyway. So the instant the lights went out I fought my way through the confusion to find one of my security team—one who hadn't been compromised by Valentin—and make sure Jenny hadn't got caught up in the panic. Sure enough, confirmation was given that she was in the room I'd set aside for our discussion.

I'd come here with the intention of announcing my plans to her. However, I hadn't expected her to suddenly bend over and throw up on my shoes.

As always, my instinct was to make sure she was all right. Sweep her into my arms and tuck her into bed, keep watch over her. But there was a reason I had to keep myself in check when it came to her, so I stayed rigidly where I was instead.

It did not enhance my mood.

I called one of my house staff to deal with the mess, and ten minutes later everything was clean, I had new shoes and Jenny was sitting bolt-upright in an armchair, a glass of water sitting on the table beside her.

She wore a cheap, chain-store black dress and cheap, chain-store black pumps, and her fingers clutched at the faded black cardigan she'd thrown over the top.

I hated everything about her outfit, since it indicated the dire state of her finances and I hated that too.

Yet again I berated myself for not sending her money over the years, to help her out. Even though I'd been trying to distance myself from her, I could still have helped her out financially.

Not that she would have accepted it. Catherine, her mother, was a gold-digger extraordinaire, and Jenny had always sworn she'd never be like her.

Jenny's dark brown hair was gathered in an untidy bun on the top of her head, with little tendrils falling down around the back of her neck and her small ears.

She was very pale as she released her death grip on her cardigan and twisted her hands together in her lap instead, looking down at them, her long, dark and surprisingly thick lashes almost brushing her soft round cheeks...

She was soft and round everywhere, her cheeks, her rosebud of a mouth, the lush curves of her breasts and the generous swell of her hips and thighs.

I remembered how soft she was, so hot beneath my hands that night in the garden here, in the grass near the roses. She'd gasped my name and sighed into my ear.

She'd been everything I'd imagined her to be, everything I'd fantasised about…

Heat shifted inside me, a thread of dark fire licking around the cracks she'd already made in my armour.

I'd repaired them and had thought I was now proof against the physical desire she always seemed to cause whenever she was in my vicinity, but apparently not.

The fury sitting in my gut coiled and twisted, demanding release, but I ignored it.

I could not feel this heat around her. It was dangerous. It had always been dangerous and that night, when she'd overwhelmed my tenuous control, only proved it.

Keeping myself firmly in check, I elected not to sit, standing by the unlit marble fireplace instead, and looked down at her, waiting for her explanation. I wanted to know why she hadn't come to me when she'd found out she was pregnant and why she was here now, because it wasn't just to farewell my father.

Even Catherine, her mother, my father's erstwhile second wife, whom he'd divorced a few years earlier, hadn't turned up for that.

Not that her reasons mattered.

I already knew what I was going to do about it.

'I'm waiting, Jenny,' I said, trying to curb my impatience. The situation with Valentin needed attending to and people would be waiting for my response. However, I had to secure this situation first. 'I assume you're going to tell me why you are here, if it's not to inform me of your pregnancy.'

Her long, delicate fingers wrung themselves in her lap. 'Does it matter?'

The clear, sweet sound of her voice hit me like a shock, though it shouldn't have. It wasn't as if her voice was unfamiliar to me, not when she had been a fixture in my life for the past twelve years.

She'd mostly been at boarding school in England, but when she hadn't been, she'd been here, small, bright-eyed and full of life. A kitten in the den of a wolf. My father wasn't known for his kindnesses, and even though I knew showing concern was a weakness he'd exploit at any opportunity, I couldn't help the concern I felt for her back then.

She was a child, and very vulnerable, and I knew better than anyone how my father loved to manipulate children.

I'd been nineteen, and working hard for Silver Inc, and even though I'd been travelling a lot on company business, when she'd been there I'd done my best to keep an eye on her.

Then one day I'd come home to find a woman standing in front of me instead of a girl, and everything— every single part of my life—had changed.

But perhaps it was best not to think about that.

'No,' I said, and it didn't matter. I would have found out about her pregnancy anyway, and the end result would have been the same. Olivia was gone, yet she was here, and that made my decision an easy one.

My intention had always been to have a wife, and then children I would guide into adulthood. Heirs to inherit Silver Inc and ensure its future. Olivia had fitted the bill perfectly to produce those children. Mainly because I felt nothing for her except respect.

I didn't love her. I didn't want her. She generated ab-solutely no heat in me whatsoever.

Which was good. Emotional distance was important

and I needed to maintain that, since I had too much of my father in me for safety.

Except my feelings for Jenny had never been distant ones, and marrying her would be a risk, but she was carrying my heir and that had decided me.

She would be my wife, yes, but in name only.

It would have to be that way.

She lifted her head then, her face drawn and pale, her big brown eyes huge and dark. There were black circles beneath them.

Protectiveness shifted inside me again. But feelings were the enemy and they had been for years, and I couldn't fall prey to them now. So I only stared back, cold and hard and detached. Giving her nothing.

Normally, the first thing Jenny did when she saw me was smile, and I'd lived for those smiles once. Small gifts she gave me…little glimmers of light in the darkness.

But there was no warm smile for me today. Her rounded chin jutted, and an expression of extreme determination hardened her soft features, stealing all her light.

You took that from her.

I shoved the thought away, along with the biting guilt that came with it. I couldn't afford it—or the disappointment that gripped me at the loss of her smile.

I'd never seen this particular expression on her face before, and if I didn't know any better, I'd have said she was angry.

Are you surprised? After what you said to her that night?

The guilt bit deeper.

'Well,' she said crisply. 'Yes, I'm pregnant, and now you know. So, if you don't mind, I'll be going. I'm sorry for Domingo's passing, and you have my condolences, but apart from that I have nothing more to say to you.'

Jenny had always been a joyful little girl, and she'd grown up into a joyful woman. A bright, optimistic woman who always saw the good in people. A soft, compassionate woman.

And, looking at all that softness, it was easy to think that she was soft through and through.

But she was not. I'd caught glimpses of the steel at the heart of her over the years, of a stubbornness that had always been there. Yet she'd never directed it at me before, nor any of the hostility currently bristling in my direction.

Which I deserved.

I remembered that night more clearly than I wanted to. Her in my arms, her face flushed and shining. She'd told me she loved me, and then I'd realised what I'd done, and my anger had escaped no matter how hard I tried to stop it.

I'd been cruel to her. I'd hurt her. Deliberately. I hadn't regretted it then, and while part of me regretted it now, another part didn't. Because it had been for her own good. To get her as far away as possible from me.

Yes, and look how well that worked?

I wasn't a man who made mistakes. But I had three months ago and now the only way forward was to fix it.

'You might not have anything to say to me,' I said. 'However, I have a few things to say to you.'

Her chin rose a fraction higher. 'Is that a fact? And what makes you think I'd be interested in listening to a single thing you have to say?'

Something flickered through me, a spark of an emotion I hadn't felt in a very long time. Curiosity. This wasn't just one of the flashes of spirit she'd shown in the past, this was something more, a glimpse of a strong will that perhaps more than matched my own.

She'd never fought me on anything before, never set her will against mine.

Dangerous.

Yes. Very dangerous. Especially when the beast in me liked a challenge.

On cue, an electric thrill darted down my spine and I had to crush it immediately. I couldn't afford any more temptations, not around her. Not when she'd already undone me so completely three months earlier.

I had to be hard when it came to her. I couldn't allow anything to get through.

'You'll be interested because this concerns your future,' I said, my voice betraying nothing. 'I've known about your pregnancy for the past few days, and I—'

'How did you know?' Jenny interrupted without compunction, a stain of colour appearing on her pale cheeks. Unlike everyone else who knew what was good for them, she'd never been afraid of me. 'Who told you?'

I let her interruption pass. 'I have someone watching you. They informed me of your pregnancy two days ago.'

Her eye went wide, her mouth dropping open. 'You have someone watching me?'

Of course I had. I might have kept my distance from her, but I still kept her protected.

'I've had someone watching you ever since you left Spain. However, I—'

'What? I can't believe this!' Her hands gripped the arms of her chair and she shoved herself out of it, virtually quivering with rage. 'You don't speak to me for four years, and yet—'

'Let me finish,' I ordered icily, my patience thinning no matter how I tried to keep hold of it.

Valentin's little display of amateur dramatics was going to take some time to contain, and containing it was the last thing I wanted to do. I wanted to take care in announcing my decision to Jenny, so it wouldn't come as quite such a shock to her, but I had no time. I had to deal with the mess Valentin had left behind which meant the sooner I told Jenny, the better.

'As I said, I was informed of your pregnancy two days ago. I'm not sure why you didn't come to me straight away, but there's nothing to be done about that now.'

'I didn't because—'

'My circumstances have changed,' I interrupted. 'I have decided I will no longer be marrying Olivia Wintergreen.' I met my stepsister's wide, dark eyes. 'I will be marrying you instead.'

CHAPTER THREE

Jenny

CONSTANTINE STOOD BY the cold marble fireplace, towering above me, his perfect features set in implacable lines, his eyes nothing but black ice.

He couldn't be serious. He couldn't... Could he?

My heart was beating hard behind my ribs, aching at the sight of him despite the shock and fury and hurt. It had been three months since I'd seen him up close and I wanted so much to close the distance between us. Lay a hand on the snowy white cotton of his shirt, feel the warmth of his broad, muscled chest and the faint vibration of his heart.

He might look as hard and icy as a glacier on the outside, but I knew how hot he was beneath it. Like a volcano, there was lava inside him, burning up through cracks in the ice.

Not that you could ever tell, but I knew. I'd always known.

I wish I hadn't. I wish I'd never marched up to him the day I met him and asked him straight out if he would be my friend. He'd looked like he'd needed one and I was an only child. I'd been desperate for a brother.

I'd smiled at him because that was what I did to people who were intimidating, or angry, or people who were sad. A smile could make them soften, forget their anger and cheer up, and Constantine had definitely looked like he'd needed one of those things.

He'd almost smiled in return. I hadn't known then just how rare that was.

He wasn't smiling now, though, and he was certainly nothing like a brother, and I still couldn't get over the shock.

'Wh-what?' I couldn't help stumbling over the word. 'What do you mean, marrying me?'

He gave me the same expressionless look he always did. 'You know what marriage means, Jenny. I shouldn't have to explain it to you.'

I hated it when he spoke like that, his tone cold and superior. But usually he only used it with other people, never with me.

'Don't be an ass, Con,' I said angrily. 'I'm not a child. I know what it means. I just want to know why Olivia suddenly isn't acceptable to you any more. Does she know? Have you told her?'

'Olivia is none of your concern. But as it happens, circumstances with her have changed too.' He glanced down at my stomach. I'd already started to show. 'And she isn't pregnant.'

For a second I thought I saw something hot gleam in his eyes, but it was gone so fast I wondered if I'd imagined it.

'What do you mean, they've changed?' I asked, because he wasn't making any sense. 'Why is—?'

'I do not have time for this.' His black gaze flicked

up again, meeting mine. 'I have a situation that needs dealing with.'

'What situation? What's happen—?'

'It's best if you stay here,' he interrupted shortly, and strode with his usual predatory grace to the door. 'A staff member will come for you. We leave within the hour.'

Wait—leave? Leave for where? And why?

I opened my mouth to ask him what he was talking about, but he'd opened the door and stepped through it before I could get a word out. It closed behind him with a sharp click and I was left staring at the white wood in shock.

This was stupid. Did he really expect me to stay here and wait for a staff member? Without any explanation whatsoever? And leaving…? Leaving for where? Why? And why was he being so cold towards me?

Back when I was a child, I'd used to escape into his study with a book and curl up in the armchair he kept in there. The book had been prop, a cover to pretend I was only interested in reading. In reality I'd been waiting for him to turn up so I could talk to him.

I'd been determined to make him if not my brother, then at least my friend.

He'd ignored me at first, but I'd persisted, chatting to him as if I'd known him for years. And gradually, over time, when I talked to him, he'd started to talk back.

At first our conversations had been simple ones, since I was only nine, and had involved school and friends, and reading and TV, but as I'd got older, our discussions had become more complicated. Books, music, politics, science. Nothing had been off-limits except for two things: the brother he'd lost when he was seventeen, and his father.

I'd never pushed, and by the time I was sixteen he'd felt like my best friend.

Until I moved London and he cut me off without explanation. I'd never understood why.

Now he was offering me marriage, and I still didn't understand why.

I turned from the door and paced over to the chair again, putting a hand to the back of it to steady myself. I still felt sick and confused, and abruptly all I wanted to do was leave.

This whole marriage idea didn't make any sense. The only reason I could think of that he would offer it was for the child's sake.

It wasn't because he loved me.

He'd been clear enough that night three months earlier, when I'd stared up into his beautiful face, seen the remains of passion burning in his eyes, and told him I loved him.

That passion had died instantly, snuffed out like a fire deprived suddenly of oxygen.

He'd ripped himself away from me and looked at me with such betrayal, as if I'd hurt him in some way. 'Well, I don't love you,' he'd told me icily. 'What a preposterous idea.' Then his eyes had narrowed. 'Did your mother put you up to this?'

I'd had no idea what he was talking about, because while my mother had told me about the party, she'd never 'put me up' to doing anything. She might have mentioned a couple of times that if I 'made an effort' I could 'snag' Constantine for myself, but I'd long since stopped listening to her. She might think men were the answer to all life's problems, but I didn't.

I'd tried to tell him that no one had put me up to anything, but he wouldn't listen.

'If you think I'm going to marry you, Jenny,' he'd gone on, even though I hadn't mentioned marriage—even though I hadn't said anything at all. 'You're sadly mistaken. You have nothing I want. Your looks might be passable, and you might be good in bed, but sex is not a basis for marriage.'

He didn't give me time to speak, finishing me off with, 'We must never speak of this again, do you understand? *Never*.'

That was when I'd burst into tears and fled.

My fingers gripped tightly to the back of the chair, more memories of that night filling me. Of arriving in Madrid late, because my flight from England had been late.

'You must have lost your invitation in your inbox,' my mother had said. 'He'll be very upset if you don't go.'

I'd eventually arrived at the Silvera mansion, finding it full of beautiful people, famous actors, politicians, models, the great and powerful—all there to celebrate.

As usual, I'd felt out of place. Because I hadn't been beautiful or great or powerful, and my dress had been from a cheap high street chain. I'd known no one, and I'd spent the first half an hour trying to find Constantine amongst the crowds.

It hadn't been until I'd stepped out into the ornate gardens at the back that I'd found him, standing near the rose garden, half hidden by a tall hedge. He'd been on the phone, talking to someone in Spanish, and he'd sounded…furious. He'd never usually allowed any emotion to show publicly, so the sound of his fury had shocked me. Then he'd cut the call, slipped his phone into his pocket and covered his face with his hands.

That had shocked me too and, unable to see him in distress and not comfort him, I'd moved across the grass to him, reaching to take his hands.

'Jenny…' he'd breathed, as if he'd been waiting all his life for me, and then…

I shoved the rest of the thoughts away. I didn't want to think about what had happened after that, the explosion of passion that had resulted in the small life growing inside me now.

My other hand dropped to my stomach, curling protectively over it.

I should have told him about the baby. I knew that. But discovering that I was pregnant by the man who'd ripped my heart out of my chest and stomped it into a bloody pulp had been shattering. Which wasn't a good enough reason not to inform him, but I'd told myself that keeping it a secret until at least the three-month mark was a good idea. Until, of course, I'd realised that I hadn't wanted to tell him at all.

He was engaged, and had made his feelings about me very clear, and I hadn't wanted to upend his carefully ordered life with the news that he was going to be a father. He had Olivia, and marriage plans, and it didn't seem fair to derail everything just because he and I had made a mistake.

I'd planned to tell him eventually, but not until my heart felt a little less raw.

My mother, on the other hand, would be thrilled if she knew—'Nothing like a child to keep a man at your side' she'd tell me, even though it hadn't worked with my father, and would likely advise me to take him for everything he had.

But I wasn't like her. I'd never be like her. I didn't want to rely on a man to keep me fed and clothed. I didn't want to end up cynical and bitter. What I wanted was stability and security, two things I'd never had growing up. Oh, yes, and love. I hadn't had that growing up either.

You won't get it with him.

I glanced over at the door.

I'd always thought Con cared for me, but that had been before he'd cut me off for four years without any reason. He'd never explained, so why would I expect anything from him now? And how was that supposed to make me feel stable and secure?

There had been no love in my childhood, no stability and no security, with my mother going from place to place and dragging me with her, looking for men to look after her. She'd never loved any of the men she'd taken up with, she'd only used them. And when she'd got sick of one, she'd found another.

I didn't want that for myself, and I didn't want that for my child. I wanted permanence, a secure home, a job that fulfilled me and a partner who loved me.

I wanted a happy-ever-after, and I knew that wasn't on the table with Con.

Which meant I was going to have to leave.

I'd wait for our child to be born and then, once I'd adjusted to being a mother, I'd contact him again and we would discuss access. But not until then.

In the meantime, I'd get out of here and get back to my hotel, find something to eat and then sleep. My flight back to England the next morning was very early, and I was exhausted.

I moved over to the door and opened it, peering down the corridor.

Silence reigned.

I stepped out of the room and walked towards the stairs, my cheap heels tapping on the unforgiving marble.

At the stairs, another security man in a black uniform appeared. 'Miss Grey?' He glanced down the corridor to the room I'd been in and then back at me. His expression didn't change but it was clear he found my failure to follow orders displeasing. 'Follow me, please.'

I didn't like to be rude, but my anger was still bubbling away inside me, so I gave him a very direct look. 'No, thank you. I was just leaving.'

'Señor Silvera's orders, I'm afraid. There is a volatile situation happening downstairs and I am required to protect you.'

A small, cold shock rippled through me. A 'volatile situation'? What on earth did that mean?

'What kind of—?'

A firm hand gripped my elbow. 'It's nothing to worry about, Miss Grey,' the man said. 'But for your own safety, please follow me.'

Before I knew what was happening I was being hustled down the sweeping marble stairs and towards not the front door, but the back. There appeared to be a large quantity of people milling about in the entranceway, all of them talking loudly.

'What's happening?' I asked, my gut twisting in sudden anxiety. Because it was clear from the looks on the faces of the people that something unexpected and maybe scary had happened. 'Where are we going?'

At the bottom of the stairs, the uniformed staff member urged me down a corridor that led to the back of the house. 'Señor Silvera wants me to tell you that he will be flying you back to England at his own expense.'

Surprise had me almost stumbling over my feet. He was flying me home? That didn't make a lot of sense—not when he'd said something about marrying me. 'But why?' I asked. 'I have a flight booked tomorrow already and a hotel for tonight.'

'He has cancelled your flight and your hotel booking. He thought you'd want to leave tonight. His jet is at your disposal.'

I blinked. We were approaching one of the back doors and I felt as if I'd been caught by a powerful current in the middle of a river and was being borne along helplessly.

This was happening too fast and my brain felt sluggish. I couldn't keep up. Something was warning me, telling me I should pull away and get back to my hotel as fast as I could, but I was tired, and I felt sick, and the thought of being home in my own bed that night was too tempting. Flying in one of Silver Inc's private jets also meant no hassle with Customs or security, no waiting in endless queues or traipsing around airports with heavy luggage. And having to do that felt like too much.

I didn't know why, after telling me he was going to marry me, he was putting me on a plane back to England, but I was too tired to think deeply about it.

Right now, all I wanted was to be home in my tiny, dingy little flat in London.

'Okay.' I tried to retain what dignity I had and not look like a complete mess. 'That sounds…very nice of him.'

The man nodded, and then I was being hurried out through the back of the mansion, where a black car waited. I was bundled into it, and a few minutes later we were driving through the busy Madrid streets.

Some time later we arrived at Silver Inc's private airfield. A jet was already waiting on the Tarmac, the Silver Inc tail livery gleaming in the runway lights.

I was rushed aboard, and I told myself I wasn't disappointed that Constantine wasn't there to say goodbye himself. No, it was a good thing, because now I could relax and put him out of my mind completely. Get back to my job and the plans I'd made for my baby and I.

Because, while I didn't have a partner who loved me, I could certainly provide the stability and security I craved on my own. I had an analytical brain and I'd already prepared carefully for the baby's arrival.

My maternity leave was all booked, as was my maternity care. I'd have to deal with childcare too, once my maternity leave was over, but I had a bit of time to work that out. I'd been saving every penny I'd earned for the last three months, so I had some savings. I could look after myself and my child, and that was the main thing.

I sank into a seat, the soft leather deliciously comfortable. After the emotional turmoil of the wake it was a welcome relief to be in the silent and warm cocoon of the plane, and I could feel myself relaxing, my heart rate slowing.

We were in the air a few minutes later, with a solicitous flight attendant bringing me a cup of ginger tea and a couple of biscuits that she said would settle my stomach. I didn't ask how she knew I'd been sick, but I drank the tea and ate the biscuits and began to feel a lot better. Dinner was brought to me, too, and it was delicious, and after that had been cleared away I relaxed even further into my seat, the low drone of the engines soothing, making me sleepy.

I'd done what I'd promised myself and I'd seen him. That he'd known about the pregnancy already was distressing, and it made me feel horribly guilty, and all his talk of marriage had been confusing, but I was on my way home now.

It was over and done with. All my secrets were out. I wouldn't have to see him again until the baby was born, and that was for the best.

I let out a breath. Perhaps I'd close my eyes and rest. Just for a moment.

CHAPTER FOUR

Constantine

BY THE TIME my jet landed at the private airfield just outside Edinburgh I was once more fully in control of myself.

I'd handled the situation in Madrid, suppressing all mention of Valentin's reappearance. I didn't want any part of that getting out, because I didn't want him controlling the narrative, not until the issue of Jenny and her pregnancy had been sorted out.

My lawyers had informed me that, as expected, he'd made a play for control of the company, but I'd instructed them to stonewall him and his team for as long as they could. And, since they were very good lawyers, they could probably stonewall for years.

I didn't need years, however.

My security staff had let me know that Valentin was now headed to the Maldives with Olivia. I'd sent some of my team after them, to ascertain her wellbeing, but I wasn't going to waste time going after her myself. Valentin wouldn't hurt her. They'd once been close friends, years ago, and Olivia was a strong woman. She'd be able to handle him. All that really mattered was that if he was in the middle of the Indian Ocean he wasn't in Europe, making a nuisance of himself, which meant that I could safely suppress the announcement of his return until I was ready.

He wasn't going to take control of this story or of my company. I wouldn't let him. I'd spent years turning myself into my father's yes-man, since that had been the only way I would eventually be able to take control of the company he'd built. Silver Inc was a powerful force in Europe, and Domingo had wanted to take it global since he'd always been attracted to power. But a psychopath—which, clinically, my father had been, no two ways about it—should never have that much control over anything as large as Silver Inc, and someone had had to steer him in order to limit the damage he could do. That someone had been me, though it had meant my being him to a certain extent, so he wouldn't see me as a threat.

However, that was irrelevant.

What was relevant was that if Val thought he could manipulate me with Olivia and undo everything I'd done over the past fifteen years then he could think again.

This was going to go my way. And while I dealt with that, I would also deal with the issue of Jenny.

She hadn't waited for me, as I'd asked, but when the jet had been offered to take her back to England she'd accepted, no doubt thinking she'd be safely deposited back home in London that evening.

Unfortunately for her, that was not going to be the case.

I hadn't had the time I'd wanted to put the idea of marrying me to her, and that had all been Valentin's fault. But I would make time now.

She would come with me, away from the situation in

Madrid. Somewhere out of reach of everyone, especially Valentin. Somewhere no one but my most trusted staff knew about, where we would have the peace and quiet I needed to discuss my marriage proposal.

That somewhere was Glen Creag, a bolthole I had in Scotland. A remote estate in the Highlands, where there was nothing but sweeping valleys and mountains and a still, deep loch. There was no internet, no TV. Nothing but the wide-open valley and the sky, and thus no distractions.

The jet I'd put her on earlier had landed about an hour before mine, and my staff had informed me that she was still on board and asleep. I forbade anyone to touch her, and boarded the jet myself to get her.

She was curled up in her seat, fast asleep, her long brown hair coming out of its messy bun and falling down around her shoulders. A curl lay across one soft cheek, and as I bent over her I couldn't resist the temptation to pull it away.

Her hair had felt like silk against my skin that night, as I'd buried my fingers in it, tilting her head back to take her mouth. Those full lips had been petal-soft and she'd tasted of chocolate… I'd always had a weakness for chocolate.

I didn't want to wake her. She looked so peaceful curled up in the seat, her hands tucked beneath her cheek like a child. Her long silky lashes fanned out over her cheekbones and didn't even twitch. The trip to Madrid and then back to England again must have exhausted her. She hadn't been well back in Madrid either, though she'd regained some colour, which was good.

A good thing, too, that she didn't know how much it had cost me to keep my distance from her the second

I saw her, not to sweep her up into my arms and carry her away, make her mine the way the beast inside me wanted to.

And she would never know.

Distance was the only way to keep her safe, and detachment the only way to control my own urges, so distant and detached I had to remain.

However, if I was going to transfer her to the helicopter that would take us to Glen Creag, the only way I could do so was to carry her. It was a physical distance I didn't want to close since I couldn't trust myself—not after that night in the garden—but I didn't want anyone to touch her either. So I braced myself against the desire she always generated in me and gathered her up in my arms.

She'd no doubt be very unhappy with me taking her to Scotland instead of London, and she'd probably have words to say, but I didn't want an argument now. She needed her sleep, and I was concerned by how sick she'd been in Madrid. I'd get a doctor to look over her in the morning, but until then she would sleep safe in my arms.

You want her there. You want to keep her there.

Reflexively, I forced the thought away. Regardless of whether I did or not, the need was dangerous and I couldn't allow it.

I bent and gathered her up gently. She was very soft, and very warm, and when I straightened she made a small sound, curling into me and pressing her cheek against my shoulder.

She trusts you.

There was a hot, tight feeling behind my breastbone, and for a second I found breathing difficult. I wanted to gather her closer and guard her against every bad thing.

But that bad thing was me, which made it difficult—

especially when I'd already made one catastrophic mistake with her already.

I would need to be doubly on my guard now.

The leftover anger from earlier in the evening knotted in my gut. Anger at myself and my inability to control my emotions, even after all these years and all the painful lessons my father had taught me. Anger at the mistake I'd made three months earlier that had led to both of us being in this position.

And, unfairly, anger at her for being who she was—the one bright spark in my life. All smiles and joy and a sharp, vital beauty that cut at my soul and tempted me beyond reason. She'd given me her trust and allowed herself to be vulnerable. That way lay only pain as I had good reason to know.

Ignoring the emotion, I carried her out of the jet and down the stairs to the Tarmac. A helicopter, our final mode of transport for the night, waited not far away, the rotors already spinning.

The sound didn't seem to disturb her. She simply snuggled into my shoulder, turning her face against the wool of my suit jacket as if the runway lights bothered her.

I tightened my grip.

Some of my staff came to assist me into the helicopter, but I refused them. I didn't want anyone else touching her and nor did I want to release her. It was a possessive urge from my baser self that I tried never to allow, but it was late, and it had already been a hectic night, so I indulged it.

He can't see you any more. He's dead.

The thought came out of nowhere, but I ignored that too. Protecting her—protecting everyone—from my father had become second nature, and apparently it didn't matter that the bastard was now gone. The reflex was still there.

Eventually we were settled comfortably in the helicopter. I didn't bother putting a headset on Jenny. If the noise of the machine hadn't woken her already then nothing would, and putting a headset on her wouldn't make her lying in my arms very comfortable. I didn't want anything to disturb that. It wouldn't be a long flight anyway.

The helicopter lifted off and soon we were flying into the darkness of the Scottish Highlands.

I allowed myself a moment to relax, automatically shifting the soft weight of the woman in my arms so she would be more comfortable. The movement made me acutely physically aware of her. The press of her rounded breasts against my chest. The curve of her rear settling against my groin.

Soft. Hot.

She smelled of something fragile and sweet, like magnolia blooms or rose petals, with an exciting, delicately musky scent beneath it. A scent that was all her and intrinsically feminine, appealing on a base level to the male in me.

Desire flared inside me, always so strong, and I found myself looking down at her, at the line of her cheek and the upturned tilt of her nose. She wasn't a typical beauty, not like her mother, but she had a warm, vital sensuality of her own that was even more attractive to me.

I'd assumed my marriage to Olivia would include sex, since children were part of the deal, but I hadn't felt any physical desire for her. We'd come together when we wanted to conceive, and perhaps for some release, but nothing more.

If she'd wanted to find passion elsewhere, I'd have had no problem with it, since she'd certainly never find it with me.

But... I couldn't do that with Jenny.

There would be no 'coming together' for the purpose of children, or even for release. My control had to be perfect, and she undermined it too much.

I should never have touched her at all, for example, let alone dragged her down into the grass and taken her like an animal the way I had three months ago. A moment of madness, that was what it had been. That and four years of holding her at arm's length, and the pressure of a constant hunger, a need I hadn't been able to get rid of.

A hunger I'd been fighting since the day I'd noticed that, at eighteen, she wasn't a little girl any more, but a soft, lush woman, with generous curves and the kind of eyes a man could fall into and lose himself gladly, the kind of mouth that could wreak havoc on his body.

And what made it worse was that it was a hunger that went deeper than merely curves and eyes and a soft, pouty mouth. Those I could find anywhere, with any woman. But her gentle warmth and kindness and empathy, the understanding that shone in her eyes whenever she looked at me, that smile... Those I could only find in one person: her.

It was shocking, that feeling. Appalling. Because Jenny was untouchable, pure. She was a bright light that had somehow never been dimmed by living in my father's house, and I couldn't be the one to extinguish it.

Distance was required, which meant our marriage would stay in name only. My self-control was equal to the task, I was sure. Sex was something I could easily do without.

What about her? What if she wants passion? Will you permit her to find it with someone else?

Somewhere deep inside, the beast roared in fury and denial, and I found myself holding her even more tightly, as if something or someone was trying to take her from me.

I gritted my teeth. This was why I had to be so very careful. I could *not* allow my possessiveness, my intense nature, to get free. It was an all-consuming thing if I didn't control it, and it would consume her if I let it.

But I wasn't going to let it.

Which would mean that my expectations of marriage would have to change.

Olivia and I had both decided that our lives would be more or less separate, even if we lived together. She had a company of her own, and while she'd needed my financial help to repay some of her late father's debts, I'd imagined that once the debts had been paid her main focus would lie with Wintergreen. As my main focus was Silver Inc. I'd envisaged us ostensibly living together, but that work and travel would mean we wouldn't spend much time together. And when we had children we'd no doubt parent separately.

However, Jenny didn't have a company. She worked in a shelter for the homeless. I had no idea about her living arrangements and whether they would be suitable for a child. There was also the question of her safety. Domingo had been a ruthless businessman and had earned himself many enemies.

I had tried to mitigate the damage he'd caused wherever I could, but I hadn't managed to prevent everything he'd done. Business deals he'd ruthlessly manipulated, companies he'd torn apart, people he'd fired...

There were people out there who hated me as much as they hated him, people who thought I was like him.

Aren't you, though? Didn't he tell you as much?

I ignored that thought completely.

I didn't care about people's opinions of me, but reputation was important, and the reputation of Silver Inc needed managing. I'd been planning to start improving that soon, but it would take time, and I didn't want Jenny to be adversely affected.

Jenny and our baby.

Something raw rippled through me at the thought of our child, another echo of that intense, possessive feeling. I ignored that too. Both of them would need to be protected, which meant I couldn't allow her to live separately from me.

I had to be there to protect her.

One lock of dark hair had fallen over her forehead and I reached up to push it back, then realised with a jolt that felt like a gut-punch that her eyes were open and she was looking up at me. In the darkness they looked black, gleaming from beneath her lashes.

'Where are we?' she asked huskily. 'What's happening?'

There was no fear in her voice, no anger either, and she made no move to get free. She sounded like a sleepy child on a long car journey.

'We're going home,' I said, conscious that a slight husk had crept into my own voice. 'Go back to sleep.'

'Home,' she murmured. 'That's nice.'

Then she closed her eyes, relaxing again into sleep, as if I was someone she trusted to hold her while she slept.

She shouldn't trust you.

I leaned back in the seat and lifted my gaze from her face, staring straight ahead, out through the front windscreen of the helicopter and into the darkness.

No. She shouldn't.

No one should.

CHAPTER FIVE

Jenny

IT WAS THE sun streaming through the window and shining directly on my face that woke me.

I scowled and tried to burrow into the pillow, because I didn't want to wake up, but that sun was relentless. Plus, my stomach was starting to growl.

The night before had been a strange fever dream, full of the comforting roar of a jet engine, before it changed to the rhythmic sound of helicopter rotors. I had a confused memory of being carried in Constantine's strong arms across the Tarmac, and then feeling warm and safe as I lay against his broad chest, my stomach dropping away as we lifted off into the air. I'd no idea where he'd come from, since he hadn't been on the jet with me from Madrid, but for some reason I hadn't questioned it.

He'd murmured something about taking me home, and I hadn't ask why, if we were flying direct to London, we'd needed to be transferred to a helicopter. I'd been too tired to do more than accept it. When the helicopter had landed, I'd had an impression of wide-open spaces and a cold night wind, and then some stairs, and a long corridor that definitely wasn't in my little bedsit. But I'd assumed it was all part of the dream and had snuggled back down to sleep as soon as I was placed in a comfortable bed with a warm quilt drawn up over me.

I felt as if I'd slept very deeply after that, and it was strange that my alarm hadn't gone off. But I often woke up before it did, so maybe it wasn't so strange. As long as I hadn't missed work I'd be fine.

I yawned and opened my eyes, squinting through the beam of sunlight.

Then I blinked and sat straight up, my heart beating very fast.

I was not in my bedroom.

The room was huge—far bigger than my bedsit— with large windows currently hidden by long, heavy, pale linen curtains. The sun was coming through a gap, lighting the cream-coloured walls. Pale carpet covered the floor, and an antique dresser stood against one wall. There was a small table near one of the windows, a glass vase full of pale camellias sitting on top of it.

The bed I was lying in was huge and wooden, with a carved oak headboard, and it was piled with white pillows, a thick white duvet, and an expensive-looking, very beautiful patchwork quilt over the top.

A shock went through me.

It was clear that what had happened the night before had *not* been a dream.

Constantine *had* been there, and he *had* held me in his arms. We'd been in a helicopter, and he'd told me we were going home and to go back to sleep. But this was *not* home.

I swallowed, my mouth dry, my heart fluttering around in my chest.

Constantine had clearly been liberal with the truth,

but no matter what he'd said to me that night in the garden, and no matter how angry I'd been with him, I trusted him. He'd never hurt me, so presumably wherever this was it wasn't anywhere terrible—there were camellias, for heaven's sake.

But…why?

I slipped out of bed, moving over to the windows and pulling back one of the curtains.

A view over a deep valley ringed by rocky mountains greeted me. There were forests at the foot of those mountains, and lying at the bottom of that valley was a pretty lake.

I shoved back the other curtain, my heart beating faster.

It appeared I was in an old stone manor house that faced the lake, with more stone buildings off to the left. The house was surrounded by green lawns that rolled into the tall, dark forests nearby and ended at the rocky shore of the lake.

The sun was shining on the lawns and the lake itself, turning the water a deep translucent green. On the foothills around the mountains purple heather bloomed, and the beauty of the little valley made me catch my breath.

No, it wasn't anywhere bad. And I was still wearing my cheap black dress, although someone had taken off my shoes and put me into bed. Had that been Con? Had he laid me in that comfortable bed? Pulled the quilt up around me?

And where was I? It looked a little like Scotland, though I'd never been there. But if it was Scotland, why was I here?

I turned from the view, smoothing my dress—a pointless task, since I'd slept in it and it was now hopelessly creased. A shower would be nice, but I had nothing to change into, and finding out what was going on was more of a priority.

Going over to the door, I tried the handle, half expecting it to be locked, and was surprised to find that it wasn't.

Outside was a long carpeted corridor with wood-panelled walls hung with landscapes and portraits. Windows at one end let the sunshine in, making it feel very light and airy.

It was very quiet.

Leaving the bedroom, I padded down the corridor in my bare feet until I came to a large, sweeping set of stairs that led downwards. The stairs were carpeted too, with more half-panelled walls, although this time the paintings on them were of a larger variety. A stag stood majestically before a green forest, his antlers glossy in the sunlight.

I went down the stairs and came to a large entrance hall. There were huge wooden double doors with glass panels to let the light in, as well as expensive silk rugs on the pale carpet. A few tables stood around, set with more flowers and a few sculptures, and—strangely for an entrance hall—there was also a big fireplace.

It was a gracious, luxurious space. A manor fit for an aristocrat.

Still not sure where to go, I went over to the first door I could see near the stairs and pushed it open.

Another large room opened out before me, a sitting room with windows on two sides, one giving a view of the rolling green lawns, the other looking out over the green water of the lake.

The room was full of light, its pale golden walls reflecting the sunshine and making the room seem warm and inviting. Comfortable couches upholstered in pale colours were scattered here and there, while a pair of worn leather armchairs faced each other near one of the windows.

It was a beautiful room, and I would have quite happily thrown myself down on one of the couches with a book, to settle in for a long morning of reading, if it hadn't been for the man standing in the middle of it.

He faced the door and his arms were folded, as if he'd been waiting a long time for me to walk through it.

Constantine.

My heart kicked hard against my ribs.

He wore one of his exquisite handmade suits, this one in dark blue-black wool and, standing there in the middle of the warm, inviting room, he seemed like a black hole, sucking away all the warmth and light, giving nothing back but ice.

His obsidian gaze swept me from head to foot, assessing me as if I was a machine that needed to be fixed or a problem he had to solve. Looking at the icy man standing before me, I thought it difficult to believe that the warm, strong arms holding me the night before had been his.

'I was wondering when you'd wake up.' His deep voice was detached, the lilt of his Spanish accent not making it seem warmer in any way.

I struggled to get my breathing under control and pull myself together, feeling like crying all of a sudden.

I'd thought I'd said goodbye to him in Spain. I'd thought I wouldn't have to see him again, or at least not for a long time.

I didn't want him to be standing there giving me the same coldly impersonal look he gave everyone else. As if that night in the garden had never happened. As if I was a stranger and not his friend. I didn't want him to be there at all.

I wanted to be over him—to give him that same look back, to feel nothing, the way he seemed to—and yet my heart ached and anger wound through me, and I couldn't decide whether to burst into tears or slap him across the face.

Neither was ideal. I'd wept humiliated tears in front of him once before, and I'd rather die than cry like that again. And as for slapping him, while that would be satisfying, like weeping it would also be humiliating. It would betray how badly he'd hurt me, and I didn't want to do that either.

I wanted him to think that I was over him, that I didn't care about him in any way. That his four years of silence didn't matter to me at all.

But it was difficult when he looked so immaculate in his suit, his short black hair glossy in the morning sunlight coming through the windows, that same sun outlining the perfect bone structure of his face.

His beauty had always made me catch my breath. And it wasn't something I'd only gradually come to see over the years. I'd always known it. Even as a child.

He seemed like an icy prince, noble and beautiful and stern, but lonely. Always lonely. Always working like a dog for Domingo, spending long hours in his office whenever he was home. I'd tried to get him to do things with me, like play card games or swim in the pool, or take me to the Prado Museum. But he wouldn't. He had no time, he'd said.

So instead I'd sat reading in his office, so he'd know that he wasn't alone. And I'd liked being near him. I'd liked the way he never told me to shut up when I talked, or that no one was interested in what I had to say. He'd never told me I had to be seen and not heard, because if I wasn't no one would want me for a stepdaughter and then Mummy and I would go hungry.

I'd liked it that he'd listened to me, and I'd known he was listening because sometimes he'd responded. But I hadn't liked it when Domingo had come in and Constantine had sent me away. He'd never talked about Domingo, and whenever Domingo had been near him, he'd tense up, go as cold as ice. I hadn't been sure why, but even back then I'd known that whatever it was, the problem was Domingo, not Con.

He might have been my prince, but I had never been his princess. And I was still just Jenny, his short, round and plain stepsister. With no shoes on her feet and her hair in a mess. Wearing a cheap dress that she'd slept in and now was all creased.

Anger flickered through me. I'd never felt pathetic in front of him before but I did now, and I hated it. It was almost as if I wasn't good enough or didn't measure up. My mother was an expert at making me feel that way and I didn't need it from him.

I lifted my chin, about to say something cutting, when my stomach growled. Loudly.

Constantine's brows twitched. 'You're hungry,' he said coolly.

'The baby is.' I sniffed. 'I'm not.'

'Don't be ridiculous.' He said it without anger, his voice detached. 'We'll talk over breakfast.'

'No,' I said. 'We won't. I have nothing to say to you.'

He ignored me, striding to the door and going out into the corridor. I heard him issue a couple of orders and then he was back, one large hand catching me beneath the elbow as he urged me over to the armchairs near the window.

My anger flickered at his high-handedness, yet I was powerless to resist. His palm was warm against my bare skin, and it reminded me of the dream that hadn't been a dream, of his arms around me, my head resting against his chest, listening to the strong, steady beat of his heart.

I forced the memory away as he sat me down in one of the armchairs, then sat in the one that stood opposite himself.

'I've ordered breakfast.' His gaze pinned me like a black obsidian spike. 'It shouldn't be long.'

I sat rigidly in the chair, trying not to be aware of how comfortable it was and how my instinct was to curl up in it. A childish instinct, borne of trying my best to avoid my mother and her lectures on my appearance and my clothing choices and how I'd never get a man if I didn't make an effort, because I was already starting at a disadvantage due to my face. How I needed to smarten myself up, get some make-up, lose some weight, wear something more flattering. Because how was I going to get ahead in life if I didn't look the part?

Now, with Con sitting across from me, staring at me, I couldn't help but feel that same sense of judgment.

It's different, though. He's not your mother.

True. And he'd never once made disparaging comments about my appearance. In fact, in the months before I'd moved to London, a couple of times I'd sworn I'd seen heat there in his eyes.

But of course I'd been seeing things. And even if he'd opened his arms to me right there, right now, I wasn't going to fall helplessly into them the way I'd had three months ago. Been there, done that. My mother might be moved by a pretty face, but I wasn't.

I stared back at him, trying not to give in to the urge to lower my gaze under the pressure of his. 'Well,' I said, trying to sound as cool as he did, 'I think you owe me an explanation for why I'm not currently in my flat in London, don't you?'

If he noticed my tone, he gave no sign. 'I never promised to take you back to your flat.'

'The man who took me to the car told me I was going back to England,' I pointed out. 'Which was the whole reason I went with him in the first place.'

'He wasn't lying. You were taken back to England.'

'But you—'

'But I what?' One black brow lifted. 'Scotland is part of the United Kingdom.'

So we were in Scotland. Good to know.

'But Scotland isn't England. And I didn't say you could take me to…this place.' I waved at the mountains and the loch outside.

'"This place" is one of my private residences. Glen Creag. It's in the Highlands.'

'That's great. But I don't recall mentioning an over-whelming urge to visit the Highlands someday soon.'

'You didn't. If you'd bothered to wait as I instructed, instead of leaving the mansion, you would know that we're here to discuss the question of marriage.'

An echo of the same shock I'd felt last night rippled through me. 'You said—'

'I said that I wanted to marry you,' he interrupted yet again. 'I meant it.'

'Why?' I was too taken aback to be angry this time.

He couldn't be serious. He couldn't. 'You can't want to marry me, Con. You're engaged to Olivia.'

'Olivia is now out of the picture.' His gaze snapped to the door as a quiet tap announced the arrival of one of his staff, carrying a tray. 'Over here, if you please.'

A smiling, grandmotherly older woman came over and set the silver tray down on the little table positioned between Con and I. On it were eggs and toast, plus a bowl of porridge topped with cream and brown sugar. There was butter and jam, a pot of tea, and a small white china espresso cup full of what smelled like the thickest and darkest of coffees.

'There you are,' the woman said in a thick Scottish brogue. 'Breakfast.' Then, somewhat shockingly, she laid a hand on one of Con's broad shoulders and gave it a gentle pat, as if he was a horse in need of soothing. 'Enough for you too,' she added. 'See that you eat. I won't have any of this "not hungry" nonsense.'

I stared at the woman in surprise, part of me tensing in anticipation of the cold, sweeping look of disdain that Con would no doubt direct at her.

Except he didn't.

'This looks excellent. Thank you, Mrs Mackenzie,' he said, scrupulously polite. Then he nodded at me. 'This is Jenny Grey. Jenny will be staying with us for a while. Please make sure that she is comfortable.'

Mrs Mackenzie gave me a big smile and patted him again. 'Don't you worry, laddie. I'll look after her.'

'N-nice to meet you,' I said, stammering slightly at the shock of Con being called 'laddie'.

'And you, lass.' Mrs Mackenzie gave a satisfied nod. 'Right. I'll leave you both to it.' Then she bustled out.

'Mrs Mackenzie is the housekeeper here,' Constantine

said. 'If there is anything you need, tell her and she'll accommodate you.'

I nodded, distracted by the divine smell of the food and the coffee, and my stomach growled yet again, reminding me of how empty it was. No wonder, considering I'd emptied most of it on Con's shoes the night before.

Ugh. That was not a good memory.

Not that I should be remembering that, or even concentrating on the food, not when he'd just told me that Olivia was 'out of the picture'.

'You mentioned Olivia,' I said. 'What do you mean that she's "out of the picture"? How? And why?'

'The hows and whys are irrelevant,' he said. 'Eat your breakfast. I'll give you the details.'

CHAPTER SIX

Constantine

JENNY WAS GIVING me a mulish look, which was unlike her. Normally there was never any argument between the two of us. This stubbornness she was directing at me was new and I didn't like it.

I'd spent at least an hour downstairs, waiting for her to get up, and while I could have woken her myself, I'd wanted to make sure she had as much sleep as she needed.

Being patient was a strength of mine, and I hadn't thought waiting would be a hardship, yet I'd found myself pacing around and glancing towards the doorway, wanting her to be up so I could see her, talk to her.

I didn't want to admit that I'd missed her these past four years, but I had. Her lack was a constant ache deep in my heart, made worse by those moments in the grass three months ago. And now she was here I wanted to…

But no. Now she was here the question of a marriage between us needed to be sorted out as quickly as possible so that arrangements could be made. Then I could get back to dealing with the Valentin issue. I'd anticipated our discussion would be straightforward, because while she'd clearly have questions, she wouldn't refuse me.

I'd ensure she'd have the best medical care for herself and the baby, and obviously finances would not be a problem. She'd also be protected legally by taking my name, as would the child.

As to the practicalities, we would work something out. I was prepared to negotiate on our living arrangements. If she wanted to live in London I had no problems moving, since the Silvera mansion in Madrid wasn't a home to me. I'd been planning to leave it anyway, so we'd find a house together that would suit us both and the child. It wouldn't be a problem.

And apart from anything else, she loved me. That was what she'd told me that night in the garden, so surely marrying me would not be a bridge too far.

Except you can't love her back.

That thought tugged at me, but it was inconvenient, so I ignored it.

Jenny, however, didn't look as if she was desperate to marry me. Sitting opposite, her black dress creased beyond all hope of an iron, with her hair in snarls over her shoulders, she looked tired and dishevelled and extremely cross.

She also looked so beautiful she stopped my heart.

The memory of her in my arms, warm and soft and relaxed, rose to the surface, making me want to pull her back into them again. But I didn't move. Distance was crucial, otherwise this whole plan wouldn't work.

'I'll eat when I'm ready,' she said firmly. 'Tell me why you're not marrying Olivia and does she know?'

'I'm not marrying her because you're pregnant and she isn't. And, yes, she does know.' Technically, that wasn't correct, but seeing as how she was with Valentin I could safely assume she wouldn't want to marry me now anyway.

You should tell Jenny the truth. Tell her Valentin is back and that he took Olivia. Tell her that she's all you ever wanted, that marrying her would be your greatest joy.

But I couldn't tell her those things. Valentin's return was a separate issue that I didn't want to get into right now, and marrying Jenny wouldn't be my greatest joy. It would be my greatest torment. Because while she'd be my wife, she would never be mine. I couldn't allow it. The possessive part of my nature—the part of me that was my father through and through—would be too strong to deny and I couldn't expose her to that. I wouldn't.

'You don't have to marry me because I'm pregnant,' Jenny snapped. 'This isn't Victorian England, you know.'

I ignored her tone. 'One of the conditions for me marrying Olivia was that she would provide me with heirs.'

'I see.' Jenny's dark eyes were sharp. She looked like a small, round blackbird, eyeing me with disfavour. 'And if someone else happens to get pregnant? What then? Would you get rid of me as easily as you got rid of her?'

You are hurting her. You know how she feels about you.

And she would hate being anyone's second choice, especially given all the lies Catherine had drummed into her about herself. And they were lies. Catherine was a career gold-digger and, while I could understand what had driven her to it, I had never understood her desire to mould her daughter into her own image.

Jenny didn't have that hard, mercenary edge. She was

softer, warmer. She trusted too easily and she gave her heart too readily. After all, she'd given it to me, the worst person in the world for her.

'No, of course not,' I said. 'No one else will get pregnant because I am not sleeping with anyone else.'

She blinked, her pretty mouth opening in surprise. 'So...what? You'll be sleeping with me?'

A thread of raw heat wound through me, making everything inside me tighten. *Dios*, I would love to sleep with her, her warm, lush little body pressed against mine. I could have her whenever and however I wanted her, sink inside her welcoming heat...

But I couldn't allow it.

'No. That is not the kind of marriage I'm offering you.'

'Then what kind of marriage are you offering me?'

'It will be one in name only.'

Her dark eyes went wide. 'What? Why?'

I steeled myself against her surprise. The beast in me wanted to tell her that I was mistaken, that it would be a full marriage in every way there was. But I couldn't.

Instead, I said, 'Because the purpose of sex would be to conceive, and you are already pregnant.'

'But I—'

'That is the kind of marriage I was going to have with Olivia, and I will not change it just for you.'

Disappointment crossed her lovely face, although she tried to hide it, and I could feel it tug at me too.

It was not what I wanted. Yet it was necessary.

'Eat your food,' I said curtly. 'You've had nothing since last night and you're looking extremely pale.'

The disappointment had ebbed from her dark brown eyes, but little sparks still gleamed there, signs of her stubborn spirit. A reminder that while Jenny Grey might look small and soft and vulnerable, she wasn't as defenceless as she seemed.

I still remembered the day my father had stormed into my study while she'd been curled up in her customary seat. I'd instantly known that he was in one of his cold, cruel moods and had tried to order her out of the room. When he'd been like that, anyone and anything had been a target, so I'd tried to make sure that the only target he found was me. I was as cold as he was, and I could take anything he threw at me.

Yet before I'd been able to speak Jenny had slipped off the chair and reached for my father's hand, taking it in hers and pulling on it. 'Mummy says you'll take me for a walk in the garden, Stepfather. Please? I love going for walks with you.'

I'd braced myself to leap over my desk, put myself between her and him, save her from whatever he was about to do. Yet before I'd been able to move, instead of raising his hand to strike her, or utter some casually cruel remark, he'd stared at her with distaste. Then he'd shaken off her hand and, without a word, turned and walked away.

She'd looked at me triumphantly and I'd realised then, with sudden insight, that she'd grabbed his hand on purpose. Somehow she'd known exactly what to do to make the terrifying Domingo Silvera uncomfortable enough to leave the room.

I'd never discovered what it was about Jenny that had stopped my father from being abusive towards her, but something had. And that was when I'd understood that if Jenny was in my office he wouldn't bother me. So I never told her to leave. And, while she'd just been a deterrent initially, I grew to like her soft, cheerful conversation and her laughter, filling up the cold silence of my study.

She had been a light to me even back then.

Now, she looked at me with exasperation and said, 'I'm your friend, Con, not a child you need to take care of. I'll eat my breakfast if I want to. And as for marrying you, the answer is no. I'm not and that's final.'

I stared at her, irritated. Her refusal was something I hadn't anticipated. I knew the idea of being looked after financially would remind her too much of her mother, but thought we could work out an arrangement where she earned her own money. And if sex was the issue…

Yes, what about sex?

The thought made me want to growl, so I shoved it away.

'Why not?' I tried not to let my irritation show.

'Because you don't love me.' Her voice was flat. 'You're only marrying me because I'm pregnant.'

'Of course I don't love you,' I lied—because I could never tell her the truth. 'We had that discussion three months ago. And what's wrong with marrying you because you're pregnant?'

The soft fullness of her mouth compressed. 'There's nothing wrong with it, but that's never been what I want, Con, and you know that. I want stability and security—especially after the kind of childhood I had with Mum—and that doesn't just mean money and a roof over my head. Those things are great, yes, but our child needs more than that.' Her chin rose a little higher. 'It needs to be loved. And so do I.'

The thread of anger pulled tight, making me tense. I didn't want to have this discussion. It was pointless when I could never give her the love she wanted. My love was too tainted, too toxic, and I would never wish that on her, never, ever.

Still, the possessiveness that had somehow woken up roaring, that wanted both her and the child, only tightened its hold.

What if I let her go and she married someone else? Someone who gave her what she wanted? Someone who would be a father to my child…

No.

The denial was so absolute there was no resisting it.

I could never trust another man with my child, or with Jenny. She saw the best in people. She never saw the worst. She might marry someone she thought was a good man, someone who could turn out to be even worse than I was, someone like Domingo…

Everything in me went cold. I would die before I allowed that to happen to any child of mine or to Jenny.

'Marrying me will give you both security and stability,' I said icily, putting all my will in my tone. 'They're a better guarantee than love.'

She gave me a strangely sympathetic look that I didn't understand. 'Are you sure about that?'

'Love is irrelevant to this conversation. You and I are friends, and that surely is enough. Do you really want to be a single mother? All on your own?'

'Are we friends, though?' Her gaze was very direct. 'When you haven't spoken to me for years?'

Guilt shifted inside me.

I couldn't tell her why I'd cut off contact with her, why I'd had to keep her at arm's length. I couldn't tell her that I longed to give her all the love she was craving, and all the passion too, but that that was a road I couldn't start down, no matter how badly I wanted to. Not when I knew how toxic my emotions could be.

So I ignored the question and said, 'I know you don't want to rely on anyone for money, but as my wife you'd never have to worry about finances again. We can come to some arrangement where you could have your own business and your own income. We can live in London, if you prefer. We don't have to stay in Madrid.'

'Con, I can't—'

'You can travel the world…buy anything you want.' I tried to think of other things that might convince her, other things she might want. 'Silver Inc already donates to and sponsors a great many charities, but more can always be given. The shelter you work at, for example. They must need money.'

She only stared at me. 'Have you finished?'

I could feel my jaw getting tight. 'Yes.'

'Good.' Her chin jutted with that stubbornness I was starting to dislike intensely. 'Because the answer is still no.'

My temper tugged at the leash I'd put on it. The beast in me was excited by the challenging signals she was sending, making bolts of heat arrow straight to my groin. I tried not to pay any attention, tried to concentrate on my detachment instead. 'What can I do to convince you? Anything at all, it's yours.'

'You can't buy my agreement, Con.' Her pretty features had softened and there was real regret amongst the sparks in her dark eyes. 'I'm sorry, but I have to be firm on this. I'm marrying for love, both for me and for my child, and that's final.'

Frustration coiled tight inside me, threatening all my emotional distance.

'So if someone else comes along,' I ground out, 'someone who says he loves you. You'll marry him?'

'If I fall in love with him too, then yes.'

'And what if you're wrong? What if he turns out to be a terrible person? What if he hurts you? What if he hurts our child? Because it's my child too, do not forget that.'

Her mouth softened. Was that pity in her eyes? 'I know,' she said quietly. 'Believe me, I've never forgotten that the baby is yours. But you don't have to worry. I will never fall in love with a man like that.'

Except she had, hadn't she? She'd fallen in love with me.

'Jenny,' I began, to say what, I didn't know.

But she only said, 'Con,' and put her hands on the edge of the table and gave me a very serious look. 'You need to take me back to London. We'll figure out something when it comes to the baby later, but right now I want to go home.'

'Jenny,' I began again. Because she had to listen to reason. I needed to explain myself further, more clearly.

'No,' she said calmly, regretfully. 'That's my final word.'

Then she pushed her chair back and got to her feet.

What? She was leaving?

My frustration intensified. Because she needed to understand. She *had* to. She was vulnerable, and so was our child, and I couldn't leave her unprotected. I had never done so before, and I wasn't about to start now.

'Sit down.' I tried to stay cold, yet that growl crept into my voice all the same. 'Sit down and eat your breakfast. I haven't finished speaking.'

Jenny merely shrugged before turning around and walking away.

I did not like that. I did not like that one bit.

'Jenny.' Her name came out low and harsh and I didn't bother moderating it. 'Sit down.'

But again she ignored me, going to the door.

'Jenny,' I growled.

She walked through it.

People did not walk away from me. People did not ignore me. People who knew what was good for them obeyed whenever I gave a command and they certainly never *shrugged*.

This concerned the safety of our child. *My* child. I wouldn't tolerate it.

I shoved my chair back before I even knew what I was doing and went striding after her. 'Don't you dare walk away from me. I haven't finished.'

But the corridor outside was empty.

I caught a glimpse of movement on the landing and started up the stairs after her, taking them two a time, gritting my teeth against the sudden and inexplicable anger that threatened to swamp me.

In the back of my mind a warning sounded. I was allowing my temper to get the better of me, that I needed to stay in control. But control had always been difficult with her. Heat and hunger consumed me whenever I was in her presence, and no matter how hard I tried I couldn't detach myself the way I normally did.

All I could think about was some other man hurting her, some other man hurting my child and me not knowing about it. Me not being able to stop it.

That had been my childhood—mine and Valentin's—and there had been no one to protect us, no one to save us.

I knew what happened to children at risk. I knew it intimately.

My anger pulsed like a giant heartbeat, and even though I tried to keep it contained I couldn't as I stormed down the corridor after her.

She reached her bedroom and disappeared into it, slamming the door behind her.

I stopped outside it, fighting to regain my control. 'Open the door. Open it now, Jenny.'

I did not like closed doors. Not at all.

'No!' she shouted from the other side. 'I'm not saying another word. I'm not marrying you, Con, and you can't make me.'

No? That was unacceptable.

She had to see reason. She *had* to.

I put my hand on the door handle and turned it.

Only to find that she'd locked the door.

A low growl formed in my throat and something dark exploded in my head.

A memory. Me, sitting outside Valentin's locked door, hearing nothing but silence from the room inside. Knowing how much he hated being confined. Knowing deep down that the reason he'd been locked in his room was because of me.

Locked doors. I *hated* locked doors.

My fury burst from the cage I'd kept it in, dark and unstoppable, propelled by the fear I could never escape.

'Get away from the door,' I ordered, my voice so low and guttural it didn't even sound like mine. And in the gap beneath the bottom of the door and the floor, I could see the shadow of her feet disappear as she did what I'd said.

Then I kicked it in.

CHAPTER SEVEN

Jenny

CON'S VOICE WAS barely recognisable, yet animal instinct had me stumbling back from the door before I could even think. Then it suddenly burst open, bouncing on its hinges and slamming into the wall with a crash, making me gasp aloud in fright.

He stood in the doorway, breathing fast and hard, and oddly, considering he'd kicked down my door, all my brief fear abruptly drained away.

There was nothing of the cold, detached man who had sat across from me downstairs, insisting that I marry him. Offering me all sorts of things except the one thing I wanted. The most important thing of all: love.

It had twisted my heart in my chest to realise that he didn't seem to understand why I'd want it. That he thought money and travel, him protecting me, would be enough. Then all that stuff about me falling in love with someone else...

As if I ever would.

As if he wasn't the only man for me and would always be.

He hadn't been listening, though, and that hurt too.

Because he'd always listened. Now it was as if I was talking in a language he didn't speak and didn't want to understand.

I hadn't been able to bear it. So I'd got up and walked away.

Some part of me had been thrilled to hear him growling at me to stop, to sit down, that he hadn't finished speaking. Thrilled to hear his voice change, to hear all the ice melting and threads of anger lace through its darkness. I'd never liked confrontation, but there was something exciting about confronting him and making him mad. It meant that he cared about the things I said, even if the only hurt was to his pride.

Right now, though, it was clear from the expression on his face that this was about more than hurt pride.

His perfect features were hard with fury, his strong jaw set, black eyes full of flames. It was a glimpse of the burning, raging furnace of emotion that lay in the deepest part of him.

I'd seen that furnace only once before: in the garden that night.

My breath caught, the heat he radiated making something in me spark like dry tinder.

He strode towards me, and before I could move he'd grabbed my upper arms in his long, blunt fingers, his grip just on the right side of painful.

'Never lock a door to me again!' His eyes blazed.

He was so tall, so powerful. He'd just kicked in the door and now he had me in his grip. He could crush me as easily as he'd crush a butterfly.

But I wasn't afraid of him. I'd *never* been afraid of him. His presence had been a cool balm to my own raw emotions, his study a place of peace. He'd never turned me away, never told me to be quiet. He'd never judged me or upbraided me for not being pretty enough, or intelligent enough, or good enough. He was a rock, a safe haven, a shelter.

He would never, ever hurt me.

And I loved this raw display of emotion. Because he never let himself go, not like this. Never, ever. The only time I'd seen him lose control had been that night in the garden. The night all the ice had melted, allowing the man he was beneath it to be set free.

A man who wasn't frozen all the way through, but who burned like the sun.

You did this to him. This was all you.

My heart was bursting with a complicated kind of excitement and a fear that he might do something I'd like, something that would make all the vows I'd made to myself about not falling into his arms go up in flames.

Yet as I looked up into his burning eyes I realised I wasn't the only one who was afraid. Underneath all that anger, he was afraid too.

Ignoring his grip, and the fury in his expression, I reached up and touched one of those perfect cheekbones, brushing it gently. 'Something's wrong,' I murmured. 'What is it?'

The look in his eyes flared, as if my reaction wasn't what he'd expected. Then his grip on me tightened, and before I could say anything else he bent his head and his mouth came down on mine.

I couldn't say that I hadn't anticipated it. And I couldn't say I hadn't longed for it with every cell of my being.

The kisses he'd given me that night I'd never forgotten, even if afterwards there had been nothing for me but humiliation. They'd been my first, hot and rough and intense. Feverish. As if all the heat inside him had been channelled into those kisses.

It was the same now.

He kissed me hard and with total ownership, his tongue pushing into my mouth, exploring me with a desperate intensity I couldn't fight. I shuddered, trembling as he let go of my upper arms and plunged his fingers into my hair, tugging my head back.

He tasted dark and hot, like strong coffee, and he ravaged my mouth like a pirate.

I shouldn't want this. I knew that deep in my heart. And allowing him to kiss me like this was a recipe for disaster. I should push him away, tell him no, say that he couldn't get around me that way.

But…he'd looked afraid. And the desperation I could taste in his kiss told me that something was wrong. He was hurting in some way and I wanted to soothe him the way I always had, ease his pain.

I didn't know what to do to help. All I could do was put my hands on his broad chest and lean into him, press myself against him. Let him know I was there and that he could take anything he wanted from me, anything at all.

For a moment that hot, dark, blinding kiss consumed my world. Then abruptly he tore himself away and turned, striding to the door and going out without a single word.

Leaving me standing in the middle of the room, trembling all over.

Instinct told me that going after him would be a mistake, that I needed to give him space to calm down, so I waited for my heartbeat to slow and the trembles to stop. My lips burned. I could still feel the pressure of his beautiful mouth on mine, still taste his heat. The imprint of his fingers on my upper arms lingered and I found myself rubbing where he'd gripped me, even though he hadn't caused me pain.

I had no idea what had happened. He'd been angry at my refusing his proposal, but something about me locking the door had set him off. And then, when I'd touched his face, I'd seen something else blaze. Then he'd kissed me hard and deep and desperate. Only to pull away the next second and leave the room without a word.

It didn't make any sense. Why had he kissed me? He'd told me that night, after he'd pulled away, leaving me lying on the warm grass, that it would never happen again. That it had been a mistake, an aberration.

But if it had, why had he kissed me again? There had been raw heat in that kiss and, yes, desperation. But was it for me? Or…had it been about something else?

Something else, it had to be. After all, he'd said that the marriage he wanted would be a platonic one. Not that I'd be marrying him anyway.

I swallowed and rubbed my arms again, ignoring how sensitive my mouth was, shoving the taste of him and the feel of his hot, hard body against mine from my head.

It was true. He could give me financial security, and stability too. A home that I wouldn't have to leave because Mum had been dumped by her latest man and we had to find a cheaper flat. And I wouldn't have to sleep with a chair wedged under the doorhandle, because her latest boyfriend was creepy and I didn't trust him.

Con could give me safety.

But it was also true what I'd told him downstairs, that security was about more than money, more than a nice house and a security detail.

My mother had spent years not only picking apart my appearance, but also telling me that I shouldn't be so sensitive, so emotional. That I needed to grow a spine and a hard shell because life was cruel, and you had to protect yourself from it any way you could.

I'd tried, because I'd loved my mother, and she'd been so bitter, and I'd only wanted to make her happy. She'd complained a lot about me being a barrier to her 'getting ahead', and even though when I was a kid I'd never known what 'getting ahead' meant, I'd known enough to realise that being a barrier was a bad thing. So I'd been obedient when she'd wanted me to be seen, and when she hadn't wanted that I hadn't been seen.

But that hadn't been enough for her. *I* hadn't been enough for her.

She'd gone from man to man, sugar daddy to sugar daddy—for money, ostensibly, but I'd known money wasn't really what she'd wanted. She'd wanted love.

I didn't want my life to turn into hers—endlessly dragging my poor child around in a vain attempt to find it—and I knew that was what would happen if I married Con.

Only it would be worse. Because while I loved him, he didn't love me, and that would only turn into bitterness for us both in the end.

Though I shouldn't be angry at Mum. It wasn't her fault she was the way she was. She'd been young when she'd had me, and my father had dumped her as soon as he'd found out she was pregnant. She'd lived a hand-to-mouth existence after I was born, subsisting on a single mother's benefit until she'd found out that having no qualifications or work experience weren't barriers when it came to charming men.

Mine had been a lonely, uncertain, unsettled childhood, and I didn't want that for my child. So no matter how much a part of me wanted to give in, to tell Con that of course I'd marry him, I wasn't going to. I needed to be strong.

Eventually I went over to where my handbag rested, on a small armchair near the window, and extracted my phone. I assumed Con hadn't let my mother know what was happening, which meant that I needed to. Then again, maybe he had. He always planned for every eventuality after all.

I also needed to let the charity who operated the shelter for the homeless where I worked know what was happening, too. They struggled to get enough help as it was.

I pulled up the number from my contact list, only to realise there was no cell phone service. Well, great. So not only had Con brought me to his Scottish bolthole without asking me, I also couldn't tell anyone I was here.

Anger joined the tangled mess of emotion sitting in my gut, but before I'd had a chance to untangle it a soft knock came on the door frame. I looked up from my phone and saw Mrs Mackenzie standing in the doorway, bearing a silver tray carrying the breakfast I'd walked away from downstairs.

'Mr Silvera thought you might prefer to take breakfast in your room.' She had very blue eyes that twinkled as she smiled at me. 'Come on, pet,' she said, bustling in and putting the tray down on a small side table. 'Eat up, there's a good girl. Then you'll want a shower and some clean clothes, hmm? I'll find you something to wear.'

My mother's parents were both dead, so I'd never had a grandmother, and Mrs Mackenzie's grandmotherly air eased my lonely soul. So I didn't protest as she poured me out a cup of tea and arranged everything on the table, keeping up a stream of reassuring chatter.

The breakfast was delicious, and I felt better for it, and after Mrs Mackenzie had taken away the breakfast things I went into the huge en suite bathroom to investigate the shower. There was a deep clawfoot bath near one window, and a large tiled walk-in shower tucked away in an alcove. Everything was white and clean. I couldn't get my clothes off fast enough.

The water in the shower was hot and the pressure fantastic, and as I washed my hair and body I let myself think of nothing at all.

After I was clean, I wrapped myself in one of the large, white fluffy towels that hung on a rail, and went back into the bedroom.

The bed had been made and a dress laid out on the thick white quilt. It was a simple wrap dress in deep red, and as I bent to examine it I saw the fabric was silk.

Mum had always insisted that 'dressing the part' was important, so she was never without her make-up or her designer clothes—when she could afford them—and never less than immaculate.

'It's all about confidence,' my mother had told me. 'No one wants a limp dishrag.'

But I hadn't had any confidence. She hadn't been interested in my marks at school, and she hadn't wanted to hear it when I'd told her of my childhood dream to become a doctor.

'You don't need all of that,' she'd said dismissively. 'Get some work done on your face, stop eating pastries, and find yourself a rich man.'

That had been the day I'd realised that the women Con was constantly photographed with were always beautiful.

They were always successful women too, models, fashion designers, politicians, CEOs. There had even been a world-renowned human rights lawyer, and I'd toyed with the idea of going to law school. But my marks hadn't ended up being good enough for medicine, let alone for law, and I hadn't been interested in fashion.

I didn't have the looks to be a model, or the contacts to be a politician, or the ruthlessness needed to be a CEO. I couldn't be one of those women at all.

Ironically, it had been a conversation with Con that had decided me. I'd been complaining about how I didn't know what to do with my life, and he'd asked me what mattered to me most in the whole world. *You do*, I'd wanted to say, but I hadn't.

Beyond that, what I'd wanted was to help people. And, after more discussion, he'd helped me figure out that charity work was definitely within my skillset. Eventually I'd found a job at the shelter. That didn't depend on looks, or school marks, and no one cared what I wore. I was good with people, and I was organised, plus I'd discovered I had a talent for fundraising, which the charity was pleased about. And that had been enough.

Gingerly, I touched the fabric of the dress. It was warm and soft against my fingers. It had been set out for me, obviously, though I'd no idea where it had come from. Did Con have a selection of women's clothes here? Was it Olivia's, perhaps? If it was, there was no way it was going to fit me.

'Here we are, pet.' Mrs Mackenzie came bustling in again, this time with an armful of silky, lacy-looking garments. 'Some smalls for you.'

I blinked as she put what she was carrying down on the bed. Underwear, from the looks of things. 'But I—'

'Don't worry.' She smiled. 'Mr Silvera had some things bought for you in Madrid. They're all your size and will fit a treat. He says you're to make yourself at home, do some exploring of the manor and the grounds. If you need anything, there's a bell on the tray in the hall. Just give me a tinkle.' She gave me the same gentle pat on the shoulder that she'd given Con downstairs. 'And don't fret about Mr Silvera. His bark's worse than his bite.'

I wanted to tell that, yes, I knew that already, but she bustled off before I could.

I stared down at the lovely clothes set out on the bed and let out a breath. Well, I had two choices here. I could refuse the clothing and keep my cheap chain store dress. Call Mrs Mackenzie back and demand to be transported back to London.

Or...

I could put on the dress and find Con, demand that he tell me why he'd kicked down my door. Why he'd kissed me. Why, when he'd taken me so desperately three months earlier, a platonic marriage was all he was offering. Why, when he'd ghosted me for four years, he was so desperate to marry me now.

Ah, but it wasn't a choice at all in the end, was it? I knew what I was going to do already.

Slowly, I began to dress.

CHAPTER EIGHT

Constantine

I SAT IN the chair in the little crofter's cottage I'd had remodelled into an office, staring out of one of its windows. It gave a perfect view over the lawns and the soft grey stone of the manor house, with the dark green of the loch beyond it.

The crofter's cottage was ancient, with thick stone walls, and I preferred it to the panelled walls of the den in the manor house since it was very private and there was less chance of someone stumbling accidentally into it.

I allowed no one in here, not even the cleaning staff.

Since there was no service in the valley I'd had it fitted out with a satellite internet link, so I could work, and work was what I should have been doing.

I'd already put in a couple of hours, first making sure news of Valentin's arrival had been contained, before getting intelligence on what was happening in the Maldives.

Olivia was still being treated well, and was apparently in no hurry to leave. I wasn't worried about her. Valentin might have stolen her from me while also trying to take my company, but he was my twin. I knew him. And he'd loved her once. If what he felt for her now was even a tenth of what I felt for Jenny, then Olivia was in safe hands.

Valentin was probably expecting me to go after him, however. Which meant I wasn't going to, especially if Olivia was in no danger. She was a strong woman. That was part of the reason I'd chosen her as a potential wife. She could manage whatever nonsense he was engaging in. Their friendship as children had grown into something more as teenagers, and it had once made me jealous. At least until I'd discarded jealousy along with all the other emotions that used to trouble me.

At least until Jenny had come along.

I'd used to feel nothing at all when I'd thought about my brother, but there were reasons I'd never spoken to her about him, mainly because she would ask questions about him, about our childhood, about Domingo, and I'd known I couldn't tell her those things. Not when she'd had the uncanny ability to reach inside me and coax emotion out of me whether I'd wanted her to or not.

As if on cue, a small figure stepped out of one of the manor's doors and stood for a moment, gazing around, a brilliant splash of red against the grey stone walls.

Everything in me clenched tight. Valentin was abruptly forgotten.

Jenny. And she was wearing the dress I'd bought for her.

I gripped the arms of the chair, my fingers digging into the expensive leather as the memory of what I'd done only that morning came flooding back. Of finding the door locked and something in my head exploding. Of kicking the door and watching it crash open. Jenny, white-faced, stumbling back.

I'd still been in the grip of that rage and I'd stormed in there before I'd even known what I was doing, grabbing her by her upper arms and roaring at her.

Her face had gone pale with shock, her dark eyes huge, and while a part of me had regretted scaring her, another had been savagely glad. Because now she would see why being in love with me was such a bad thing, why opposing me, pushing me, was dangerous. I would never hurt her physically, but I had no emotional control around her and I could hurt her in other ways. Ways I'd learned at my father's knee.

Except then she'd put her hand to my cheek in the gentlest of caresses. And she'd looked straight at me, past the anger, right down to the pain and fear I kept locked away inside. And she'd asked me what was wrong.

She'd always been able to do that. She'd always been able to see past my detachment, see the boy I'd once been years and years ago. The boy who'd rescued chicks from fallen nests and cried over dead kittens. The boy who'd once wanted to be a pirate or a cowboy, who'd loved his twin brother and had tried his best to protect him.

Jenny had reached out to that boy, and that boy wanted to reach out to her in return.

But I couldn't allow it. My anger and my stunning loss of control had been proof enough of that.

I shouldn't have kissed her, either. But I'd already been undone by the touch of her fingers on my cheek, and the depths of my own anger and fear had only undone me further.

Kissing her had been instinctive. The beast in me had been tired of distance and it had wanted her, it had needed her, and so it had taken what it could.

I'd expected her to protest or struggle, yet she'd melted

against me the way she had that night in the garden, all soft and hot and giving. Making me want to take and take and take.

Dios. I'd thought my control around her was iron-clad, that the distance I'd put between us these last couple of years had done its job. Yet every time I was in her vicinity that control failed, and nothing I did seemed to prevent it.

The figure in red moved away from the manor, following one of the white gravel paths that led down to the loch's pebbly beach. The wind whipped the dress around, flattening the red silk against her luscious curves. Even from here I could see them, full and rounded, inviting a man's hand.

I could feel myself hardening—a reminder of her physical effect on me—and every muscle in my body went tight.

I needed to do something about it because distance wasn't working. And that only left me with two options: either I gave that possessive part of me what it wanted— which was her, in every way possible—or I sent her away from me for good.

But how can you allow that? When she's pregnant with your *child? What about if she falls in love with someone else?*

That thought made me want to growl with fury and denial, yet I couldn't force her to marry me if she didn't want to. And the more she resisted, the more the beast in me found it a challenge. It kept whispering that there were ways to make her see reason, ways I *could* force her, ways that my father used.

I could use her emotions against her, threaten to take

our baby from her when it was born if she didn't marry me, for example.

Except that was the kind of tactic my father would have employed, and my entire being rebelled at using those kinds of tactics myself.

But if I sent her away I would never see her again. And I would never see my child either. Because if she fell for someone else... Well, I'd probably do something I'd regret, and neither of them needed to be exposed to that.

Perhaps she'll fall for someone good. Someone who'll treat her better than you will.

That was true. That was a possibility and one I couldn't deny her.

Still, I'd have to have them both protected in some fashion.

I would never leave them with nothing.

A weight shifted in my chest at the thought—a heavy, dull ache which I ignored.

The figure in red moved away from the loch, wandering over the rolling lawns surrounding the manor. Then she paused and I could see her turn her head, glancing in the direction of the crofter's cottage where I sat. Her curiosity must have been caught, because she started towards it.

I cursed under my breath. Clearly Mrs Mackenzie hadn't warned her not to come near the cottage, which meant I was going to have to warn her off myself. She couldn't be in here, not in my private domain. It was mine and I guarded it jealously.

Shoving back my chair, I crossed to the door, pulling it open and stepping outside.

She stopped dead as soon as she saw me, and didn't move as I went striding across the lawn towards her.

I found myself staring hungrily at the dress, pleased that, firstly, she was wearing it and secondly it fitted her deliciously. The wrap style suited her curves, highlighting her hourglass figure to perfection, while the red made her skin look creamy and struck warm tones from the deep chestnut of her hair. It flattered her eyes too, lightening the liquid brown into a beautiful copper.

As I came closer I saw her cheeks had gone pink, and she brushed a strand of dark hair behind her ear in a nervous gesture. Was she still remembering that kiss? Was it lingering in her memory the way it was in mine?

Fool. You cannot lose control again.

No, and if I couldn't even look at her without feeling as if I might, then the situation was even worse than I'd suspected. Sending her away was my only option.

My jaw ached, tension flooding through me as I forced my attention from her pretty mouth, meeting her gaze instead.

'Oh,' she said breathlessly. 'I didn't know you were—'

'The cottage is out of bounds,' I interrupted. 'No one is permitted there.'

She glanced at the cottage, then back at me again. 'Okay, sorry. No one told me.'

'I'm telling you now.'

Her luscious mouth flattened, those intriguing sparks of temper glittering in her eyes again. 'You can be polite about it, Con. You don't have to bark orders at me like a drill sergeant.'

I was being an ass to her, and I knew it. Which wouldn't help matters.

'I apologise,' I said stiffly. 'I also apologise for scaring you before.'

She eyed me for a moment, as well she might, since

apologising didn't come easily to me and I didn't do it very often. 'You didn't scare me,' she said. 'You never have.'

'Nevertheless. I should not have kicked the door in.'

Her chin lifted. 'And are you going to apologise for that kiss too?'

A flash of heat went through me. 'Do you want me to?'

Colour stained her cheeks and her gaze wavered, then flicked away.

I stared hungrily at her, noting the goosebumps rising on her arms. That slight breeze came directly off the mountains and was chilly. Perhaps we needed to be inside, where it was warmer, to have this discussion.

Taking a step forward, I caught her gently beneath the elbow. 'Come with me. We need to talk.'

She resisted. 'Do you really have to be so bossy?'

'Well, if you'd prefer to freeze to death then by all means let's continue this conversation out here.' I relented slightly. 'Please, Jenny. The wind is cold and your dress is thin.'

A complicated expression flickered over her face. 'Well...' she murmured after a moment. 'Okay, then.'

I should have let her go then, but I couldn't quite bring myself to do it. Her skin beneath my fingers was warm, and very soft, and I wanted to keep touching it. This might be the last time I ever got to touch her, so I kept my hand beneath her elbow as I urged her towards the manor.

'I'm sorry if I intruded,' she said again as I hurried her along. 'I thought it was okay to explore.'

'It is. I just don't want anyone going near the cottage.' I wasn't looking at her, my attention ahead, but I could feel her curious dark gaze on me.

But there was no point explaining—not when I was going to send her away—so I said nothing.

I thought she might ask why, but she didn't, remaining silent until we stepped through the front doors and into the entrance hall. Then I let her go, turning to face her.

Being outdoors had flushed her skin and made her dark eyes sparkle. She hadn't inherited any of Catherine's delicate blonde beauty, and neither had she any of Catherine's poise. Jenny was always fidgety, biting her lip and tugging at her clothes.

But she was beautiful to me all the same and standing in the hall, in the red dress I'd bought her, giving me a smile, she was even lovelier. Her skin reminded me of delicate pink roses washed by rain. Her chestnut hair lay in loose, glossy waves around her shoulders. There was a vitality to her, a sensuality I'd first noticed that day on the stairs, when she'd been waiting for me to come home.

She'd been all of eighteen, a woman grown, and my body had noticed even if my head had refused to acknowledge it.

All very good reasons to let her go now.

'So, what did you want to talk about?'

The flush to her skin had deepened. She'd noticed me looking at her. Which meant I needed to say my piece and get her out of my immediate vicinity.

'Speaking of that kiss,' I said. 'Yes, I apologise for that too. It should not have happened.'

This time there was no denying the emotion that flickered over her face. Disappointment. 'Do you really think that? Because I don't.'

I didn't want to hear that she'd liked it, that she still wanted me, even though I knew both things were true. I'd tasted the evidence in the heat of her kiss, in the way she'd melted against me, malleable as warm candle wax. I didn't want to feel the satisfaction that turned over inside me at the memory. It made me think of the garden, and the deep pleasure of her arms wrapping around my neck, of her body arching into mine, pressing all those sweet, soft curves against me. And it made me want to push her against the wall and take her now, ease inside her, keep her here in the manor house like the most precious treasure in my hoard.

She kept doing this. She kept undermining my control.

'I'm sending you back to London,' I said, ignoring her question. 'I'll arrange for transport to collect you in the morning, and you'll be home by tomorrow night.'

Jenny's lovely mouth dropped open, her eyes going wide. 'What? But before you were insisting that I marry you. In fact, you wouldn't take no for an answer.'

'I've changed my mind. I'm not going to force you into it if that's not what you want.'

I thought she'd be pleased, yet it wasn't pleasure or relief that rippled over her face, but shock. 'Why?'

'Isn't it obvious? You were very clear that you didn't want to marry me.'

'Yes, but…you were so insistent.' The pretty stain of pink had drained away, her cheeks now pale. 'Why did you change your mind?'

'As I said: you refused me, and I do not force women.' I searched her face. 'You should be pleased. You were clear that marriage isn't what you want.'

Abruptly, she looked away, smoothing down the red silk of her dress. 'It's not. I mean, one day. But…' Her smoothing hands paused, and she glanced back at me. 'What about the baby?'

'You and the baby will be taken care of. We can arrange the details later.'

'Details?' she echoed faintly, as if the word held no meaning for her. 'Right.'

I frowned, trying to follow the expressions on her face, because she wasn't acting at all the way I'd expected her to. 'This is what you want,' I said again. 'Isn't it?'

'Oh, yes, it is.' Her smile had returned, but it looked forced. 'Yes, absolutely.'

Yet from her expression it appeared to be the opposite. Curiosity tightened inside me. Why wasn't she pleased? She didn't want to marry me—not when I couldn't give her what she wanted—so why was she disappointed?

But I couldn't start thinking like that. I had to cut her out of my life and that started now.

'Good.' I made my voice cold and hard. 'Once you're back in London we will not see each other again.'

Her forced smile faded. 'What do you mean?'

'I mean, apart from being the mother of my child you will no longer be a part of my life.'

She searched my face as if she didn't believe me. 'You're serious?'

There was a dull ache behind my ribs, growing stronger, becoming pain. I knew this wouldn't be easy—not for her or for me—yet there was no other option.

There was too much of my father in me.

'I wasn't myself this morning, and I cannot risk you being harmed or scared by my behaviour. I'm not an easy man to be around, Jenny, so it's better for your sake if you are not.'

She was still pale. 'You *are* an easy man to be around,' she insisted. 'I've been around you for years. I mean, not the past four years—which you haven't explained, by the way—but still… I don't understand. Is this an ultimatum? If I won't marry you, you won't see me any more?'

A thin thread of anger wound through me. As if I would stoop to using Domingo's tactics. Except he had couched his ultimatums with charm, so that the person he was giving them to wouldn't realise what he was doing until it was too late.

Domingo Silvera had been a charming psychopath, and no one had ever known his real nature except Valentin and I. We'd had to survive any way we could.

Valentin had survived by disobeying him at every turn.

I had survived by becoming him—at least on the outside.

Are you sure it's just on the outside?

Well, that question was why Jenny had to leave.

'I do not give ultimatums,' I said coldly. 'And I've already made the decision. You will be leaving for London tomorrow morning.'

Her face was white, her eyes very dark, and she opened her mouth to say something. But the pain inside me was too great.

I couldn't stand to be in her presence any longer, knowing that it would be the last time.

So I turned on my heel and went out.

CHAPTER NINE

Jenny

I COULDN'T SETTLE. It was a beautiful day, with the sun shining brightly in the dense blue sky above the valley, the loch reflecting back a perfect dark green. The purple heather on the hills around us was glorious and I contemplated going on a long ramble to explore. Yet I knew I wouldn't enjoy it. Not when all I could think about was what Con had said about sending me back to London. About me no longer being part of his life.

Mrs Mackenzie served me some lunch in a cheery dining room, which had a long, dark oak table and a huge fireplace at one end. It was pretty during the day, with the sunlight streaming in, but I could imagine it at night, with candles in the big brass candelabra flickering and a fire in the fireplace, all warm and cosy.

I'd had a lovely day exploring the manor and its grounds. It was such a beautiful place. And I should be pleased about returning to London. And yet…

Something cold sat inside me.

I'd had all those questions I'd wanted to ask Con, and had faced him expecting a fight. Yet all he'd had to do was tell me he was going to send me home and my questions had gone straight out of my head.

I hadn't expected him to just…give me up.

He can't want you. Why would he?

I knew that was the truth, yet it hurt all the same. After that kiss I'd hoped… But, no, he didn't. It was only my stupid optimism. After all, he'd never given me any sign that he was attracted to me in particular, and that night in the garden, when he'd turned on me so ferociously, he'd been angry and upset. I'd thought afterwards that had been the reason he'd taken me. Not because he wanted *me* but because I was…what? Simply there?

Upstairs this morning, that kiss had been the same. He'd been angry and, again, I'd been there. It wasn't me he wanted, not *me*.

My gut twisted and my heart ached, but I ignored them.

I couldn't think about me. Our child was more important. And if Con was sending me home then that was a good thing, right? I would be the one to provide all the security and stability our child needed, and all the love too. Our child would grow up safe and secure and happy, the way I'd initially expected right from the start.

But shouldn't a child know its father?

Glumly, I moved a tomato around on my plate. I wanted to tell myself that of course a child didn't absolutely need to know its father. I'd never known mine and I was fine, wasn't I?

Then again, perhaps if my father hadn't left my mother I'd have had a more stable upbringing. Perhaps if he'd stayed for my birth he might have wanted me. I might have gone to live with him, and things might have been different...

Except that hadn't happened, and things weren't different.

And by refusing marriage to Con you're denying your child the chance to know him and for him to know his child.

My fork dropped onto my plate with a clatter and I stared down at it, unseeing.

I couldn't deny him that. It wasn't right. Yes, it had been his decision to take himself out of my life and out of our child's, but there had to be a reason for it.

He hid it from most everyone, but he had a deep, caring nature that he'd never hidden from me. Once, back when I was eleven, I'd found a tiny nest of sparrow chicks that had fallen out of a tree in the mansion's garden. The mother bird had been nowhere to be found, so I'd picked the nest up and taken it straight to Con.

I'd known he would help and he had. He'd taken that nest to his study, kept the heat cranked up so the chicks would be warm, and then we'd both sat down at his computer to look up what to feed them. The nest had stayed in his study for a couple of days, and we'd looked after those chicks together until he'd managed to find a local bird sanctuary. Then he'd transported them there himself.

He was a protector, a caregiver. And not just with birds. He'd always made sure that I had a blanket to snuggle under, and he'd made sure that my favourite drinks and snacks were always stocked in the mansion's kitchen. When I'd got older, we'd discussed his plans for Silver Inc, and how he'd wanted to improve conditions for employees. It hadn't seemed to be a simple thing, though I hadn't been sure why.

What I was sure of now, though, was that he'd be a wonderful father, and I couldn't deny him the opportunity to have that connection. Some part of me sensed that he even needed it. Which meant I couldn't allow my own conflicted feelings about him get in the way.

Yes, I wanted love. But my child was more important than my feelings. Con could give me everything I'd always hoped for except love, and while he might not love me, he would love our child. I was sure of it.

Then there was the issue of his donations. The shelter always needed money, and plenty of other charities did too. I could help a lot of people if I married him.

I picked up my fork and shoved the tomato around a bit more. I would be like my mother, of course, marrying a man for his money, and she'd be very pleased to know I was even contemplating it. She'd been encouraging me to get closer to Con for years. But, again, refusing him just because I didn't want to be like her was all about me. It wasn't thinking of our child.

I bit my lip, then speared the tomato with my fork and popped it into my mouth, chewing slowly as the determination that had driven me to Madrid to catch one last glimpse of him hardened inside me once again.

Marriage. It had to be marriage. But I wasn't going to let him have it all his own way. I had to demand a few things of my own, set some boundaries. Otherwise he'd think he could tell me what to do. I wasn't the little girl who'd curled up in his chair and had only wanted to please him. Who'd rushed to get him drinks or snacks, or talked to him when he was sad. The little girl who'd once thought he could walk on water.

No, I wasn't that little girl any longer. He'd seen to that.

If I had to give up what I wanted, then he'd have to give up what he wanted too.

The idea of a platonic marriage, for example.

He might not want me, but he'd had no problem pushing me down on the grass and taking me, just as he'd had no problems taking that kiss this morning.

And I wanted more. I didn't want a platonic marriage, not with him. And I suspected he didn't truly want one himself. Seriously, was he really expecting us to stay celibate for the rest of our lives? Did he think that one time had been enough for me, and as for himself he'd take his pleasure discreetly, with other women?

A burst of possessiveness swept through me and I very deliberately targeted another poor tomato, stabbing it viciously with my fork.

Absolutely not. That would not be happening. The molten core of passion at the heart of him was nobody else's but mine and I would have it.

He was *not* going to deny me.

Full of renewed determination, I got up from the table and helped Mrs Mackenzie clean up—even though she told me not to—then went in search of Con so I could inform him of my decision.

He wasn't around, however, which meant he must be still in the crofter's cottage near the trees by the loch. He'd been very clear that the cottage was out of bounds, which was annoying.

Part of me wanted to go charging over there anyway, just to show him that he couldn't tell me what to do, but I decided that this time he could come to me, so I amused myself in the library that led off from the living area instead. It was a small but cosy room, with bookshelves lining every wall and a small window seat piled with cushions. Unable to resist, I grabbed a book and curled up with it, spending the afternoon reading as the sun warmed me.

I must have dozed, because the next thing I knew it was dark outside, and I was blinking up into Con's dark and disapproving gaze.

He stood beside the window seat, looking down at me, his arms crossed over his broad chest. His expression was as hard and cold as I'd ever seen it. He was virtually radiating ice.

'I've spent the past twenty minutes looking for you,' he said in frigid tones. 'Mrs Mackenzie is going to be serving dinner soon.'

I pushed myself up on the cushions, my heart thumping. I'd wanted to be ready and poised when I told him I'd changed my mind, not groggy from an unexpected nap.

He was already turning away from the window seat, clearly his duty to call me to dinner done, so I slipped off the seat and said, 'Wait. I need to talk to you.'

He paused and glanced back, his black gaze sweeping over me like a chill winter wind.

My red dress was creased, and my hair was a mess, so it came as a shock when that same cold black gaze lingered on my breasts, where the fabric had slipped, and then flicked lower, to where the silk had parted, revealing my thigh.

Instinctively, I went to adjust the fabric, then stopped. Because there wasn't ice in his eyes any more, but…heat.

My breath caught. The air between us was abruptly gathering weight, becoming dense and shot through with electricity.

A muscle ticked in the side of his strong jaw, his eyes gleaming with a dark fire.

Did he…want me? Was that what I was seeing in his eyes? He wasn't upset or angry, and yet…

A wild, intoxicating heat swept through me as I realised that, yes, it was definitely fire in his eyes, and it was directed at me. Short, plain, dumpy Jenny. Then hard on the heels of that realisation came another: I'd assumed I had no power when it came to him, that all the power was on his side. I'd always wanted him, but he didn't want me, and that was the end of it. He was beautiful, powerful and rich, while I was none of those things.

But that wasn't quite true, was it?

My mouth went dry, my heart rate through the roof. I'd thought I'd have to work at convincing him to give me a full marriage, but maybe I wouldn't.

Maybe I had some effect on him after all.

To check, I bent to adjust the silk around my thigh, while at the same time allowing the fabric around my breasts to gape. When I glanced up at him from beneath my lashes, trying to be covert about it, I noted where he was looking. And it wasn't at my face.

A thrill went through me, electric and hot.

It was me, wasn't it? I did affect him.

Do you, though? Or is it just your breasts? Your mother always did say that men are easily distracted by a low-cut dress.

I shoved that thought away. It didn't matter whether it was me or not; what mattered was the small amount of power my femininity afforded me. And while it felt wrong to use it, since it was the kind of power my mother had always thought so important, it was still power. And I'd never had any before.

'What is it, Jenny?' he asked, his voice not quite as cold as it had been a second ago.

Slowly I adjusted the silk at my breasts, not missing how his gaze followed the movement of my hands. 'I've been thinking,' I said breathlessly, 'about your marriage proposal and about leaving, and I think I might have been a bit…premature.'

Constantine went very still, and this time his gaze met mine with the force of a hammer-blow. 'What did you say?' His voice was quiet and icy and deadly.

I lifted my chin, looked him straight in the eye. 'I said, I've changed my mind. I don't want to go back to London. I think I'll accept your proposal and marry you instead.'

CHAPTER TEN

Constantine

JENNY STOOD WITH the window at her back, the red silk dress now firmly wrapped around her curves, her hair in a loose dark skein hanging down over one shoulder.

I should have been paying attention to what she'd said, because it was important. But I couldn't get the sight of all that pale, creamy skin she'd flashed as she'd adjusted her dress out of my head. Or the glimpse of the red lace bra she was wearing underneath it.

The night we'd had sex, I hadn't seen her naked. She'd been in a dress that hadn't suited her, and all I'd wanted to do was strip her bare, see her glory for myself. Except that night there hadn't been time.

There was time now, though, and I could see myself tugging the tie at her waist and pulling away the red silk. Noting how the red lace of her bra cupped her pretty breasts, then putting my hands on them, stroking her satiny curves, tasting her. I'd lift her onto the window seat and rip away her underwear entirely, so she was naked, and then I'd—

'You did hear me, didn't you, Con?'

I blinked, ruthlessly grabbing my thoughts from the

gutter and directing my attention back to her. Because, yes, what she'd said was important. Vitally so.

'You've changed your mind,' I said. 'You want to marry me after all, correct?'

Her cheeks were flushed, as if she'd read my mind and seen all the dirty things I wanted to do to her, and her warm brown eyes darkened.

'Yes,' she said. 'I've been thinking about it. It's not right for our child not to know you. I never knew my father, and maybe if he'd stayed things might have been different. But he didn't, and I... I don't want that for our baby.'

Heat flashed through me, an electric current that seemed to charge every part of me. My heartbeat was fast, my body hardening, that possessive, animal part of me already howling in triumph.

I wanted her. I wanted my baby. I wanted a family. I wanted *everything*.

But you can't. You're going to send her away because that's your best option.

Yes, that *had* been the best option when she'd refused me. She wasn't refusing me now.

I didn't move, keeping myself very, very still. 'I have said I will provide for you. Marriage isn't a requirement.'

'I understand that.' Her delicate hands fluttered. 'But it's not just about our child needing its father. I think you might...need your child, too.'

Every muscle in my body ached with tension, with longing, because she wasn't wrong. I had no idea what kind of father I'd be, but I knew exactly what kind of father I *wouldn't* be. And whether I needed a child or not was beside the point.

I would have one.

A child that was mine to protect. Mine to keep safe. I could not give that up.

'Very well,' I managed, forcing the words past the urge to growl that rose up inside me. 'But I still won't ever be able to give you love. That hasn't changed, Jenny.'

'I know.' Her fluttering hands stilled. 'But that brings me to another point. I don't see why you get to have it all your way. If I have to give up something, then you have to give up something too.'

My patience was thinning, my blood running too hot for me to be near her. 'And what should I give up?' I demanded gracelessly, needing to be away from her.

Her dark gaze was direct. 'A platonic marriage.'

I froze, every muscle, every cell in my body, electrified. 'What?' My voice sounded hoarse, unlike mine.

The colour in her cheeks deepened. 'I don't want to be celibate for the rest of my life, and I don't want another man. I don't want you going elsewhere for s-sex either.'

The beast shifted inside me, acquisitive, possessive. The hunger of a boy who'd been denied everything precious to him. The desperation of a man who now realised there had only been one thing he'd ever truly wanted.

Her.

As a child, I'd been forbidden any emotional attachments, and as an adult I still had to be careful. Because my father had had no compunction in using emotional attachments to get what he wanted. He hadn't cared who he hurt in the process, but I had, so I'd made sure that no one got close to me. I'd kept my distance by being hard, by being ruthless, by being cold.

But Jenny had somehow got past all my defences and found her way into my heart.

I still remembered the day I'd fallen in love with

her. I'd returned to Madrid after an extremely hard six-month stint in the States, setting up a new Silver Inc company office.

I'd come home very late and headed straight to my room, only to find Jenny sitting at the top of the stairs dressed in nothing but an oversized T-shirt. The moment she'd seen me she'd leapt to her feet and her face had lit up as if someone had turned a light on inside her.

It had been me she was waiting for. Me who'd turned on that light.

'I just wanted to tell you that I'm so glad you're home,' she'd said. 'And that I missed you.'

People were afraid of me. They never lit up when I walked into a room. They were never glad I was home, and they certainly didn't miss me.

How could I not have fallen in love with her in that moment? How could I have resisted?

And I hadn't resisted. But I'd known that there could be nothing at all between us. She'd been only eighteen and I nearly ten years older. My emotions had been intense, toxic things that I would never expose her to.

So I'd distanced myself from her. I'd pushed her away.

That had hurt her, I knew that, and I knew if I denied her now I would hurt her again.

I didn't want to do that. I didn't want to hurt her, not any more. And my own denial wasn't working.

We didn't *have* to have a platonic marriage. Not if I was careful. I was a master at cutting my emotions off, and maybe allowing myself a physical relationship with her would even help matters. It might be a safety valve.

I could still keep her safe. I could.

'Are you sure that's what you want?' My voice had deepened, got rough, and I let it. 'A physical marriage?'

She was blushing furiously. 'Yes.'

'You must be sure,' I said roughly. 'You must be very, *very* sure.'

Some of my desperation must have shown in my voice, because she gave me a worried look. 'Yes, of course I'm sure. Why?'

I couldn't keep still any longer. If she wanted to know why then I would show her.

I stepped forward, crowding her against the window seat, luxuriating in the sexual tension that pulled taut between us. She gave a little gasp, her dark eyes widening. Then I leaned forward, putting my hands on the cushions either side of her, caging her with my body.

'This is why,' I said, and gave her a glimpse of the beast that lived in my heart, the one that wanted her with a desperation that bordered on madness.

I heard her breath catch, saw her pupils dilate. A hectic flush bloomed over her cheeks, the pulse at the base of her throat accelerated.

Disappointment was already gathering inside me because I knew that one glimpse would be enough. She'd change her mind. I would frighten her and she wouldn't want any part of me, not again.

She smelled delicious, fresh and sweet. Pushing myself away from her would be difficult. But I would do it. I'd already frightened her twice since we'd arrived here.

There wouldn't be a third time.

'If you're trying to scare me,' she said huskily, 'you're doing a terrible job.'

My whole body went taut. 'Jenny—'

'I'm not afraid of you. When will you believe me?'

The chains on my control began to loosen and I leaned forward even more, unable to help myself. I inhaled her scent, my breath against the soft, tender skin of her cheek. 'Sex is all I have to give you.' I tried not to growl. 'There won't be anything more than that. Not ever. Do you understand?'

'Yes.' Her voice was patient, as if she was trying to soothe me. 'I understand.'

But I didn't want to be soothed. I wanted to let go of my control, my restraint, let go of everything and take what was mine.

I angled my head, brushing my mouth along her jaw, intoxicated by the scent of feminine arousal and her own intrinsic sweetness.

'Tell me to stop and I will,' I murmured, easing forward, my body almost pressing against hers, a delicious agony. 'I will not hurt you. I will never hurt you.'

'I know you won't.' She took a ragged breath. 'Ask me, Con. Ask me, please.'

I could hear the note of desperation in her voice. It was the same desperation that lived in my own heart, and even though the logical part of me was telling me this was a mistake, I couldn't refuse.

'Marry me, Jenny,' I said. 'Be my wife.'

She gave a husky laugh. 'It's supposed to be a question, not an order.' But she must have seen that I was beyond amusement at this point, because her smile faded. 'Yes. Yes, I will be your wife, Constantine.'

A deep satisfaction swept through me. All the tension in my muscles faded, the beast inside me quietening. As if now she'd agreed to be mine it was content.

The man, however, was not. The man was starving.

I leaned in again, putting my mouth near her ear. 'Stay still,' I said. 'Stay very, very still.'

She did as she was told and I inhaled again, breathing

in her scent, indulging myself utterly. I was hard, and I didn't resist, letting desire tighten its grip.

'You're mine now.' I bent to nuzzle against the side of her neck, brushing my mouth over her skin. 'Every part of you is mine.'

She was shaking, but she didn't move.

My satisfaction deepened, a sharp, intense pleasure I'd never allowed myself. It was addictive to have this, to indulge myself so completely, and perhaps it was a mistake. But, no, I could have her and keep my emotions separate. That was what I'd spent my life doing, after all.

I nuzzled into her throat, enjoying how she trembled, then put my mouth over her leaping pulse, the sweet, salty flavour of her skin on my tongue.

A breathy sound escaped her, honing my desire.

I sucked gently, tasting her frantic heartbeat. There would be a mark there in the morning and the thought pleased me.

I lifted my head and glanced down into her face. Her dark eyes were black and glittering as they met mine. I lifted one hand from the cushions and took hold of the tie of her dress, tugging on it.

She shivered, but made no move to grab the fabric as it fell away from her body, the red silk slipping open to reveal her.

My breath caught.

She was so very, very perfect. Even more so than I'd anticipated. Full breasts and rounded hips and thighs. She wore the red lace underwear I'd bought for her, the gaps in the fabric giving me a glimpse of soft pink nipples and the dark curls between her thighs.

Now she moved, lifting her hands as if to cover herself, but I grabbed her wrists before she could and held them down at her sides.

'No,' I ordered roughly, unable to tear my gaze from her beautiful body. 'I want to look at you.'

Another shiver went through her, but she didn't try to pull away. Her breathing was short and fast and ragged, and that red flush was creeping down her neck and over her chest.

'Beautiful.' I let my gaze sweep slowly over her creamy silky skin, her full breasts, her elegant, narrow waist, her curvaceous hips and thighs.

Her lashes fell, veiling her gaze, and I wasn't sure why. But then I had an inkling. It was Catherine and all the lies she'd told Jenny about herself.

It made me furious to think how she wasn't valued by the one person who should value her, but it wasn't the right time to talk about it. I was impatient, and hungry, and I could think of better ways to let Jenny know how beautiful she was.

I let go of one of her slender wrists and put my fingers against her throat, stroking over her frantically beating pulse and the red mark I'd left on her skin there.

'You are exactly what I want,' I said fiercely. 'Exactly.'

She felt so soft, and she made another little sound as I let my fingers trail down over her chest, brushing lightly over the curve of her breast and then down further, following the line of her hip to her rounded stomach.

I stroked the little bump where our baby lay, allowing the fierce possessiveness to grip me, and then I let my fingers move over it and down further.

'C-Con...' she whispered as my fingers grazed over

the lace between her thighs. It was damp, the evidence of her arousal slick against my fingertips.

Hunger wound its way around my soul, tightening until I could hardly breathe.

I dropped to my knees in front of her, pushing her back against the window seat, then tore apart the thin silk that was in my way.

She gasped as I touched her, stroking the soft, sensitive folds between her thighs, feeling soft curls and moisture and heat, and then she gasped again as I leaned forward, pressing my mouth to her stomach, trailing kisses down over it until I reached the salty heat of her.

'Oh… Con…' Her voice was ragged, a tremble shaking her.

When I licked my way inside her she jerked against me and cried out.

She tasted delicious, a delicate feast I couldn't get enough of, so I hooked her thighs over my shoulders, gripping her hips as I tasted her, deeper and more fully.

She fell back onto the cushions, crying out yet again as I pushed my tongue deep inside her.

She was mine now, every part of her, and I was going to take my own sweet time exploring her.

Her fingers curled in my hair, gripping me tight, and she shook beneath my hands. But I didn't rush. I feasted on her, making her cry out and sob.

And only when I was ready did I give her what she was begging for, making her sob my name as the orgasm came for her.

CHAPTER ELEVEN

Jenny

I LAY GASPING against the window seat cushions, pleasure still cascading through me. I couldn't move, could only stare at the ceiling, feeling as if I'd been shattered into a million tiny, glittering pieces.

Con had broken me, and I wasn't sure I wanted to be put back together again. Or maybe I did, if only so he could break me again like he had just now.

I'd told him I didn't want a platonic marriage and I'd thought I understood what that meant. Except I hadn't. Not really.

Oh, I'd seen the flare of black fire in his eyes as I'd told him I'd changed my mind, that I'd marry him after all. And I'd sensed the tension in the air growing tighter, hotter, as I'd said he'd have to give up the idea of a sexless marriage.

He'd asked me if I was sure, and I didn't know why he'd bothered to ask.

So he'd shown me.

It was as if I'd poured petrol on a smouldering fire. Flames leapt in his eyes and he'd come closer, pressing me back against the window seat, letting me know that it wasn't just a fire that burned inside him, it was a volcano.

Perhaps he'd thought his passion would scare me, but that had been impossible, because all I'd wanted in that moment was him.

I'd ignored what he'd said about love. All I'd been able to focus on was the heat in his gaze, and when he'd whispered that every part of me was his my soul had shivered.

I'd felt self-conscious as he'd pulled away my dress, because he'd never seen me naked and I wasn't anything like the other women he'd been with. I wasn't tall, willowy Olivia, for example.

Except then he'd told me that I was exactly what he wanted, and then he'd touched me so softly, delicately, making me feel precious. He'd kissed me. He'd dropped to his knees before me. He'd…tasted me, making it very obvious that he was enjoying every second…

It had been the most erotic thing I'd ever experienced.

I shut my eyes, conscious that I was wearing only a bra and he was still kneeling on the floor, my thighs over his shoulders, my most secret places laid bare for him to see.

I tried to move, but he laid a firm hand on my stomach, pinning me. 'Don't,' he said, his voice rough with desire. 'Open your eyes, Jenny. I haven't finished.'

Unable to resist the command, I opened them in time to see him rising from his position on the floor, his eyes blazing.

There was nothing left of his cold armour, nothing left of the glacier. He was burning with a raw heat that ignited me, burning my self-consciousness abruptly to the ground.

I had done that to him. While he might have broken

me, and left me shattered, I had also broken him. I—short, plain, Jenny Grey—had broken the most powerful and feared man in Europe.

I pushed myself up, not bothering to cover myself. I didn't look away. I met his gaze and held it.

He didn't look away either, his hands dropping to his belt. He didn't rush. He took his time undoing it.

My mouth was dry, desire gathering inside me despite the shattering orgasm he'd already given me not moments ago.

This is a mistake. You know this will never be enough for you.

Maybe. But it was too late now. He'd asked me to be his wife and I'd accepted. And no power on earth would make me take it back.

'I want you, Jenny. Right here. Right now.'

Ferocious intensity burned in his eyes and I knew it was for me. *Because* of me. And that gave me power, a confidence I hadn't known was inside me until now.

'Yes,' I said thickly. 'Yes, please.'

His hands dropped away, his belt undone. I leaned forward, my fingers shaking as I undid the button on his trousers and unzipped his fly. I could feel the pressure of his gaze on me. He was watching me so avidly it was amazing I didn't combust on the spot.

'Your hands are shaking.' His voice was deep and laced with heat. 'Are you nervous?'

'No.' And it wasn't a lie. 'I just…want you.'

'Then take what you want.' His hands drifted to my hair, his fingers curling gently through it as if he relished the feel of it. 'I will be your husband and you can take from me as I take from you.'

Yet more confidence filled me, and I spread the fabric

of his trousers, reaching to touch the long, hard ridge I could see beneath the fabric of his underwear. I felt him tense as I stroked him, my fingers trembling a little at being able to. That night in the garden everything had happened so quickly. It had been over before I'd known what was happening. But now I could touch him. Now I could see him.

I'd fantasised about him for so long, and now he was here the reality was…indescribable.

I drew him out. He was hot in my palm, and satin-smooth, and as I curled my fingers around him he made a harsh, very male sound. He reached down and pulled my hand away. The look on his face was drawn tight, his cheekbones etched, his jaw hard. He looked fierce, and hungry, like a wolf who'd gone without food for too long.

He didn't speak, pushing me gently but firmly back onto the cushions of the window seat. Then he slid his large, warm hands beneath my rear and lifted me, positioning himself. He pushed inside me in one smooth, hard movement, filling me completely, tearing a gasp of agonised pleasure from my throat.

He leaned forward, easing deeper, his gaze on mine as he placed his hands on the cushions on either side of my head. His black eyes were a furnace, burning me alive, while the pressure of him inside me made it hard to breathe. I'd forgotten how big he was, how the pressure and the exquisite stretch of my sex around his made everything sharper and more intense.

It was glorious. He was glorious.

He didn't speak, only looked fiercely down at me as he began to move, and I didn't look away. I couldn't. I was locked in his gaze, held there as surely as his body pinned me to the cushions.

He set a hard, relentless rhythm, sending fierce pleasure spiralling through my veins, and I reached up to
grip his wrists, bracing myself against the shocks of his
hot, hard body. He was still fully dressed, while I was
only in a bra, and I found that so erotic. Especially as
his gaze raked down my body, watching as I writhed beneath him, every movement he made coiling the pleasure tighter and tighter.

I could see he liked it, that it gave him pleasure to
watch me, and that fed my pleasure too. I'd never had a
man watch me the way he did, obviously liking what he
saw. I'd never had anyone look at me with such possessive ferocity either.

He moved faster, harder, his teeth bared in a savage
smile as he leaned down. 'Come for me, my Jenny,' he
growled, before his mouth covered mine and his hand
reached between my thighs to where we were joined,
and he stroked me. Once. Twice.

I detonated, screaming his name against his mouth
as the orgasm swept over me, turning me over and over
and dragging me under.

Dimly I heard him make a harsh, guttural sound, felt
his body slamming hard into mine, before he slumped
on top of me, crushing me into the cushions.

He was heavy, but I didn't care. Once again he'd shattered me, all the pieces of me scattered on the winds and
his weight the only thing holding those pieces together.

I didn't move, content to lie there under him, secure
and safe beneath his heat.

Yet after a moment I wriggled under him and eventually he shifted, pushing himself up and away from me.
I tried to sit, but he put a hand out, pinning me in place.

'No,' he ordered, his voice still husky. 'Stay there until I say.'

Puzzled, I did what he said, waiting as he adjusted his clothing and ran a hand through his short black hair. Then he bent, gathering my dress from the floor before pulling me off the window seat. He shook out the fabric and wrapped it around me with expert hands, tying the tie at my waist in a bow then smoothing down the silk.

He was so careful, so gentle, it made my heart ache.

Then he cast around for my underwear and picked them up. 'You can't wear these,' he said, examining the torn lace. 'I'll get you some new ones.'

Much to my shock, he folded them up and put them in his pocket.

I opened my mouth to ask him what he was going to do with them, but he took my face between his palms and examined me carefully, and every word went clean out of my head.

His black brows were drawn down, his gaze sharp. 'Are you okay? Did I hurt you?'

'No,' I said. 'No, not at all.'

His gaze narrowed for a second, as if he didn't believe me, but then he nodded. 'You need to eat. You have a long night ahead of you.'

A thrill arrowed down my spine. 'I suppose that doesn't mean a night on the couch, watching TV?'

'No, of course not. After dinner I will be taking you to bed, where I can explore you properly.'

I shivered, anticipation collecting inside me. 'We don't have to have dinner. I don't mind if you want to go straight to bed now.'

His eyes gleamed, the banked flames leaping.

'Tempting. But food is important, especially when you're pregnant.'

I should have been thinking about what was going to happen next, about what exactly I'd insisted on when I'd changed my mind and told him I'd marry him. About weddings and living arrangements and all kinds of things...

But I didn't want to think about that. I couldn't even remember why it was important.

And when he took my hand, his fingers lacing through mine, I let him lead me to the dining room without thinking about anything at all.

CHAPTER TWELVE

Constantine

I NARROWED MY gaze at the computer screen, noting all my unread emails and deciding to respond to only two. One was to give a direction to my legal department to keep stonewalling Valentin's continued attempts to take over the company. The other was to remind my management team at Silver Inc that no mention of Valentin's return was to appear anywhere in the media, on pain of instant dismissal.

I didn't like being so autocratic with my staff, but I didn't want that leaked, not until the situation with Jenny had been well and truly handled.

It had been five days since she'd agreed to marry me and I'd kept her in bed, allowing my hunger free rein. I couldn't remember the last time I'd allowed myself such an indulgence, and it made me greedy. It made me want to cast all thoughts of wedding arrangements and the discussion of other practicalities aside so I could concentrate completely on her.

It was mid-morning already, for example, and I could feel the persistent ache for her begin to build. I'd taken my time with her in bed this morning, hoping that would satisfy it, but it hadn't. The pull towards her, the demand for more of her presence, more of her time, just more of *her* was relentless.

So I'd taken myself off to the cottage to put some distance between us, thinking to immerse myself in work. But I couldn't concentrate. My head was too full of the satin feel of her skin and the silkiness of her hair draped across my chest. The tight clasp of her body around mine and the sounds she made when I was inside her.

I'd agreed to a full marriage thinking that I could master my emotions and that sex would be a good way to release the pressure. It wouldn't complicate matters. Except…that was turning out not to be the case.

Instead, sex had only opened up another avenue of fascination. I'd wanted to be careful with her because she'd seemed vulnerable, and I hadn't wanted to scare her. Yet I needn't have been concerned. She had a seam of pure steel that ran all the way through her, and a hunger that matched my own.

It was endlessly surprising to me that something so soft and unguarded should secretly be so strong. Perhaps, though, I shouldn't have been quite so surprised, considering how she'd had no hesitation in arguing with me since we'd got here. Whatever the case, I wanted to explore this hidden strength of hers in other, more interesting ways. Perhaps tonight I'd—

I growled, realising I'd been staring at my computer screen for a good ten minutes.

Unacceptable. I was supposed to *not* be thinking of her.

Shoving my chair back, I got up and turned to the line of bookshelves along one of the cottage's thick stone walls. Behind the books, hidden beneath a panel fashioned to look like a stone in the wall, there was a button. I flicked open the panel and pressed the button. A section of shelving slid to one side, revealing a door in the wall with a pad on it. I put my hand on it, my palm print unlocking the door.

The door opened and I stepped into the room beyond, hidden and protected from everyone but myself.

No one knew of this room's existence except the people who'd built it for me, and I'd paid them handsomely never to reveal its secrets.

The room housed my collection. Treasures I'd collected over the years and kept hidden from everyone, but most especially from my father. He hadn't liked us to have attachments to anything, even inanimate objects. No toys or books or games No friends. No pets. Even our mother had been taken from us when we were young, having died after going for a walk along a local trail in the mountains, her body later found at the bottom of a cliff.

My mother hadn't liked hiking—that I remembered about her. So God only knew what she'd been doing on that trail. I'd had my suspicions, but I'd never voiced them. And there had been no point thinking about it. My father had ruled with an iron fist, and fighting him had been a lesson in futility.

A lesson Valentin had never learned, but I'd had to.

I'd had no other option.

The room was blessedly quiet, the non-directional lighting giving it a relaxing glow. Spotlights illuminated special pieces I'd had mounted in climate-controlled cases, plus other, less sensitive items that were no less important.

This was *my* place. *My* things. And I could be as possessive of them as I liked because there was no one to observe me, no one to note how important they were to me and no one to take them away.

Here, in this room, I could allow myself to feel.

I stopped in front of one shelf, looking down at the small green plastic toy soldier illuminated by the spotlight shining on it. An insignificant piece of plastic. Worth nothing.

It had been the first and only toy I'd ever had. A housekeeper, taking pity on me, had given it to me and I'd loved it. I'd played with it every day. Valentin had told me to be careful and not to let our father see, but somehow Papa had found out anyway. He'd tried to force me to throw it in the fire, but Valentin had got hold of it and run away with it, throwing it up onto the roof of our house, where Papa couldn't get it. He'd earned a beating for that.

Valentin had never understood that sometimes it wasn't about the battle but the war. And it had been a war, my childhood. *Our* childhood.

That night I'd had to listen to him trying not to cry in pain, his body bruised from the beating. I'd been so furious with him—that he'd been hurt and all for a ridiculous piece of plastic.

But of course I'd known who'd really been at fault and it hadn't been Valentin.

He was my older brother by a couple of minutes, and he'd only been trying to protect me. But the fault had been mine. If I hadn't taken that toy from the housekeeper, if I hadn't let my father see me playing with it, then Valentin wouldn't have got hurt.

That was the night I'd decided there was only one way for us both to survive Domingo's parenting, and it hadn't been to rebel against him the way Valentin did. It had been to learn his lessons. Cut off the source of pain. Our feelings had been weaponised by our father to hurt us, so the best thing to do was not feel them.

Nothing could matter to me, not even my own brother.

Eventually I'd retrieved the toy solider and hidden it under a loose floorboard in my bedroom. I never played with it again.

'Con?'

The voice that came from behind me was feminine, light and clear and sweet.

For a moment it felt as if I'd been wandering in a dark maze, unable to find my out, and suddenly a light had flickered into life, shining through the darkness, showing me the way.

My Jenny was here. My Jenny had found me.

Then reality flooded back in—the reality of where I was and what it meant that she was here.

She'd not only come to the cottage, after I'd expressly forbidden her to, she'd come into my secret collection room.

An instinctive territorial anger swept through me, so strong that for a second I couldn't speak. I didn't want to get angry with her, she didn't know how private these things were, how personal, because I'd never told her about my childhood, not any of it. Yet I still felt like an animal whose safe and secret den had been invaded. A dragon whose hoard had been discovered.

She shouldn't be here. She shouldn't be seeing this. All these things were mine and *only* mine.

My hands clenched as I tried to leash the rage, freeze it solid and not let any of it escape, but I could feel it trickling through my fingers.

I needed to get her out of here before I said something I regretted.

I turned sharply.

She stood in the doorway in one of the dresses I'd bought her, this one fitting closely around her breasts before flowing out around her in a waterfall of dusky pink. It was flattering to her curvy figure, the colour warming her skin and making her eyes seem darker and more liquid. Her hair was loose in glossy waves over her shoulders. She'd taken it to wearing it like that because I'd told her I preferred it that way.

The morning sunlight streamed through the windows behind her, catching threads of caramel and toffee in her hair and shining through the material of her dress, illuminating her luscious figure.

She was glowing. She was absolutely beautiful.

I stood frozen, staring at this glowing pink vision. She'd always had the kind of presence that made any room seem lighter and warmer.

'You shouldn't be here.' Anger laced my voice even though I tried to stop it. 'The cottage is forbidden to anyone but me. I told you that.'

Colour stained her cheeks. 'I kn-know. I'm sorry, but—'

'Please leave.'

'Con, I—'

'Get out!' Suddenly I couldn't stand her being there. Couldn't stand the thought of her seeing what was in this room, the evidence of the vulnerable, stunted little boy I'd once been. It felt like a violation. It made me feel ashamed. 'Get out now.'

But she didn't move, and she didn't look anywhere

else but at me. She was frowning, her chin taking on that tell-tale stubborn cast. 'No,' she said.

More fury trickled out, and I'd taken a step in her direction before I could stop myself, my grip on my temper loosening. I felt the way I had a few days ago, when she locked the door against me and some part of my brain had exploded with fury. Then, I'd kicked the door down.

This is why you should never have touched her. This is why you should have sent her away. She draws all kinds of emotions out of you and you can't stop her.

She had done even back when she'd been a child, sitting in that chair in my study, swinging her legs and telling me funny stories about the boarding school she'd gone to, making me smile.

I should have known then that she had an ability to touch a part of me no one else had, and I should have guarded myself against her. But she'd been a child, and I'd thought Domingo had killed laughter in me for ever.

I didn't feel like laughing now. My territory had been invaded and I was furious about it.

'Jenny,' I growled, 'you really need to leave.'

She ignored me, her frown deepening as her warm, dark gaze searched my face. 'Are you okay?'

I'd crossed the room before I knew what I was doing, lifted my hands and taken her upper arms in a gentle grip. Her breath caught audibly. There were dark circles beneath her eyes, as if she hadn't slept well.

What are you doing? Why are you manhandling her? She's Jenny...she's your *Jenny. Remember what happened to Domingo. Remember what you did.*

I couldn't move. She felt breakable in my hands, fragile as a china shepherdess. I'd already lost control with her once before, and now here I was, laying hands on her again…

She was still frowning, looking up at me, and yet there was no fear in her lovely face, only a concern that gripped me by the throat.

She shouldn't be concerned for me. Not when I hadn't shown any concern for her.

'I know you don't want me in here, and I'm sorry,' she said. 'I didn't mean to intrude. But…you've been gone all day and I… I was worried for you.'

I struggled to contain my anger, to keep it locked down. She had intruded into my private space, but not so she could discover my secrets and use them against me.

She'd been worried about me.

'You don't need to worry,' I said through gritted teeth. 'I'm fine.'

CHAPTER THIRTEEN

Jenny

HE DIDN'T WANT me here, and if the look of fury that had momentarily crossed his face when I'd stepped into the room hadn't been enough of a sign, then the tension radiating through every line of his body and the fierce heat in his black eyes certainly was.

He wasn't fine. He wasn't fine at all. He was furiously angry. And now, of course, I wanted to know why.

I also wanted to know why he was always gone when I woke up in the mornings, and why he stayed here in the cottage the entire day. Why he only came back in the evenings, and why he'd then take me to bed and keep me there until dinner time.

And, most importantly, I wanted to know why he wouldn't talk to me. Because we hadn't discussed the wedding, or when we'd return to London, or what would happen after that. He'd told me he'd instructed one of his staff members to tell my mother where I was, and to contact the shelter where I worked. But we hadn't discussed anything beyond that. We hadn't discussed anything at all.

Those first few days I'd been too dazed and a little

drunk with the effects of sex to notice the distance he'd put between us. But then, as the fifth day came around and he'd left me alone, I'd had enough. I couldn't let this distance between us continue, not when we were going to be married and had a child to raise together.

So I'd crossed the rolling green lawns to his cottage. If it had only been about myself, maybe I'd have left him to his privacy, but it wasn't only about me. It was about the baby, too. I couldn't let him dictate everything. I couldn't let him walk all over me.

I had to make a stand.

His stare was fierce, his heat surrounding me. He was in a white shirt and charcoal-grey trousers, the stark colours highlighting his dark beauty, a perfect foil to the rage burning in his obsidian eyes.

'Don't be ridiculous,' I said, ignoring the hard grip he had on my arms. 'You're not fine. If you were fine you wouldn't have been skulking in this cottage for the past five days.'

It was an unwise thing to say, but someone had to say it to him. And since I was apparently the only person who wasn't afraid of him, that someone had to be me.

He stared at me for one long second, then muttered a curse under his breath and let me go, stepping away, withdrawing his heat. A chill crept through me at the loss of his warmth. I tried to ignore it.

The ice was back in his eyes, the fierce expression fading, his perfect features hardening.

I didn't like it. I preferred his anger to his cold detachment, because at least that was honest. At least that was more him than this ice was.

'In there,' he said curtly, nodding his head in the direction of the office.

Shoving away the feeling of disappointment, I turned and stepped back through the doorway, leaving him to shut the door on that fascinating secret room. A wall of shelves slid back into place, and I had to bite down on my urge to ask him what was in there, because I hadn't looked when I'd had the chance. Not when all I'd seen was him.

Once the shelves were back, Con came over to me and slid a hand beneath my elbow, guiding me over to a couch and sitting me down on it.

The tiny cottage had been converted into a large, comfortable office, with that big desk and lots of shelving. The wooden floor was very old, dark and pitted, yet gleaming. A few hand-knotted silk rugs covered it, and under the window opposite the desk was the comfortable-looking couch in dark leather. The walls were undressed stone and very thick, giving the place a cosy, contained and secure atmosphere.

Con folded his arms over his broad chest, looming over me, staring at me with those cold eyes.

I was beginning to hate that expression, the one he showed to everyone else. Didn't he know he didn't need to be that way with me? Didn't he know he could be himself when he was with me?

Abruptly, I felt close to tears, though I wasn't sure why. Perhaps it was the way he'd turned on me, because, regardless of whether I'd invaded his privacy or not, I hadn't expected that. He'd never been angry with me before, yet in the space of the past five days cold and angry was all he seemed to be.

It didn't start five days ago, and you know it.

That was true. He'd been cold and distant ever since I'd left Spain to live in London. Apart from that night in the garden, when we'd both crossed a line we hadn't been able to come back from.

And then you both broke what you'd once had. You broke it irretrievably.

Maybe. But I suspected something had broken before that night. And I still didn't know what it was, because he wouldn't tell me.

I bit my lip hard, shoving away the tears and reaching for anger instead. 'What was all that about?' I demanded.

'What was what about?'

'You, in that room. Getting so angry with me.'

A muscle ticked in the side of his hard jaw. 'I don't want to talk about it.'

'Okay, fine. So is that how it's going to be? Our marriage? Sex whenever you want it and then you disappearing off God knows where and refusing to talk to me?'

His dark brows twitched. 'What more do you want?'

'I want you to be there!' The words came out far more vehemently than I'd expected, and I tried to moderate my tone. 'I don't want this distance you keep putting between us. I don't understand it, not when we have so much we need to talk about.'

Something flickered behind his cold black eyes, a glimpse of an emotion I couldn't read. 'Fine. Let us talk about the arrangements now.'

His voice was expressionless, blank as a stone wall.

It made me even angrier.

'I don't want to talk about the "arrangements",' I snapped. 'I want to talk about why, for the past five days, you've done nothing but have sex with me and leave.'

The muscle in his jaw leapt again. 'I have work I need to do.'

'You ignored me, Con,' I said flatly. 'Funny how you

were able to work years ago in your office and you didn't mind talking to me then.'

The ice in his expression cracked, another emotion I couldn't name flickering across his beautiful face. He turned abruptly and strode over to the desk, looking down at the stack of papers neatly piled on top of it. 'I told you that sex was all I could give you, Jenny. I meant it.'

I stared at his tall figure, his broad shoulders rigid with tension, and part of me wanted to go to him and put my arms around him. But I was also angry, and I couldn't give in to the need to make him feel better, not all the time. Not if I wanted to close this distance between us.

Because it wasn't a physical distance, it was emotional. He was pulling away from me and, sure, he'd told me he couldn't give me love, but he could at least be the friend he'd once been to me. Couldn't we go back to that? Didn't I deserve that? Didn't our baby? What if he pulled away from our child? Would he put this distance between them too?

'What happened to being my friend?' I asked, my hands tightly clasped in my lap. 'You can't be that either?'

There was a long silence.

'No,' he said.

A cold current of shock rippled through me.

Are you really that surprised? He hasn't been a friend to you since you left Madrid.

'Why not?' I asked hoarsely. 'You never told me why you cut me off. Was it me? Did I do something? Con, I—'

'No.' He glanced at me all of a sudden, his gaze fierce. 'It's nothing you did. It's not your fault.'

I felt bewildered. 'Then…why?'

He looked back down at the stack of papers and placed one hand carefully on top of them, as if to protect them from a non-existent wind. 'I never spoke to you about my childhood, did I? I never talked about Domingo.'

As soon as he said the words, a knowledge that had always been there twisted deep inside me. He had always been tense when his father had been around, always cold, detached. And, no, he'd never spoken about Domingo, or the twin brother he'd lost at seventeen.

There is probably a reason for that.

'No, you didn't,' I said softly.

'I did not want you to know. I did not want it to… touch you.'

Foreboding gripped me. Domingo hadn't been an easy man, and he certainly hadn't liked me. I'd tried my best to be a good stepdaughter, but he'd avoided me for some reason.

'What did he do to you, Con?' I whispered.

'It's better if you don't know.' His voice was completely expressionless. 'Suffice to say that I decided long ago it was better for me not to form any…emotional attachments.'

I blinked, taken aback. Then immediately I wanted to know why he'd decided that and what had made him choose something so extreme? But I knew from the look on his face that he wasn't going to tell me.

So instead I said, 'Is that why you said you couldn't give me love?'

'Yes.'

'But…you were my friend before,' I pointed out. 'What changed? Because something did.'

He turned his head, his black gaze pinning me to the

couch where I sat. 'You did, Jenny. It changed because of you.'

A cold little shock pulsed through me. 'What do you mean?'

'Did you never wonder why, for the past four years, I never visited you? Never called you? Never replied to your emails or texts?'

'Of course I wondered.' My voice had gone hoarse. 'I wondered all the time.'

'It was because I wanted you.'

I sat on the couch, my heartbeat loud in my ears, four years of silence shifting and altering and finally falling into place. 'And you were…what? Keeping your distance?' My voice sounded faint and slightly cracked.

'Yes, I was keeping my distance.' His gaze burned. 'I was too old for you, and you were my friend, my step-sister. My duty was and still is to protect you, most especially from myself.'

It made sense, so much sense. The years of curt, cold messages, and finally no messages at all. And then that night in the garden, how he'd fallen on me like a beast let out of a cage…

I swallowed, the cold shock slowly fading to be replaced by heat.

He'd wanted me all those years. He'd wanted me the way I'd wanted him.

'But you don't need to protect me any more,' I said. 'You can—'

'Yes, I do,' he interrupted. 'And it's even more important now. You don't want a platonic marriage, Jenny, so I can promise you that it won't be. And if you want to talk about our living arrangements, our wedding, how we will raise our child, then we will. We can organise all of that together. It will not be an issue. But I cannot be your friend again. The relationship we once had is over.'

Tears prickled once again, loss throbbing behind my breastbone. But I ignored the sensations. Because all of this was *his* decision, not mine. He was the one who'd decided on distance, who'd thought he had to 'protect' me, or some such nonsense. Who now seemed to think that sex was an adequate replacement for his friendship.

Even though the sex was very good indeed, I discovered that I'd been right. It *wasn't* enough.

I wanted him. And it wasn't only about me, it was about our baby as well.

'What about our child, Con?' I asked flatly. 'Will you distance yourself from them too? Will you tell them that you can't give them love?'

That muscle in the side of his jaw jerked and jerked again. 'That's not—'

'How do you think they'll feel when they say *I love you, Daddy* and you don't say it back?'

CHAPTER FOURTEEN

Constantine

THE WORDS HUNG in the air, the sharp edges of them glittering like knives.

I turned away from her, looked back down at the papers on my desk, struggling to contain the fury and anguish twisting deep inside me.

I love you, Daddy. They were words I'd said once to my own father, back when I was very young. Too young to know yet how painful those emotions could be.

Domingo had laughed. 'You really are a stupid boy, aren't you?' he'd said. 'You should be more like your brother. He doesn't bother with any of that nonsense.'

That had been the start of the wedge he'd driven between Valentin and I. Valentin had been rebellious, confrontational. Never doing what Papa said and constantly fighting with him. While I… I had found such confrontations distressing. They'd been painful and I'd hated conflict.

I had been weak back then. Vulnerable. I still remembered the cruel edge to his laugh and the lazy amusement on his face as he'd called me stupid. Reducing my feelings to something shameful and humiliating.

The only way to protect myself from him had been to become him, and I couldn't allow the same thing to happen to any child of mine.

I would never intentionally do anything to hurt them the way Papa had hurt me, but if I was finding it difficult to control my feelings around Jenny, then controlling my feelings around my child was going to be impossible.

How could I expose them to that? I couldn't trust myself.

'I will tell them the truth,' I bit out. 'That I will protect them with everything I have, but love is something they will only be able to get from their mother.'

'Oh, Con…' Jenny didn't sound angry now, her voice full of a compassion that made me ache. 'What happened to you?'

Unconsciously I closed the hand resting on top of the papers into a fist.

She was still on the couch, her hands clasped in her lap, the sunlight from the window behind her streaming in, making her glow, illuminating all the dark spaces in the cottage.

Illuminating all the dark spaces in my heart, too.

I'd told her the truth, that I hadn't wanted her to know about the war zone that had been my childhood. I hadn't wanted any of that to touch her. I'd wanted her to stay the bright light that I turned to when things were dark.

I'd thought I'd never have to tell her, and yet… I couldn't keep it from her, not now. Not when we were going to be married and would have a child to bring up. It wasn't fair to her, and it wasn't fair to our child either.

Both my hands were now clenched tightly, and no matter how hard I tried to relax them, they wouldn't.

'What happened to me?' I echoed, my voice sounding strange and hollow in the silence of the cottage. 'Domingo was a psychopath, Jenny. You wouldn't have known, because he hid it well, but he was a smiling, charming psychopath. So I suppose you could say that what happened to me was him.'

'A psychopath?' The words were a soft, scraped whisper as horror rippled over her lovely face. 'Con...'

I looked away, unable to bear her expression, staring down at the dark wood of my desk. 'I think Catherine sent you away to school because she didn't want you anywhere near him and with good reason. My childhood was a war zone. Domingo wouldn't allow Valentin and I any kind of attachments. Not to anything.'

I wanted the words to be flat and toneless, the facts issued and nothing but. Yet anger tinged them no matter how hard I tried to prevent it.

'We had no toys. No friends. No pets. We only had each other, and Domingo would use that bond against us. He would manipulate us, turn us against each other. Valentin responded with argument and rebellion, while I...' I took a breath. 'It seemed safer not to feel anything at all.'

There was a long, shocked silence.

I didn't want to look at her. I didn't want to see what was on her lovely face. Deep down, I'd thought that now Domingo was gone his poison would have gone with him, but it hadn't. It was reaching beyond the grave and now it was touching Jenny. My Jenny.

That was my fault. I poisoned everything I touched, too.

I needed to get out of the cottage, away from her gentle presence, away from the consequences of my own actions just for once.

I turned from the desk, ready to stride out, only to

have warm arms wrap themselves around me and soft curves press against my chest. Jenny looked up at me, her dark eyes liquid with tears, with sympathy, and a compassion that made my entire being clench tight.

I went rigid in her grip, but she didn't let me go, softness and heat to the sharp edges and ice inside of me.

'She kept me safe,' Jenny said thickly. 'But who kept you safe? Who, Con?'

We both knew the answer to that, and when I didn't speak she pressed her face to my chest and held me tight, as if her embrace would ease the toxic mixture of emotion inside me.

And it did. I felt the moment all the rage and pain I'd turned inward shift, the press of feminine curves altering it, turning it into a volcano of something hotter, more intense, and far more welcome.

Desire leapt high, consuming me, and for a second all I could do was stand there in a futile attempt to take control.

But there was no controlling it. My hands were in her hair before I could stop myself, pulling her head away from my chest, turning her delicate face up so I could bend and take her mouth like a man possessed.

She didn't pull away and she didn't stop me. Her arms tightened and she went up on her toes, kissing me back as hungrily as I was kissing her.

Her mouth was hot and sweet and generous, just like her soul, and I clenched my hands tightly in her hair, holding her fast as I gorged myself on her, letting the taste of her flood through me, blotting out all the rage and pain I'd told myself I didn't feel.

She held nothing back, giving me everything, and I took it. I couldn't stop.

I lifted my mouth from hers only so I could tear her pretty pink dress from her body, and then her pretty pink underwear too. Her fingers fumbled with my shirt buttons, pulling at them as if she was as desperate for that skin-on-skin contact as I was.

I helped her, getting rid of my shirt and then dealing with my trousers and the rest of my clothing, wanting nothing more than to be rid of any constraints. Then, naked, I picked her up in my arms and took her over to the couch, laying her on the cushions before following her down and pinning her beneath me.

Her hair was in wild curls over the cushions and tangled over her shoulders, her face flushed. Her eyes were liquid and there were tear tracks on her cheeks. I bent and kissed away the tears, drowning myself in the taste of salt and the sweetness of her skin before finding her mouth again and kissing her deeply and with hunger.

She tasted of summer and sunlight, champagne and strawberries. Of long, warm twilights and perfumed rose gardens. Of all the fantasies I'd ever had about her. I couldn't get enough. The scent of her arousal was driving me mad.

I kissed my way down her throat to the curve of her breasts, flicking my tongue over her nipple, licking her, teasing her. Then I drew the hard bud into my mouth and sucked. She gasped, arching into me, her hands gripping my shoulders.

She tasted delicious. I wanted to spend time feasting on her, but my own needs were becoming too much for me to control. I shifted between her soft thighs, easing the hard length of my shaft through the hot, wet folds of her sex, feeling her shudder against me.

She whispered my name and then, as I nipped the sensitive bud of her nipple, she groaned aloud.

I was losing myself in the taste of her, the sound of her gasps and the feel of her heat, and all I wanted to do was lose myself more, get rid of all the emotion inside me and leave nothing behind but pleasure.

I moved again, holding her hips as I positioned myself, then pushed into her, a groan escaping me at the feel of her hot flesh parting around mine, only to grip me tight, holding me inside her. Welcoming me. She was slick and tight and perfect. I slid my hands beneath the softness of her rear, tilting her so I could go deeper, making both of us gasp.

Then I was moving, unable to stop, my mouth on hers, kissing her harder as I moved inside her, a relentless and intoxicating pleasure driving me on.

Her nails dug into my shoulders and I relished it, glorying in how she could be as demanding as I was, her passion burning hot and strong.

I poured myself into her, all my pain and my rage, and she took it and changed it, giving me back only ecstasy and heat and wild passion.

It was magic. It was like nothing I'd ever had from anyone in my entire life. It was too much.

I slipped my hand down between her thighs, giving her back what I could before all conscious thought left me and I was driving myself deep into her, hard and fast, feeling her convulse around me as the climax took her and she screamed my name.

And then I followed, annihilated by the pleasure that swept over me with all the force of a tidal wave, knocking me over and pulling me under.

CHAPTER FIFTEEN

Jenny

I LAY BENEATH HIM, parts of me utterly shattered while other parts of me were hungry for more. And yet my heart ached.

He'd lowered his head, his face turned against my neck, his warm breath ghosting over my skin. He was a heavy weight on me, pinning me to the couch, but I didn't mind it. I never had. Beneath him I felt safe and secure, as if he was sheltering me from the world.

Except…who sheltered him? Had he ever had anyone? Had he ever had someone who'd brought him the same kind of solace and understanding he'd brought me? I had tried, but from what he'd said about his childhood I knew it hadn't been enough.

I ran my fingers through his short, thick black hair. It felt like raw silk against my skin. My body might feel utterly sated, but inside I hurt.

I hurt for him.

I'd always wondered why my mother had sent me away to boarding school, and I'd assumed it was because she hadn't wanted me around. I hadn't realised—

and why would I?—that she'd sent me away to protect me from Domingo.

That made sense, given what I now knew about him. But my safety paled in comparison to the realisation of what it had meant for Constantine.

His father had been a psychopath, using him and his brother. Using their bond to hurt them and manipulate them. And all the while denying them all the things a child needed in order to grow.

No friends. No pets. Not even any toys.

I couldn't imagine it. It horrified me to my core. Yet it also explained things. Con had said it was safer for him not to feel anything at all, and I could see now why he thought that. Why he'd always been so distant and so cold. Why it had always seemed as if he was armouring himself. Because he had been. He'd been armouring himself against his father.

I'd stayed out of Domingo's way, mostly, but whenever I'd noticed Con getting very tense around him, I'd tried my best to distract him. Domingo had never responded to my attempts to befriend him, shaking me off as if I was insect and walking away. I'd never discovered why I'd made him so uncomfortable, yet I felt pleased about it now. If only I'd known at the time I would have tried even harder to make sure Domingo stayed away.

Con had relaxed, his big body covering me like a heavy warm blanket. All the tension from before had bled out of him and now he lay on me unmoving.

Out of his suit he was a glorious specimen of manhood. Wide shoulders, broad chest and chiselled abs, all that muscled power covered with smooth, velvety olive skin.

Touching him was a delight and I didn't deny myself, dropping my hand from his hair to stroke down his back.

'I'm sorry.' My voice sounded thick in the heavy silence. 'I'm so sorry you had such a dreadful childhood.' It was a useless thing to say, but I couldn't think of anything else. And I wanted him to know that I felt for him.

He let out a long breath, its warmth chasing over my skin, and I thought he might move. Might cover himself in ice, detach himself once again. But he didn't.

'You do not know how much I valued your friendship, Jenny Grey,' he murmured. 'You were the first friend I ever had.'

Tears rose in my eyes at the realisation of what that must have meant for him. 'I was?' I asked shakily.

'Yes.' And then, as I was recovering from that, he added, almost casually, 'Valentin has come back.'

I went still. 'What? No, Valentin's dead. You told me that—'

'He's not dead.'

Slowly, Constantine lifted his head and looked down at me, his eyes full of some complicated emotion I couldn't read.

'That night in the garden, when you found me, I'd had a call from a source informing me that he was alive, that he hadn't died in a car crash after all.'

I stared at him in shock. 'I don't understand. If he's not dead, then what happened to him?'

'It looks like he spent a few years in hiding—my sources weren't able to tell me where—before appearing suddenly as the head of a multi-million-dollar security firm.' He reached for one of my curls, winding it slowly around one finger. 'You wanted to know why the power went out that night in the mansion last week? It was Valentin. He created a…disturbance. He kidnapped Olivia.'

More shock pulsed through me. The lights had gone out as I'd waited for Constantine in that room. And then he'd appeared, telling me he was going to marry me. That he'd changed his mind about Olivia.

But he hadn't changed his mind. He'd decided to marry me because his twin brother had come back from the dead and taken Olivia.

'Oh, my God…' I breathed, struggling suddenly to sit up. 'He kidnapped her…? Then what are you doing—?'

'Be still,' Con said quietly, not moving an inch, holding me down on the couch with the weight of his body. 'Valentin won't hurt her, though she might very well hurt him. He's told me he's going to take the company from me, but I don't think it's Silver Inc he actually wants. I think it's Olivia.'

I was still trying to process what he'd said, my heartbeat racing. 'Why didn't you tell me?'

He let go of the lock of hair he'd been playing with, brushing his fingers carefully over my collarbone, his touch making me shiver. 'I didn't want you to know. I didn't want anyone to know. Not until I'd decided how I was going to deal with the situation.' His gaze flicked to mine. 'He's in the Maldives at present, with Olivia.'

It was…a lot. Everything he'd just told me was a lot. Firstly that his father had been an abusive monster, and then that the twin brother he'd thought dead was very much alive and now with his erstwhile fiancée. Not to mention the fact that he'd kept all of this secret from me.

I wasn't sure of what to say. 'Have you…spoken to him?'

Con shook his head. 'He keeps leaving messages for me, but I haven't responded.'

'Why not? Aren't you pleased that he's not dead?'

His stroking fingers descended lower, tracing the curve of my breast, his attention on what he was doing. 'That's an interesting question,' he murmured.

I shoved away the delicious prickle over my skin that his touch drew, concentrating instead on his beautiful face, trying to read him. There were emotions there, deep and strong, but untangling them was difficult. Then again, I'd had years of watching his face. Years of seeing beneath his cold detachment—which I understood the reason for now—to the volcanic heart of him. And I could hear the thread that ran through his voice, that coloured every word.

'You're angry with him,' I said softly. 'You're furious.'

He flashed me one hot black look and, yes, I was right. The fury that I'd seen before, that had been in his every movement as he'd taken me on the couch, was there, starkly burning in every line of his perfect features.

'He let me think he was dead,' Con said, his lilting Spanish accent turning every word into angry poetry. 'He left me alone with that monster for fifteen years. And he never contacted me, not once.' His mouth was hard. 'He made our lives a misery, Jenny. His constant rebellions, his resistance to our father's rules, made everything worse. If he'd only done what Papa had said, even once. If he'd—' Con broke off, glancing back down at his fingers, still stroking the curve of my breast. 'I had a plastic toy soldier, given to me by a housekeeper. It was the only toy I'd ever had and I loved it. Valentin told me I had to be careful with it, that I couldn't let our father see me with it. But I didn't listen. Papa found out and he was angry. He tried to make me burn it in the fire, but Valentin took it and threw it on the roof so Papa couldn't get it.'

I lay there very still, my gaze fixed on his face, not daring to breathe in case he stopped talking.

'That enraged Domingo. He beat Valentin badly for disobeying him.' Con let out a breath. 'Valentin took the beating intended for me and… Papa broke his ribs.'

An anguished sound escaped before I could stop it, the horror of it settling inside me. But Con didn't look up, too lost in his terrible memories.

'I shouldn't be angry with him,' he went on after a moment. 'Not when all of it was my fault. I should not have accepted the toy and I should have listened to Valentin when he told me to be careful with it. I should not have let my father see it.' He paused. 'I should have put it in the fire. If I had it would have been one less beating Valentin took for me. But…'

He didn't need to go on. I could already see why he hadn't wanted to give up his toy. He'd had nothing, so a plastic toy soldier must have seemed worth the risk. Yet it had ended up with his brother being beaten.

I ached for him. He was a man who felt deeply, I already knew that, and I suspected that as boy he must have been the same. A loving boy who'd had to protect himself in any way he could. And he'd cut himself off from his emotions so completely he didn't feel anything at all.

Yet that boy was still there, beneath all that ice. He'd looked after a nest of chicks for an eleven-year-old girl and had always remembered to send her postcards from all the countries he'd been to. He'd given her a birthday card when everyone else had forgotten and he'd listened to her chatter inanely, and he'd always taken her seriously. He'd never judged her, and he'd never criticised her. He'd made her feel that she wasn't alone.

But that loving boy had lost the only person he'd ever loved and who'd ever loved him. The brother who'd left him alone with a father who'd twisted him into something he never should have been.

No wonder he was so lonely.

I'd never developed the hard callus my mother had. I'd never been able to hide my own loneliness away. My mother had channelled hers into an endless succession of men who didn't love her and whom she didn't love. But I couldn't do that. Just as I couldn't do what Con had done, cutting himself off from his emotions completely.

I'd always thought that feeling so deeply was a weakness in me somehow, a flaw. Yet it didn't feel like a flaw now. Now, looking at Con and the anguish I saw deep inside him, it felt like a gift I could give him. He'd forgotten how to feel, how to process emotions, so they were harsh and jagged and painful inside him. But I could help. Whether he wanted my friendship or not, he needed it.

He needed to talk to someone he could trust.

I was that someone.

'Years ago,' I said huskily, 'I told you that I was your friend.'

He glanced up at me and this time I couldn't read his expression at all, his black eyes fathomless. He didn't speak, only stared at me.

'I'm still your friend, Con. You don't need to distance yourself. You don't need to protect me. I know you. I have known you since I was a child, and there is nothing in you that scares me. You can trust me. I'm here for you. I always have been.'

He said nothing for a long moment. Then abruptly he leaned down and brushed his mouth over mine in a featherlight kiss.

I dug my fingers into the hard muscle of his shoulders, wanting more, but he didn't deepen it, only lifted his head, staring down into my eyes. His hand curved over my stomach, where our baby grew. 'I will not hurt our child,' he said, with all the certainty of a vow. 'I became like Domingo in order to survive, but I will never be like him as a father. Never.'

'I know,' I said simply. 'And you're not him. You never were.'

His hand was large and warm, resting on my stomach.

'You're going to make a wonderful mother, Jenny. I couldn't ask for a better mother for my children.'

A flush of heat went through me, my whole being responding to his praise like a flower opening its petals to the sun. I felt as if I was back in his study and he was telling me very seriously that my mother didn't know what she was talking about and that if I wanted to try for med school I should, because I had both the intelligence and the work ethic.

'I don't know...' I felt oddly hesitant. 'I didn't have the best role model for a mother. I have no idea of how or what you're supposed to do, or...or anything, really.'

They were fears I'd had, but never wanted to acknowledge. That for all my determination to provide a stable and secure home for my child, I wouldn't be able to.

There had been so many things I'd wanted to do, and I'd never succeeded at any of them, so how was I supposed to succeed at this?

'Does anyone the first time they become a parent?' His hand lifted and cupped my cheek, his thumb brushing over my cheekbone. 'You're beautiful, you're successful, you're—'

I snorted. 'I'm not successful.'

'You are,' he insisted. 'You wanted to work with charities and that's exactly what you're doing. Isn't that success? Working in a job that makes you happy and fulfils you?'

'I suppose so.' I sighed. 'I never got into med school, though.'

'So?' One imperious black brow rose. 'You can try again, you know. Plenty of people go back to university years after they leave school.'

I rolled my eyes and gave his shoulder a little push. 'That's not the point.'

He ignored the push. 'Then what is?'

'You know… I think I'm just unsure. I badly want to be a better mother than mine was. I want to give our child the best start in life that I can.'

Something in his hard face softened, his beautiful mouth curving. 'And you will. You already know what *not* to do, correct?'

'True.'

'And, apart from that, you're warm, you're empathetic, you're giving. And you care. You have so much love to give our baby, Jenny. You will be the best mother a child could have.'

There was so much conviction in his voice that my throat closed with emotion. He'd always had the ability to make me feel better about myself. Always.

'Thank you,' I said huskily, reaching out to touch his face. 'That means a lot to me.' Then, to lighten the atmosphere, because I didn't want to cry, I said, 'She always thought I should marry you. That since she had Domingo I should get in there and snag you.'

It was a risk to tease him with that, because I had no idea how he'd take it. I hoped he'd understand that it wasn't something I'd ever have done, but who knew?

Yet his dark eyes glittered with amusement, the lines around his hard, carved mouth relaxing. 'Well, you did snag me, didn't you?' He shifted against me. 'And now that you have, what are you going to do with me?'

My heart fluttered. I'd thought I'd lost the ability to make him smile and, while it wasn't quite like the smiles he'd used to give me, the potential was there.

'I suppose I have a few options.' I lifted a hand to his broad shoulder, stroking it then trailing my fingers down his hard, carved chest. 'I could try seducing you.'

'That's true,' he agreed. 'You could try. But I warn you: I'm rather difficult to seduce.'

My heart fluttered even harder. Oh, yes, that was definitely amusement. 'No, you're not.'

One corner of his mouth turned up and my heart turned over. 'Prove it, then.'

So, I did.

CHAPTER SIXTEEN

Constantine

I WOKE EARLY the next morning, coming to consciousness instantly, a warm and very naked female body in
my arms. I was hard, and all I could think about was
waking her up then putting her on her back and sinking
inside the tight, wet heat of her body.

But she was sleeping peacefully, and I had kept her
up late the night before, so instead I raised myself on an
elbow and allowed myself the total indulgence of gazing down at her, studying her sleeping face.

She looked so young, her soft rose petal skin pink
with warmth, her features relaxed in sleep. Her eyelashes
were thick, and darker than the hair on her head, a sable
colour that looked just as soft to the touch as the rest of
her. Her nose was slightly upturned, and her mouth was
full and delightfully sensual.

She was beautiful. I knew she felt that she didn't have
her mother's looks, but she did. Catherine's beauty was
cold and hard-edged—a bit like Olivia's—but Jenny's
was different. Jenny's was soft, and had a deep and
generous sensuality that both Catherine and Olivia had
lacked. Or at least when it came to Olivia I hadn't seen it.

But I saw Jenny's. It came from the deep well of empathy inside her, her warm, unselfish spirit. She was a giving person—she'd always had been, ever since she'd turned up that day in the mansion and declared that she was going to be my friend.

I touched her cheek very lightly, her skin satin-smooth beneath my finger.

I hadn't wanted to tell her about Domingo and my childhood, yet now I had I couldn't bring myself to regret it. It felt as if a weight had been lifted from my shoulders, a weight I hadn't realised I'd been carrying. Even telling her about Valentin and his return had been…good.

She hadn't been angry with me for not telling her. She hadn't turned it into a battle. She hadn't used the confession to get something out of me, and she hadn't pressed for any more information than I'd been willing to give her.

She'd simply let me talk, her fingers playing with my hair and stroking my back as I lay on her warm body. I should have moved to make her more comfortable, since I was heavy, but she hadn't insisted and so I hadn't moved. She was wonderful to lie against. She was soft and she smelled like heaven.

You trust her.

Perhaps it shouldn't have been so surprising. I wouldn't have told her everything if I hadn't trusted her on some level.

'You can trust me. I'm here for you. I always have been.'

Her words from the day before echoed in my head, along with the conviction I'd seen in her dark eyes.

She *had* always been there for me. But I hadn't been there for her, had I? I'd cut her off for four years, kept

myself emotionally distant from her without an explanation. Then I'd told her yesterday that we could never
go back to being friends and she'd looked so stricken...

A tight feeling coiled in my chest and I stroked the
side of her cheek.

I couldn't keep doing that to her. I couldn't keep holding myself apart. Every decision I'd made for the past
four years had hurt her, and that wasn't fair.

Telling her about the night Valentin had left, when I'd
lost my temper, going to Domingo in a rage, was impossible. That she must never know. But surely I didn't
have to keep the rest of it from her. Surely I could stay
being her friend. As she'd said, we'd managed it before.
And, while things were different now, I didn't see why
we couldn't manage it again.

I could stay in control of myself, and while she might
be vulnerable, she also had that thread of pure steel running through her.

It fascinated me how she could be so open and yet so
strong. As if the emotions she wore so honestly were a
strength and an armour in themselves, not a weakness
that could be exploited and weaponised.

She stirred, giving a sigh, and those long, silky eyelashes of hers fluttered, then lifted. Her eyes were such
a warm brown, like hot chocolate, and when she smiled,
as she did now, I swore I could see rays of sunshine
dancing in them.

'Good morning,' she murmured sleepily, a pink flush
spreading over her skin. 'Exactly how long have you
been lying there watching me?'

'I'm not sure.' My fingers trailed over her jaw and
down the side of her neck. 'Does it disturb you?'

'No.' She put her hand on my chest, her touch warm

on my bare skin. 'Though I didn't realise I was quite so fascinating.'

'You are.' I looked down into her eyes. 'How do you do it, Jenny? How do you walk around with your emotions so close to the surface? So everyone can see exactly what you're feeling? Aren't you afraid?'

Her brow furrowed. 'Afraid of what?'

'Afraid someone will take advantage of you.'

'Well, I didn't have the kind of childhood you had so, no, that has never been my first thought. Though Mum was always telling me I was too soft for my own good, that I needed to be colder, more calculating.' Her fingers brushed over my chest in a gentle caress. 'I just… couldn't. It felt dishonest and wrong.' Her gaze flicked up to meet mine. 'She uses men, you know. Manipulates their emotions in order to get access to their money. In fact, now I think about it, she's more than a little like your father.'

I, too, had thought that. The two of them had seemed well suited. And that made Jenny all the more fascinating. Because while I had tried to make myself like my father, she had done the opposite. She had rebelled.

Like Val. And you always had a sneaking admiration for him.

Yes, that was true. Part of me had loved his blatant opposition. Loved how it had enraged our cold father. It just hadn't been my choice.

I frowned with a sudden suspicion. 'Did Catherine ever hurt you? Did she ever try to make you—?'

'No,' Jenny murmured firmly, pressing her fingers against my chest as if to emphasise the word. 'No, she didn't. But you know she was never very…loving. She didn't even seem to like me all that much. I used to wonder sometimes if it was because I wasn't planned, and because my father left her when she found out she was pregnant with me.' Her gaze dropped from mine, her attention on her hand. 'There were a few times I wanted to ask her why she didn't just get rid of me, but I... I never had the courage.' Jenny let out a soft breath. 'I think I was afraid of the answer.'

I hadn't really thought Catherine would have hurt Jenny physically, but I knew she'd hurt her emotionally... that her treatment as a child had left scars. That they weren't quite as dark as the ones that my father had left on me didn't matter. What mattered was the pain they'd left, and the fact that I could do something about it.

I had been working hard at Silver Inc, trying to change the culture of fear Domingo had instituted, but sometimes I feared that the damage he'd done was beyond repair. He'd destroyed the few relationships I'd had, after all.

Yet while Valentin was lost to me, Jenny wasn't.

'Anyway,' Jenny went on quietly, 'she thought I should marry you. That I was stupid for wanting to work at a charity when I could simply seduce you and be your wife.'

Shouldn't you not *be discussing this? What happened to emotional distance?*

No, I couldn't do love, but I could certainly do friendship. I could certainly do reassurance. And for Jenny I would do just about anything. Besides, apart from anything else, no one had needed me before, and I wanted to hold on to that feeling for as long as I could.

'Simply seduce me, hmm?' I murmured, amused despite myself. I wasn't angry at the confession. 'Sounds easy.'

She gave me a teasing look from underneath her lashes. 'It was yesterday.'

I liked how she flirted with me, yet I had a sense that there was more going on, that she wasn't telling me quite everything.

I reached down and slid a finger beneath her chin, tilting her face up so I could see her, and caught the doubt that flickered in the depths of her deep brown eyes. 'There's more, though, isn't there?' I said softly. 'Tell me what worries you.'

'A lot of things.' She paused and swallowed. 'I want to give our child safety and security and stability, like I told you. But this baby wasn't planned, and I know you wouldn't ever have married me if I wasn't pregnant. I just worry that I'm not…successful enough to be your wife. That one day you'll see it and…' Her voice had gone husky. 'I don't want you to be disappointed in me and I don't want you to regret marrying me.'

My chest tightened, an ache sitting behind my breastbone. Because I understood. Her childhood had been chaotic and lonely, and of course she wouldn't want that for our child—I didn't want that for our child myself.

'You won't disappoint me,' I said huskily. 'It's impossible. You were the one bright spot in my life. The only good thing. You never lied to me or tried to manipulate me. You distracted me when I needed it and you made me smile. You always cared, Jenny. You always cared so much. So why would I *ever* regret marrying you?'

Her eyes filled with tears. 'Don't make me cry, you horrible man. I swore I would never cry in front of you again.'

Ah, yes, that night in the garden. When she'd told me she loved me and I'd said those awful things to her.

She'd cried, and even though I'd tried to tell myself I felt nothing, in breaking her I'd broken a part of myself, too.

I stroked her cheek with my thumb, then bent and kissed away the tears. 'I'm sorry.' They weren't words I said often, if at all, but if anyone deserved them it was her. 'I'm sorry for the way I've treated you for the past four years, for cutting you off without explanation. And I'm sorry for what I said to you that night. You didn't deserve it—not any of it. The only excuse I can give was that it was the day when I'd found out Valentin was alive, and I was…not myself.'

Her fingers spread on my chest, a soft warmth sitting on my skin. The endless well of compassion and sympathy that was Jenny's spirit glowed in her eyes.

And what have you done to deserve it? Nothing. You've done nothing.

I hadn't. I'd forced her to come to Scotland with me. Forced her into accepting marriage. I'd seduced her and then shut her out. Shouted at her. Kicked down her door. I'd been a bastard, and yet all I could see in her eyes was forgiveness.

'I know you weren't,' she said. 'It made me angry with you for months, but even back then I knew something was wrong. It makes sense now.'

I could feel it twist inside me then, the need to tell her everything. The one thing I'd left out, that I'd let fester inside me like a thorn.

But how could I tell her about what I'd done to Domingo? And what he'd done to me in return? It wouldn't help things. It wouldn't make them better.

And she wouldn't look at me with compassion any longer, but horror.

Because the other thing she'd always given me was

hope. Hope that one day I could be the man she saw when she looked at me. Hope that I could leave Domingo behind in the past for ever. And he wouldn't be if I told her what I'd done.

He'd be between us always.

So, no truth. But I couldn't keep shutting her out and locking myself away. That wasn't fair on her. That was about my own baggage, not hers, and she shouldn't have to bear the brunt. Besides, I wanted to be with her. I wanted to spend time with her. I didn't care what we did, just being together would be enough.

'I'm not going to the cottage today.' I brushed my finger over her cheek once again. 'I will spend it with you. That is, if you'd like that?'

Her smile was like dawn breaking over a delicate landscape, illuminating everything. Illuminating me. 'Oh, yes, I'd love that. What would you like to do?'

Warmth glowed inside me, as if the light in her face had somehow transferred itself into me. 'Well,' I said, 'I'm not sure. I've never done things with a friend before, so I was hoping you could tell me.'

'Idiot.' Her voice was full of affection. 'Of course you've done things with a friend before. We looked after a nest of sparrows together, remember?'

I raised an eyebrow. 'Jenny, I'm sorry, but I'm not looking after birds with you today. Or tomorrow. Or possibly ever again.'

She laughed, as if the sunshine had turned into sound. 'Good. Because I have other plans.'

CHAPTER SEVENTEEN

Jenny

IT SOON BECAME very clear to me that Con had put sex at the top of his list of things to do with friends, and he was puzzled when I suggested that we didn't have to spend all day in bed.

'But what else should we do?' he asked, and I could see that he genuinely didn't know.

Luckily for him, I did.

The thought of him being around all day, doing the kinds of things friends did with each other, filled me with happiness. Yes, I'd always been his friend, but that had been limited to the mansion in Madrid. We'd spent time with each other, but only in his study. Then I'd always wondered why he was so different with other people, but now I knew. It had been because of his father.

Today, though, Domingo was dead and Con wanted to spend time with me. I didn't want to think about the past. I didn't want to think about the future either. I wanted to enjoy the present while I could, because I had a sense that we had some difficult conversations ahead of us, about marriage and living arrangements and raising our child.

I'd voiced my worries about that, about my yearning

for the kind of security and stability I'd never had grow-ing up. Plus the doubt that underlaid all of that, which was the fear that he'd regret marrying me and leave me, the way my father had with my mother.

Some part of me knew he wasn't that kind of man and never had been, but I'd needed to hear his reassurance all the same. Except it hadn't completely eased all doubt. Some was still there, like a shard of ice in my heart.

He didn't love me, and he'd said he'd never be able to give me that, and somehow that made everything feel precarious.

But I wasn't going to think about it. And while spend-ing time with him was probably a bad idea for my poor heart, I decided to ignore the danger. The future could take care of itself. I just wanted one day with the man I loved.

The weather was beautiful, so after we'd got out of bed—or rather when Con finally let me escape—and we'd had breakfast, I went off to speak with Mrs Mack-enzie. Together we organised a picnic basket full of all Con's favourite foods—I was thrilled to find some choc-olate-covered strawberries lurking in the fridge, since he did like chocolate—and some of mine, plus a bottle of champagne for him and some sparkling grape juice for me. Then I asked her where the best picnicking places were around the loch, and she patted my hand and told me she'd get someone to arrange the picnic for us, so we didn't have to lug a heavy basket around.

When I told Con I'd organised a picnic, he made a show of being miffed that he hadn't arranged it himself, but I could tell he was secretly delighted. Which in turn delighted me.

Then he went and changed into some casual clothes—

worn jeans and a black T-shirt—and every thought went out of my head.

I'd never seen him wear anything but handmade suits and formal wear, and he was to die for in those. In jeans and a T-shirt he was quite simply devastating. The cotton of his tee clung lovingly to his wide shoulders and broad chest, and the denim of his jeans hugged his powerful thighs. It almost made me consider scrapping the picnic and spending the rest of the day in bed, the way he'd suggested.

I'd looked around in the drawers for something casual to wear for myself, but found nothing. Apparently he hadn't thought I'd want to go traipsing around the loch. I didn't mind, though. Especially when he told me he'd prefer me to wear another wrap dress, since they were much easier to take off.

There was a trail around the loch, and at first he set a blistering pace, prompting me to grab his hand to slow him down. I told him that the whole point of this walk was to look at the scenery and talk to each other. He seemed mystified by that too, but he didn't let go of my hand, his fingers entwined with mine warm and strong.

The setting was beautiful, the deep valley and the loch, the heather blooming on the slopes turning the whole valley purple.

'What made you buy this place?' I asked as we walked. 'It's a long way from Madrid.'

He gave me an enigmatic glance. 'That's exactly why. Because it's a long way from Madrid. There's no cell phone service either, which makes it the perfect place to retreat to.'

'From Domingo?'

'*Sí.*' He looked away from me, out over the loch. 'In

the past when I came here I would dismiss all my staff for a week or so. Live in the house completely alone.' His mouth twisted wryly. 'Well, apart from Mrs Mackenzie.'

'Oh, you let her stay?'

He glanced back at me, wry amusement clear in his gaze too. 'I didn't "let" her do anything. She refused to leave. Said I needed someone to look after me.'

I grinned, charmed at the thought of Mrs Mackenzie bullying one of the most feared businessmen in Europe into being looked after. 'She's difficult to say no to, it's true.'

'Stubborn women plague my life.'

'Poor you.' I squeezed his hand, then after a moment asked, 'Why did you stay in Madrid? Why didn't you ever leave and go somewhere else?'

Something furious glittered briefly in his eyes. 'What? Run away like Valentin? No. I couldn't leave. Silver Inc is one of Europe's largest companies, and that made Domingo powerful. His influence spread everywhere, affecting many other companies and many other people. And no one knew what he was really like except me, so I had to stay to mitigate the damage he could do, to manage him.'

'Did that person have to be you?'

'He listened to me. I'd spent years turning myself into a carbon copy of him and, while I don't believe he was capable of trusting anyone, he certainly gave more weight to my opinions that anyone else's. I was able to guide him on certain policy changes.'

That didn't surprise me, not considering Con's deep protective streak. But I could also see that he was very angry with Valentin, and I wanted to know why. Obviously pretending you were dead for fifteen years wasn't going to endear you to anyone, and I could understand why Con was upset with him for that. But…there was more. Even when Con had spoken about Valentin rescuing his toy soldier he'd been furious. He'd said that Valentin had made things worse, and I could see that too, but… I was curious. I wanted to know more.

I wanted to know everything.

Still, there was a time and a place, and while I knew I could push him if I wanted to, I didn't want to right now. This was supposed to be a nice day for the two of us, so I squeezed his hand and changed the subject.

We talked about other things, such as how he preferred riding to hiking, and that there were stables here if I wanted to ride too. I'd never ridden a horse before, and of course he insisted that I needed to learn and that he would teach me himself. Then he went off into a long description of the whisky distillery he'd had built on the other side of the loch, an interest he'd been pursuing for a few years, and how their first single malt was due to be released soon.

It was clear from the gleam in his eyes that this was something he was passionate about, and I loved listening to him talk about it. That passion coloured his voice, softened the hard planes and angles of his face, making him even more ridiculously beautiful than he already was.

The picnic place Mrs Mackenzie had recommended was half an hour from the manor—a lovely flat area just across from the pebbly beach of the loch. A thick rug had been spread out over the heather, and all the picnic things laid out. There was no sign of paper plates or plastic cutlery and plastic glasses. Instead, the plates were porcelain, the cutlery silver, and the glasses cut crystal.

I watched Con's face as he examined the picnic and

saw him smile. And when he looked at me his dark eyes were full of intensity. 'This is wonderful, Jenny. Thank you.'

He meant it, and that made me glow with pleasure.

I tugged on his hand to lead him to the rug. 'Come on. Let's have something to eat.'

He sat down and I insisted on serving him, putting on his plate all the delicacies I knew he liked—including the strawberries—then handing him a glass of champagne that was already opened and sitting in an ice bucket for us.

I loved doing things for him. I loved looking after him.

A peaceful silence reigned as we ate, and then, when Con finally put down his plate, he said, 'These are all my favourite foods. How did you know what I liked?'

'I paid attention to you,' I said, pleased that he'd noticed. 'And I remembered what you like.' I paused, then added, 'I always liked taking care of you, too.'

The expression in his eyes shifted. 'Why did you sometimes take Domingo's hand? Those times he came into my study, when I'd tell you to leave and you wouldn't. You started talking to him instead.'

I shrugged. 'Domingo didn't like me. I made him uncomfortable. I'm not sure why. When I tried to talk to him he'd ignore me and just…leave. So when I noticed that you didn't seem to like his visits, I did it more.'

The look on Con's face was impenetrable. 'You were protecting me?'

I had my legs tucked under me, my plate at my side, sipping on my grape juice—which was delightfully dry and not at all as sweet as I'd dreaded.

I blushed. 'I know, it's stupid. It's not like I'm tall or powerful or anything, but... Well, I tried.'

His eyes were as black as space and they watched me keenly, though I couldn't tell what he was thinking.

'Domingo had an estate in the Caribbean that he used to take Valentin and I to,' he said after a moment. 'Valentin got to know a girl from a neighbouring estate and she became his friend. He used to meet her on a secret beach, very much against our father's wishes.'

I wasn't sure why he was telling me this, but there was no way I was going to interrupt him so I stayed silent, watching him.

'That girl was Olivia,' he went on. 'Her family used to holiday on the same island.'

A shock of surprise went through me. 'Really?'

'Yes. I was...jealous. Not of Valentin, but of her. She took away the one person I had, because he didn't want to spend any time with me when she was there, he only wanted to spend time with her. I was angry with him for choosing her over me. And he always made our situation worse by not doing what Domingo said and making him angry. I felt that Domingo even liked it when Valentin rebelled, and that somehow he preferred Valentin's rebellions to me doing everything he said.' Con paused, looking down at the champagne in his hand. 'He preferred resistance. He liked it... Anyway, I was furious that Valentin was disobeying Domingo by continuing to see Olivia, by developing a friendship we weren't allowed and by preferring to spend time with her than with me. So, I...went to Domingo and told him what Valentin was doing.'

A thread of tension wound through me.

'Papa was furious. He ordered Valentin to stop seeing

her, but Valentin wouldn't. So Domingo locked him in his room. He wasn't allowed to come out until he agreed to stop seeing Olivia. But Valentin refused.' Con's perfect face was hard, his mouth a grim line. 'I pleaded with him to agree, because I knew Domingo. He'd keep Valentin in that room for ever if he had to. But Valentin kept saying no. He stayed in that room for six months.'

Ice pooled in my gut. Six months? He'd stayed in his room for six months?

'He wouldn't listen to me,' Con went on, his accent deepening. 'He refused. I needed him, but his battle with Domingo was more important than I was. Even protecting Olivia wasn't as important. I didn't understand him—I never did. And in the end all I could do was find the key and give it to him, because I knew he'd never give in. And I was the one who'd put him there.' Con looked at me, his gaze sharp enough to cut. 'You wanted to know why I kicked down your door? Because I spent hours, days, sitting outside Val's locked door, desperate for him to come out. And he never did.'

There was anguish in his eyes, and grief.

'Con—' I began.

'No, I haven't finished.' His voice was hoarse. 'I'm telling you this because you asked me a few days ago who protected me, and the answer is that you did. You protected me, Jenny. And you will never know how much that meant to me. But you have to understand that you also need protection. I always thought the danger came from my father, but it doesn't, not any more.' He took a breath, then caught my gaze. 'It comes from me.'

I blinked at him, not understanding. 'What do you mean, the danger comes from you?'

'Emotions are grenades. They can explode at any

time. You saw what happened when you locked the door on me. And when Valentin refused to give Olivia up. When he left me—' Con stopped, darkness in his eyes. 'I am that grenade, Jenny. I am unstable when I let my emotions get the better of me. And when that happens, you are at risk.' He took another breath. 'I want to be your friend. I don't want to cause you any more pain than I already have. But when we get back to London you will have to allow me to keep some emotional distance from you.'

I stared at him in shock, trying to process what he'd said. 'I don't understand. You're not unstable. You're not a danger. What on earth makes you think that?'

He glanced down at the heather in bloom all around us. 'Kicking down your door. Getting Val locked in his room. Being so angry with him. There have been other instances.'

'Con—'

'No, please.' He glanced up again. 'Not now. Let's have this day just for us.'

I wanted to push. I wanted to tell him he was wrong, that he wasn't unstable or volatile or a grenade. He was only a man who felt deeply and who'd never learned how to deal with his emotions. Who'd been scarred by his childhood. That was all. He wasn't a danger, not to me.

But he was right. This day was for us, not for the past, so I put down my grape juice, then went over to him and relieved him of his glass. Then I wriggled into his lap, winding my arms around him. I didn't speak. I simply pressed my face to his throat, holding him tightly.

He was still a moment, his big, powerful body tense. Then his arms closed around me and he crushed me to him, burying his face in my hair.

We stayed like that for a long time, and then Con released me. But only so he could pull me down on the picnic blanket beside him. Then he tugged open the tie of my dress and spread the fabric out, baring me to the deep blue sky above. He bent his head and kissed me, his mouth tasting of champagne and the delicious dark flavour that was all him. Then he got rid of my clothes and turned his hunger on me, making a meal of my body, feasting on me as if he'd never had anything quite so delicious.

Only when he had me quivering in delight and shaking with need did he strip his own clothes off and rise above me, naked and magnificent, his olive skin burnished by the sun. Then he thrust into me in one hard movement, making me cry out his name.

And when he moved, deep and slow, turning my pleasure into white-hot passion in seconds flat, I cried out his name again.

Perhaps it was then that I knew, even though consciously I didn't want to admit it. Knew that no matter how many months had passed, and no matter how many promises I'd made to myself, no matter how many stern talking-tos I'd given myself, I was still in love with him.

And friendship would never be enough.

CHAPTER EIGHTEEN

Constantine

I FORGOT ABOUT going to the cottage. I forgot about the company. I even forgot about Valentin. All I wanted to do was spend time with Jenny.

I taught her the basics of riding, making sure to put her on the gentlest horse, and took her for a walk around one of the fields. She turned out to be a natural on horseback, which thrilled her since, as she told me, she hadn't been a natural at anything before.

Another day I took her on the tour of my distillery. The business of whisky-making took time and care, and I'd found it the perfect escape from the day-to-day running of Silver Inc. It had also helped that it had nothing whatsoever to do with Domingo.

It mattered to me more than I'd thought that she was interested in it, and asked all kinds of questions on the tour. I'd wanted to give her a taste of our first batch, but obviously that would have to wait until after the baby was born.

She was so easy to be with. Easy to share with. She made every day brighter, and I'd forgotten how simply being around her brought me joy.

Except it made the beast in me hungrier and hungrier. As if all the time in the world with her wouldn't be enough. Nothing would. I wanted to keep her here in Glen Creag, never let her leave. We could bring our child up here and it would be perfect. I could have them both all to myself for ever.

But that was what the beast wanted, not the man, and I would never give in to it. No matter what Papa had said to me that night, I wasn't just like him. I was different, I was better, and even though it was getting harder and harder to be better where Jenny was concerned, I had to be for her sake.

When we finally left Glen Creag I would have to be ruthless with myself. I'd warned her that I would have to retain a certain amount of emotional distance but, since I wasn't willing to hurt her, I couldn't completely withdraw my friendship from her, not again.

It would be difficult—torture—but I could do it.

I also had to be strong with regard to my other little secret.

Since that day of the wonderful little picnic she'd arranged for me, when I'd nearly told her about it, I'd managed to keep it locked down.

She had to keep believing I was a good man, keep thinking that I would make a good father. Because if she didn't I would be lost. I would have nothing to aim for, nothing to strive for. I wanted to be the man she saw when she looked at me, both for her and for our child, which meant I could never tell her.

Which was fine. She might get under most of my defences with pathetic ease, but not that one. That one would have to remain obdurate.

A few days after I'd taken her on a tour of the distillery, and after another riding trip, where this time I brought a picnic for her, I decided that there was one last place on the estate that I wanted her to see.

My collection room.

I hoped that sharing it with her would make her feel at ease. I'd caught her looking speculatively at me a couple of times, and wondered if it was to do with my slip at the picnic, but she hadn't broached the topic again. Perhaps if I gave her this last piece of myself she'd forget about the thing I didn't want to tell her.

I found her curled up in one of the armchairs in the small library a few days later, with her nose in a book. It reminded me very much of how she'd used to be in my study, tucked away in the armchair, reading. She'd look up from her book and see me, and then she'd smile, and her face would light up.

My chest tightened as she did that now, putting down her book and looking up at me, her smile lighting the room in the same way it always did.

'What are we going to do today? Please tell me we're going riding.'

I smiled at her eagerness. 'This afternoon, perhaps. Right now, though, I have something I want to show you.' I held out my hand.

Instantly she got up and came over to me, her fingers threading through mine. 'Oh, what?'

Her hand felt small and delicate and warm, so I held it gently. 'You'll see.'

I let her out of the room and headed towards the front door.

'You know, Con,' she murmured as we stepped outside, 'we've skirted around it, but we need to talk about a few things.'

We did. Our wedding loomed, and so did the question of where we would live and other such practicalities. I needed to deal with the Valentin situation also. But I didn't want to think about those things right now. They could wait.

'We will,' I said. 'Later.'

I led her across the grass towards the cottage and she didn't speak, although her fingers tightened around mine.

Inside the cottage, I went to the shelving unit and pressed the hidden button to reveal the palm lock. I unlocked the door, pulled it open, and gestured for her to go in first.

She gave me a worried look, her beautiful brown eyes questioning. 'Are you sure?'

'Yes.'

'Okay.' She went to the doorway and stepped through it into the room beyond.

I'd thought I'd feel tense at her presence there, the way I had before, but I didn't. As soon as she stepped through the doorway something clicked into place. A sense of rightness. As if she belonged there, along with all of my other precious items.

I followed behind her, watching as she stared around at the glass cases and shelves of my collection. At the things that were precious and the things that were not. Things worth millions and things worth nothing at all.

'What…is this?' Her voice was quiet as she stared around, her eyes wide.

'You know I told you that I wasn't allowed anything as a child? No toys. No friends. No pets. Only school materials and the clothes on our backs. We weren't even allowed books to read. So when I was finally old enough to be out from under Domingo's thumb, I decided I would collect things that I liked.'

She paused beside a case that contained coins. I had some old Spanish doubloons, a few from Ancient Roman, one or two Greek. I even had a *daric*, a gold coin from ancient Persia.

'Why didn't you want me to come in that day I found you in here?' she murmured, gazing at the coins. 'You were furious with me. I know you were.'

'Because this collection is private, and some of these things are very personal to me. I suppose hiding them is a habit I've got into. With Domingo, you couldn't let him see that anything was important to you, because he'd take it away. So I found it easier to keep everything hidden.'

Perhaps I hadn't needed to in the past few years, but by then it had become a habit too hard to break.

Jenny moved on to my small collection of mechanical toys, mostly from the Victorian era, staring at them in wonder. 'I can understand that. You have so many different things…'

'I collect anything that takes my fancy.'

She examined the collection of swords and knives from different parts of the world—some historic, some modern—that I'd had mounted on the wall. Then went on to another case full of gems, crystals and geodes. A few were very valuable, while some weren't. Some were just ones I liked.

She paused, staring at them, and her mouth curved. 'You have a rock collection, Con.'

I loved it when she teased me. There was so much affection in her tone.

I raised a brow, mock-stern. 'Yes. What of it?'

She grinned. 'And coins and swords and toys and—'
Abruptly, she broke off, her expression changing, her
smile fading away, leaving her looking almost stricken.
Her dark eyes seemed liquid in the light of the room.

Tension gripped me. 'Jenny? What is it?'

She turned away, moving over to one of the other
shelves before pausing again. I knew what she was looking at. My toy soldier.

She didn't say anything, staring down at the piece of
plastic sitting on the shelf.

I went over to where she stood, coming up beside her.
'What's wrong?'

'That's your toy,' she said quietly, ignoring my question. 'That's your toy soldier, isn't it? The one Valentin
threw onto the roof.'

'Yes.' I wasn't sure where she was going with this.

'And all of this…' She turned, looking up me, tears
in her eyes. 'Rocks and coins and swords… You missed
out on so much.' Her voice went hoarse. 'And you were
hurt so badly. I can't…'

A tear slid down her cheek, making my chest feel so
tight I could hardly breathe.

Reaching out, I pulled her into my arms and gathered
her close. 'I didn't bring you here to upset you.' I pressed
a kiss to the top of her head. 'I only wanted to share it
with you. Something important to me.'

'I know.' The words were muffled against my shirt.
'And I'm honoured, Con. But it makes me so sad to
think about the little boy you were and what you never
got to have.'

'That's all in the past now,' I said gruffly.

She looked up, her face flushing pink with emotion.
'I don't want this for our child. I don't want him or her

to miss out on a single thing or to feel as if they're not loved. Not even a little bit. We can't let that happen. We can't. Promise me.'

The tension gripped tighter. 'I can promise you that they won't miss out on anything.'

Her gaze flickered and she bit her lip. 'You said that love isn't something you can give. Do you still mean that?'

A blade slid between my ribs, so sharp I barely felt it go in. Yet it was there, deep in my gut, radiating pain. But ever since I'd met her I'd spent my life protecting her, and I wasn't going to stop now. Especially not now we were expecting a child.

She must have read my expression, because the look in her eyes changed. 'Oh, Con, please don't say—'

I let her go abruptly and took a step back. I hadn't wanted to hurt her—not again—but this was unavoidable. 'Yes,' I said. 'Yes, I still mean it.'

Anguish flickered over her face. 'Why? I don't understand.'

'Because love isn't something I can—'

'No,' she interrupted, her voice quivering. *'No.'* The anguish disappeared, leaving fury hot and bright in her eyes. 'Don't tell me you can't, or that you're not able to. Don't lie to me, Constantine.'

'Jenny—'

'No,' she said again, her hands in fists at her sides. 'There's something you're not telling me, something you're hiding. I think you almost let it slip at our picnic, but you didn't want to talk about it.' She took a step towards me. 'What is it? It's something to do with these lies you believe about love, isn't it?'

You have to tell her. You can't hide it.

Ice sat in my gut, hard and jagged and sharp. I hadn't wanted to tell her. I hadn't *ever* wanted to tell her. But there was no escaping it now. I could have given her some ridiculous excuse, some meaningless justification, but I couldn't do that to her, not when it concerned our child. She deserved better than that.

I had to tell her the truth. Even if it changed things. Even if it meant putting her and our baby beyond my reach for ever. And maybe it would even be better this way. Better a short, sharp pain now, so that she could heal, rather than a prolonged agony, especially an agony that might have the potential to affect our son or daughter.

'You're right,' I said, ignoring the pain that lay deep in my heart. 'There is something I'm not telling you. I didn't ever want to tell you. I wanted to keep you and the baby safe. But… You deserve to know. It's not fair to keep you in the dark.'

Her face had gone white. 'What is it?'

'The night Valentin escaped his room I knew he was gone for good. That he wouldn't ever return. He had… left me.'

I could still feel the rage. It was still there. Rage at Valentin, rage at myself, rage at my father.

'It was my fault. If I hadn't told Domingo about him and Olivia then none of it would have happened. I was… furious. At myself, at Val, at Papa. I went to Papa's study and I stormed inside. I hadn't ever rebelled against him, not like Val. I did everything he said usually. But…not that night.'

Even to my own ears my voice sounded harsh, metallic.

'He was sitting in a chair, reading a book, and I lost

my temper. I was tall at seventeen, and I was strong, and so when I pulled him out of his chair he came easily. I'd surprised him.'

Jenny's eyes darkened, but she didn't look away and she didn't speak.

'I don't remember much of what happened then, just an explosion of rage and the feel of my fist connecting with his face. The next thing I was aware of was him on the floor, his face a bloody mess.'

Every part of my body was tight, the pain radiating outward, but I forced it away. Turned myself cold, hard. Impervious.

'My fists were bloody too, my knuckles raw, and he… he was laughing. He was laughing at me.'

My jaw ached, everything ached.

'And do you know what he said, Jenny? He said "Finally. I was beginning to think you had none of my blood. But you do, boy. Deep down, you're just like me."'

Jenny blinked, a small crease between her silky brows. 'But…you're not, Con.' She said it as if it was self-evident. 'You're nothing like him.'

Of course she would say that. She liked to see the best in people, and that was one of the wonderful things about her. But that meant she minimised the worst. Especially the worst that could do harm.

'Aren't I?' I stayed very still, so I wouldn't give in to the need to pull her into my arms and hold her, never let her go. 'I thought I was. That night I decided never to lose myself to anger again, never to lose myself to *any* emotion again. And for years I managed to do that. To not be the man *he* saw. Until you came along. When you were a child it was easy to distance myself, but… not when you grew up.'

'Con—'

'That night in the garden I lost all control,' I went on, over the top of her, because I had to get this out, she had to know. 'I hurt you. I got you pregnant. Then I kidnapped you and stole you away to come here. I kicked down your door, laid my hands on you. I…' I stopped, breathing hard, feeling as if all the air in the room had been sucked away. 'You bring out all these feelings in me, feelings I cannot control. And it's dangerous. Don't you understand? It's dangerous.'

She stared at me, so pale and lovely, her eyes dark. 'No, actually, I *don't* understand. You've never made me feel afraid, not ever. You're not dangerous and neither are your emotions. You just…feel deeply. Besides, everything you do is about protecting other people, about protecting me.'

I shook my head, my heart beating too fast. Because it was clear that she didn't understand. 'I'm not dangerous now because I remain in control of myself. But I have no control around you. And the more time I spend with you, the more I want. And I can't want. I can't feel so hungry, so desperate. Because I would never forgive myself if I hurt you, and I'd rather die than hurt our child.'

She took a step towards me, her hand outstretched, but something in my gaze must have stopped her, because she lowered it all of a sudden. 'You wouldn't, though. I know you wouldn't. Those birds that you looked after—'

'A child is not a nest of birds,' I ground out. 'And I didn't feel anything for those birds.'

'But you feel something for me, don't you? And for our baby?'

I didn't say anything. I didn't have to.

'Oh, Con,' she murmured, her voice hoarse. 'Why didn't you tell me this?'

'I didn't want you to know. I didn't want you to see…' I gritted my teeth. 'I didn't want you to see Domingo when you looked at me.'

'And I don't.' She closed the distance between us, so small, yet indomitable. 'I never have. Do you know what I see when I look at you, Constantine Silvera? I see the man I've loved for as long as I can remember.'

I could see that love in her eyes. It shone so bright. She didn't hide it. She didn't control it. It radiated from her like heat from the sun.

That love was her light, and I couldn't dim it. I couldn't bear to be the one who made it go dark. And I would. At some point in time, I would.

I was too much like my father and I knew it. I'd always known it.

The pain inside me turned to agony, but I crushed it. Pain had been a constant in my life anyway. It was nothing new.

'I'm sorry,' I said, my voice frozen all the way through. 'I cannot risk it. I cannot risk you.'

'What does that mean?'

The pain had gone now. There was only the ice settling around my heart and it was a relief, so I let it. It was the only way I could survive the decision I had to make, and I knew it.

'It means you have to leave. Go back to London. Go back to your life. I will arrange a flight for you. You can be home by tomorrow night.'

She was staring at me now as if I was a total stranger. 'Go home? But for how long? What about the wedding?'

'How long? For ever, Jenny,' I said gently. 'Because there will be no wedding. I cannot marry you.'

CHAPTER NINETEEN

Jenny

I STARED INTO Con's beautiful hard face, looking for some sign that he didn't mean what he'd said, even that this was some elaborate joke. But it was clear that he did mean it. He meant every word.

Pain collected inside me, tears in my eyes already from the evidence of a destroyed boyhood all around us in the rocks and coins and weapons and toys. A collection of things a little boy would have loved. A little boy who'd have kept them in a shoebox under his bed or in his closet. His favourite rocks and a coin or two. A wooden sword and a mechanical toy. A plastic soldier...

A combination of rare and common, priceless and worthless, and all kept behind a locked door in a vault, as if they were the most precious things on the earth. It broke my heart.

Con broke my heart.

He had lost so much, and although he was the successful CEO of one of Europe's biggest companies, at heart he was still a lonely little boy. A little boy who surrounded himself with things because it was easier to love a thing than a person.

I ached for that boy. Because I knew him. That boy was like me. The kid who felt everything so deeply, whose emotions were big and painful and raw. Who cared so much and who wanted more than anything on earth to love and to be loved in return.

That boy thought his emotions were dangerous, thought *he* was dangerous.

He wasn't, though, I knew that. All his life he'd been protecting people, protecting me, and he hadn't done that because he didn't care.

He cared too much, that was his problem. And he didn't know how to handle it.

But I did. I could help him. I could show him how.

I ignored what he'd said about me leaving and him not marrying me, and said, 'So you'd believe your psychopathic father over me?' I didn't try to hide the growing anger in my voice. 'Is that what you're saying? He told you that you were like him and so you believe him.'

Con's obsidian gaze glittered, sharp and unyielding. 'You think it was just what he said? I have always battled to stay in control—'

'Because you were never taught how to deal with your emotions!' I interrupted, suddenly furious. Not at him, but at the father who'd scarred him and the brother who'd left him. 'You were brought up by a psychopath, Con. No wonder you think all your feelings are toxic.'

'I can't put you at risk.' There was iron in his voice. 'I have done nothing but make your life miserable for years and I will not do it any longer. Especially now we have a child to consider.'

I felt as if there was stone stuck in my throat, making it hard to breathe, to swallow, and what I wanted was to throw myself into his arms. Tell him it was okay, that we could talk about this later, just let us have another few days of happiness.

But I couldn't do it. I couldn't give in. If I wanted to have him—if I wanted to have any kind of relationship with him at all—I couldn't let him pull away from me.

If he wasn't going to fight for us, then I would.

'I'm sure that sounds great in your head,' I said, steel to his iron. 'I'm sure that all sounds very noble. But it's just an excuse, isn't it? It's just an excuse so you don't have to deal with difficult things.'

Black fire flared in his eyes. 'You think I haven't had to deal with difficulties? You really think you can say that to me?'

But I wasn't having that. I wasn't going to have him walk all over me, tell me I was wrong, break my heart, because he thought he was protecting me. He wasn't protecting me. He was protecting himself. And if I wanted him it wasn't just him I'd have to fight, but Domingo too.

'I can say whatever I like to you,' I said fiercely. 'Because I love you and I want you. I want to spend the rest of my life with you. I want us to be a family and I think you want that too. I know you do. You're desperate for it, just like me.' I stared at him, letting him see the depth of what I felt for him, see my love for him in all its painful, ecstatic glory. 'But you're still letting your father make your decisions for you, Con. And you're still believing his lies. And if you can't see that, it's because you don't want to.'

Anger flashed in his gaze, and a deep pain.

Suddenly he was in front of me, his warm hands cupping my face with such gentleness I nearly wept. Even in a fury he was gentle.

'I can't,' he said, as if the words had been ripped from

him. 'I can't take the risk. You and our baby…you're precious. I can't… I don't…'

'You can take the risk. You can. And if you can't trust yourself, then trust me. Trust my love for you. When have I ever let you down?'

His gaze searched mine and I could see the desperation in it. I wanted to tell him that it was okay, that he could let go, that his love wasn't something to be afraid of, but something to celebrate. But I saw the moment when he made the decision not to make that leap, to step back from the edge. To trust in the lies of a psychopath rather than me.

And wasn't that the story of my life? I hadn't been enough for my father, who'd left, or my mother, who'd gone searching for something she'd never been able to get from me. Why would it be any different with Con?

My heart broke then, into tiny, jagged pieces. Because as much as I wanted to push him further, I didn't have the will for it. His whole life had been a battle, so why make this just another fight? He wasn't going to change his mind. He'd decided. And there was nothing I could say that could convince him.

He thought he was doing this to protect me and our child, so why not let him believe that? Why not let him have that peace of mind?

It hurt. It hurt so much. But this wasn't about me, and I didn't want it to be.

It was only and had only ever been about him.

It was only a broken heart. Nothing major.

'Okay,' I said croakily. 'If that's what you feel you need to do.'

I'd sworn I'd never cry in front of him again, and yet more and more tears were gathering in my eyes, and no matter how hard I tried I couldn't blink them away.

A muscle ticked in his jaw, but he was already retreating from me, ice in his gaze. Ice right the way through his soul. 'Don't cry, Jenny.' He let me go and stepped back. 'It's better this way.'

I could have turned around and walked away right then. I could have given in to anger and kept everything inside, met him ice for ice and not allowed him a thing.

But I didn't want that for him. What I wanted was to give him one last thing to carry, a piece of myself he could take with him wherever he went. So he'd know that at least there was one person in this world who cared about him.

I lifted my chin and let the tears fall, because those tears were for him and what did it matter that he could see them? What did it matter that this was agony? This agony was love, and I couldn't keep it inside me any longer.

'I love you,' I said clearly. 'I love you so much, Constantine Silvera. I always have and I always will, and there is nothing you can do to change it. Nothing you can do that will make me love you any less.'

His expression shifted then, a crack in his icy detached mask giving me a glimpse of something molten and raging beneath it. 'Jenny, I—'

'No,' I interrupted. 'No. I haven't finished. I'm telling you this because I want you to know. I want you to be absolutely certain. If you think you're alone in this world, you are not. There will be two people in it—' I touched my stomach so he'd know who else I meant '—who love you utterly and without reservation.'

That raging volcanic thing in his eyes burned bright for one shining moment. Then he glanced away briefly, and when he looked back it was gone. Ice-cold Constantine Silvera was in charge again.

'Please do not worry about money,' he said, as if I hadn't spoken. 'You and the baby will be financially secure. I'll see to it. And I'll also see to it that you will be well protected.'

The tears slid down my cheeks. 'You probably won't want to hear this either, but I'm going to say it anyway. You deserve to be loved. And you deserve to love in return.'

His face remained expressionless. 'Maybe,' he said blankly. 'Maybe not.'

That night in the garden, where I'd felt so destroyed, so broken, I felt those same things now. Yet I could also feel a determination inside me, a steel that perhaps had always been there. A steel that came from love. Love for my child, and love for the man in front of me, and last but not least, it came from hope.

Hope that one day he'd find his way out of the darkness.

Hope that one day he'd come back to us.

I closed the distance between us, going up to him and lifting a hand, wanting to touch him one last time. I brushed my fingers along his hard jaw, feeling the warmth of his skin that was the truth of him, not the black ice in his eyes.

He said nothing, his big, powerful body tense as a wound spring.

'I'll go, but know that I'm not leaving you,' I said softly. 'I will never leave you, not in spirit. I'll be there whenever you need me, Con, and so will our child.'

I wasn't going to change his mind. If he was going to come to me he'd have to make that decision himself. I couldn't make it for him.

I let my hand drop away from his face and moved past him to the door, stepping out into the office. Then I went out across the grass to the manor.

I didn't do anything about the tears that poured down my cheeks.

I let them fall.

CHAPTER TWENTY

Constantine

THAT NIGHT, AFTER THE helicopter had come to take Jenny back to Edinburgh had gone, and there was nothing left for me but the echoing corridors of the manor and the last, elusive threads of her scent hanging in the air, I went out to the cottage and called Valentin.

I'd been putting it off for too long. He had to be dealt with.

Unfortunately, the conversation was not a productive one. I was angry, and in pain, and I allowed my temper to get the better of me. Another reason that it was better that Jenny wasn't here.

Every relationship I had, I seemed to break.

I tried to bury my emotions with work, mobilising my legal team to fight Valentin's claim. Then I went about making sure that Jenny and our child were taken care of.

I didn't think too deeply about her, didn't think about that phone call with Valentin either. Neither of those things would touch me. Neither of those were going to matter.

Instead, I found the detachment that had kept me

going for fifteen years and held on to it as tightly as I could.

Three days passed with aching slowness.

I stayed in the cottage. I couldn't bring myself to be in the manor, where Jenny's scent still lingered. Where everywhere I looked I could see her. Curled up in an armchair. Sitting on a dining chair telling me about some book she'd been reading as she ate ice cream. Squealing on the pebbly beach of the loch as she tested the icy water with small bare toes. Lying naked in my bed and lifting her arms to me, welcoming me into her warmth and her softness. Her understanding and her compassion.

I ached and nothing could ease it. All I could do was distract myself from my empty house, and my empty bed, and the emptiness in my heart that ached and ached right down to my bones.

In the end I spent a lot of time in my collection room, adjusting the displays and unpacking new items. Normally I got tremendous satisfaction out of those small tasks, and yet as I flicked open a box containing an emerald I felt…nothing.

I put the box down on a shelf and looked around at my collection with growing disquiet. These things were all mine, and yet now they all seemed…ridiculous.

What had Jenny said? *'Rocks and coins and swords… You missed out on so much.'*

I had missed out. I had missed out on everything. And now I was trying to fill that emptiness inside me with things. With a little boy's pathetic collection of rocks and coins and toys. A leftover from the childhood he'd never managed to leave behind.

'You're still letting your father make your decisions

for you, Con. And you're still believing his lies. And if you can't see that, it's because you don't want to.'

I took a shaken breath, her words before she'd left echoing in my head as I stared around at the remnants of my childhood. Seeing them finally with new eyes.

This wasn't a collection of things I'd always wanted and never had.

These were reminders of what Domingo had done to me. Reminders of Domingo's hold on me. Things I was clinging to, to fill up that emptiness inside me. An emptiness that could never be filled. Not while Jenny wasn't here.

She was the only one who made me feel I wasn't the same kind of psychopath Domingo had been. The only one who made me feel I could be a good man. The only one who'd made me *want* to be a good man.

'So you believe your psychopathic father over me? He told you that you were like him and so you believe him?'

I paused beside the toy soldier sitting on its shelf. The soldier Domingo had tried to make me burn, and that Valentin had taken and thrown on the roof.

Why had I kept it? Why had I kept any of these things when they were reminders of all the ways Domingo had hurt me? And not just me, but Valentin too.

He had hurt us, twisted us, turned us into his image.

Val escaped, but you never did. You're still that lost boy with bloody knuckles, listening to a man you hated telling you that your worst fear is true.

She was right, my Jenny. She'd been right all along. He still had a hold on me, even all these years later, and I'd never be free of him until all these reminders were gone.

I picked up the soldier, the edges of the plastic cutting into me, then slowly and deliberately I crushed it.

Then I turned and systematically smashed every case in the room.

'Feel better?'

I stopped dead, surrounded by broken glass, my breath heaving, my hands bleeding from all the cuts I'd received.

That voice. It was familiar.

I turned.

Valentin stood in the doorway, leaning against the frame. The brother I'd last seen three weeks ago, striding into the ballroom to tell me he was going to relieve me of my company. Stealing my bride.

His posture was casual, but the look on his face—the same face I saw every day in the mirror—was not. His gaze burned.

I couldn't speak. I couldn't trust myself, not after our last conversation on the phone.

He gazed dispassionately around the room and then looked back at me. 'Are you done?'

He spoke in Spanish, our mother tongue, and he looked the same as he always had. He looked like my brother, my twin.

'What are you doing here? How did you—?'

'I came back to London with Olivia. We're married, by the way, and blissfully happy. You can congratulate me at any time.'

I stared at him, my knuckles stinging, shock resounding through me, unable to think of a single word to say.

'Fine, don't, then.' He shoved himself away from the door frame and took a couple of steps into the ruined room, not paying any attention to it. 'Jenny contacted me.

I like her, by the way. She and Olivia got on like a house on fire.' He took another step, his footsteps crunching on the glass. 'She told me that you've hidden yourself away and are refusing all calls. That you're quite certain that it's safer for her and your baby to be far away from you. She's worried about you.' He took another step. 'So I thought I'd better come up here and check, to make sure you're okay.'

I'd thought about this moment, the moment when I'd see Val again. Thought about all the things I would say to him. Cutting things. Hurtful things. Furious things.

Yet seeing him, with the last remains of our twisted childhood lying in ruins around us, all my rage drained suddenly away.

'I'm sorry,' I said hoarsely. 'For the last conversation we had. I was angry. I've been angry at you for a long time. But all of that was my fault. Olivia…what Papa did to you…shutting you in your room… It was my fault.'

All the polished charm dropped from Val's face and his eyes darkened as he looked at me. 'No, Con. No.' There was anguish in his words. 'I'm to blame as much as you. I left you alone with him. I let you believe I was dead. And… *Dios*, you will never know how sorry I am for that.'

Such a simple thing to say, and yet it made the pain in my heart ease somehow.

'I had to go,' he went on, his voice getting rough. 'With Domingo it would never have ended—only with one of us dead.' He took a breath. 'That phone call… I am sorry for that too. I still had issues to work out as well.'

'So what changed?' I asked. 'Between now and three days ago?'

His mouth curved, his face softening, his eyes lighting up. 'Let's just say that being with Olivia changed me. Made me think about the past and realise a few things.' His gaze focused on me. 'You're right to be angry with me, Con.'

'No,' I said, straightening. 'No, I'm not. You were a victim as much as I was.' I looked down at my hands, at the blood on them, remembering another occasion where my hands had been bloody. 'I need to escape him somehow. But I... I don't know how to move past this.'

'I think you do. I think the way to move past this is in London, pregnant with your child.'

The words cut through me like a knife.

Valentin didn't look away. 'I know you,' he said quietly. 'We're twins, remember? Once something is ours, we never let it go and I don't think you want to let her go.'

I looked away, the beast in my heart desperate. 'How can I? There are things I haven't told you. Reasons she needs to be protected. No one can know that I—'

'No,' Val interrupted quietly. 'What she needs is to be loved.'

The words fell into the stillness like a stone in a quiet lake, creating ripples.

She *did* need to be loved. And I had loved her. No, I *still* loved her—deeply, madly, without reservation.

Except that wasn't right either. Because it *wasn't* without reservation. I was holding a piece of myself back.

The piece of myself I'd always thought was my father.

'Do you know what I see when I look at you, Constantine Silvera? I see the man I've loved for as long as I can remember.'

I'd told her what I'd done, what Domingo had said to me all those years ago, yet nothing had changed for her.

She still loved me. She still saw the man I wanted to be for her. So why did I still believe him?

But I knew why. She had been right about that, too.

I was protecting myself. Distancing myself so I didn't have to face up to the fact I had no idea how to manage the emotions inside me. The deep, hot, possessive yearning for her. The beast I couldn't control.

I'd told myself I hadn't wanted to expose her to that, but the truth was I hadn't wanted to expose myself.

Vulnerable Jenny. Fragile Jenny. Soft Jenny.

Yet she was none of those things. Soft on the outside, but steel and strength down to her core.

It was me who was the fragile one.

Me who could break.

'I don't know if I can.' My voice was as cracked and jagged as shattered glass.

Valentin let out a soft breath. 'You can. Our father broke us, but that doesn't mean we have to stay broken. We can choose to heal.'

And suddenly all I could see was Jenny's lovely face. Jenny standing in front of me, her brown eyes full of warmth and compassion. Full of love. A complicated mixture of strength and vulnerability I hadn't thought possible.

She was vulnerable, yes, but strong. Fearful, yet full of courage.

Love had given her that. Love had made her vulnerable, but love had also given her bravery. Love had made her powerful.

I'd told her I could never give her love and yet she loved me, and she'd told me she always would. I might have sent her away, but she hadn't left. I could feel her still in my heart, a warm, glowing light that refused all my efforts to freeze it. That was starting to melt the icy edges of my soul.

Was it really that simple? Could I really make a choice? The choice to stay broken, as Val had said, because I was broken. Or choose Jenny. Choose our child. Choose love.

She was so strong, my Jenny. How could I be any less? And Val was right. She *should* be loved. She *needed* to be loved. She was always so concerned about everyone else's feelings. She never put herself first.

But she should. *Someone* should.

And that someone should be me.

She was in my heart, in my soul. She was part of me. And I loved her.

The warmth inside me glowed brighter, stronger, melting away the ice around my heart, cracking all my armour. And I couldn't bear it. I couldn't bear being without her one second longer.

I turned to the doorway and without a word headed straight for it.

'I take it you're going to London?' Val asked from behind me. 'I'll just clean up here, shall I?'

I didn't answer.

I left him to it.

CHAPTER TWENTY-ONE

Jenny

I HADN'T BROUGHT an umbrella, so I got soaked on my walk from the tube station to my flat. My dress was clinging uncomfortably to my skin as I put the key in the lock and opened the door, chilling me to the bone.

I was feeling very low. It had been a long day at the shelter, which always took it out of me. I often felt emotionally drained afterwards, and for the past few days I'd felt even worse.

I missed Con so badly. Every minute I'd think staying away wasn't worth it, and I'd nearly go to book myself a ticket to Edinburgh, only to remember that I wasn't doing this for me, that I couldn't go to him.

It was his decision to remain alone, not mine, and forcing myself on him would only make things more difficult.

I went into the kitchen and made myself a hot cup of tea, shivering in my damp dress and trying to fight the memories that always claimed me whenever I was alone. Memories of purple heather and Con's black eyes. Of the way they'd light up whenever he talked about something he was passionate about. Of the way his mouth would soften into an almost-smile when he was amused. Of the way he'd touched me, sometimes with such demand he'd set me on fire, and sometimes with such tenderness he'd made me cry.

Of that room full of things that were precious to him.

He was a man desperately in search of something to ease the loneliness inside him, just like my mother. And, just like her, he couldn't see that that something had been right in front of him all this time.

The flat was dark, and when I felt the baby give a little kick, tears started in my eyes. I put my hand on my stomach. 'It's okay, little one. We have to hope Daddy will change his mind one day. And he will. I'm sure of it.'

Except I wasn't at all sure he would.

A knock came on the door and I sighed, debating whether or not to answer it, since I wasn't up for visitors. But when the knock came again, and louder this time, I pulled a face and went into the hall to open it.

A man stood on the steps outside, rain soaking his expensive suit and catching in his eyelashes, turning his hair into watered black silk. He was looking at me as if I was his last chance of salvation.

My heart almost stopped beating.

'Jenny,' Con said hoarsely, before I could speak. 'I've changed my mind. I don't want you to leave. I never want you to leave.'

Tears blurred my vision and that stone was back in my throat, preventing me from speaking.

'You're in my heart,' he went on, dark eyes searching my face. 'You're part of me. You always have been. And I'm sorry I let you go. I'm sorry I sent you away. I truly thought that I was protecting you, but…you were right. You were right about all of it. Domingo did still have a hold on me. I wanted to believe what he said about me because…' Con took a deep, shuddering breath. 'I was afraid. Afraid of how deeply I felt about you. How deeply I loved you. I've loved you since you were eighteen.'

I blinked back the tears and my whole body was trembling with shock. And then, as that began to fade, reality began to sink in.

He *was* here. He really was. And he loved me.

Wordlessly, I reached for his hand and pulled him into the hall, out of the rain, shutting the door behind him.

He stood there, dripping on the threadbare carpet, not seeming at all bothered by how wet he was, staring only at me. His eyes burned with that dark fire I'd come to love so very much…the dark fire that lay at the heart of him.

'Val came to see me,' he said into the heavy silence, because my voice had stopped working. 'And he told me that I could choose to stay broken or I could choose to heal. And I…'

Con took a step towards me, his hands in fists at his sides, as if he was holding himself back from reaching for me.

'I didn't think it could be that simple. I didn't think I could just…choose it. And I thought of you, Jenny.' His gaze intensified. 'I thought of you, and how honest you are with your emotions. So giving. You never hold anything back.'

He took another step, no ice at all in his fierce gaze now.

'But you always put what you need and what you want last, and that ends now. Someone needs to put you first, Jenny Grey, and I want that someone to be me. I want to be brave enough to heal, to let my father go to his grave, where he belongs, and I want to be strong enough to love you the way you should be loved. The way you *deserve* to be loved.'

My heart was a flower, opening up, spreading its petals wide to catch every drop of sunlight, reaching towards the light. Reaching for him.

I couldn't wait for him to close that last bit of distance, so I did. Going to him and putting my hands on his chest, not caring about his wet clothes. Not caring about anything but him.

'Then I'm yours,' I said simply, looking up at him, drinking in the sight of his beloved face. 'I've always been yours, Constantine Silvera.'

He took a sharp, ragged breath and lifted his hands, cupping my face between them. '*Dios*, I love you, my Jenny. I love you so much. I want to marry you. I want you to be my wife. And when our baby is born I want us to be a family. I want to make you happy.' His thumbs stroked over my cheekbones, the look on his face blazing bright. 'That's all I want. Just…to make you happy.'

I cried. I couldn't help it. The tears were streaming down my cheeks, but this time they weren't from pain, but from happiness.

'I want that too,' I said thickly, and then, because words were too difficult, I went up on my toes and kissed him.

And he ignited.

Because Constantine Silvera had never been ice. He'd always been fire.

And so was I.

EPILOGUE

Constantine

THE DOOR TO the birthing suite opened and Valentin came out. He was carrying a small white bundle and looked completely shell-shocked.

I knew the feeling. Two years and three children later—a boy and twin girls—I still remembered the way it felt to hold your child in your arms for the first time. It was like being hit very hard over the back of the head.

Jenny launched herself out of the seat in the waiting room, where we'd been sitting, and flew over to him, cooing over my new nephew.

Our children were being looked after by the nanny. We'd been at a function to celebrate the launch of Jenny's new project—a children's charity I'd helped her set up, though only in a very limited capacity. Jenny was the most competent organiser I'd ever seen, and the charity was mostly her own work. I was just the backer.

Val had called me towards the end of the function, to let me know that Olivia had gone into labour. So we'd left the party early and come straight to the private hospital where Olivia was.

Jenny, still in her evening gown of soft, flowing

golden silk, gave Val an enquiring look and then, when he nodded, gently took the baby into her arms.

She looked like a goddess in gold, cradling my nephew, and all I wanted was to take her home and worship her the way she deserved. And I couldn't deny that seeing her with a baby in her arms, made me want another of our own.

Laurent, our son, loved his sisters to distraction, but it would be nice if he could have a brother. I approved of brothers.

Mine, however, looked as if he needed some support, so I got up too, and went over to my dazed-looking twin, glancing down at the baby boy nestled in Jenny's arms.

'He's beautiful, Val,' she murmured, stroking his downy forehead. 'He's perfect.'

'Yes,' Val said, clearly unable to say anything else.

Jenny glanced up at him, then back at me, her dark eyes knowing. She eased the baby into Val's arms, then said, 'I'll go and see how Olivia is,' before slipping away into the birthing suite, allowing me some time alone with my brother.

She always knew what I needed, my Jenny, without me even having to say. Just as I knew what she needed too. Our connection was deep, strong, and as time went on it only got stronger.

'How do you do it?' Val asked, staring down at his newborn son with a fearful kind of awe written all over his face. 'How do you stand having your heart outside your chest like this?'

I put my hand on his shoulder and gave it a squeeze. We had walked a long, hard road, my brother and I, and it had taken time to rebuild our relationship. But now we were back where we'd first started. Together. Brothers for ever.

'Oh…' I said. 'You get used to it.'

I hadn't, not quite. But with Jenny's help I was getting there.

She'd put together the broken pieces of my soul and made me whole. And if sometimes the places where those pieces were joined ached a little, I'd learned to accept it. As she often told me, healing could be painful sometimes.

She was so full of wisdom, my Jenny.

I would love her until the end of time.

'You really get used to it?' Val asked with some disbelief.

'No,' I said, and smiled—another thing she'd taught me. 'You just learn to live with it.'

And I'd learned.

Love was a choice, and I chose it every day.

* * * * *

COMING SOON!

We really hope you enjoyed reading this book.
If you're looking for more romance, be sure to
head to the shops when new books are
available on

Thursday 1st September

To see which titles are coming soon, please visit
millsandboon.co.uk/nextmonth

MILLS & BOON ®

Coming next month

THE KING'S CHRISTMAS HEIR
Lynne Graham

Her cheeks were pink, her striking eyes downcast as she disconcerted him by reaching for the pen and scrawling her signature on the document that Dario had given him.

"You shouldn't sign a legal document without your own lawyer at hand to represent your interests," Gaetano remarked tautly.

"That's your world, not mine," Lara parried in a tone of scorn. "I don't require a lawyer to tell me I want to be free of you. You have disappointed me in every conceivable way, Gaetano –"

"I regret that you feel that way," he breathed curtly.

"No, your only goal is that I sign this form so that you can shed any responsibility you might have for me as discreetly as possible. That doesn't surprise me but I'm angry on my son's behalf!" Lara countered, throwing her head back. "He is an innocent party here and you didn't even look at him at the park!"

"You're trying to say that your son is also... my son?" Gaetano framed in open disbelief.

"He's sixteen months old, Gaetano. Who else could be his father?"

Continue reading
THE KING'S CHRISTMAS HEIR
Lynne Graham

Available next month
www.millsandboon.co.uk

MILLS & BOON

THE HEART OF ROMANCE

A ROMANCE FOR EVERY READER

MODERN

Prepare to be swept off your feet by sophisticated, sexy and seductive heroes, in some of the world's most glamourous and romantic locations, where power and passion collide.

HISTORICAL

Escape with historical heroes from time gone by. Whether your passion is for wicked Regency Rakes, muscled Vikings or rugged Highlanders, awaken the romance of the past.

MEDICAL

Set your pulse racing with dedicated, delectable doctors in the high-pressure world of medicine, where emotions run high and passion, comfort and love are the best medicine.

True Love

Celebrate true love with tender stories of heartfelt romance, from the rush of falling in love to the joy a new baby can bring, and a focus on the emotional heart of a relationship.

Desire

Indulge in secrets and scandal, intense drama and plenty of sizzling hot action with powerful and passionate heroes who have it all: wealth, status, good looks…everything but the right woman.

HEROES

Experience all the excitement of a gripping thriller, with an intense romance at its heart. Resourceful, true-to-life women and strong, fearless men face danger and desire - a killer combination!

To see which titles are coming soon, please visit

millsandboon.co.uk/nextmonth

LET'S TALK

Romance

For exclusive extracts, competitions
and special offers, find us online:

 facebook.com/millsandboon

@MillsandBoon

@MillsandBoonUK

Get in touch on 01413 063232